Advance Praise for *The Ne*

"What do you get when you pair the subve
pulp with the in-your-face sass and sexuɛ
stories? You get this thrill ride of an anthology. ..ᴛ .ᴀᴜ᎐᎐
savory depths are the perfect antidote to the bitter political realities of
the present day."

**—SUSAN STRYKER, author of *Queer Pulp: Perverted Passions
from the Golden Age of the Paperback***

"How badly do we need to escape into worlds of lesbian hijinks, outlaw
sex, evil man murder, thievery and subterfuge? This collection is a gift
of angst and longing, of thrill and delight across the ages that comes at
exactly the right time."

—SAM COHEN, author of *Sarahland*

"*The New Lesbian Pulp* delights in its benders and its sprees, its littery
glittery streets and its sapphic power play, and all of the adjacencies of
pleasure and pain that make lesbian pulp so irresistible. Reading this
collection was like being witness to the dirtiest, sexiest, grittiest, gayest
game of truth or dare, where there are only dares, and no one is remotely
afraid to take them. This book is the sauciest kind of treasure trove, and
we are so lucky to have it."

—TEMIM FRUCHTER, author of *City of Laughter: A Novel*

"*The New Lesbian Pulp* is one of the hottest and daring-est anthologies of
sapphic stories I've read (and I've read a lot). These new and vintage tales
deliver all the tension, plenty of torment, and a perfect excess of steam
and surprise. Did I say hot? I'll say it again: This book is hot, dangerously
hot! When not in use, it should probably be stored in a cool space with
the rest of your queer pulp canon."

**—MEGAN MILKS, author of *Margaret and the Mystery
of the Missing Body***

"*The New Lesbian Pulp* perfectly balances literary and pulpy sensibilities
to create an unforgettable collection. At turns wild, tender, shocking,
creepy, romantic, sexy, and strange, each story grabbed me by the throat,
held me down, and left me wanting more. Long-loved authors and emerging talent both shine in this instant classic."

—JEN ST. JUDE, author of *If Tomorrow Doesn't Come*

"*The New Lesbian Pulp* channels the illicit thrill of 1950s dyke-noir. This
is a world of deserts and dive bars and back alleys, where women are
willing to risk everything for a glance held too long. These stories of
danger and defiance hone pulp fiction to its sharpest edge."

—NAOMI KANAKIA, author of *The Default World*

"*The New Lesbian Pulp* brings together such a range of outstanding
stories—classic and new, aching and daring, subtle and sensational, and
all of them drumming with a shared pulse. Truly a collection for the ages."

—L. T. THOMPSON, author of *Devils Like Us*

The New
LESBIAN
PULP

Edited by Sarah Fonseca and Octavia C. Saenz

FOREWORD BY TRISH BENDIX

THE FEMINIST PRESS
AT THE CITY UNIVERSITY OF NEW YORK
NEW YORK CITY

Published in 2025 by the Feminist Press
at the City University of New York
The Graduate Center
365 Fifth Avenue, Suite 5406
New York, NY 10016

feministpress.org

First Feminist Press edition 2025

This book is made possible by the New York State Council on the Arts with
the support of the Office of the Governor and the New York State Legislature.

This book was published with financial support from the Jerome Foundation.

First printing August 2025

Cover illustration by Leslie Hung
Cover design by Drew Stevens
Text design by Drew Stevens

Library of Congress Cataloging-in-Publication Data is available for this title.
ISBN 978-1-55861-346-1

PRINTED IN THE UNITED STATES OF AMERICA

Contents

Foreword

TRISH BENDIX

WHEN I FIRST told her I was in love with a woman, my mother insisted I had been "sought out." She spat it like I'd somehow been lured down the wrong dark alley, falling into an untoward lifestyle by way of some demonic, lecherous dyke who could see I was an easy mark. It was not only untrue—finally attuned to what I wanted, I'd been the aggressor—but comical, how uncharacteristically convinced she was in her narrative about my private motivations. She couldn't grasp that I'd simply left home and discovered my sexuality skewed sapphic (tale as old as time!). But still, she felt hope: If I'd fallen prey to someone, I might still be talked out of it. After all, a lack of sense and self-control could be fixed. Did I want to speak to the family therapist? "You're selling yourself short," she said.

Like most, I didn't come out with any fundamental knowledge of gay history, so it took some time for me to understand how cheap lesbians were when my mom was growing up in the 1950s. Back then, it was only twenty-five cents to purchase a life of pure depravity from the drugstore on the corner. For the brave and curious, that quarter would grant entry to French women's barracks during wartime, the seedy dyke bars of Greenwich Village, the bedrooms of a North England sorority house, or a chance to ride "*a tortured merry-go-round with this passionate Lesbian who jumped on young . . . and is too frightened to climb off!*"

A quarter seems like a steal for a Choose Your Own Lesbian Adventure, but the real cost was all there was to lose should you be caught reading one. A preteen in the 1990s, my first palpably pulpy experience was seeing the cover of *Bound* at the local Blockbuster, staring at it lustfully without knowing why, wanting so badly to rent it but feeling just as strongly that

I shouldn't. I'd already intuited what it might say about me that
I was drawn to a photo of two sultry, dark-eyed women wearing
black leather jackets, rope-tied breast-to-breast, parallel pairs
of lips parted in pouts. *"In their world, you can't buy freedom,
but you can steal it."*

Mom may have been too square to read a pulp, but even that
couldn't save her from all the lesbians — or, as the books of the
time had it, Lesbians. Cheap and easy, at least five hundred
lesbian-themed paperbacks sold millions of copies nationwide
between 1935 and 1965. That's a lot of lesbians. In the fifties
and sixties, these voyeuristic stories about lesbians could be
purchased at all the same public venues you'd find in an episode
of *Leave it to Beaver* or *The Patty Duke Show*, but you wouldn't
see *Satan is Lesbian* on television, nor her more successful
sorority sister, *Spring Fire.* Considered immoral, explicit homo-
sexuality was forbidden on film courtesy of the Hays Code, and
even the thinly veiled queer characters written by clearly sapphic
authors of the McCarthy and Cold War eras were loath to be
so bold for the cause. It was pulp novels that were the first to
name lesbians on their covers with that capital *L* and sometimes plural, which indicated there was more than one and that
they'd managed to find each other. That alone was enough to
send a guy to his fly, or an isolated gay woman to imagining
new possibilities.

Hyperbolic and hypersexual, lesbian pulp novels could
famously be identified by their suggestive titles and salacious,
punishing taglines. Typically, at least two women appeared,
generously endowed and in various states of undress, posed
between sheets and slips of lust and terror. Accuracy was neither
attempted nor attained. Even when characters were described
with traditionally assumed Lesbian characteristics, such as
masculine haircuts or butch demeanors, it was femmes only on
the front, a loaded precursor to lesbian chic. Inside, storylines
followed a formula with frequently dire consequences for the
twisted woman who dared indulge in, by today's standards,
some pretty tame lovemaking. More often than not, the lost
women teased on the cover found their way back to heterosexu-
ality, while the committed capital-*L* Lesbians faced certain death
or ended up in mental institutions. This was the path taken to
circumvent the same censors who'd given Radclyffe Hall hell
with the 1928 publication of *The Well of Loneliness*, which also
eventually received the pulp treatment once lesbians were all

the rage: *"Denounced, banned, and applauded—the strange love story of a girl who stood midway between the sexes."*

Not surprisingly, many of the pulps were written by straight male authors who let their crude imaginations run wild, and publishers, also straight and male, imagined the audience would be similar. However, a crucial part of the lesbian pulp readership mirrored the estimated one-third of pulp authors who were gay women. Their success highlighted how many readers were here for something beyond skimming the dialogue to reach the sex scenes, getting off, and trashing the books. It's thrilling to know just how many different women discovered lesbian pulp novels at their corner store, and within them a name, proof of a shared identity, community, and history for the first time—even if, as Dorothy Allison once wrote, the Lesbian of lesbian pulp novels wasn't exactly "true," she was "true enough."[1]

In 1982, during the height of the Feminist Sex Wars, Allison, no stranger to trash or depravity herself, published an essay about the summer she spent house-sitting while exploring the owner's secret shelves of saucy paperbacks poolside. She discovered the pulps hidden in a closet, their spines shamefully facing the wall, with titles like *Valley of the Lesbo, Midnight Orgy, Make it Sting*: "Well, what other kind of books do people keep in their closets?"[2] The collection included all the typical softcore material, but then there was what Allison called "pseudo-porn," the psychological and political paperbacks from authors explaining lesbianism from an outsider's perspective of "exotic titillation and moral superiority."[3] Cringey as those "reports" could be, Ann Aldrich's gay girl's guide, *Carol in a Thousand Cities,* with its oft-depressing possibilities presented for any woman who chose to be a lesbian, sent Allison "back to the house for Kleenex and aspirin."[4]

Years later, we have the context that Ann Aldrich was a pseudonym for Marijane Meaker (a.k.a. Vin Packer, a.k.a. M. E. Kerr), and that the book's title was a line pulled directly from her former girlfriend Patricia Highsmith's novel *The Price of Salt.* The book that would later become the Oscar-nominated

---

1. Dorothy Allison, "A Personal History of Lesbian Porn," in *Skin: Talking about Sex, Class, and Literature* (Firebrand Press, 1994), 187.
2. Allison, "A Personal History of Lesbian Porn," 183.
3. Allison, "A Personal History of Lesbian Porn," 189.
4. Allison, "A Personal History of Lesbian Porn," 184.

Todd Haynes film *Carol* was first released under Highsmith's pen name, Claire Morgan, as the lesbian author lived mainly in the closet and initially had difficulty finding a publisher for her queer book. Despite significant success with a hardcover debut and subsequent paperback, Highsmith's experience—she wouldn't take credit for the 1952 novel until 1990—underscores how discretion and secrecy were paramount to even the most successful lesbian authors. They, among many others, enjoyed a rousing sapphic life in secret, so it makes sense that many of the stories centered on women leading double lives and weighing the pros and cons of self-realization and sexual fulfill-ment within the constraints of capitalism and conservatism. In retrospect, the high stakes arguably heighten the excitement of seeing how these writers dared and got away with it.

The remaining living legend of lesbian pulp is Ann Bannon, whose famed Beebo Brinker series brought Dorothy Allison back to her college dorm in Florida, where she read her copy locked in the dorm bathroom and harbored a crush on a girl down the hall who shared Beebo's "close-cropped hair and an eternal sneer." "When that girl disappeared from the dorm one myste-rious night full of shouting and confusion, I ripped Beebo cover to cover and spread the pages over eight garbage cans and one dumpster," Allison recalled. "Suddenly, I wasn't reading porn, I was paging my own history."[5]

It's fair that many queer women found lesbian pulp to be shameful, vulgar, and off-putting, fair to argue that the plea-sure taken in our pains was neither positive representation nor adequate visibility, no matter who held the pen. It's well docu-mented that the publishers of *The Ladder* considered even (or maybe especially) the novels written by lesbians "trash," and later they removed lesbian pulp entirely from their annual guide to *The Lesbian in Literature.* At least *The Ladder* reviewed lesbian pulp; nowhere outside of lesbian publications deemed them worth the low-grade pulp paper they were printed on. Some women seemed to read them begrudgingly, as what writer and Lesbian Herstory Archives cofounder Joan Nestle famously referred to as "survival literature." But to women like Allison, who could decipher enough truth from the fiction,

> It didn't matter that almost all the books were awful—intermit-tent sexual escapades paced by eight to twelve pages of plot

5. Allison, "A Personal History of Lesbian Porn," 184.

pretense and rare paragraphs of "socially redeeming value" —
nor that sometimes I'd lose track of which one I was reading.
Suddenly, the bushes seemed thicker, the texture on the dogwood
trees rougher, the smell of flowers and chlorine overpowering,
while my dreams produced men who searched the garden for
their detachable genitals and women who sat on the window
ledges and slowly licked their greasy fingers.[6]

Faithful to the heat of the originals, *The New Lesbian Pulp* main-
tains that same hot drip of anticipation and action on every
page, with considerably fewer fucks to give. The modern-day
protagonists are no longer the kind of lost souls my mother
assumed I had been, what Allison described as "startled sleepy-
eyed women . . . taken by surprise when confronted with the
sexual."[7] *The New Lesbian Pulp* luxuriates in the sexual without the anxieties that plagued the original pulp fiction era. There
is no longer the same preoccupation with being discovered as
a lesbian at the center of the sex. The lesbian agenda is less
taboo, making way for stimulating new circumstances between
two women, including but not limited to heavy sexting coming
to sweaty fruition in the back seat outside of an Orlando gay
bar, or a simmering truckload of tension while hunting roadkill
for revenge. Gay shame may be present, but it's no longer filling the room with its stench.

And to *The New Lesbian Pulp*'s credit, sometimes it's not
even sex so explicitly, but rather an erotic energy exchanged
in front of one's husband, no less, as in Lorraine Hansberry's
story "Chanson du Konallis." Initially published in 1958 under
the nom de plume Emily Jones, it appeared in *The Ladder*,
which is what's so fun about *The New Lesbian Pulp*: the chance
to revisit, reframe, and expand lesbian literature in new ways,
thanks to the hindsight and hot takes time has afforded us. *The
New Lesbian Pulp* introduces trans femmes and butch-on-butch
dynamics to the otherwise butch–femme, femme–femme inter-
actions that only perpetuated confusion among sapphics in a
wider society that had yet to differentiate gender from sexuality or allow for deviations from what one source defined as
Lesbian, with a capital *L*.

It's exciting to find modern-day stories with the promise and

6. Allison, "A Personal History of Lesbian Porn," 184.
7. Allison, "A Personal History of Lesbian Porn," 191.

payoff of the originals sitting alongside uncovered sapphic-themed work from earlier writers like Alice Dunbar-Nelson, whose "Natalie" offers an enduring romantic friendship across race and class lines. How rich it is to see Gertrude Vanderbilt Whitney included in this queer context, with an excerpt from her unearthed 1934 sapphic murder mystery novel, *Walking the Dust,* under the name L. J. Webb. The inclusion of Eve Adams/Evelyn Addams serves as a fitting tribute to the Polish Jewish immigrant who both published her book *Lesbian Love* and ran a lesbian tea room in Greenwich Village before she faced entrapment and deportation in 1927.

Some original pulp fiction provided enough specifics to help readers navigate real-life lesbian locations, and *The New Lesbian Pulp* does the same. There's dyke sex in an alley outside of Ginger's and inside the bathroom at Metropolitan, just like there is every weekend in Brooklyn. Closeted women still cling to men they don't love but believe they need, until they finally decide they don't—and this time, there is no forced course correction at the end. Kink parties, a femme top's funeral, an Airbnb outside of Palm Springs, rural family farmland, and performances at a jazz club—*The New Lesbian Pulp* is not afraid to publish what others have refused. (See: "Cottonmouth.")

By the end of her time at the house that summer, Allison decided to go home and put all her "Lesbian porn" out on display, wondering where all the books she'd published and still had yet to write would end up. Forty-some years later, and twenty-one years after coming out to my mother, I keep my lesbian pulp books directly under the television, where everyone can see them, alongside the rest of my "porn" collection—lesbian history, biography, fiction, photography, art. Audre Lorde's "Uses of the Erotic" shares space with *Lesbian Nuns: Breaking Silence* and copies of *On Our Backs*; work from writers like Andrea Dworkin, Michelle Cliff, Kathy Acker, Camille Paglia, Alice Walker, Nikki Giovanni, and Heather Lewis, each challenging in their ways. I go to bed with explicit images by Catherine Opie, Tee Corinne, and Kate Millett on my walls, a blue silicone facsimile of Eileen Myles's fist taking up prime real estate on a center shelf for the curious to ask about. From the poetry of Sappho to the journals of Susan Sontag, a case could be made for either lesbian porn and lesbian history. But like Dorothy Allison, I don't find them mutually exclusive.

I hope *The New Lesbian Pulp* will be proudly displayed in libraries and bookshops, pulled daily from bookbags, totes, and Telfies, spotted in profile photos on dating apps and in the text of personal ads (*ISO a smokin' top to dig her fingernails into my skin, shoot and skin a beaver, kill a man, and tie me up, not necessarily in that order. Must love snakes.*) But in true lesbian pulp tradition, and at a time when book bans, censorship and anti-LGBTQ sentiments are at a fever pitch, some will inevitably read *The New Lesbian Pulp* covertly, concealed in closets or under the bed. Whether out of shame or safety, they too are a part of the time continuum of lesbian history and porn.

So let me be the first to welcome all you wayward women who stumbled blindly into this twilight sisterhood. You surely had to go out of your way to be here—thank you for seeking us out.

—Trish Bendix
Los Angeles, CA
April 28, 2025

Introduction

The typewriter rattled under her long, strong, agile fingers.
She had a well-formed hand, a college girl's hand with flat,
clear fingernails, masculine in its length.
—Tereska Torrès, Women's Barracks, 1950

IT WAS OCTOBER 1960, and the girls were fighting. A reader in California who went by C. L. had written to the lesbian magazine *The Ladder* to express her dissatisfaction with the artlessness of Ann Aldrich's newest pulp paperback, *Carol in a Thousand Cities*. "I thought there was too much ado over Ann Aldrich-Bannon," C. L. offers, snarkily merging Aldrich's name with that of another lesbian pulp writer, Ann Bannon. "She's proof that automation has reached the literary (?) field. I don't believe she exists at all but is really a creation by I.B.M."

Now approaching seventy years old, C. L.'s complaint remains fascinating for a handful of reasons. For one, it reveals the lively underground that this era's gay girls had built for themselves. For another, C. L. exposes a tension between the sophisticated lesbian and the popular dyke literature that was increasingly available to them. There is also the writer's choice of language—*automation*—which feels wildly modern in a moment when technology is being actively trained to write books. Finally, lesbians, faced with finite media outlets and means of connection, have always wanted more: This can and does lead to infighting about high versus low culture, rather than appreciation for the undergrounds we've forged and considerations of the systems that keep our hands more bound than those of our straight contemporaries.

With the printing of Tereska Torrès's novel *Women's Barracks* on cheaply pressed paper in 1950, the lesbian pulp movement was launched in mail-order catalogs and drugstores around the country. And though they were subjected to censorship by publishers and the postal service alike, these texts were plainly written and relatively accessible, affording covert readers chance encounters with their own desires. Pulp also provided a roster

1

of authors, from Anns Aldrich and Bannon to Patricia Highsmith, the opportunity to publish transgressive, candid, dreamy, and lustful work.

We, the editors, recognized a need for a present-day equivalent to the incognito, liberatory, and connective sensation of reading lesbian pulp in the 1950s and 1960s, and we took to heart the lives of early pulp readers, particularly those whose experiences strayed from those of pulp's traditionally pale ingénues and equally pale brunette toughies—readers who inhabited society's underground because race, class, or gender identity forced them into it. The voices of Black and Brown lesbians, including the late Mabel Hampton and Georgia Brooks, were at the fore of this preliminary investigation. One critical wellspring was the late writer and dancer Donna Allegra, who wrote, "No matter how embarrassed and ashamed I felt when I went to the cash register to buy these books, it was absolutely necessary for me to have them. I needed them the way I needed food and shelter for survival." In the same breath, Allegra articulates the inadequacy of the available materials, noting, "I look back now and see where those books and their ideas rotted my guts and crippled my moral structure." It feels imperative to do right by Allegra and readers like her.[1]

Between the conception and publication of *The New Lesbian Pulp*, much has changed: in the world, in the United States and its territories, and in our own lives. If the current moment were summarized as a sordid golden-era dyke pulp novel's tagline,

---

1. While undertaking the creative, intellectual—and at times corrective—project of reviving lesbian pulp for modern readers, the editors have kept one critical appraisal especially close to the chest. In *Lesbian Rule: Cultural Criticism and the Value of Desire* (Duke University Press, 2003), Amy Villarejo takes to task the wanton nostalgia for bygone gay eras and the racial and socioeconomic inequalities such fantasies can perpetuate. Writing in response to the pulp-styled documentary *Forbidden Love: The Unashamed Stories of Lesbian Lives* (dirs. Lynne Fernie and Aerlyn Weissman, 1992, Canada), Villarejo makes several essential points: that "lesbian bar culture has been and is involved in the production of racist enclaves, hallucinations of urban life which depend for their existence on street culture (drinks, drugs, sex work, and pornography), which provide a sense of outlawry, but yet that very culture is frequently denied or disdained by white lesbians seeking community"; that "the labor of the streets, particularly sex work, is often performed by lesbians. Lesbian bourgeois culture has hitherto ignored that labor"; that "participation in subcultural leisure activities does not guarantee a politic, much less an anti-racist agenda"; and, last but not least, that "when we think we are 'odd girls out' on the town, to borrow one of Bannon's titles, we remap the streets of that town, since it has always belonged to others, both to capital and to struggles we don't necessarily see in our lesbian chic finery." Without the bravery of scholars such as Villarejo, this text would not exist as it does.

it might be *Story of a woman behind bars* (Wenzell Brown's *Prison Girl*, 1958). Or, *Their flaming desire could only be satisfied by breaking every rule and ignoring every taboo* (Rea Michaels's *Duet in Darkness*, 1965).

We've seen the commercialization of artificial intelligence—not unlike the sort C. L. compares to Aldrich's prose—take hold of the publishing industry; we've seen queer media outlets, abandoned by advertisers, flounder and shutter; we've seen geopolitical tensions meet a fever pitch, in which one nation's tolerance for LGBTQ individuals can be wielded as a propagandistic license to indiscriminately bomb another nation; we've heard new talking points—stand-up routines, really—from electeds, pundits, and other public figures, some once vocally supportive of marriage equality and other "love is love"–type declarations, yet now imploring us to join them in mocking and disenfranchising nonbinary and trans-identified persons; we've seen new dyke bars come and go, and an ex–drag queen stage the performance of a lifetime as a Republican representative from Long Island. At the same time, we've seen a cornucopia of new songstresses mount the pop charts with songs that convey a desire to mount other girls.

To that end, *The New Lesbian Pulp* has rolled with the punches of culture and, more importantly, with our storytellers: What potential do prospective contributors see in this collection that we, focused on the genre's and lesbian fiction's literary inheritance, could not? How do they wish to define "lesbian pulp" in the twenty-first century?

In order to fully convey the relief, admiration, and excitement we felt in encountering these operant yet deliciously modern tales, it's necessary to go back in time and inventory what the lesbian storyteller faced, post-pulp. Lesbian pulp's circumvention of censorship in the 1950s and 1960s is well documented, as is the corollary advent of lesbian/feminist presses in latter decades.[2] By the 1980s and 1990s, a new generation of

---

2. It is impossible to overstate the role such lesbian and feminist presses played in the publication, distribution, and preservation of lesbian fiction throughout the decades. Now recognized as a landmark work printed by Random House, Rita Mae Brown's *Rubyfruit Jungle* (1973) was among the first titles published by Daughters, Incorporated, an independent press helmed by June Arnold and Parke Bowman and based in New York, New York. Likewise, the 1991 reissue of *The Price of Salt* by the Tallahassee, Florida–based Naiad Press included Claire Morgan, the pseudonym under which Highsmith originally published the pulp in 1952, as well as her legal name, on its cover. The book featured an introduction in which the author "came out" as its mastermind.

storytellers was entering the mainstream, as works like Rita Mae Brown's *Bingo* (Bantam Books, 1989) and Carol Anshaw's *Aquamarine* (Houghton Mifflin, 1992) were published by major presses. Though this breakthrough looks great on paper, two issues cropped up that resembled those faced by pulp's pioneering broads: Queer sexuality was chastity-belted on the page, and writers were still getting shortchanged in the way of funding.

Some fifty years after the pulp paperback revolution, and thirty years after the women's press movement, the queer think tank and grantmaker Astraea Lesbian Foundation for Justice had a pressing question: How were gay girls in the US faring in the literary world? Specifically, the babes with brains at Astraea wanted to know whether lesbian writers were benefiting from the funders that make it possible to meaningfully devote time and energy to one's craft, never mind write the proverbial Great American Novel: the MacArthur Foundation, the Guggenheim Foundation, the Whiting Foundation, and so on.

Compiled in a report titled "Does Lesbian Content Discount a Writer's Artistic Merit?" in June 1998, Astraea's findings were bleak—so bleak that, had either of us weighed them during the rose-colored-lens days of our own writing careers, we might have put down our pencils, like Ann Bannon or Lorraine Hansberry, to pick up well-to-do husbands.

Among those financially supported by six titans of institutional literary funding from 1990 to 1998 were only two dykes, white and well educated: Blanche Boyd and Jeannette Winterson (a Brit).[3] Courtney Gillette, director of the Writing Institute, summed up Astraea's findings best: "Two! Crunching my own numbers, I figured that these six fellowships over ten years had 370 awards for women writers. Two lesbians out of 370 women writers! (Gay men, for the record, got 18 out of their respective 370 awards for male writers). In a word, it's despicable."

---

3. Author Susan Sontag's 1990 MacArthur Fellowship was omitted from Astraea's lesbian writers report, ostensibly because Astraea "found that lesbian writers who are not 'out' personally and in their creative work are the most likely to receive funding." This rationalization is a bit spurious in hindsight, given the queer legibility of Sontag's prose and the misogyny she weathered (most notably that of MacArthur board member Saul Bellow, who took it upon himself to prevent her from receiving the "Genius Grant" for years). This to say, some nuance is better than none when evaluating the past. No point in kicking a closeted writer when she's down, particularly one who had a soft spot for Highsmith's *The Price of Salt*.

Be they "literary" or "popular," writers cannot write if they are not meaningfully recognized, championed, and remunerated. Time is money, and the labor of literature extends beyond writing to editing, researching, workshopping, rewriting, connection-forging, pitching, submitting, and—perhaps most vitally—reading, the results of which take time to be actualized. Without the assurance of material stability, ingenious and unapologetic concepts languish in unpublished manuscripts, or are never written to begin with.

Some twenty-five years after Astraea's report gestured toward the ways in which institutional biases, racism, classism, and puritanism exclude lesbian writers, we—committed to honoring pulp's iconic penwomen and making sense of our fragmented literary lineage—take our own lay of the land. This brings us back to what lesbian storytellers want today. It's very simple, really: They want to forget the identity-based dissatisfactions of day-to-day life. They want to not have to fitfully consider the consequences of having written before even setting pen to paper. They want purposeful nostalgia. They want to surprise and titillate through effortlessly heterogenous casts of characters. They want freedom, escape, pleasure, revenge; they want girl gangs. They want the cloak-and-dagger, the morally gray. They want to disrupt tropes through fierce engagement. They want to disarm the most fickle of adult readers by invoking the sensations of opening a comic book, viewing a classic exploitation flick, or sampling one's choice guilty-pleasure fan fiction.

They want, in essence, lesbian pulp.

The stories before you—some brand new, others newly unearthed—are organized into four sections, each embracing a different lesbian-pulp-fiction tradition, ranging from the sentimental to the profane. This collection opens with *Women's Work*, a selection of four new exceptionally ribald stories, plus one rarity from 1932, in which heroines and antiheroines take matters into their own hands, forgoing emotional labor and rereads of *The Feminine Mystique* in favor of vigilante justice. Lillian James's violent and enticing "Smoke and the Sea Breeze" cozies up to Remy, a philanderer's trophy wife who, with the help of his femme fatale executive assistant, terminates the relationship—*and* the husband. Excerpted from a little-known novel, "A Parlor Game" underscores the suspect's queer character without explicitly naming it. A freshly unearthed classic,

L. J. Webb's[4] *Walking the Dusk* follows the aftermath of a New York society girl's fatal poisoning. Suspecting the mature Katharine of entering a jealous rage and murdering the girl, the narrator initiates an independent investigation, eventually discovering that Katharine is not a murderer—but that she *was* the dearly departed's lover.

In *Coming of Rage*,[5] four young heroines undergo formative erotic and intellectual transformations that will carry them into queer adulthood. Sarah Schulman's "New York City, 1967" is told through the eyes of Anita, an urban teen experiencing the first flushes of estrangement and idol worship against the backdrop of a city on the cusp of detrimental change, with fatal implications for her gay best friend. Famously censored by Cleis Press's *Best Lesbian Erotica* in 2014, Ella Boureau's "Cottonmouth"—not unlike Schulman's tale—finds inspiration in the life and work of a legendary Southern writer. Left to their own devices on a sweltering provincial day, Rose and Lou turn their backs on a God-fearing world to share an unforgettable, verboten experience in the Eden that is their backwoods.

In our third section, *Best You Never Had*, five authors take us on a prismatic journey through chance encounters, missed connections, and failures to launch. Each of these short works boasts and basks in that quintessential dyke emotion: *yearning*. Grace Byron's "Rookie Mistake" features a white-knuckling

---

4. L. J. Webb is the pen name of the artist, heiress, philanthropist, and Whitney Museum namesake Gertrude Vanderbilt Whitney. *Walking the Dusk* is the only book she published within her lifetime. The novel remains historically remarkable for exploring lesbian subject matter with relative compassion in the early 1930s, in the years between the creation of the very first LGBTQ rights organization and the so-called "Pansy Craze." By the same token, the high stakes of publishing such a novel remain palpable. The book was written by Vanderbilt Whitney in the shadow of "The Trial of the Century," in which the stoic heiress fought for custody of her young niece, Gloria Vanderbilt, in a Manhattan courtroom. During the course of *Vanderbilt v. Whitney* in 1934—a case Vanderbilt Whitney would win—Gloria's mother, Gloria Morgan, was accused of having a lesbian affair with second-degree royal and socialite Nadejda Mikhailovna Mountbatten, Marchioness of Milford Haven. The revelation scandalized the court, the public, and weighed heavily on the verdict. In the years following her death, Gertrude Vanderbilt Whitney's own sexuality has been pondered by biographers, who've detailed a passionate friendship she had with another girl in adolescence and alleged affairs with women in adulthood.

5. It is a serendipitous delight to unite Sarah Schulman and Ella Boureau in *The New Lesbian Pulp*, and particularly among the *Coming of Rage* selections. The editor of Cleis Press's *Best Lesbian Erotica* for 2014, Schulman hand-selected Boureau's story for publication and subsequently resigned from the post when the anthology's publisher refused to print the fantastical, fearless story.

heroine, Margo, who approaches a reckoning upon realizing she enjoys sex with a beguiling fellow t-girl, Hannah, more than she does with her milquetoast boyfriend. First published by playwright Lorraine Hansberry under her pseudonym Emily Jones in 1958, "Chanson du Konallis" forays into a Parisian nightclub with Konnie and her husband, where our heroine grows quietly besotted with a chanteuse who appreciates Konnie more than her mate does.

The New Lesbian Pulp closes with *Some Like It Fraught*, a selection of tales that challenge dogmas of queer representation and visibility by leveraging narrative truth over palatable optics and by reevaluating tropes identified in media criticism as "unsavory." Set at a funeral for Anaïs, a beloved queer femme, August Clarke *literally* buries their gay in "Pale Horse." Like its dearly departed, this darkly comedic short story is forgiven its sins because those in attendance are all gay girls, immaculately coiffed and conflicted about Anaïs's legacy. One of two vintage pieces contained in this section, Dora Rosetti's[6] "The Perfect Pair" waxes poetic about lesbian codependency at a time when there was negligible language for the psychological pitfalls of queer sexuality, and when scarcity of possible romantic partners only served to increase despair and determination. Pseudonymously published in Athens, Greece, in 1929, as part of a longer work, and lost to time for nearly a century, the story is told from the perspective of Dora, an impoverished medical student who is besotted with her friend Laura.[7]

Collectively, this anthology—from its greatest disasters to its most fevered desires—serves to broaden what one thinks possible within lesbian fiction, as well as readers' knowledge of where we've already been. It remains a delight and an honor to

6. Dora Rosetti is the pen name of Nelli Kaloglopoulou-Bogiatzoglou, a gynecologist and friend to the Greek poet Constantine P. Cavafy. After the publication of *Her Lover*, from which "The Perfect Pair" is excerpted, Kaloglopoulou tried to ensure that all copies of her book were destroyed. A century later, two copies were discovered, one of which was inscribed to Cavafy. This is the first presentation of the late author's work in the United States.

7. In addition to the selections mentioned in the introduction, "Some Like It Fraught" contains "Diana Thornton," an excerpt from Eva Kotchever's *Lesbian Love* (1925), a recently rediscovered collection of portraits of queer women. Kotchever, a.k.a. Eve Adams, a Jewish immigrant and tea room proprietor, was an ardent communist. Her politics and sexuality were the grounds on which she was deported from the United States. Later working as a Parisienne saleswoman of groundbreaking literature banned stateside, Kotchever was subsequently deported to Auschwitz, where she perished in 1943.

share these works with audiences in partnership with Feminist Press, a publisher who has honored pulp fiction's lesser-known origin stories through its Femmes Fatales imprint for nearly two decades.

Whether you're reading this book behind your family's back or femme-flagging with it on Fire Island, we hope you get out of it even one-tenth of the heart we've put into it over the past few years.

We've been here for millennia. We've only just begun.

—Sarah Fonseca   —Octavia C. Saenz
   New York, NY   San Juan, Puerto Rico
                                      August 2024

Works Cited

Astraea Lesbian Action Fund. "Does Lesbian Content Discount a Writer's Artistic Merit?: Examining the Lack of Foundation Support for Lesbian Literature." June 1, 1998. https://archive.org/details/lack-of-foundation-support-for-lesbian-literature.

Boureau, Ella. "Lesbians Who Eat Their Young: How Sarah Schulman and I Got the Boot From Best Lesbian Erotica 2014." *HuffPost*, December 13, 2013. https://www.huffpost.com/entry/lesbians-who-eat-their-yo_b_4426552.

Brooks, Georgia. "Georgia on Lesbian Pulp Fiction." Interview by Tiona Nekkia McClodden for *United Black Lesbian Elder Project*. Posted November 6, 2011. https://vimeo.com/31704911.

"Bury Your Gays." TVTropes.org. August 10, 2010. https://tvtropes.org/pmwiki/pmwiki.php/Main/BuryYourGays.

C. L. "Readers Respond." *The Ladder*, October 1, 1960. https://digitalassets.lib.berkeley.edu/sfbagals/The_Ladder/1960_Ladder_Vol05_No01_Oct.pdf.

Friedman, B. H. *Gertrude Vanderbilt Whitney: A Biography*. Doubleday, 1978.

Gillette, Courtney. Review of *The Gentrification of the Mind: Witness to a Lost Imagination* by Sarah Schulman. *Lambda Literary Review*, March 13, 2012. https://lambdaliterary.org/2012/03/the-gentrification-of-the-mind-witness-to-a-lost-imagination-by-sarah-schulman.

Goldsmith, Barbara. *Little Gloria . . . Happy at Last*. Knopf, 1980.

Hansberry, Lorraine (Emily Jones, pseud.). "Chanson du Konallis." *The Ladder*, September 1, 1958.

Harker, Jaime. *The Lesbian South: Southern Feminists, the Women in Print Movement, and the Queer Literary Canon.* University of North Carolina Press, 2018.

The High Bar. Episode 302, "The High Bar with Warren Etheredge and Ann Bannon." Aired February 10, 2012. https://vimeo.com/36583112.

Highsmith, Patricia (Claire Morgan, pseud.). *The Price of Salt.* Naiad Press, 1991.

Katz, Jonathan N. *The Daring Life and Dangerous Times of Eve Adams.* Chicago Review Press, 2021.

Keller, Yvonne. "Was It Right to Love Her Brother's Wife So Passionately?: Lesbian Pulp Novels and US Lesbian Identity, 1950–1965." *American Quarterly* 57, no. 2 (2005): 385–410.

Khatib, Rasha, Martin McKee, and Salim Yusuf. "Counting the Dead in Gaza: Difficult but Essential." *The Lancet* 404, no. 10449 (2024): 237. https://doi.org/10.1016/S0140-6736(24)01169-3.

Lambda Literary Foundation. "Previous Winners: Lambda Literary Awards Finalists and Winners, 2020." https://lambdaliterary.org/awards/previous-winners-3/.

Lavietes, Matt. "George Santos Says He Will Revive His Drag Queen Persona on Cameo." *NBC News,* April 29, 2024. https://www.nbcnews.com/nbc-out/out-politics-and-policy/george-santos-says-will-revive-drag-queen-persona-cameo-rcna149867.

Moser, Benjamin. *Sontag: Her Life and Work.* Ecco, 2020.

Perry, Imani. *Looking for Lorraine: The Radiant and Radical Life of Lorraine Hansberry.* Beacon Press, 2019.

Rosetti, Dora. (Nelli Kaloglopoulou-Bogiatzoglou). *Her Lover.* ETPbooks, 2017.

Torrès, Tereska. *Women's Barracks.* The Feminist Press at CUNY, 2005.

Villarejo, Amy. *Lesbian Rule: Cultural Criticism and the Value of Desire.* Duke University Press, 2003.

Women's Work

Smoke and the Sea Breeze

LILLIAN JAMES

I

THERE WERE ONLY the stars and the light of Remy's cigarette. It had been a short while since she last took a drag, and the embers had traveled up the paper, ash accumulating in their wake. Remy appreciated the symbolism, even if she couldn't decide who precisely it applied to. She moved the cigarette so it wouldn't shed on her coat and continued to stare at the water, barely discernible against the black of the sky.

Annabeth grunted beside her.

The night was too cold for sitting on a dock in a sleeveless gown, no matter how heavy her coat was. She had thought to put on only a second layer and change from her heels to a pair of sensible shoes, but now wished dearly that she had taken the time to change completely. At least her coat pocket still had both a pack and a lighter despite her attempt to quit smoking months ago.

Remy put her cigarette between her lips and picked up the phone in her lap. Charlie's lock screen was near blinding in the darkness, making the AI-generated "make your own reality" image even more insipid than it was during daylight. She input the access code—9078.

The lock screen transformed into a photo of Charlie and Tony standing over the lifeless body of a stag, its blood still fresh on the ground. Annabeth stood to their side, their rifles laying at her feet, while her hand dripped from having slit the wounded beast's throat.

"Charlie couldn't do it," Annabeth had said the day the stag's stuffed head was mounted on the wall of Remy's dining room. *"Didn't want to get blood on his jacket."*

Charlie hadn't been able to do a lot of things. Remy thought it was endearing, at first, then bearable, before she grew to find it (and him) insufferable—but of course, people changed.

Charlie hadn't been able to do that, either.

HER AND ANNABETH'S first date was the day they met: Remy and Charlie's wedding anniversary.

The reservation had been made for seven p.m., and by ten, Remy had ordered herself a steak and a bottle of wine to be left at the table. Divorce papers sat next to her empty plate, and for the first time, she had signed one of the pages.

It was the humiliation that had her finally grabbing a pen— the acidic taste in the back of her mouth as she waved off the waiters several times, habitually checking her watch, until the staff were giving her sympathetic glances and a complimentary dessert. All because Charlie couldn't find the time to pull out of the nubile blond in his office.

Well, Charlie never hired his assistants for their time-management skills.

Remy poured another glass. The restaurant was almost empty, but no one was rushing out to exile a woman who spent 250 dollars on a steak and some Bordeaux. In fact, they were more than accommodating, and their eagerness settled on her like oil.

Annabeth had not offered any such consideration. Instead, she had sat down in the chair left for Charlie, like everything of his was already hers to claim.

Fuck it, Remy thought. She could have him.

"Are you here to give the simpering apology, or a victory speech?" Remy clutched the stem of her wine glass in her hand. It would shatter with one strike on the table. She could use it as a weapon—she was even tempted to.

"Neither, ma'am," Annabeth answered, her regional accent unexpected but not ill-fitting. "At least, not on my behalf."

Remy groaned inwardly. "What's his excuse this time?"

"His meeting in Tokyo ran late," Annabeth said. "And the jet had to take a detour for poor weather conditions."

"I see." Remy took a swill of her wine. "So, he got distracted by fucking an air hostess."

"Two, actually," Annabeth said, and poured herself a glass of Remy's wine.

Remy's teeth itched as Annabeth put the glass between her plump, glossy lips and swallowed.

"Usually, his girls think they're the only one." Her eyes felt stuck to the glass, to the lip gloss on the rim, to the lips that put it there.

"Aside from you, of course," Annabeth said with a laugh.

Remy wanted to make her scream.

"Doesn't Jesus have a problem with you fucking married men?" Remy used her wine glass to gesture at Annabeth's cross.

Annabeth's hand jumped to it, rubbing the corners that had been left sharp. It left scratches on the surface of her hands, but she didn't stop doing it. A nervous habit, under that shameless veneer.

"Oh please," Annabeth waved her other hand in feigned dismissiveness. "The man was having sex with at least eight of the twelve disciples. And some of them were married."

Remy barked out her laughter, enough to make a waiter behind her drop their tray.

"Sacrilege," she said through her giggles.

Annabeth just sighed. "That's why they kicked me out of the nunnery."

There was a mischievous twinkle in her eye.

"Listen." Annabeth drank the rest of her wine like a shot, then grunted her displeasure. "Let me give you a ride home."

"I can handle my liquor," Remy said, taking another drink for good measure.

"That wasn't why I was asking," Annabeth replied, something strange hiding in the smirk on her lips.

Remy blamed exhaustion for her acceptance. Intoxication, for the slap she gave Annabeth when they arrived.

Desire, for why she dug her fingernails into Annabeth's face as they fucked in the driveway.

AFTER ENOUGH CAREFUL scrolling to make her thumb ache, Remy found *the* photo.

It was well taken for a selfie. Carefully angled to show only Annabeth's bottom lip, still plump and glossy and curled into a smile, while catching the light of the sun in her blond hair as it curved around her bare breasts. It was a very pleasing photo, Remy had to admit, stirring her libido and her anger in equal measure. Annabeth's stupid cross was nestled against her cleavage, a gold flashing sign begging for corruption.

Poor Charlie. He'd thought Annabeth needed more corrupting.

Remy admired the photograph a few moments more before

deleting it and continuing to scroll. Annabeth's wasn't the only nude picture he had saved, but it was the only one that stirred something within her. The other photos were just nameless tits and faceless asses, not women but body parts for her husband to salivate and masturbate over. She deleted them all.

Annabeth made some more noises from beside her. Remy ignored them.

When she was certain there were no others, near the bottom of the gallery, she found one of herself, not sexual, but somehow more intimate; a photo from their trip to Paris for their second anniversary. His face was buried in her hair while she laughed into the camera (the words he'd been whispering in her ear had been absolutely filthy, not that the sweet lady taking the photo could hear them). They were young and happy. His arms were wrapped casually around her waist, as if he could will into existence the child she had already known she didn't want and wasn't going to give him.

She deleted that too.

"WHAT DO YOU even see in him?" Remy asked, when the buzzing of a phone led Annabeth from her arms.

Fucking Charlie again.

"Same as you, I guess," Annabeth replied, squeezing her bare ass into a pencil skirt.

"That's different." Remy ran her thumb over her ring finger, as naked as the rest of her. "I was young, dumb, and in love."

Annabeth chuckled. "If that was true, you would have thrown him out years ago."

"I've tried. He's a fucking boomerang."

Annabeth hummed, her fingers deftly doing up her bra. "Maybe you want him to come back."

Remy's hand twitched. She clenched it into a fist to stop Annabeth from noticing, but already knew she hadn't been fast enough. *Don't*, she wanted to say, but the problem with giving orders was that they had a habit of making you more vulnerable than receiving them.

"You didn't answer my question," Remy said instead, and prayed that Annabeth wouldn't notice the bruise she was pressing on.

"You're jealous," Annabeth giggled.

"Not at all." Not once, not ever. Not when she found two used tickets to *Hamlet* in Charlie's suit pocket. Not when a condom wrapper fell out of Annabeth's purse. Not jealous, not left out, not lonely.

Liar, Annabeth said with her smile.

"What can I say?" Annabeth leaned in for a kiss, and Remy gave it to her, hot and hungry and possessive. The place where Annabeth had scratched herself a little too deeply on her cross was nestled against Remy's chin. "I guess I'm young, dumb, and in love."

"BASTARD'S FUCKING HEAVY," Annabeth said through gritted teeth.

"Unless his stamina has gotten considerably better in recent years, you should know that already." Remy smashed the back of Charlie's phone into the cement block she was sitting on until she could pull it off.

"He could at least take some of his weight then." Annabeth sat on the edge of the dock, panting. She wiped the sweat from her forehead with her sleeve.

Pink with exertion and breathless, Annabeth was still the most beautiful person Remy had ever seen.

"I'll help in a minute," Remy said. It was hard to find the SIM card in the dark, so she began to pull whatever part she could from the phone. Battery, memory card, every small chip she could wrangle from it. Each part she managed to pull free, she threw from the dock and into the ocean, each in a different direction.

"Why bother deleting everything if you were just going to do that?" Annabeth asked.

"Satisfaction." Remy threw the scraps of the phone into the water.

"That's littering."

"And that isn't?" Remy pointed to the lumpy rolled up rug at Annabeth's feet.

"It's biodegradable," Annabeth answered. She got back on her knees and resumed tying rope around the rug.

HER CHEEK STILL stung from the slap. Her palm stung as well. The reflex to twenty years of insult and fresh physical pain was to return the pain in kind. It was a good feeling—satisfying, like when she slapped Annabeth's ass, and just as erotic.

Charlie looked at her with wide, wet eyes, clutching his cheek. There was a scratch from her wedding ring. He looked—weak, almost. Frightened. For all his faults, he had never been violent with her, nor she with him. Maybe the possibility had never occurred to him before.

It had occurred to her, though. Even in college, she had fantasies about wrapping her fingers around his neck, digging the nails in until he gasped the way Annabeth did. He had recoiled the one time she pinned down his wrists. If Remy had ever brought out her strap, Charlie would have turned a brighter red than he had just now, when he found her fingers-deep in Annabeth.

Some strange emotion ached deep inside of her, a similar hurt to when she found out he had cheated on her for the first time, and the second. Yearning. She yearned to walk forward and kiss his stupid face, push him to his knees and order Annabeth to bind his hands behind his back. *I love you*, she almost said. *Did you know that? I'd forgotten*.

Charlie raised his hand. Perhaps to strike her again, so she could wrestle him to the ground. Or kiss her tenderly, passionately, the way she had been kissing Annabeth when he walked in. She yearned, yearned for both, yearned to show him his place and how happy they all would be if he would just let her hurt him, dominate him, drive him out of his mind—

His small grunt of pain was so like his grunt near orgasm. His eyes rolled into his head, and when he fell, she leaned in to catch him, cradling him as her hand reached for the sharp letter opener she had dropped to the floor.

Annabeth looked down at them, panting heavily. She seemed almost frozen, until her tongue darted out to lick the cut on her lip.

The bookend in Annabeth's hand started to drip onto the rug.

PERCHED ON HER cement block, Remy watched Annabeth tie the knots to keep the rug closed—her face calm despite the aggression in her movements—and wondered if she'd ever be able to look at Annabeth on her knees again without thinking of this moment. She tilted her head, and the Annabeth working in front of her began to sweat for another reason, her clothes all but melting off her, the rope in her hands turning into rope around her wrists. No, Remy thought, she wouldn't have to worry about that particular problem.

With the phone dealt with, Remy walked over to where Annabeth was working and began to kneel beside the rug. Annabeth flung an arm out and stopped her descent.

"You'll ruin your dress," Annabeth said.

"It's already ruined," Remy replied, moving away from Annabeth's arm so she could kneel anyway.

"I *liked* that dress," Annabeth complained quietly.

Remy bit the inside of her lip to keep the myriad comments she wanted to make from slipping out. She was certain that at last she was as calm on the inside as she was on the outside, the tempestuous storm within her settled, but she couldn't be as sure about Annabeth. So she dampened her usual behavior to keep Annabeth certain of her support, lest she run off or worse, become emotional. Remy wasn't very good with emotions.

She could see some of Charlie's hair in the shadows of the rug, and the glint of something gold. His glasses must have fallen out of his breast pocket. Bizarrely, she was struck with the urge to reach in and fix it, like she would fix his tie when they were young and happy.

Annabeth's hands brushed past hers as Annabeth trussed up the rug.

"You're very good with that," Remy noted as Annabeth deftly coiled the rope.

"Don't tell me this is bringing out your inner submissive," Annabeth said.

Remy smiled and tapped her fingers against Annabeth's cheek.

"Merely admiring your skill, dear," she replied.

Annabeth visibly relaxed, humming a song Remy didn't know as she set about finishing her masterpiece, looping the final knots around each other. For a moment, Remy even thought that she was going to finish with a neat little bow.

No bow, but still satisfied, Annabeth stood up.

"It's going to be a bitch getting this into the water." She tapped the rug with the toe of her shoe. The contents clumsily collided against each other.

"What strength I have won't help much, I'm afraid." Remy waved her thin arms.

"We should have stolen a boat."

"How many felonies are you wanting to commit tonight?" Remy asked.

"Is boat theft a felony?" Annabeth shrugged at her own question. "Doesn't matter. Give me your cigarette."

Remy did.

Annabeth put the cigarette between her own lips, her gloss

and the last of Remy's lipstick intermingling on the surface. She bent down and began to shove the rug, heavy as it was, to the edge of the dock.

Remy quickly followed, pushing as much as she could but unable to shift much of the weight. Her bones had never been particularly strong, even as a young woman. Now, in her fifties, they were unsettlingly fragile, and her exhaustion from the events of the night did little to help. She tried to shove, but there was little movement on her side.

Annabeth was a woman made of curves and muscle. Still, it took considerable effort for her to get the rug and its contents over the edge.

Oh Charlie, Remy thought, watching as the rug sank. *I love you. I love both of you. Why couldn't you have let this end another way?*

II

WHEN ANNABETH WAS sixteen, there was a new priest at her school. He was young, only in his late twenties or so, with soft brown hair and shining blue eyes that he hid behind old-fashioned glasses. If he knew he was attractive, he did his best to downplay it, but his awkward demeanor and shy smiles suggested to her that he did not.

And he had been nice to her. That was the worst part. Annabeth was smart, but a troublemaker, and everyone else at her Catholic school had long since given up on her short skirts and class disruptions. But he wrote encouraging notes on her papers, and whenever she would—deliberately, but also sincerely—push the envelope of religious teachings, he would only follow her train of thought, not shut it down.

She and some of the other girls gossiped about how cute he was, and collected whatever kind comments he gave them in their uniform pockets. Every night, Annabeth would open the notes, read them, and smile, until the old notes began to crumple, and new ones took their place.

And then. Oh, and *then*.

At the time, she hadn't interrogated the impulse much. All she knew was that something was irritating her brain, like a leaky faucet driving her mad with one drip at a time. Soon enough, the drip became a puddle, and Annabeth sat in the confession booth next to the priest she adored and spilled every fantasy she had, the ones that kept her awake and throbbing at night, of him bending her over the desk and pulling up her skirt and—

The first time, he had been understanding. The second, forgiving. Even if he could no longer meet her eyes, they would go into confession, and he would absolve her of every sin, no matter how graphically detailed the sins became.

Eventually, he asked for a transfer, and was replaced by a seventy-two-year-old narcoleptic who smelled of hard candy.

That summer, when that same itch returned, she pushed her best friend off the dock to see if they would still be friends afterward.

Her therapist—who, on threat of expulsion, she'd been forced into seeing—had called it "self-destructive tendencies."

Annabeth wasn't self-destructive. She was sure of it—so sure that she stripped to her underwear in front of her dad's new girlfriend and asked her to smack Annabeth around a little. It was a reckless masochism that had gotten out of control, but Annabeth had remained adamant that it wasn't self-destructive.

But she would admit that it was compulsive. A driving need that had gotten her kicked out of school, out of her house, onto the other side of the continent just to escape all the burning bridges.

"If you're not careful," said her teacher, an old nun who hadn't yet realized she was missing the jar of Vicodin hidden in her robes, "you'll end up choking on the smoke."

It had been that same compulsion that drove her to pass a hotel-room key to her married boss, just to see if he would follow her there.

CHARLIE'S BLOOD DRIPPED onto Annabeth's shoes.

Annabeth released the marble carving in her hands, the bookend silencing the drops with a satisfying *thud*. She had planned what she was going to say, even practiced sobbing it in front of her bathroom mirror, but now she wasn't even able to speak.

Remy was looking at Charlie, splayed groaning on the floor, in a way that Annabeth had, perhaps boldly, assumed was a fondness reserved only for her. The thought that Remy could still care about him, maybe even *love* him—it made Annabeth feel sick.

All her frightened pleas died in the wake of what felt a lot like jealousy, more acidic than the blood from her wounded lip, and she regretted dropping the bookend on the rug and not Charlie's face.

But then Remy smiled at her, and raised the letter opener in her hand like it was a knife.

Annabeth knelt and laid Charlie's head in her lap, one knee pinning his shoulder while her hands pressed down on his mouth. She shushed his cries of pain, pressing kisses into his hair as he failed to free himself from her.

Remy straddled his waist and held her hand over his breast, and Annabeth could feel the heat radiating from Charlie as Remy thrust the letter opener in and out of him. Blood spilled from his chest and down Remy's thighs, then spread into the rug below.

ANNABETH THOUGHT SHE loved Charlie.

She had just assumed it was true, the way she assumed the sky was blue and gravity existed. Uninterested, uninterrogated, like something she read in a book somewhere and obediently committed to memory. Why wouldn't she love him? He lavished her with gifts, took her to see her favorite plays. They had been together for two years now. So when he had said, "I love you," she had said it back, and that was all there was to the matter.

Maybe she would have kept thinking she loved him if he hadn't dragged her to that hotel room.

She hadn't even been planning to see Charlie that evening. Her plans had been with Remy; Charlie was supposed to be out of town, so they were going to cuddle on the couch and watch a movie, and, if time allowed, break in Remy's new flogger. Annabeth had been looking forward to it.

But Charlie had called in a state about something or other, and hopelessly pleaded with her to meet him at the Dresden Hotel, in their usual room.

She expected to find him disheveled and panicking, having been robbed or drugged, or maybe fresh from committing vehicular manslaughter. When she opened the door to find the hotel room covered in rose petals, it didn't occur to her what it meant.

"Darling." Charlie reached out to her, looking like a waiter in his overpriced tux. "Are you surprised?"

Well, yes. See, I expected you to be dying or something.

"What's the occasion?" she asked, tentatively shutting the door.

It didn't feel right to cross the room to him, so she didn't. Eventually, he came to her, wrapping her in his arms.

Charlie chuckled. "Usually, it's the man forgetting the anniversary."

Oh. Shit. She was usually so good with dates.

"Annabeth." Charlie stood back, still holding her arms. He looked drunk, with his watery eyes and pink cheeks. "These past three years with you have been the happiest of my life. You've made me feel—" He stopped for a sharp breath. *Oh, god, was he crying?* "—feel things I've never felt before. Happier than I knew a man could be. Oh, Annabeth, my love—"

Charlie moved, lowering himself down. Instinctively, she tried to help him. He had no practice at kneeling.

Oh, she thought as he reached into his pocket. *Oh no, oh shit, oh fucking Christ!*

"Will you marry me?"

Charlie, for god's sake. Why are you like this?

"Marry you?" Annabeth repeated. "But what about—you're already married!"

"I'm getting a divorce." This, too, had him reaching in his pocket. Annabeth half worried he was going to bring out a second ring, but instead it was just divorce papers, creased from the haphazard way he had folded them. "I'm leaving her, so that you and I can be together."

Annabeth could feel the beginning of a headache, a stabbing pain right behind her eyes. "You can't do that," she said, her mouth slack with disbelief. "The company—your assets will be split in half, at least. What if she proves adultery? She could take everything you've got!"

"Hardly." Charlie rolled his eyes to prove it. "Even if she did—look!"

Charlie held out his phone, open to a bank account that even she hadn't known about. "It's offshore. My private funds, all stashed away somewhere she will never find them! All you need is the code—9078, the hotel room we always get!"

It sank into her like a boulder in water: Charlie was so fucking stupid. So stupid that neither of them had thought to check what he was up to.

"Where did you get this?" The words scratched her throat, like she was trying to speak through needles. The number in the account bored into her eyes—millions. That was millions. "Did you steal it?"

"It's *my* company," Charlie told her. "Remy micromanages every dollar that we make—so I skimmed a little. Big deal."

Annabeth laughed. She couldn't help it. It bubbled up from within her, spilling out until all of the air in the hotel room was taken up by loud, cackling laughter.

"We'll take the money. More of it, even. Disappear, and send her the divorce papers from Cuba. Look—I've already booked the flights!"

Still, Annabeth laughed.

I hate you.

She hadn't realized it before, but now that she did—clutching his phone in her hands, memorizing the details of his secret account, unsure whether to be mad about his fuckery or that she and Remy didn't think of it first—she felt that she always had. Every day, every touch, every sight of him repulsed her. He tried to kiss her, and she almost jumped to escape him. His face, wide-eyed and hopeful, gazed up at her like he could dare hope for her affection.

I hate you, I hate you, I hate you.

"Wait to make any announcements," she said, her voice sounding unnaturally sweet to her ears but seemingly unchanged to Charlie's. "I want us all to end things the right way."

III

THEY WATCHED THE rug sink into the dark water while Annabeth took a last pull of the cigarette, then ground it beneath her shoe. Her work done, Annabeth collapsed against Remy, her back coated in sweat and radiating heat even when Remy shivered against her. Annabeth's exhausted panting soon became a tremble, and Remy prepared herself for the tears. She did not prepare herself for the laughter—relieved, manic, even slightly exuberant—that made Annabeth's entire body shake.

"Y'know, Charlie brought me here on our fifth date," she said, before breaking into giggles again.

"This is where we came for our twentieth anniversary," Remy responded.

Annabeth turned to look at her, eyes full of concern, but that concern was nothing against the mirth that still consumed her. She began to laugh again.

It *was* funny.

"Poor Charlie," Annabeth said through her laughter. "Can't even think of somewhere new to take his girls!"

"Couldn't," Remy corrected. "Past tense."

Annabeth snorted.

Remy pulled Annabeth close to her, using Annabeth's heat to warm her own body. She so desperately wanted to bring their mouths together, to steal Annabeth's laughter with her lips and put her hand around the girl's throat. Even here, on an abandoned dock covered in grime, she wanted to finish what they had started in her office and strip Annabeth naked so she could bury herself in her warmth.

"Do you think I would have been a good nun?" Annabeth asked, turning away from the spot where Charlie's body had been sinking.

"What? A—a nun?"

"Charlie didn't think so." Annabeth said, smiling as if it was a private joke. "He kept complaining about it being a 'boner killer.' My parents didn't think so, either. And the priest at my convent school—"

"Are you planning to become a nun?" Remy interrupted, tightening her arm around Annabeth's waist, digging her fingernails into Annabeth's wrist.

"Of course not, silly." Annabeth laid her hand over Remy's, gentle even when Remy's fingers began to puncture. "I'm not *planning* anything."

"Then why . . . ?"

Their fingers interlocked like bodies twisting in bedsheets.

"Oh, it's nothing," Annabeth answered, voice lilting like she was going to laugh again. "Shakespeare."

"Shakespeare?"

"Mmm." Annabeth leaned back into Remy's body, shivering slightly as the wind lapped at the sweat still dotting her skin. "Going my way to a nunnery."

"That would be—" Terrible. Lamentable. Tragic, even. "Lonely."

"Don't worry," Annabeth said. "Ophelia drowned herself. I drowned Horatio. That makes it a whole new play."

Jouissance

NADINE SANTORO

"ANOTHER ROUND?"

Priya tore her eyes away from the swirling wood-grain pattern of the bar and blinked twice. "Yeah. Thanks, Mel."

The bartender cracked a smile as she swept Priya's rocks glass off the bar and filled a fresh one with ice. "You're in a mood today, huh."

Priya shrugged and picked at the frayed hem of her denim jacket sleeve. She watched Mel grab the bottle of whiskey off the shelf, manicured nails clacking against the glass, and top her up with a heavy pour. "What makes you say that?"

Mel laughed as she slid the glass back across the counter. "Honey, I can't tell you the last time I saw someone sit and drink for half an hour without even glancing at their phone." She leaned her elbows on the edge of the bar and tucked a loose curl behind her ear. "What's eating you?"

Priya frowned and scrubbed a hand through her short-cropped hair. "I'm fine."

Mel's eyebrows quirked up, but the tinkling of the bell over the door saved Priya from having to elaborate. "Suit yourself," Mel said, rapping the bar twice with her knuckles before striding away to greet the new guests.

The chill from the street had Priya glancing over her shoulder, appraising the new arrivals. The bar had filled up a bit in the last thirty minutes—she could hear the clack of billiards from down the hall, laughter bouncing off the dark, wood-paneled walls. The group filing in through the door was mostly femmes, sliding out of rain-glossed trench coats and stacking sleek, see-through umbrellas by the door. Priya took a sip of her drink and watched the women unstick flyaway strands of hair from their lips and pull at the hems of their skirts as they approached the bar: that femme magic that Priya admired but never really understood, a

27

fluent performance that always read more succubus than house-
wife, even in the same clothes as a straight woman.

It was the next woman through the door that caught her eye.

Tall and androgynous, with an effortless-looking blond under-
cut and a sharp jaw, the last one in the group let the heavy
door swing shut behind her as she shrugged out of a well-
worn leather jacket. She ran a hand through her damp hair
and grinned at her friends with the easy confidence that Priya
had envied and prayed for her entire life. It was maddening,
magnetic. Priya downed half of her drink in one gulp.

"First round's on me," the butch said to Mel. Her hair flopped
down as she leaned over the bar, wet strands just brushing the
tops of her high cheekbones. "Y'all better not order the expensive shit—Angie, I'm looking at you."

Her voice needled Priya, kicked up some old feeling in the
corner of her mind as the other women burst into laughter.

"Wow, and people say chivalry is dead," one of the femmes
teased, shoving the blond woman's shoulder. She just shook
her head, fished a wallet out of the back pocket of her dark
jeans. Her skin was pale enough that Priya could see the blue
of a vein that snaked down the back of her hand.

Priya knew she was staring, but she couldn't stop. Drunken-
ness had snuck up on her, had turned everything syrupy slow.
Heat rose to the tips of her ears as she watched those long, pale
fingers pry a credit card from a black leather wallet, jarring an
ID out onto the scratched-wood surface of the bar.

Priya felt her blood drain all at once. She recognized the long-
haired, picture-perfect girl smiling up at her from that photo.

"Charlotte *fucking* Montagne?"

The butch woman turned her head sharply to the left, brow
furrowed, and then her face dropped and her lips went slack.
Priya felt hot under the collar in a whole new way as she stared
down that maddeningly perfect face—a face that was, somehow,
ten times more gorgeous now that it was framed by short-
cropped hair.

"Oh my god—Harris? Priya?"

Charlotte was not returning her glare. Charlotte was, inex-
plicably, smiling and moving toward her, eyes roving to take in
Priya's buffalo-plaid flannel and well-loved boots with an expression that would've read as appraising, almost interested, if Priya
didn't know better.

"It's been—god, ten years? Twelve?" Charlotte laughed the

same polite, tinkling laugh she'd used to win over friends and teachers and coaches and worm her way out of every detention.

Priya ignored her question and fired back one of her own: "The whole time?" Her voice was thick as she spat out the words. "Charlotte, the whole time?"

"I go by Charlie now," the blond said, grinning almost sheepishly.

"Of course you do," Priya replied flatly, picking up her glass and draining it. She pushed herself up off her stool in a huff, face-to-face with Charlie, forgetting that the other girl—woman, now—had a good four inches on her. She straightened her back and exhaled sharply. "I just have one question."

"Okay," Charlie said, looking down at her, her eyebrows raised, her mouth twitching at one corner, like she was amused.

"Was it all to throw people off the scent?" Her voice was hard, but her hands shook at her sides. "Writing 'Priya likes pussy' on the bathroom stalls as, what, a red herring?"

Charlie's friends were all watching; a hush fell among the group. "Well," she said carefully, glancing askew and then back to Priya. Her mouth curled into a cold smile. "I was right, wasn't I?"

Priya balled her hand into a fist and punched Charlie right in her perfect, chiseled jaw.

"YOU GOT *thrown out* of Ginger's?!"

"Don't look at me like that," Priya said miserably, shrugging her shoulders up to burrow deeper into the collar of her jacket. "I feel bad enough on my own."

"I'm not, I'm just—you made me get the humane kind of mouse traps, Priya," Kelsey said, walking faster to match her friend's pace. "Since when are you the kind of person who punches girls at the bar?"

"I'm not!" Priya replied, a desperate edge to her voice. "Not—not anymore, anyway. It's just . . . her. She always got under my skin like that."

The wind picked up. It was unseasonably cold for the first week of October, and Priya shivered, glancing across the field where a group of elementary schoolers played soccer. It had been years since she played, but she missed it now, watching the girls run and sweat and get their aggression out on the ball streaking across the muddy grass.

"I punched her once before, in high school," she blurted,

turning as Kelsey scoffed beside her. "We got in a full-blown fist-fight at practice. I almost got kicked off the team."

Kelsey was staring at her incredulously, wind blowing her long brown hair around her face. "Who are you?" she asked, but she was grinning. "What did she do?"

"Pulled my ponytail," Priya said reluctantly, and Kelsey burst out laughing. "No, but it was more than that—she was always out to get me. We hated each other. Always, almost at first sight." She kicked at a pile of dead leaves on the edge of the dirt path and then stomped on one, relishing the crunch under her scuffed-up boot. "You should've seen her at the bar. She looked so smug."

"Did she, or are you just harboring a fifteen-year-old grudge on the hot popular girl?" Kelsey said, gentle but pointed, nudging Priya with her elbow.

"You wanna know what the worst part is?" Priya said. She glanced back at the soccer game.

"What?"

"She goes by Charlie now."

"No," Kelsey gasped. She grinned again. "Not Charlie."

"I know," Priya groaned, watching storm clouds roll in on the horizon. "Devastating."

IT RAINED FOR four days. Priya spent most of them brooding, haunted by memories of those pale hands, that godforsaken smirk that dimpled on just one side. The way her cheekbone had bloomed pink with the impact of the punch. And other memories, too—Charlie, back when she was still Charlotte, knocking books out of Priya's hands in the echoing linoleum hallways, waving over her shoulder as her blond ponytail swung behind her. Chucking erasers at the back of Priya's head in class, always a picture of girl-next-door innocence when the teacher turned toward the commotion. Shoving Priya up against the peeling red lockers in the gym, breath hot, so close, jeering to the rest of the girls that they might want to get changed in the next row over to avoid wandering eyes.

Those teenage memories twisted in her dreams, morphed as the adult Charlie emerged, her hair still damp from the rain, almost brown. Her breath hot on Priya's face. Her icy eyes, searching, searching.

Priya woke up in a tangle of sweat-soaked bedsheets with her hands curled into fists, just looking for something to punch.

Whatever this part of her was, whatever demons she had buried for so long, they were awake again. Wide awake.

"YOU'RE A WOMAN possessed," Kelsey said, exhaling cigarette smoke into the night air.

"Shut up," Priya muttered, lighting up her own.

"You saw that girl for approximately forty-five seconds a week ago, and you've managed to bring her up in almost every conversation we've had since."

Priya didn't respond; she took a drag of her cigarette. The door to the bar opened and a group of beanie-clad bros spilled out onto the street, laughing. The jarring, nasally vocals of the band playing on the dive's tiny stage lingered on the crisp air for a few moments before the door swung shut. Priya's phone buzzed in her pocket, and she scanned the text on the screen.

"What's the word?" Kelsey asked, leaning over her shoulder.

"I'll be unbanned in November." Priya sighed and tucked her phone back in her jeans. "Mel vouched for me."

"Well, thank god," Kelsey said, raising her cigarette in a cheers. "Imagine if we had to keep coming to this place forever."

"You can go back to Ginger's any time," Priya said, a little testily, and leaned against the brick wall. "And I'm not the one who lives in goddamn Gowanus." She watched ash fall off the end of her cigarette and onto the pavement, one glowing ember sputtering out as it drifted down.

She hardly noticed the footsteps approaching until they stopped just beside her.

"Got a light?"

Priya coughed, heart lurching.

There was Charlie, washed out in the sepia glow of the streetlamp but still unfairly striking. She wore a sleek black bomber jacket and a simple silver chain. There was the faintest yellow-green tinge to her left cheekbone. Priya felt pride surge through her chest, soured slightly by Charlie's calm, expectant demeanor.

"Are you stalking me?" Priya asked, pushing herself off the wall to stand at her full, completely undaunting, height.

"No, just unlucky," Charlie responded coolly. Between the fingers of her left hand, she loosely held up an unlit cigarette. "Gonna punch me again, Harris?"

Priya gritted her teeth. "No." She paused. "Maybe."

Charlie laughed—that terrible, charming laugh. "God, you're

still so stubborn." She eyed the lit cigarette in Priya's hand. "So. How about that light?"

When Priya didn't move, Charlie sighed and ran a hand through her hair. "Look, I was a royal bitch in high school. I'm not proud of it. But you can't pretend it was one-sided." After a tense moment, she held out her right hand. "Can we bury the hatchet?"

Priya felt Kelsey's eyes on the back of her head. She let Charlie's non-apology hang in the air and glanced between her outstretched hand and her face. Charlie's mouth was set in a hard line, but her eyes were open, earnest. To be fair, she was right—it never really had been one-sided. Maybe the punches Priya had landed had been in self-defense, but the rumors she'd spread, the tires she'd slashed . . .

Priya sighed.

"Here," she said, fishing her lighter out of her pocket and placing it in Charlie's right hand.

Their eyes met for one long, searing moment. Then Charlie nodded and lit her cigarette, cupped her hand to shield it from the wind. She handed the lighter back to Priya as she exhaled, smoke clouding the air between them.

"So, uh." Priya gestured to her left. "This is my friend—" The sudden sound of music made her turn, and she saw Kelsey disappearing back inside the bar, her cigarette left half-smoked on the pavement. ". . . Kelsey."

"She's cute," Charlie said with a little nod to the side, one eyebrow raised.

"Not my type," Priya replied with a shrug.

"Hm." Charlie took another drag of her cigarette, her expression unreadable. "How long have you lived in New York?"

"Been here since college," Priya answered. "You?"

"Five years."

Priya huffed out a laugh. "And now we run into each other twice in one week."

"It always happens that way, doesn't it?" Charlie said with a wry smile. "I won't see any of my ex-girlfriends for years, and then I'll see three of them in the same weekend."

Priya smiled, eyebrows raised. "You have a lot of exes running around this city?"

Charlie grinned, looked her up and down. "You don't?"

Priya burned under her gaze, her own eyes darting back up to the night sky. "God, this is fucking weird."

"What is?"

Priya almost glared at her, gesturing with both arms. "This. You." She took a drag of her cigarette and exhaled sharply. "Hearing you talk about all the women you've dated. You made my life hell, you know."

A moment of tense silence stretched between them.

"I know."

Priya watched Charlie, who was staring up at the sky, blowing smoke, her expression blank. "And?" Priya demanded, crossing her arms.

"And what?" Charlie asked, looking back at her steadily. She was so cool, so solid—it made Priya want to punch her again. "High school was hell for a lot of people. You don't have a monopoly on it."

"Oh, right," Priya scoffed. "I'm sure it was so hard to be everyone's favorite blond Barbie princess." She held out her hand and started counting off on her fingers, ash flying off the end of her cigarette. "Little miss rich girl. MVP three seasons running. Honor roll. Prom queen. Life was just so hard for you in high school, wasn't it?"

"Sounds like you were a little obsessed with me, Harris."

Priya flung her cigarette butt to the ground and shoved Charlie backward, against the brick wall, her forearm locked across her chest. "What the fuck is your problem?" she hissed. She was hardly tipsy this time, but something about Charlie got her blood boiling anyway, made everything blur at the edges. "Do you get off on tormenting me?"

"I don't know." Charlie couldn't quite maintain her cool facade anymore, her voice a little breathless from the impact of being shoved against the wall, her mouth twitching up at the corner. "It's pretty hot that I can rile you up this easy."

"Fuck you," Priya spat, her cheeks burning.

"You wish," Charlie countered, grinning.

Priya let out a roar and moved to swing at her again, but this time Charlie was ready. She caught Priya by the wrist and spun them around so that Priya was the one against the wall, knocking her head hard against the brick. Priya winced and pushed against Charlie's shoulder to shove her off, trying to pry her hand free, but the other woman's grip was firm, so she swung wildly with her other arm, hitting Charlie in the ribs. Charlie let out a sharp gasp and grabbed at Priya's arm and then they were grappling, locked in and unwilling to let go. Priya struggled, her head banging against the brick again, and managed to reach up and grab a fistful of Charlie's short hair, yanking her head down.

Their foreheads knocked together, and she could feel Charlie's hot breath on her face, smell the stale smoke and the warm, woodsy scent of her cologne beneath it. She felt sixteen again, out of her mind with loathing, brawling on the soccer field, two bodies tangled together as she relished every bruise, every bit of skin contact, every moment of this, just like this, and—

She wasn't sure who started it. One moment they were struggling and panting, and the next their lips crashed, teeth clacking, the impact almost painful. Priya's wrist was still pinned under Charlie's tight grip, Charlie's hair was still clutched tightly in Priya's fist, and they kissed with violent desperation. Priya's body responded before her mind could fully catch up—her lips parting, one leg slotting in between Charlie's thighs. There was still a part of her that wanted to punch, to bruise. But then Charlie let out a soft groan as Priya tugged at the roots of her hair, and Priya had to bite back a whimper in response.

Charlie let go of Priya's wrist, and Priya's hands jumped to Charlie's waist, grabbing at her hip bone, her ass. Priya was dizzy with desire. She felt like her brain was on fire, like all that existed was Charlie's mouth and her lithe frame that surged forward, seeking friction. She despised her; she'd never wanted anyone more in her life. Her hands roamed down Charlie's body, hungry, and she wanted, she wanted, she wanted the one person she'd spent half her life hating. The fact of that had her coming up for air.

"Fuck," she mumbled, her wet mouth pressed to Charlie's jawline. "What—"

"Shut up," Charlie replied, silencing her with her lips. Priya gladly let her. She didn't want to reason things out, not really—not if it would put a stop to whatever this was: Charlie's hands at her hips, thumbs skimming under the edge of Priya's well-worn T-shirt. She wanted more, more than they could do in the middle of the sidewalk under a streetlight. She pulled away again, glancing around quickly, and then grabbed Charlie's hand and tugged her into the narrow alley behind them.

The farther they went down the alley, the darker it was. Priya blinked as her eyes adjusted. Broken glass crunched underfoot, and a few rats scurried out from some black trash bags, squeaking as they rushed behind a pallet of crumbling bricks. Satisfied they were far enough out of sight, Priya cornered Charlie back up against the wall.

Charlie grinned. "Romantic spot," she whispered.

Priya didn't dignify the jab with a response, just kissed her harshly, pressing her into the brick. Charlie kissed back with equal fervor. They were both too rough, trying to dissolve the years of bitter rivalry with their tongues. Charlie's hands snaked under Priya's shirt, cool against her skin. Priya pressed her thigh between Charlie's legs, pinning her closer to the wall, shivering at the choked-off noise that spilled from her throat. Priya followed that sound down, kissing the hard line of Charlie's jaw, pulling at the collar of her shirt, biting the taut muscle where her neck met her shoulder. Priya's heartbeat roared in her ears. If she could, she would devour this woman whole.

But Charlie was giving back just as good, her hand pushed up under Priya's sports bra, pinching her nipple at that perfect threshold between pain and pleasure. The nails of her other hand dug into Priya's back, hard. This was what Priya loved about butches, about being a butch with other butches—or at least the butches she chose. Every fuck was a competition, a race to see who would unravel the other first.

Tonight, she was particularly determined to win.

She pulled at the button of Charlie's jeans with one hand until it came free, yanked down the zipper. Charlie gasped in her ear and Priya paused, biting at her neck again, her fingertips trailing the elastic waistband of Charlie's boxers.

"Want something?" Priya murmured against her skin, grinning.

"Oh, fuck you," Charlie hissed, digging her nails deeper into Priya's back.

"You first."

She felt Charlie's whole body shudder the moment she touched her, and her body responded in kind, thrumming as it did when she brought a woman to the edge.

"Wow, you really are desperate for it," she whispered, fingers slick.

Charlie groaned and brought a hand up to yank Priya's short hair—a sharp, painful tug. "I hate you," she muttered, but her hips keened forward for more.

Priya indulged her, spurred on as Charlie's cool facade crumbled at her touch, the choked whimpers she let slip. Whatever this was, Priya felt high on it—she finally had a little bit of power over Charlotte Montagne.

She leaned back a few inches and grabbed Charlie's jaw in her free hand, tilted her face toward her own.

"Look at me."

Charlie's eyes fluttered open, pupils blown wide.

"You have to keep looking at me if you wanna come."

She didn't say anything, didn't nod, just thrust her hips harder against Priya's hand. Her gaze was burning, open—Priya lost herself in it, drunk on her submission. Before long Charlie was shaking, gasping, nails scabbering at the back of Priya's neck as she tumbled over the edge, muscle clenching around Priya's fingers. Victorious, Priya didn't stop until Charlie yanked her hand up by the wrist, overstimulated, chest heaving.

"Okay," she breathed, scanning Priya's face, almost laughing. "Okay."

Priya hardly had time to catch her own breath before Charlie spun them both around, shoving Priya roughly against the wall, and dropped to her knees on the concrete.

"Fuck," Priya hissed, watching Charlie unbutton her pants and tug them down. She hardly had time to process what was happening before Charlie's mouth was on her, and her hands leapt immediately to the other woman's hair, her glassy eyes gazing over the scene behind them—

"Oh my god," Priya yelped, jerking Charlie back by the hair.

There was a man watching them.

Engulfed in shadow, he was barely visible but for the flutter of movement at his waist, his pale fist pumping. Priya felt bile rise in the back of her throat.

"Wha—" Charlie started, indignant, trying to lean back in.

"Get the fuck out of here," Priya yelled, and Charlie whirled around, scrambling to her feet. Priya tugged her pants back up, feeling inside out, like her guts were exposed, defenseless in the cold night air. When the man didn't immediately move, she grabbed a small rock on the ground and hurled it at him, missing by barely an inch. It hit the dumpster behind him with an echoing, metallic clang.

That set him off. He stumbled out of the darkness. He was taller than both of them, young, pale, with long brown hair pulled back in a bun. He lunged for Priya and shoved her back against the wall, his hand at her throat.

"Fucking bitch," he slurred, breath beery and sour.

"Get off her!" Charlie shouted. She grabbed at the man's arm, trying to pry him away, but even with his drunken, uneasy footing, he was too heavy to move.

"You wanna be a man?" he jeered. His fingers pressed against Priya's windpipe.

Priya struggled, trying to dislodge her knee enough to kick

him in the groin, but the weight of his body pinned her to the wall. She could feel him hard against her hip, and she wanted to projectile vomit in his face.

"I'll bite your fucking dick off," she wheezed.

Charlie kicked the man in the back of the knee and he buckled slightly, just enough for Priya to partially unpin one of her arms and land a punch to the side of his ribs. A moment later, there was a shatter and green broken glass rained down on them both.

The man stumbled back, clutched at his head. Blood trickled from his ear as he turned toward the mouth of the alleyway. Charlie cast the broken bottle neck aside, kicking him in the knee as he retreated, and he changed tack, swinging out and punching her solidly in the gut. She tripped from the impact, crying out as she struck the slat metal fence behind her. Priya surged forward, blind with rage, kicking the cowardly piece of shit in the groin as he tried to stumble away. He crumpled to the ground. His dick was still hanging out, a pale, pathetic worm, and she stomped on it hard with her boot, leaving him howling on the concrete.

She rushed over to Charlie, slumped against the fence and struggling to her feet.

"Are you okay?" she asked, pulling her up, but Charlie just shook her head and shoved Priya roughly aside.

Priya saw the man's shadow on the fence and froze, half turned back toward him, unsure if he'd risen to his feet to strike again or to flee. Charlie didn't wait to find out. She palmed a brick and swung. The brick met his temple with a sickening crack.

The man collapsed with a moan, and Priya shouted out in shock, but Charlie was still moving. Bearing down on him with empty eyes, she brought the brick down again—another dull crack. Again. The wet sound of flesh rending. Again. Charlie's anguished cry. Again.

Priya grabbed Charlie by the arms and hauled her off the man, who was no longer making any noise, no longer moving at all. Charlie was sobbing, shaking, her hands slick with blood, and she dropped to the ground, her fingers loosening on the gory brick.

"What—" Priya rasped, doubled over. "Charlie—"

She'd known he was dead by the second swing of the brick— it was overkill; it was bound to be gruesome. But she looked anyway.

He was spread-eagled on the ground, one hand still curled

into a loose fist, a muddy boot print branded across his pale crotch. His skull was caved in, more pulp than face. Blood spattered around what was left of his head, a halo of dark stains seeping into the cement. One eye was still intact, staring blankly up at the sky.

Priya turned and retched onto a pile of broken glass, hot acid burning her throat.

"Fuck," Charlie whispered, looking at her bloody hands like they weren't her own. "Fuck, fuck, fuck."

"We have to go," Priya croaked, wiping her mouth on the back of her sleeve. Panic was hardening into resolve, a lead weight in her chest. "Charlie, we have to go right now." She whirled around, scanning the eaves of the building. "No cameras. Okay. Okay. Fuck. Let's just—let's make it seem—" Avoiding looking at the man's face, she shoved a hand blindly into the front pocket of his jeans, pulling out a leather wallet, and then into the other pocket, retrieving his cell phone. The screen looked freshly cracked, shards of glass crumbling off its face. "Fuck. Okay. Let's go."

Charlie got to her feet, trembling. There was a spatter of blood across her cheek. Gore clung to her eyelashes.

"Here—" Priya reached up and wiped her clean sleeve across Charlie's face, leaving a pale pink streak near her hairline. It was good enough to make a getaway. "Put your hands in your pockets. Come on."

"But—" Charlie hesitated, glancing wildly around the scene. "But—"

"They won't find us," Priya said, a desperate edge to her voice. She grabbed Charlie by the crook of the elbow and pulled her toward the hazy streetlights. "We were never here."

THE HOT WATER was out again in Priya's apartment. They stood under the icy blast, shivering, watching pink runoff swirl down the drain. Their clothes were in a pile in the tub around their feet, rust-tinged denim and black cotton. Charlie leaned her head back against the tile wall, her eyes glazed and empty.

"They're coming for us," she said, voice hollow.

"Stop it," Priya muttered, soaping up the loofah and scrubbing her hands for the fourth time. "No one saw."

"This isn't fucking 1950, Harris," Charlie said, her eyes sliding back into focus as she glared. "It doesn't matter if no one saw. They have forensics. They'll put it together eventually."

"Don't," Priya warned, dunking her head under the frigid stream of water again. She surfaced sputtering, blinking to clear her eyes. "If you hadn't gone psycho on that guy . . ." She turned the squeaky faucet knobs off more aggressively than she needed to.

"He would've killed you," Charlie said. Her voice echoed off the tiles, too loud without the rush of water.

Priya looked up at her. She was shivering, arms wrapped around her torso, but her gaze was steady. After a frayed, tense moment, Priya looked away. She pulled the shower curtain back abruptly, its plastic rings rattling across the metal bar.

"Here," she said, handing Charlie her bath towel. "I'll grab some clean clothes."

She turned to leave the bathroom, but Charlie grabbed her by the wrist.

"Why didn't you just leave me?"

Priya paused. She didn't want to turn around. It felt too intimate, suddenly, to see Charlie's naked body like this, to be seen. She wished she had the towel back, so she could cover herself up.

"You could've run," Charlie continued, her voice strained. "You could've turned me in."

"Don't be stupid," Priya said, glancing back at her at last. "I wouldn't do that."

Charlie clutched the towel over her chest uselessly as water from her hair dripped down her temple, over the sharp bridge of her nose. "Why not? You hate me, don't you?"

"You hate me," Priya countered, afraid Charlie could feel her pulse jumping in her wrist. "You could've just let me die."

"No," Charlie said. She shook her head almost desperately, a hard crease in her brow. "No."

The distance had closed between them without Priya even noticing. Had she taken a step forward? Had she grabbed Charlie's waist? This time when they kissed, it was with all the same frantic energy, but for none of the same reasons. In the alley, she was catching fire. She was summiting a mountain. She was coming alive. Now, when Charlie's teeth grazed her tongue, when the towel dropped to the floor and they clung together, dripping wet and swaying with their bloodstained clothes soaking in the bath behind them, they were tending a wound. They were making a pact. They were digging a grave.

BANG BANG BANG.

Priya's eyes shot open.

Bang bang bang.

"Motherfucker," Priya hissed, her stomach lurching violently. Charlie stirred beside her beneath the dark green duvet, eyes bleary and then wide, her hair sticking up in three different directions.

"I know you're in there," a familiar voice called, accompanied by another set of loud raps on the door. "I have your location on."

Priya exhaled, flopping bonelessly back onto her pillow. "Jesus. It's just Kelsey."

Charlie pushed the blankets down and propped herself up on her elbows. "*Just Kelsey* can't be involved in this."

Priya frowned and nodded, scrubbed a hand over her face. "I'll get rid of her."

She pushed back the covers and stood up, every muscle in her body groaning and sore. Weak, pale sunlight filtered in through the sheer curtains, bathing the small, messy room in a sickly glow. Priya grabbed a T-shirt and boxers from the pile of clean clothes on her desk chair, tugging them on as she tottered out into the hallway.

"Go away," Priya called through the door.

"She's ali-ive!" Kelsey replied, sing-song. A pause, and then: "Oh shit, you've got her in your bed, don't you?"

Priya groaned, letting her head rest against the door. "If I say yes, will you go away?"

"Not a chance. Open up, slut."

Priya turned the deadbolt and cracked open the door, peering out into the hall. Kelsey had her hair tossed up in a messy bun with her pink hoodie pulled up over the top of it, paired with matching track bottoms. She looked like a Conehead. It was a classic hangover fit.

"Wider."

"I'm not letting you in, Kelse."

"Then I guess I'll just stand here in the hallway while I tell you about the fucking dead body I saw last night."

Priya's blood turned to ice. She wrenched the door open and ushered Kelsey inside.

"I was freaking out, by the way, and you didn't answer any of my calls, and then I was more—woah." Kelsey paused, ogling Priya's neck. "Your girl's into choking?"

Priya frowned as she locked the door. "What?"

"Your throat, dude."

Priya's hands jumped to the tender muscles around her windpipe, stomach churning once more at the ghost of the man's touch "I, uh. Fuck. You—you saw a dead guy? Did the cops come?"

"Yeah, the cops came," Kelsey said. "This dude was like—he was squashed like a bug. It was awful. Half his face was gone. I almost threw up." She flopped down on the couch, grabbing a lumpy throw pillow to hug across her lap. "You'd think I'd've watched enough *SVU* to be over this kind of thing, but it's different in real life."

Priya swallowed and nodded, leaning one shoulder against the wall.

"Anyway," Kelsey continued, "did you guys leave soon after I went inside? You might've even seen the guy who did it—have the cops called you?"

"Why would the cops call me?" Priya demanded, a little too sharply. "Did you tell them I was there?"

"Jesus, Pri. Fuck the police and everything, but—"

"What do they think happened to the guy?" Priya interrupted. Her palms were sweaty. "Like, what was the deal?"

"I dunno. They talked to a bunch of people, closed the whole block down. I don't even remember exactly. I was pretty fucked up, and then I saw the inside of a dude's skull, and you abandoned me, and—" Kelsey was counting grievances on her fingers now, "—Sammy left me on read again. So basically it was the worst night ever."

"Great," Priya said distractedly, leaning against the edge of the kitchen counter, trying to even out her breathing.

"It's not great, asshole," Kelsey said, with less bite than she probably hoped. "Meanwhile you've just been fucking your high school nemesis for fourteen straight hours—is that right?" She leaned forward, peering down the dark hall. "CHARLIE!"

"Okay, you're leaving now." Priya hauled Kelsey up by the arm and pulled her toward the door, held it open, and gestured over the threshold.

"I'm traumatized," Kelsey pleaded halfheartedly, leaning against the doorframe. "You'd really kick me out?"

"I love you, and you're leaving."

Kelsey sighed, glancing back conspiratorially in the direction of Priya's bedroom before she stepped out into the hall. "Seriously, though, it's almost four p.m. That hate sex must be fucking amazing."

"Goodbye, Kelsey."

When she returned to the bedroom, Charlie was sitting at the foot of the bed, flipping through a thick book she'd pulled from Priya's shelf. Her pale skin was mottled with red and purple bruises, blooming on her stomach and shoulders. Bite marks trailed from her neck to her chest. It was overkill, but Priya hadn't been able to stop herself.

"I didn't take you for a poetry girl," she said, turning the Audre Lorde collection over in her hand.

"What kind of girl did you take me for?" Priya asked, closing the door gently with her back.

Charlie shrugged and slid the book back into its place on the overstuffed shelf. She glanced around the room, at the haphazard stack of unopened mail on the desk, the small pile of cardboard boxes that gathered dust in the corner, half unpacked, nearly two years after Priya had moved in. Priya fidgeted with the hem of her T-shirt, a souvenir from a 5K she'd run in college.

"I'm gonna go for a walk," she said, before Charlie could finish her thought. She turned to her dresser and pulled out a pair of jeans, tugged them on. "We should get rid of the clothes."

Charlie let her eyes fall on Priya at last, lingering over the bruising on her neck. She nodded slowly. "What about the wallet? And phone?"

"Maybe—cut up the cards in the wallet and flush them?" she said, tossing fresh clothes at Charlie. "The phone—I don't know. Flush the SIM, too, I guess. I can ditch the rest in a different dumpster."

It was easier to think about it like this—detached, just a puzzle to solve. But when she saw the deadened, fear-hardened look behind Charlie's cold blue eyes, her pulse jumped in her neck. She looked so small, naked on the edge of the bed, clutching Priya's clothes to her chest.

Priya turned abruptly and left the room, ignoring the tenderness swelling in her chest as she grabbed their crumpled clothes out of the bathtub. Charlie's leather jacket was still waterlogged, and Priya hesitated for a moment before she tossed it into a tote bag with the rest of their things. She emptied the man's wallet onto the bathroom floor without looking at its contents— she didn't want to see, didn't want to know his name. When she returned to the bedroom, Charlie was dressed, tightening the drawstring cords of the sweatpants to keep them up on her narrow hips.

Charlie's eyes fell on the collar of her jacket peeking out of the bag. "Damn. I loved that thing."

Priya swallowed. She avoided Charlie's gaze. "Yeah, well."

THE AIR WAS cooling, and Priya zipped up her jacket, cast her eyes to the darkening sky. She'd visited five different dumpsters, just to be safe. It had occurred to her on the second-to-last one that they should get rid of their shoes, too, but that was a problem for later—assuming they'd managed to buy themselves enough time.

On the corner of Dean Street, Priya bounced on the balls of her feet, waiting for the crosswalk sign to change. The cars' headlights moved across her body like helicopter searchlights. The imposing metal obelisk of the LinkNYC pillar beside her played an ad for the new exhibit at the MoMA in which a man in a flamboyant yellow suit stood in front of a large painting. The figure in the painting was cast almost entirely in silhouette but was clearly female, her dark hands up as if pressed against a pane of glass. Her only illuminated feature was a pair of open, cold blue eyes.

As the last car whizzed through a red light at the intersection, Priya's eyes wandered to the top edge of the screen, where the bright glow of the ad gave way to the smooth black of the pillar's face. And there, in a small, round opening behind the glass was the steady, beady lens of a camera.

"WE'RE FUCKED," she said, slamming the door behind her. "Charlie, we're fucked."

Charlie was pacing in the kitchen, eating tortilla chips out of the bag. "What?" she asked, freezing with a handful of chip fragments halfway to her mouth.

"Those stupid Link things they've been installing all over the place, you know, those things with the ads and the weather and the free Wi-Fi?" Priya twisted her carabiner of keys in her hand, fidgeting with the metal hinge. "Well, they also have surveillance cameras."

"Jesus," Charlie said, blanching. "We must've passed—"

"Dozens of them." Priya dropped her keys on the counter, the clattering noise too loud. "Fuck."

"This is your fault," Charlie blurted.

Priya looked up at her, jaw slack.

"You said we were good," Charlie said. Her voice was tight with desperation. Her fists clenched, unclenched, clenched again. "You said—fuck, we should've just—"

"We weren't thinking." Priya crossed the room cautiously, like she was approaching a wild animal. She reached for Charlie's arm. "What else could we have done?"

Charlie flinched away, shrunk in on herself. "Claimed self-defense in the first place! I don't know!"

"Self-defense?" Priya's pulse jumped in her neck. "Charlie, you bricked him in the face. Maybe if you'd had a little self-control—"

"Fuck you," Charlie spat. She spun and shoved Priya up against the wall and put a hand to her throat, her thumb pressing into the bruise the dead man had left the night before. "You wanna talk about self-control, huh? You wanna lecture me about self-control, Harris?"

"What the fuck does that mean," Priya rasped, swallowing against Charlie's fingers. Heat pooled in her gut absurdly, the spike of danger and adrenaline tipping over into arousal.

"God, your victim complex is insane," Charlie scoffed. "You slashed my fucking tires because I called you a dyke in the locker room *once*, and you want to talk to me about self-control."

"You're the one who killed a man," Priya said. "You're the one who's insane."

Charlie exhaled sharply, then released Priya's throat and stalked across the room. "You fucking cunt. I saved your life."

"But you didn't have to kill him," Priya shouted. It was too loud, the walls were paper thin, but all she cared about was putting Charlie down.

"Yes, I did!" Charlie practically shrieked. She looked crazed, breathless, her eyes wild, her hair hanging limply across her face. "He hurt you, he threatened you, he would've—"

"Why the fuck do you care?!" Priya yelled.

"I was in love with you!"

The words pierced the air of the kitchen like the wail of a siren.

Charlie swallowed, pushed her hair out of her eyes. "In high school. I was in love with you."

Priya let out a breath she didn't know she'd been holding.

The shrill trill of a cell phone ringing made them both jump.

Charlie strode forward and grabbed her phone off the couch. It was an unfamiliar number with a 718 area code. It kept ringing—two, three, four times, and then it went silent. Both women waited, barely daring to breathe. After a minute, a voicemail notification popped up with a cheery chime. Fingers shaking, Charlie played it on speaker.

"Charlotte Montagne, this is Detective Patrick Morgan from the 76th Precinct. I'd like to ask you a few questions regardi—"

Charlie closed out of the voicemail and dropped her phone back on the couch.

"I have to go."

"Where?" Priya asked, suddenly sweating through her shirt. "If they have your number, they definitely have your address by now, too."

"I don't know. I just—" Charlie crouched down, her hands over her ears, as if to shield herself from what was coming. "I need to think. I need air."

A BITING WIND blew off the East River. Priya had worked up a sweat on the walk over, and now she was chilled, shivering, her flannel damp under her jacket. It was quiet on the pier. They'd followed Atlantic all the way down to the water, hardly speaking, feeling the eyes of traffic cameras and corner bodega security systems on them with every step. Now that they'd reached the end of the street, Charlie paced in front of the chain link fence where the ferries docked, her eyes blank, seemingly unaffected by the sharp breeze that pinked her cheekbones.

"I have to turn myself in," she said finally, staring out at the Manhattan skyline.

"No," Priya said immediately, stepping into her field of view. "They don't know anything, they might just think you were a witness—"

"Come on, Harris," Charlie said, her eyes flickering over Priya's face. "There's only one way this ends, and I can make it easy on everyone, or I can keep running."

"Then let's run," Priya said.

Charlie leaned against the fence, her gaze steady as she stared at Priya. After a moment, she huffed a laugh. "God, you're stubborn." She folded her arms across her chest. "You're not coming with me."

Priya scoffed. "Fuck you. Yes, I am."

A half-cocked plan formed in her head: a vision of them on the bus out of town, lying low in a cottage on the Cape, empty streets and winter waves cresting on the sand. Make it seem like a romantic getaway and let Kelsey's big mouth do the rest.

Charlie rocked forward onto the balls of her feet, pushing away from the fence and shouldering past Priya. "You don't want this. Just—let me take the fall, all right? Let me do this for you."

"Don't be chivalrous right now," Priya said, marching down the pier after her. "Let's go. Let's get out of here, together." When Charlie didn't answer, Priya grabbed her wrist and yanked her back around. "Stop! Just stop! I'm not the one you need to be running from!"

"Yes, you are," Charlie said, reeling back out of Priya's grip. A siren wailed in the near distance. "You—I'm insane when I'm around you." Charlie let out a watery laugh. "I mean, look at what I did. I need to get away."

"No, Charlie—please—" Priya reached for her again and felt a surge of relief when she didn't pull away. The siren wailed louder now, and Charlie's pulse beat frantically in her wrists, leaping against the pads of Priya's fingers. "I'm not letting you take the fall for this alone."

"Priya—" Charlie's eyes widened as tires screeched to a stop at the end of the pier. Her face was bathed in the glow of blue and red.

"Hey!" a rough male voice called from the car. Priya turned slowly, letting go of Charlie's hands.

Two officers stepped out of the car. The one on the passenger side stayed back, his hand hovering near his right hip, while the driver took a few paces forward, drawing his gun. The barrel glinted in the moonlight.

This is it, Priya thought. A perverse sense of calm washed over her.

"Let's go, guys, it's over," the driver yelled out, peering down at the shadowy corner where they stood. "Put your hands up."

They stepped forward, their hands rising into the air. Priya edged in front of Charlie and drew herself up to her full height.

The officer approached them warily at first, but as he got closer, his expression shifted.

"Oh—sorry, ladies," he said, lowering his weapon halfway, scanning their features. He glanced back and nodded at his partner. "It's not them, Rod."

Priya felt a cold rush of relief flood her chest.

"What're y'all doing out here?" the cop asked, eyeing them as he holstered his gun.

"Just—uh—hooking up," Charlie said, her voice suddenly shy

and sweet, as sickening as it had been in high school.

The cop cleared his throat, eyeing them up and down one more time.

"Well, find another spot," he said after a moment. "You seen anyone else down here?"

"No," Priya said. She finally let her arms drop slowly to her sides. "Just us. But we haven't been here long."

"All right." He tipped his head toward the street. "Get lost. I'll let you go with a warning."

"Thanks," Charlie said, plastering on a smile. She grabbed Priya's hand and they hurried back down the pier. The man waved to them and got back into his car, where his partner was talking to a dispatcher, the radio held up to his face.

"Keep walking," Charlie said, still smiling as she pulled Priya down the sidewalk. "Pretend to laugh at something I said." Priya could feel the cops' eyes on them, that prickling sensation at the back of her neck, so she laughed, a forced, jarring sound. They passed a looming warehouse, jaywalked across a quiet late-night street. It wasn't until they'd walked beneath the highway overpass and past a locked-up playground that Charlie finally let go of her hand.

"Holy fuck," she gasped. She slumped against the side of a shuttered office building. "I thought that was it."

"I know," Priya whispered, almost laughing. "Oh my god."

"I thought you were going to confess," Charlie said, wide-eyed, grabbing Priya's hands.

"I was," Priya said, surprising herself with her certainty. "I know, I'm insane," she added, cutting Charlie off as she started to open her mouth.

Charlie laughed, tilting her head up to the vast night. Priya looked up, too. It was clearer than usual, and she thought she spotted Mars beaming down on them from the heavens.

A siren wailed again at the corner and they both jumped, ready to bolt. But it was just an ambulance whizzing through the empty intersection, headed toward some other emergency.

"Fuck," Charlie whispered, grinning. She squeezed Priya's hands.

Priya watched her for a moment. There was a small cut on one of her cheeks, probably from the broken glass, and it was already starting to scab. Priya resisted the sudden urge to reach out and touch it—to pick the wound open again. To put her mouth to the bloody mess she'd leave behind.

"God," she muttered, and Charlie looked back up at her again.

"You make me feel . . ." She trailed off, floundering. A cold gust of wind whipped around them, rustling Charlie's hair.

"Like you're dying?" Charlie finished.

Her pulse jumped in her neck. A dark vein twitched, violent blue against her skin. Priya met her gaze and held it.

"Yeah," she breathed. "And I want more."

Revenge of the Roadkill Bodysnatchers

ROSE JEANOU

A MAN CALLED the Highway Maintenance Department to report a dead moose off 1-A. Sharon was going to have to hack the animal up herself because her boss, Stuart, a desperate, piss-his-pants alcoholic, was too hungover to come to work again. This wouldn't be Sharon's first moose, but it would be her first moose alone.

She drove down in the clunky white PHMD pedo-van, bringing her chainsaw and mechanical scraper, plus several large buckets and body bags. She also packed her hunting rifle, which wasn't province issued. Sharon hated Medicine Hat, but she loved driving through it in the summer, noting the slices of sediment embedded in the mountain, its slopes failing, slumping down.

At the spot the caller'd told her she'd find the dead moose was only a moose-sized puddle of blood with tire marks running through it. The missing moose marked the fourth time Sharon had been called about a large animal, then pulled up to find the roadkill gone. Stuart theorized people were growing desperate for meat due to rising grocery prices. The receptionist, Ronnie, said maybe it was vultures. In the four years Sharon had been with the PHMD, disappearances were unheard of, yet this was the fourth in as many weeks. And vultures had always been around these parts, as had poverty. Scavengers usually picked at the carrion instead of carrying the whole body off the road, and your average vulture couldn't cart away an entire moose.

Sharon thought it was likely there was some kind of bodysnatching operation going on. She had thus far kept this thought to herself. From a docuseries about a mortician she'd watched with Mom, she'd learned that gravediggers and bodysnatchers often had some kind of financial motive. A local university who needed animal corpses for experiments. Some abnormally depraved high schoolers.

Sharon drove down the road a little farther and kept an eye out. She got lucky; it was only about half an hour before she saw a beaver ambling down the other side of the road. Sharon climbed out of her truck and crept over to where the beaver sat, sniff-sniffing its little nose. The smiley round face of Mr. Orange, her favorite barn cat from Gramma's farm, flashed into her mind. But she pushed the memory away and shot the beaver three times with her hunting rifle.

Her shot was good—well, it was okay, but good enough. The beaver fell dead. She picked up its body, swung it between her legs and threw the dead beaver underhand into the middle of the highway. It landed in the middle of one of the dashed white lines and lay, staring up into the sun. Then Sharon sat in her car and watched the road. After a couple minutes, someone ran over the beaver's head with their car, squashing it flat.

It was a small animal, so she figured it might not be enough of a nuisance for someone to call in to the PHMD about it. Half an hour passed. Sharon grew restless and called in herself from her personal cell phone. Ronnie picked up.

Sharon made an attempt to disguise her voice: "Hi, PHMD?"

"Yep, speaking. What's the problem, sir?"

Having been mistaken for a man, Sharon lowered her voice even more. "I'm driving off 40-A right now and I've just hit a beaver. I assume this is the number to call?"

Ronnie confirmed and asked for her location. Within a minute, a text appeared on her work phone from Ronnie, sending her to where she already waited. Sharon settled in. She suspected someone had access to their phone lines.

Sharon sat in the van, looking at one-bedroom apartment listings on her phone and occasionally glancing back into the rearview mirror. Rent would eat nearly half her paycheck, let alone utilities. Who wanted to live here? Why would anyone stay?

Mom would say Sharon lived here because she was irresponsible. She would say Sharon should be working full time at PHMD, if she wasn't too disgusted to mention her line of work. She would say Sharon shouldn't buy so much gear and eat so much junk food. Maybe if she had a partner to share the rent with, or God forbid a good friend, she could get out of her mom's house. But Sharon didn't want roommates. Her last roommate was a sorority-girl type who had accused Sharon of leering at her. The one before that was a member of a neo-Maoist cult. So Sharon had been forced, at the very old age of twenty-seven, back with

Mom. She felt this urge to put herself in horrible situations, like this one, working for the city government of the saddest place in all of Canada, her hometown, scraping roadkill off the side of the highway.

That morning, as Sharon was walking out the door, Mom had said, "I know you did this just because it was the most disgusting thing you could think of."

Mom was right. She was a loser, worse even than Stuart, by some measures. Plus, she hadn't had sex in almost three years. She'd been with a few men, mostly smaller and mousier than she, discards from dive bars who still chewed tobacco. She did not particularly enjoy the feeling of their penises, nor their rough, jabbing hands. And she bled lots. At first, she'd attributed all the bleeding to her being a virgin. But by the sixth man, she decided she had a fucked-up pussy, or maybe her hymen had never popped, or whatever. It didn't really concern her. She had always known that sex was not really for her. Sex was painful and lame. What was the point? She'd once done it out of some sense of obligation, but now she was content to grind against a Hitachi wand and think about abstract concepts, like financial success or home ownership.

Though Sharon was not a psychopath or a sociopath or anything, she was admittedly into some weird shit. A teacher had once said she had a taste for the macabre. She liked gory movies and taxidermy and putting metal in her face (eyebrow, lip, ears, and nose, thrice). Blood and guts, if not sex. That was why she didn't mind the roadkill job so much. This, and she liked to drive. She liked driving out of the suburbs and through the prairies, past the billboards with guns on them, and the billboards with oil and Jesus on them, and the ones with the bleeding weeping skinless fetuses on them, and the ones telling her to repent for her sins, and the ones that showed her more cars and more cars.

When she looked up into the rearview mirror again, she saw a baby-blue van approaching. The bright color caught her eye. The van got closer, a dinged-up Astro van with a long key mark down the side and a big hammer and sickle spray-painted on the passenger-side door. The Astro van pulled up behind Sharon. She turned all the way around in her seat and looked out the back window. It was funny—she knew that van. It looked just like the van they'd used at Camp Pembertyn.

Why was that van here? It didn't make any sense to Sharon.

It made her feel strange and knotted up inside to see that van. She'd traced a lot of her weirdness back to her days at that camp. Camp Pembertyn was an all-girls sleepaway camp in Victoria. Her mom had mistaken it for a church camp because they'd advertised as such—the advertisements, Sharon realized at some point, were painfully, obviously ironic. It was sometimes a lucky thing for Sharon that her mother was not all there.

The Pembertyn girls had not invited her into their little friendship bracelet circles. The girls did not talk about their boyfriends back home with her. She had lurked and sharpened sticks with rocks into spears. Yet, thinking back on it, Sharon couldn't recall a less lonely time in her life. Her furry body and lurking largeness made her a curiosity, a presence that the girls begrudged and mocked but privately found endearing, like a moose-head trophy mount at their funniest uncle's house. She would braid their hair because she was very good at French braids and the inside-out Dutch ones, and she had strong, nimble fingers that felt good on the girls' scalps. But they would never touch her hair. They would shriek and laugh at the prospect. But the same girls, having just learned what the word *motorboat* meant, would ask Sharon to motorboat them in their bathing suits, and then again with nothing on. Sharon attributed her effect on the girls to her being a tomboy.

She had not thought about Camp Pembertyn in years.

A woman climbed out of the van. She wore a leather jacket covered in patches and pins, and big black boots. She was very butch, with a shock of pink hair on the top of her head and the sides all shaved off. A punk or faux-biker type, or something. The pink-haired butch waited a while for cars to stop driving by, then she ran onto the road with a scraper and a bucket. She scraped up the beaver and dropped it in the bucket, then sprinted back to the van.

This was them! Sharon hadn't really planned what she'd do if she actually caught the culprit. She put her hand in her pocket to make sure she had her pocketknife. Then she got out of her truck and approached the baby-blue van.

"Someone's coming," a voice from inside the van said. Sharon almost thought she could recognize it, so she answered before they could.

"Highway Maintenance. We've noticed that roadkill's been going missing."

"The government? You've gotta be shitting me," said the voice—Sharon was sure now, this was Missy—who by now probably knew it was Sharon from her voice.

"Well, it's just me," Sharon said. "I do most of the collection. I'm alone. I just noticed them going missing, and I killed this one by myself and made a fake call. I figured someone was tapping my phone lines."

The lady with the pink hair watched this exchange from inside the van as if recording Sharon with her eyes. She was big, and butch, and unforthcoming. She noticed Sharon looking.

She told Sharon her name, then added, "But don't go spreading that around. Lady X is what most people call me."

Lady X! Sharon vaguely remembered her. She had been a spectral presence at the camp. Campers saw her only slightly more regularly than other ghosts like the Bukwus or the Sonokawa, who were rumored to haunt the land. Lady X was the camp director. She was visible twice per summer, once to bless the land at the beginning of camp, and again at the end.

"We missed you, Sharon," Lady X said.

Sharon had not remembered what she looked like, not at all. All she could do was shake her head.

"Just get in," said Missy. "We're gonna take you on an adventure."

Sharon looked back behind her at her pedo-van. She couldn't abandon it here. But—did she care? Did she really care about keeping this job? She shook her head again, then nodded.

"Yes," Missy said, "yes."

As the back of the van lifted open, Sharon was stunned by the stench of dozens of dead animal bodies, a truly unmistakable smell to which she was no stranger, a putrid and bloody stink that got into your skin and clothes and the air. She could see into the back of the car. The interior was stripped and renovated, a shabby living room on wheels, filled with body bags and hairy corpses, soaked with blood.

In the passenger seat was another person who introduced themself as Winnie. Sharon could mostly see the back of their head, but from what Sharon could see, Winnie was jacked, like, shredded, and had those sick Indigenous chin tattoos that Sharon would've gotten for sure if it wasn't cultural appropriation. Neither she nor Lady X spoke as they drove. On the radio a punk woman spat words in a strange pseudo-English tongue:

Well it's a big big big big SECRET
No no nobody understands except you I hope
O wall-ee-dee, und den tauvis
Sigmund Freud frog 9

Though she considered herself the least squeamish broad in the world around roadkill, the stench was enough for her to pull the neck of her shirt up over her nose.

The van's walls were covered in old flyers for queer liberation meetings, dyke nights, and grrl bands with names like Tribe 8 and See You Next Tuesday and Dickless. The moose Sharon had been looking for was half-covered by several body bags and lying on the floor in the middle of the van. It was a female, though still massive enough to fill most of the space inside the large van's interior. The moose was delimbed and decapitated, the way Sharon and the boys always did it. Sharon took a peek under the bags. This was clean, impressive work.

Lady X dumped the beaver from the buckets into a pile in the corner. A line of muskrats dangled by their necks from the ceiling, like stemware hanging on a drying rack. She settled into her place in the driver's seat without another word of explanation.

Winnie read out directions from a real paper map in her lap while working her long hair into an intricate French braid. Skilled fingers. The group whispered between each other. Sharon only caught on to a few key words—"security," "pedo," "ether."

Wedged between a stack of body bags and Missy's left thigh on the couch, Sharon's eyes kept drifting away from the dead animals to focus on Missy's features.

Missy was wearing a tank top, more of a scrap of fabric really, that showed off her arms—she'd bulked up. The arm holes in her tank top were so wide, Missy's breasts were visible as she moved around. Ugh. Missy's tits were so big now. What the fuck? She got nipple piercings? Nipple piercings went crazy.

She had serious, way-back history with Missy. What had happened between them—Sharon couldn't exactly remember the timeline of events. First, she and Missy had been friends. They'd been pen pals when camp let up. Sharon sent letters from Albertan suburbia to Montreal, which she'd always imagined was very sexy. When she was twenty-two, they had planned to go on a road trip together. Missy would fly to her, and then they would drive back together to Montreal. But this had never happened because Missy got a butch lover with whom she went on the road trip instead. Sharon never really forgave her. She never forgave at all, in general.

"Where are we going?" Sharon asked.

"We're going to Mr. Sly's house," Missy muttered, slipping her hand under Sharon's.

"Why?" asked Sharon. The others in the van exchanged looks. There was a long minute of silence.

"Are you sure we shouldn't explain?" Lady X finally asked. "Goddamn, I feel bad, Missy."

"I never got the chance for anyone to explain anything to me beforehand," said Missy. She had this strange, squeaky, girly voice. It sounded weird coming out from her. "Why should she get an explanation?"

Now Sharon felt that violent jolt of rage she'd inherited from Mom. "You—fucking—you kidnapped me. I think you need to explain something to me."

"First of all, my love, you climbed in here all by your lonesome. And you know it. And you wouldn't understand. It's better that way," said Missy.

"It is ideal that way," said Winnie. "But Missy, be nice."

"Sharon's a big girl," muttered Lady X.

"Can't you at least tell me something?"

"Think of it this way," said Winnie. "You're about to be radicalized."

"Radicalized how? Are we going to do something violent?"

No one responded for a moment. "It's complicated," Missy whispered.

She looked crazy, Sharon noticed, her bug eyes wild with something like vengeance or lust (Sharon projected). She had a new tattoo on her bicep in red ink, a symbol Sharon didn't recognize: a globe crossed out with an X, superimposed with a double-sided axe, each blade bleeding black blood.

"We can be as violent as you'd like," Lady finally replied.

A word came into Sharon's mind: *desecration*. "What are we going to do with all this roadkill?"

As the van slowed, Sharon recognized where they were: Mr. Sly's house. It had been a long time since Sharon had seen Mr. Sly. He had been her swimming instructor, just one of those quintessential pedo jobs. He hadn't ever done anything physical to Sharon, at least not that she could recall. And still, and still.

"I see the vision," Sharon muttered. The carcass fumes had gone to her brain.

Missy laughed. "Wait," she said. "You're serious? You're down? You understand?"

"Well, I guess we're getting revenge, right? I'm fine with that. I just want to be told what's going to happen. Are we killing them?"

"Would you want to?" Missy asked.

The house was one ugly and modern with geometric architecture, all square and sterile with beige faux brick and slate-gray paneling. "SIX" was written out in the same blank, minimalist font as the street number marker. The lawn was laid with Astroturf and littered with plastic children's toys.

"God," Missy drawled from behind her. "Rich folks have no taste."

Winnie shushed her.

"Okay, everyone," X said. "Y'all head out and find an entrance. I'm going to explain to Sharon what it is we do."

She explained that she had a wealthy benefactor. "I can't tell you who, but you probably have heard of them. They were the victim of a high-profile sexual assault case," Lady X said, taking a drag of her cigarette, an illegal menthol. "They lost. They wanted revenge. And, see, their rapist had a really bad case of necrophilia."

"Which is?" Sharon asked, head spinning.

"Like, the fear of death," said Missy.

"The *love* of death," Winnie corrected.

"Right, right," Missy said. "Not phobia. Philia."

X continued, "The benefactor wanted us to get taxidermied animals and put them all over his house. Give him a scare. But we couldn't easily find a bunch of animals for a cheap enough price. We still wanted to pay ourselves, see? So we asked her if we could use roadkill. She said yes, and when we sent the pictures she was overjoyed.

"Anyway, we smeared it all over everything in the guy's house. We fucked up his walls. We left three dead wolves in his nice car. Dead raccoons everywhere. It was glorious. And we spray painted 'rapist' on everything. He'd have to clean it up himself, or people would see. We also sent letters to his wife and kids. And then, when Winona told me she had someone, we did the same thing to him.

"I had someone, too. For mine, we left a live badger in there— he mauled the guy. It was dark, and he ended up dying. One of our girls got PTSD from that. We stick to roadkill now."

"Oh," Sharon said.

"So, we put roadkill in rapists' houses. That's all," Lady X clarified. "We've already done three, and we have two more. One for each of us."

Winnie turned around. They were almost perfectly androgynous, with a round square face and doe eyes, like a gentle mother cow, and a soft mustache. "It's okay," they said. "It's like a ritual. You feel all right after—purged. But if you don't want to . . . If you don't want to, we'll turn around right now and drive you right back to your van."

No, Sharon thought. "No," she said. "Let's do it."

"Didn't I say she'd be game?" Missy said. Sharon felt a surge and put her hand on Missy's thigh. Missy squirmed closer.

How had Missy known? Well, Sharon used to talk all the time about killing Mr. Sly. She wanted to kill him so bad because he had probably molested her as a child, she thought, though she could not remember exactly what had happened, and it was to this that she attributed most of the bad things in her life. Her desire to kill Mr. Sly was like a childhood dream of becoming a superstar—a dream that was childish not because it was immature, but because it was instinctual and universal. Children want to be stars because they want admiration, love, beauty, style, wealth, and security—worthy and understandable aspirations. Our drive to avenge those who have wronged us is, too, worthy, and perfectly understandable. Most of us still harbor some desire to be stars as adults, after all. Most of us still need revenge on someone, Sharon thought. We just so rarely get the opportunity.

"Are you two coming in with us?" Sharon directed her question to the front. She felt nervous. These were unknown entities to her. She had hardly interacted with Lady X, back at camp.

"Winnie is going to stay outside. We need someone in the car. I'm going to keep watch at the door," said X. "Don't worry. We've dismantled all the security systems. We've done this before."

The night was cold, blank, and flat. Mr. Sly's lawn was wetter than it should have been. Behind the house was a goose pond. The geese squawked and ruffled their wings as Sharon and Missy walked back and forth, van to car, bringing out body bags and animals, while Lady X picked the locks. Once they had access, Missy and Sharon racked and stacked up the bodies in the dark sunroom. They lugged in the goodies from the van's stockpile: weapons, spray paint cans, chemicals, garbage bags, extension cords, crude oil canisters, car parts.

The two crept all the way in. The house was way bougier than Sharon's, but hellish and Alberta-plain, with heavy gray curtains over the windows, clunky and characterless furniture on white carpet, stained with piss from the crusty white dog Missy immediately tranqed for yapping. Nice hardwoods, though. Sharon looked at the condition of the floors and had a sudden urge to remove her shoes. This was, of course, ridiculous, because she was carrying their biggest intact catch, a dead coyote, draped over her shoulder, its body still hot from the baking car, the blood seeping warm onto her back. But her first thought was of her father yelling at her not to ruin the floors of her childhood home. These were unscathed dark hardwoods with no visible dirt in the corners, so uniform they looked fake.

Then they crept upstairs to the bedroom, which was wheezing and alive with the sound of machine-assisted breath. They were lucky; Sly was a heavy sleeper. In Sharon's mind's eye, Mr. Sly was still young, a leering predator with thick sideburns and a healthy, fat body, a virile, veritable threat to little boys and girls at YMCAs everywhere. But now he was an old white man, white-haired and surprisingly decrepit, pathetic and weak even in sleep. The side table was littered with little orange medication bottles and pill organizers. He was hooked up to a sleep apnea machine. It was bad to do something like this to someone like this.

"He takes Trazodone," Missy said, à voix haute. She was rummaging through the pill bottles. "And Klonopin. Holy shit. Usually they wake up and we gotta tranq them. This guy's gotta be out like a rock."

"I wanna put him out anyway," Sharon said, trying to copy Missy's badass tone. She set the coyote down near the door, saving it for later. "Where's that ether at?"

Missy let Sharon do the honors. Mr. Sly woke up, sputtered, and gagged when the napkin was placed over his face, then fell back again, limp on his back. His eyes were closed but his mouth was open, as if he was stunned, and he was drooling.

"Should we lay him on his side?" Sharon asked.

"Nah," Missy said. "Let him choke."

He probably won't die, Sharon thought.

The fun began. They started in the bedroom. Missy dragged the decapitated head of a possum, smearing gore all over the nice books in the floor-to-ceiling bookshelf. Then she removed the top of an urn and stuck the possum head on top of it, so it looked like one of those Egyptian urns. They dragged in all the limbs off the moose. The blood splattered over every corner of the bedroom. In the bathroom, they smeared shit over every porcelain surface. On the mirror, Missy painted—with her bare hands, no less—two female symbols in blood. Sharon dipped her hands into the warm, sticky, thick, blood and scrawled next to it FUCK YOU. Then she went above his head and wrote I FUCKING DESPISE YOU!!!!! The blood dripped all over his ugly headboard and white pillows.

In the hallway outside the bedroom, Missy dissected three raccoons one by one with surgical precision, taking out the intestines and pulling another one's stomach inside out. Sharon distracted herself by looking at Missy's chest to calm her nausea. Her nipple piercing glinted in the light from the tacky chandeliers in the hallway.

Then they stuck organs in the worst places; as Sharon moved through the house, she strung guts along walls like Christmas lights, sprinkled paws and ears on the floor like an evil witch's breadcrumb trail, and hung intestines from curtain rods.

Finally—Sharon didn't know what came over her—she swung the coyote onto the glass coffee table. Its body hit the table and the glass top shattered everywhere. Only the table's weird geometric legs stood, impaling the poor coyote, whose blood began to pool on the floor.

"Holy shit," Missy said from behind her.

"Thanks," Sharon said. She was bloody but not bleeding, safe, amped the fuck up, and panting with her tongue out like a dog. She was hot. She wanted to vomit, or fuck, or fight someone.

"My shirt is sticky," Missy said, pulling it off. Sharon could fuck a woman. This was, somehow, the first time the thought had occurred to her for real, for real.

Missy's perfect tits were out, and Sharon stared at them without shame, because she was far beyond shame at that point.

"You're looking at me," Missy observed.

Sharon stepped forward, kissed her, then pulled back. Missy smiled and pulled Sharon's hair at the back of her neck. Sharon leaned down, kissed her with tongue, and held her face in her hands. Missy tugged at Sharon's hair at the back of her neck and kissed her back. This was okay; there was an adrenaline-rush situation going on, and she wanted to fuck Missy, for lack of a better word. How did lesbians fuck? They went down on each other, Sharon knew. They ate pussy. They wore strap-ons.

60 Rose Jeanou

Scissoring was a myth—or was it? Sharon wasn't really sure, but she definitely wanted to do some of those things with Missy.

She had been with men before, quite a few of them, actually. And Missy ate pussy better than any of them had, not that most of them had gone for it. There were men at work who liked her because she was grimy like them and talked about similar things, and she had tried out those sexual relationships, lying still on her back, being ripped in half from the inside. They were always short-lived, because Sharon didn't really feel the need to keep going, and she always bled when they tried to stick something in her.

Kissing Missy, lying down on the couch with her, taking off her pants and feeling Missy's wet pussy rub against her leg, Sharon realized that she was probably not going to go back to having sex with men. This just felt more like what she had envisioned she should feel like when she was having sex.

Missy moved very fast, and before Sharon knew it Missy's face was between her legs. She was really good, doing a lot of flicking stuff and using her hands. Sharon came quickly, which made her feel embarrassed, but Missy seemed like she was into it.

When she tried to eat Missy's pussy, she just pretended to know what to do. First, she made out with it, just because that's what she was intuitively drawn to do. That was hot. She had heard a rap lyric once about tracing a girl's name on the clit, so she also tried that. M-I-S-S-Y M-I-S-S-Y. But her tongue got tired and she began losing focus, so she just started tracing O-O-O-O and applying some pressure and Missy really liked that. So she just kept doing it for a while, because she was getting off on Missy getting off.

When they were done, Missy kissed her with the taste of her pussy still in her mouth. They were both wet in the mouth with the taste of pussy and spit. Jesus Christ, Sharon thought.

Missy's face suddenly looked like that of a man who Sharon had once slept with. The man had called Sharon ugly during sex, pulled her hair, and called her a desperate slut while he choked her without asking. She gagged. Missy pulled back from her mouth and said, "Are you okay?"

Sharon thought about her dad calling her a dyke. Then she imagined her mom walking in on her in this position. She remembered how hard her mom had cried when she asked if she could take a girl to the junior prom. She gagged again and her body stiffened. In the end, she had taken no one.

Missy scrambled up and her eyes widened with horror. "Don't—"

She remembered wanting it, because it made her feel normal. To have sex with him. Wanting that, but not badly enough that her body did too. She had hated the smells of it, more than anything.

"No, it's—let's just stop, okay?"

Missy scrambled to put on her clothes while Sharon lay, shaking a bit.

"I think it's just all this roadkill," Sharon said after a long pause, during which neither dyke looked at each other.

Missy looked down at her and they both looked across the fancy living room covered in dead animals, stinking like hell. They looked down at the massacred coyote in front of them, impaled on the coffee table, then looked back at each other and cracked up, gasping with laughter.

"Yeah. Kind of a vibe kill," Missy said. "God. Let's get dressed. Goddamn dyke shit."

They threw on their clothes and walked out.

Lady X and Winnie were already in the back of the truck. They had the warm exposed lightbulbs on and were washing themselves off with peppermint castile soap and rags in a bucket of warm water.

Sharon sat in the car and tried to hold back a smile as the van got moving.

"Where do you live?" Missy asked. She sounded angry.

Sharon sat on the floor of the vile-smelling van, rocking side to side, her body jumping when the van hit a crack in the road. Missy had gotten a real seat and was sitting above her. Several times, Sharon's face bumped against Missy's knees and she looked up to say sorry. But Missy never looked back at her, just stared out the window without turning her head, so Sharon stopped looking at Missy.

Then Missy said: "Do you want to come up here?"

Sharon looked up. Missy was looking down at her. She didn't look angry; she was frowning with big, concerned eyes.

"Come on," Missy said, reaching down to let Sharon grab her arm. "You're rattling around down there."

Sharon grabbed at her limply, and Missy pulled Sharon up with surprising force.

"I'll crush you."

Missy positioned Sharon onto her lap, drawing her arms

around Sharon's waist and clasping her hands at the front. Sharon looked down at Missy's profile: her sweet freckled nose, the long eyelashes curling over the side of her cheek.

Sharon whispered, "I'm sorry about that back there."

"No, don't."

"It's just that, I've had a lot of experiences with men, okay? And I've never had an experience with a woman—"

"Uh."

"—and my mom is homophobic, and I live with her right now. But I think it's this really bad experience for me. Sex."

"Oh. I didn't—God. I'm sorry."

"Don't be. Like, it's actually fine, but I just have memories and—"

"The same thing happens to me. I mean, I don't wanna make it about me. And I'm sure for you it's worse—"

"No, don't say that—"

"I mean, my parents are really accepting and everything. Of my sexuality. They've taken me to Pride parades since I was a toddler. I can remember it, kind of. But I just meant, the memories thing has happened to me. I have other stuff. Like, assault stuff."

"Oh, yeah."

"Well, you know what I mean. It was a decade ago. And he didn't really touch me or anything. It was just who it was. In relation to me. And I felt . . . I don't know."

". . ."

"Well, never mind. I just wanted you to know it's okay. It's happened to me, too. Don't feel weird about it."

It was light out when Sharon woke up. Her head pounded from the back—migraine. She was lying on her back in her own white pedo-van. The roadkill bodysnatchers had taken her back. How could they? She didn't want this. Had they ethered her? No. She'd rejected them. She'd fallen asleep. Or—was that a chemical feeling in the back of her throat? Missy had kissed her when she climbed out, said she hoped to see her again sometime, but didn't say where.

Outside the window a tiny animal was looking at Sharon. Brown, small, with a long, pink tail, sniffing nose. It stood up, sniff-sniffing its little pink nose, rubbing its ears with its little pink hands. A rat? A rat! But—there were no rats in Alberta. Rats famously did not exist in Alberta. They'd all been eradicated. Sharon reached into her pocket to pull out her phone to capture the rat. As she did this, she noticed on the back of her hand an address scrawled in red Sharpie. The address was in French, province, PQ—Quebec. Missy must want her to find her!

Thank God, thank God! They wanted her after all. She snapped a picture of the rat, just to prove it was there and that she'd really seen it. A rat in Alberta. Picture that! She slammed the van into first, then fourth—right onto the highway. She was late for work, but she wasn't going back to the station. She was headed east, to Montreal.

Palm Desert

ANNA DORN

BLUE'S HANDS ARE tied. Literally. I've tied her up in the garage of the Airbnb in Palm Springs. Well, Palm Desert, technically, as Blue rudely noted when we arrived. *Sophia, you said we were going to Palm Springs.* My name isn't really Sophia, but Blue really is a fucking brat. It's what I like about her.

No, it's what I love about her.

I'm sitting in a metal chair across from Blue, waiting for the Rohypnol to wear off. She looks so beautiful unconscious, her body limp and peaceful, thin arms crossed delicately against her chest. Her skin appears smooth and unblemished even under the light of the exposed overhead bulb, which hits her lashes and casts little shadows on her cheekbones. I can't see her eyes, but I can imagine them: blue, like her name, like the cloudless desert sky outside the garage. Wispy blond hair frames her face like a halo.

Right on schedule, her eyes start to open.

"Hello, Angel," I say.

Blue always looks so innocent when she wakes up. Serene, like a baby deer. She attempts to move her arms and panic dawns on her face as she digests her surroundings. I hate when she looks scared, but what's the phrase?

No pain, no gain.

"What the fuck?" Blue asks, pulling her bound arms. "What the actual fuck?"

"It's okay," I tell her, voice calm like I'm putting a baby to bed. I've dreamed of this moment for a long time, reuniting with my sweet Blue. She still doesn't know it's me. "You can trust me," I tell her, and it's true. I walk over and untie her, just the hands. She lunges at me but can't do much: Her legs and torso remain tied to the chair. I fetch her a La Croix, key lime flavored, her favorite. She's from Florida.

65

When I hand her the seltzer, she knocks it from my hand. The can hits the concrete floor and explodes. "No big deal," I tell her. "I have a whole case." I point to the fridge behind me. "I also got dark chocolate, salted almonds, figs, Gruyère." I know Blue's favorite foods. I know everything about her.

Blue squirms and shouts. "Help! HELP!!" I've never seen her so animated.

"No one will hear you," I tell her. "Don't you remember the drive? Nothing but sand and rocks for miles."

Perhaps unconvinced, Blue continues to scream.

I go to the back of the room and rummage through my alligator-skin bag of tricks while Blue's shouts increase in volume. I'm not too concerned about someone hearing her. As I said, the place is isolated. I suppose a hiker or a car driving by could hear. But I'm not too worried about being caught either. I've already lost everything. I have . . . what's the phrase?

Nothing to lose.

I pull a red vintage Hermès scarf from the bag. As I walk over to gag Blue, she tries to fight me, but I'm ultimately stronger. I don't exercise, and I'm not muscular—I find muscular definition on a woman to be gauche—but I have grit. When we were together, Blue liked me to dominate her. She wanted to be tied up and gagged; it got her off. Part of me believes this is foreplay, even though it's technically nonconsensual, and I'm still not sure Blue knows who I am. She's at least pretending she doesn't know who I am. Blue was always very good at playing dumb. Most pretty women are.

She continues to shriek through the scarf, and I wonder if I should sedate her further. I've dreamed for so long about having her to myself, really talking about what happened, but I didn't realize how hard she'd fight. It hurts my feelings a little, but I also like watching her exert some effort for once.

"You should channel this energy during auditions," I tell Blue. We're both actresses, although she thinks I'm an agent. I knew if I told Blue I could make her a star, she would do anything I wanted, like come to an isolated rental in Palm Desert with someone she met online just a few days prior. I knew Blue wouldn't bother to look me up to confirm I do in fact work at ICM—she's too desperate—but I did my research. Sophia Bell works in the talent department, and we look enough alike: raven-colored hair, wide-set eyes, a wry smile. On her first date with "Sophia," Blue went down on me in the parking structure at the Grove in my leased Mercedes. Like I said, she's desperate.

The problem is, Blue is a terrible actress. She's pretty, sure. But it's a quiet, listless beauty. She has long and thin limbs, dainty features. She modeled for money, probably still does. I also suspect she has a trust fund. When we were together, I resented that Blue didn't need me. And she resented my success. But she shouldn't have been resentful. My wild eyes lent themselves to the silver screen. But I'd much rather be Blue. Unbothered and gliding through life like a swan.

I PLAY PATSY CLINE on the portable speaker Blue brings with her everywhere. She needs music playing at all times. I've always suspected this is because she lacks a complex inner life, which is frankly exactly what I'm looking for in a partner: white noise between the ears.

Crazy, I'm crazy for feeling lonely, I sing to myself along with Patsy as I pour two glasses of aged scotch, very expensive scotch, in the garage kitchenette. *I'm crazy, crazy for feeling so blue.* When we were together, I used to sing to Blue all the time. I have a classically trained voice that Blue must recognize. My face is different, but my voice is mostly the same. Although I smoke more now, so it's a little huskier. The doctors say in some rare cases, nicotine can be a blessing.

I hand Blue her glass, and she doesn't knock it away. I remove the red scarf from her mouth and she doesn't scream. "Good girl," I say. We clink glasses and both take sips. Her sip is more of a gulp; she empties the contents of the glass into her throat. Mixed with the lingering Rohypnol, the scotch will surely calm her down.

I turn back to go sit in my chair. As I'm walking, a thud lands against my head. Glass shatters on the concrete floor beside me. I reach to touch the back of my head and it's damp. There's blood on my fingertips. My head throbs in a way that isn't entirely unpleasant. Blue has always been so good at hurting me. I turn toward her and smile, lick the blood from my fingertips.

Blue starts yelling again and I go to gag her—gently, of course. I need to wash the blood off my head. I'm wearing Prada. It's new and expensive, a little black dress I got just for this occasion, and I don't want to stain it.

"I'll be back, Angel," I say to Blue as I leave through the back door of the garage into the main house.

THE KITCHEN IS bright with desert sun. My eyes start to burn, and then I see orange spots. The back of my head continues to throb. I can't believe the bitch threw a glass at my head. Actually, I can. Like I said, she's a brat. I love Blue, and she loves to torture me.

In the shower, I watch pink water circle the drain and consider my next move. I could tell Blue who I really am. But I have a few concerns. First, I'm worried she won't believe me. Like I said, I look different. And I'm not saying I gained five pounds or got highlights. I got facial reconstructive surgery. It's a dramatic story. I told you; I was a successful actress. I had a flair for melodrama. Still do, I suppose. Still acting. Only one thing has ever felt fully real to me, and it's my feelings for Blue Vandewald.

These feelings caused me to act, well, a little extreme. I did some things I'm not proud of. We don't have to get into all of it, but this leads me to my second concern: Blue does believe me. We didn't end things on a good note. I might have a better chance as Sophia. I'm in a pickle. Unsure what to do, I continue to sing, *And I'm crazy for loving you.*

THE DEVIL WINDS make it impossible to light my cigarette. I'm in the yard trying to clear my head. As is typical in Southern California, the sun is bright in a sinister way, seemingly designed to alert the nervous system that something is wrong. Rather than clear headed, I just feel more on edge. The Santa Anas are said to make people go crazy. But I already did that a long time ago.

I cup a hand around the cigarette and try to light it again, but it refuses to take. I suppose I could smoke in the garage, give Blue a cigarette. Blue loves to smoke indoors. That's something we have in common.

The wind nearly knocks over a palm tree. A large frond flies off and falls into the pool, where it floats in a circle. I feel the back of my head for blood, and it's dry. Blue will have to try harder to thwart my perfect little plan. On second thought, I shouldn't give her a cigarette. Blue gets nothing that can be used as a weapon. I should have bound her hands before I left. At least she's tied to the chair.

IN THE KITCHEN, I find a plastic cup and return to the garage, where Blue is twisting her hair between her fingers. Her face is always calm but she has a nervous energy that manifests in constant fidgeting, smoking, chewing, hair-twirling, nail-biting, doodling, et cetera. I imagine one—the fidgeting—allows the other—the calm face.

"Hi Angel," I greet Blue and hold up the plastic cup. "I found a solution to our little issue." Blue rolls her eyes. I pour Blue some scotch, then hand it to her and remove her scarf. She doesn't yell. She sips, glaring at me.

"Why the long face?" I walk backward to my chair, facing her, so she doesn't try any funny business. In my chair, I light a cigarette. "You used to love when I tied you up."

Hostility brews on her face. "I should have listened to Dillon," Blue says. "He said you were sketchy."

An invisible dagger sinks into my chest. Dillon. Fucking Dillon. Blue's boyfriend. Blue's beard. Blue's beard doesn't like me so much. "Never listen to Dillon," I say. "He knows nothing."

Blue takes a slow sip. "You know nothing about him or me." Her voice is calm but stern, concealing a soft rage.

"This is what you need to get a role, Angel," I tell Blue. "The thinly veiled rage. It's working."

Blue smiles. "Dillon said you were going to kill me."

I shake my head. "I'm not going to kill you." How dare Dillon accuse me of something so crass? I'm not violent. Not toward people. Or, well, not people I love. Except when absolutely necessary. Like now.

Blue is still smiling. "Dillon said you're an unhinged dyke who wants to kill me." Now I'm certain she knows it's me because Blue knows just how to hurt me. And she wants me to hurt her back.

Playing along, I walk over to her and lift my leg above her head. I'm very flexible, and, thankfully, so is this dress—it's nylon, and I'm not wearing underwear. In an act that would impress the most advanced of yogis, I plant my stiletto on Blue's forehead. My heel digs into the space between her eyes. Blue swats my leg but fails to disrupt my balance. I press harder. "Say my name," I tell her.

"Sophia Bell," she says.

"Don't play dumb," I say, pressing harder.

She winces. "What do you want from me?"

I remove my shoe, then slam my heel onto the concrete. A clink echoes.

"The truth," I say.

BLUE IS GAGGED again. I'm smoking a cigarette and thinking. Watching her sit still in the chair—the stillness, I assume, a combination of sedatives and boredom—I get an idea. It's time to up the stakes. "Excuse me," I tell her, walking backward to retrieve my phone. "I have to make a call."

I begin dialing, saying the numbers out loud as I press them. "9-0-4," I say. As I hoped, she perks up at hearing her home-town area code. "6-8-8. 2-9-0-4."

Blue squirms, surely recognizing her mother's number.

"Oh come on, let's have some fun," I say, putting the phone on speaker. It rings.

Blue has a terrified look in her eyes.

The call goes to voicemail. *Hi, you've reached Suki Vande-wald. I'm not available to answer the phone right now. Please leave a message and I'll get back to you as soon as possible.*

Blue looks relieved.

"Damn," I say. "Let's try again."

I redial the number.

Panic reenters Blue's eyes as the phone rings. Once, twice, three times.

On the fourth ring, a woman answers. "Hello?" Suki's voice is froggy, tired.

Muffled screams escape from Blue's gagged mouth.

"Hi there," I say into the phone. "Did you know your daughter is a pillow princess?"

"A pillow *what*?" Suki is awake now, and a hint of Southern accent creeps into her voice.

Blue squirms more frantically, yelling louder, and I hear muffled words I can't quite recognize. I walk over to Blue and start to untie the scarf. But first I mute my side of the call.

"Excuse me?" Suki asks. "What is this about?"

"We're muted," I tell Blue and show her the phone to prove it. "If you tell me who I really am, I'll end the call. If not, I'll tell your mom the truth."

"Hello?" Suki says. "Are you still there?"

I remove the scarf, and it drifts to the floor in slow motion.

"Nora Frost!" Blue yells.

I unmute the phone. "This isn't Domino's?" I say to Suki. "I must have the wrong number." Click.

ON OUR FIRST date, I took Blue to a cemetery. Blue said it was morbid. I thought it was romantic. I figured she'd want to see

Elizabeth Taylor's grave. We'd met at a party a few days before. I was young and stupid, celebrating my first starring role. The party was at my manager's house, and I'm not sure how Blue ended up there, but I was thrilled to see her. I wasn't as excited about the role as everyone else was. Acting had always come naturally to me, and I had no doubt I would succeed. I was less certain about romance. My romantic pursuits had been . . . what's the word?

Tragic.

When Blue glided up to me that night, I knew I couldn't mess it up. There are lots of beautiful women—I'm one of them— but Blue also had something I wanted: ease. It was as though she'd been floating through life in a protective cloud. Meanwhile, my life had been nothing but heartbreak and trauma. She wanted my success; I wanted her insouciance. I took her home that night.

In the morning, she revealed she had a boyfriend, Dillon. She showed me a picture on her phone, a sadistic act, in retrospect. Dillon looked like every other guy in Silver Lake: emaciated and emasculated, wearing a T-shirt featuring a band I'd never heard of. He didn't threaten me. I knew Blue was gay, know she's gay. But she's closeted—who knows why. I can't believe people are still closeted, that Blue is still with Dillon. I blame Suki, Florida, and the Episcopalian church. Luckily, I have no relationship with my parents or with god. Blue is all I've ever worshipped.

Blue said we were just "messing around," like naughty children breaking the rules on the playground. It was so strange. It was the twenty-first century and Blue was acting like we were closeted lesbians in 1950s Greenwich Village, which I grew to see as hot because I had no choice. Shame and secrecy became aphrodisiacs.

I knew Blue liked me in part because I was succeeding in the field she aspired to succeed in, but it was also more than that. When we fucked I left myself behind; I knew what it was like to be inside her protective cloud and never wanted to leave. I loved watching her sleep, I loved watching her wake, I loved watching her do just about anything, even pick her nose when she thought no one was watching. But I was always watching.

In fact, it was one night while I was staring longingly at her clipping her toenails that she first told me I was "too intense," which of course I'd heard before. But I didn't expect to hear it from Blue. I thought our connection was too deep for my standard relationship bullshit, but it turned out to be the same bullshit. Blue told me she "needed space" like they all do. She said Dillon was "catching on." She said a lot of things that day, and I stopped hearing her, tuned out, saw red. Like I said, I did some crazy things. And again, we don't have to get into it.

"I TOLD YOU to stay away from me," Blue says, and I feel that familiar knife in my heart. "I thought you were dead."

I nod. Everyone thought I was dead, still thinks I'm dead. They honored me at the Indie Spirit Awards and everything. *Nora Frost: 1989–2019*. I watched it on TV from the hospital. "That looks like you," my nurse said. "Everyone says that," I responded.

If Blue were smart, she would have cashed in on my "death." She would have pitched a documentary or a Netflix special. She would have said she knew why rising star Nora Frost took her own life. Tabloids speculated it was because of a little tiff I had with a costar. As if. I didn't give a shit about that man. I got aggressive—so what? It was ephemeral rage. My feelings for Blue are forever.

When I got out of the hospital, I rented a cabin tucked away in the woods of Topanga. I scrolled the ICM website for a talent agent who looked most like me and landed on Sophia Bell. I took photos that made me look even more like her. In them, I wore a blazer. I made an online dating profile. I swiped for hours a day until I came across her: Blue Vandewald. I knew I'd find her. Dillon was a little clueless, still is (more on that later). I put "ICM talent agent" on my profile to be sure she would swipe right. It worked.

Blue and I met at a dive bar on the East Side. She hadn't changed at all, hadn't aged a day, although it had been several years. Even her uniform was the same: striped T-shirt, jean shorts, Converse sneakers. After her second drink, I told her I wanted to rip off her stripes. She said she had to go home, but texted me late the next night, surely drunk. Blue was only her true self after a few drinks. Uninhibited and extremely gay, with an insatiable hunger for seductive brunettes, for me. *Meet me at the Grove*, she'd texted. Like I said: We ended up in the parking structure, doing what we are meant to do. Afterwards, she told me about Dillon like she did the first time. Again: Blue has always been so good at hurting me.

"You drove off a bridge," Blue says.

I nod again. Erected in 1913 and built in the Beaux-Arts

style, the Colorado Street Bridge has a distinctly European appearance despite its location near Pasadena. During the early twentieth century, it became known locally as "Suicide Bridge" after dozens of people leapt from the structure. It was the perfect place to fake my death. I didn't actually drive off the bridge. I flipped my car though. Fucked up my face enough that I needed reconstructive surgery. I shattered every bone in my face. That's—count them—fourteen bones. Unconscious on impact, I felt nothing. I entered the hospital with a fake name. I told the plastic surgeon to make me look like Sophia Loren. He did a pretty good job; I have the cat eyes and everything. I was pretty before, but I'm even prettier now.

"I thought I was safe," Blue says. Surprising me, tears well up in her eyes. And it kills me to see her upset, it really does, I mean that.

I walk over and graze her cheek with my hand. "You are safe, Angel," I say.

For a second, I feel our connection, the electric current between our bodies. Then, abruptly ending our beautiful moment, Blue spits in my face. Saliva lands in my eye; it burns. I need to go to the main house to rinse it. But first, I walk over to gag Blue.

To my shock but not surprise, she takes the scarf from my hands and ties it around her mouth herself.

THE SUN IS setting over the pool. The wind has calmed. The palm frond floats eerily still in the murky water. I easily light a cigarette, revel in the inhale. Blue knows who I am. She said *Nora Frost*. She knows it's me, and she is playing along. She's pretending to cry, pretending to be afraid, pretending she thought I was dead, but like I said: Blue is good at playing dumb. When she tied the scarf around her own mouth, she told me everything I needed to know.

I read online that being overprivileged depletes dopamine. I use this fact to comfort myself when I envy people like Blue, who grew up with everything handed to them. They're miserable. That's why Blue was constantly meditating and getting ketamine infusions and going to acupuncture and buying crystals and smoking two packs a day and hiding and lying and dating someone she didn't even like. She couldn't act because she'd never known danger. But now she's adrenalized, and some emotion has blossomed on her face. I knew I could save her.

And this is only phase one.

"I HAVE A little surprise for you," I announce as I enter the garage, rolling the shopping cart I found in the abandoned lot next door, very convenient. Also fortuitous, Blue's beard is petite enough to fit easily inside. He's easy to lift too. Such a weak little man. "I know how much you love Dillon." Blue's beard was tied up in my trunk for so long, I'm glad he's still alive. If he were dead, it might ruin the fun. I roll the cart over to Blue. "Ta-da! What do you think?"

Blue doesn't react, embodying the woman I fell in love with—bored, unbothered. She simply looks at her boyfriend, blinks, then nods. I imagine how turned on she is under this disaffected facade. My bored captive is the role Blue was born to play.

"Don't worry," I say, even though I know Blue isn't worried; she's excited but hiding it. "He's not dead." I recheck his pulse just to confirm and feel a slow but present heartbeat. "Yet!" I remove the surgical gauze from Dillon's mouth—only Blue gets gagged with Hermès—poke him a bit, tug at his Joy Division T-shirt, and ruffle his mousy brown hair, which leaves a film of grease on my fingers. "Rise and shine, Dillie boy!"

"What the fuck?" Dillon says, gaining consciousness. He looks at Blue, gagged and strapped to a chair. "Blue? What's going on? Who is this?"

Blue shrugs, then takes the rope I tied earlier and begins tying her hands together. Something pulses between my legs. It's like we're back together. This scenario is the foreplay of my wildest dreams. Blue secures the knot with her teeth and then holds up her hands, tugs to show they're bound together.

"Blue?" Dillon says. "What's happening?"

"She's gagged, silly," I tell him. I walk over to untie the scarf.

"It's Nora," Blue says flatly. "She's Nora."

"The dyke who killed my cat?" Dillon asks. I shudder. Like I said, I did some crazy things. But it was all for Blue. Everything I did was for Blue. She's allergic to cats. And she was always over there, in his creepy little studio apartment, struggling to breathe. I would watch them through the window, crouched in those goddamn rose bushes, getting stabbed by thorns and heartbreak. "What the fuck, Blue?" Dillon appears frantic. A pussy, like his dead cat.

Blue is calm in comparison, a delicate angel living in a cloud far above us mere mortals.

I go back to my alligator bag, remove the butcher knife. I walk over to Dillon while he screams like a little bitch. As I'm grazing the blade against his throat and fantasizing about handing the knife to Blue, watching her finish the act, there is a knock in the distance. It sounds like it's coming from outside. Someone is knocking on the front door of the house.

Curious.

Dillon screams, and I stuff the gauze back in his mouth. Again, Blue ties the scarf around her own mouth. While she does, I kiss her on the head. Then I put my knife in Blue's tied-up hands.

I trust her.

"CAN I HELP YOU?" I say to the muscled man at the door, surely a gay who's lost his way from Palm Springs. He's shirtless and sweaty and wearing short-shorts. Beats headphones hang around his neck.

"I was on a run and heard screaming," he says. "Just wanted to make sure everything is okay."

"Oh," I say. "I'm screening *Bound* in the garage. I got a sound-bar, very expensive." I laugh. "How funny, you thought someone was in danger?"

"Oh my god," he says, the register of his voice moving up an octave, as if he knows he's safe to go full faggot in the presence of an obvious dyke, screening *Bound* midday in a Prada dress in Palm Springs, or near Palm Springs. "I fucking love that movie. So hot."

I sense that he wants an invitation. "Have a nice run!" I shut the door.

BACK IN THE garage, Blue is free.

Shredded ropes lie on the floor beneath her. Blue faces Dillon and holds the knife in the air. The shiny surface of the blade reflects light from the overhead bulb right into my eye. For a second, I can't see. But I hear Dillon. "Blue, hurry!" The cart rattles.

My vision returns and I watch Blue walk over to Dillon. She tucks the knife under his ropes. I consider grabbing the knife from Blue but decide instead to trust her. I pop open a La Croix as Blue saws Dillon free. I slowly eat a fig. I turn the music back on. *Just remember all the while.* I tap my heel on the concrete. *You belong to me.*

When Dillon is free, he jumps out of the shopping cart, grabs Blue's hand, and tugs her toward the exit. Blue doesn't budge. Dillon drops her hand and runs toward the door. "Are you crazy? She's going to kill us."

Blue glances at me and winks. Shivers trickle down my back.

"Let's kill her first," Blue tells Dillon. "She'll follow us. She's dangerous."

"I'm not that dangerous," I say, playing along. I set down my drink and meet Blue's gaze. "You're the one with the knife."

"She's bluffing." Blue runs over to her beard. "Come on, Dillon," she says. "Be a man." With her free hand, Blue grazes Dillon's cheek. She pleads with him, then whispers something in his ear that appears to change his mind.

Dillon approaches me slowly. I prepare to let him take me. He opens his arms and charges into me. He's so weak I nearly laugh. For Blue, I go spaghetti. Let him tackle me to the ground.

"Yes, Dillon!" Blue shouts. "Hold her down!"

The concrete is cold on my wrists. Dillon is straddling me, and his breath smells like pizza. I feel like I'm going to vomit. Blue walks over with the knife and stands over me. Her hair glows in the light from the bulb above her.

"Get her, Blue," Dillon shouts, frantic. "Quick!"

Blue squats down and grazes the knife along my cheek.

"Blue!" Dillon shouts. "Hurry! I can't hold her down much longer."

God, I'm not even resisting.

Blue whispers into my ear. "You ready?"

Dillon's eyes bulge.

Eager to end this charade, I knee Dillon in the nuts. He yelps and I flip him over. I'm on top now, where I belong.

Dillon starts to cry.

I put one hand on his throat and offer my other hand to Blue.

Blue places the knife in my hand.

Dillon screams.

I lift the knife above his body and prepare to plunge, basking in the melodic sounds of Dillon's cries for mercy.

"Wait." Blue grabs my arm. I worry she's had a change of heart. I look at her, afraid, prepared to convince her. But instead Blue smiles at me. "I want to finish the job."

With glee, I hand her the knife.

BLUE AND I are covered in blood, speeding down the darkened road, nothing visible but the glowing red lights of windmills in the distance. Dillon is dead in the trunk, and Blue holds my hand on the center console.

I remove my hand, roll down the windows and light a cigarette. After a drag, I pass the cigarette to Blue, who blows smoke into the night. When she hands it back to me, she starts to laugh.

"What is it?" I ask.

"Nothing," Blue says. But she's still laughing, and it borders on maniacal. Being bound awakened something in Blue. She's alive.

"Tell me," I say.

"We're insane," Blue says.

I laugh too, and soon we're both laughing, and it's so romantic. Blue lights fill the car, almost like a movie. But then I realize they're police lights. I'm being pulled over. With a dead body in my trunk. Fantastic.

The patrol car glows behind us.

"Fuck," Blue says. "Fuck, fuck."

"It's fine," I say. "I'm an incredible actress, remember?" It's true. "So are you." I squeeze her hand.

The cop emerges from his vehicle with a flashlight. As he approaches, I lean out the window preemptively. "Hello, officer." I'm glad I'm still in my Prada dress, which frames my cleavage like art. Blue and I both have something men want. I have perfect tits and an irresistible joie de vivre. Blue looks like someone who would get tortured and killed in every man's favorite movie. Recalling the past twenty-four hours, I stifle a laugh.

"Where are you all headed this late?" the officer asks.

"Back to LA," I say.

"LA's the other way, miss," the officer says, pointing behind him.

"God," I say, leaning over, giggling, clutching my chest. "Women and directions! The stereotypes are true, goodness."

"Your left taillight is out," the officer says. "And you were speeding." He pauses, looks us over, shines his flashlight in the car.

"Are you bleeding, ma'am?" He points the light at Blue, who is very still. "Are you both bleeding?"

I giggle again, even breathier. "We're actresses," I say. "Well," I pause, squeezing my arms together to reveal the perfect slit of cleavage. "Adult film stars," I whisper as though embarrassed. The cop's eyes move to my chest, right where I want them. "We had a shoot in the desert." His eyes remain fixed on my chest. "People have strange fetishes, officer, and that's none of my business, but I have bills to pay."

The officer clears his throat and looks up at my face. "License and registration."

"Can't you let us off with a warning?" I ask.

Blue reaches over and circles my kneecap with her fingertip. "Please, officer?" She rests her head on my shoulder and runs her fingers through my hair, sending chills down my back. "Our husbands are waiting for us."

"Yes, officer," I add, pulling Blue's head onto my bosom. "Our husbands are waiting."

A voice shoots through the officer's walkie-talkie, and we all jump. He shakes his head and says, "I'll be right back," then walks back to his patrol car.

Once the officer is gone, Blue leans over and whispers in my ear. "You ready?"

I press the gas.

WE'RE DRIVING TOWARD Los Angeles now, but it doesn't matter where we're going because I have Blue. Losing the officer was challenging, but I knew I could do it. I leased this car in part for its speed. The Mercedes-AMG GT 63 S is one of the fastest cars on the market, far faster than the Ford Crown Victoria used by the Riverside County Police Department. It took a few dangerous maneuvers to lose him, but I'm a fairly fearless driver, and to be honest it was exciting—driving 190 miles per hour with Blue gripping my thigh.

I assume there is a warrant out for my arrest, but I'm unbothered, like Blue by my side. We ditched and replaced the plates before dumping the body in Lake Hemet, a water storage reservoir at the foot of the San Jacinto Mountains. It was a nearly three-hour detour, including lifting and dragging the body, and afterward we fucked on the beach. Blue made me tie her up first.

Windmills spin overhead, the sun rising behind them. Blue tells me she has to pee, so I pull over. "When did you know it was me?" I ask Blue while she pulls down her pants behind the car. "Be honest."

"Give me a second," Blue says. I walk to the other side of the car and lean against it, listen to the stream of liquid hit the dust. I look out at the pinkish desert expanse and my eye catches something slithering in the dirt on the other side of the road. A rattlesnake, I think.

The stream stops and Blue walks over to me, leans beside me on the car. We watch the rattlesnake slither onto the pavement.

Blue takes out her phone and films the serpent writhing on the concrete. "I knew it was you almost immediately," she says while looking at the snake on her iPhone. The snake stops moving, and Blue puts her phone back in her pocket. She looks right at me, her blue eyes igniting something in my chest. "No one else calls me Angel."

A hawk circles overhead. The snake starts slithering toward us again.

"Do you still think I can be a star?" Blue asks, watching the snake.

I nod. "Of course I do," I say, and for once I'm not lying. Blue was very good at playing the victim. I almost believed her.

Blue looks up from the snake and smiles at me. I smile back, proud of her, me, us. My little experiment worked.

Suddenly, the hawk swoops down and picks up the snake in its mouth. We watch the bird disappear into the dim purple sky with the snake hanging, struggling to escape.

BEEP. BEEP.

"Nora? Nora?"

Beep. Beep.

I blink and see a fuzzy outline over my head. Several blurry figures. They sharpen into view. A nurse. My mom. A doctor.

Beep. Beep.

I scan the hospital room. There are wilted tulips on the table. On the TV screen above my head, a man holds a rattlesnake on a stick. "She's a feisty one," the man says in a South African accent.

Beep. Beep.

Just three bodies. A nurse. My mom. A doctor.

Tulips. A snake on the TV. A feisty one.

No Blue.

Beep. Beep.

No Blue.

Beep. Beep.

No Blue.

The nurse jams a needle in my arm. I blink and—

A Parlor Game   Excerpt from *Walking the Dusk*

L. J. WEBB (Gertrude Vanderbilt Whitney)

SINCE THE DRESS-UP party there had been a sense of dramatics in the air. A climax was pending, but in the meanwhile the interest was suspended, the orchestra was playing, and the personnel of the play were sauntering about awaiting their clues.

The evening after Ronald and I had taken our supper out on the lake was to be our last one in camp. At dinner Walter, Valentine, and Ronald became very excited over the theatre and books.

We had our coffee before leaving the dining room and I noticed Katharine asked for a second cup. She had eaten hardly anything. Vally looking around the table said, suddenly, "What we suffer conversationally from the Victorian times, the gay nineties, nudity, the younger generation and the eighteenth amendment, is enough to drive anyone to suicide."

A dead pause followed the careless sentence. I glanced across the table and met Ronald's eyes fixed on me.

"Suicide is a dull proceeding," Vally continued innocently. If he had not been intent on his argument, he might have seen that at least five of the persons seated around that table were electrified by that word, but there had been no mention of Mabel and he had not been through that experience with us.

It was Katharine who broke in with an untroubled voice, "Someone ought to invent some new topic, the way Dr. Munthe invented a new disease after everybody had had their appendix out." She got up from the table and we all went into the living room.

Stephen was near me.

"You were very quiet tonight," I said to him.

"I'm not much good on the theatre and books. Besides, I'm restless."

"Come and sit with me on the piazza," I said. "I meant to tell you Sylvia did try to butt in on this party."

Everyone else stayed in the big sitting room and we had the porch to ourselves.

"What's the big idea about Sylvia?" I asked.

Stephen's color unaccountably changed. "Women are the devil," he said, changing his position.

"You attract females like a trap baited and set and then when they are caught, you let them loose and wonder why they are lame or halt."

"Don't be an idiot, Di. Sylvia—"

"I wasn't thinking only of her—."

He drove straight to the point. "So you think Mabel was in my trap? As you so kindly put it."

"I know it is horrible for a woman when she stops caring to have the man go on. It must be even worse when it's *vice versa*."

"It is," he said shortly.

Sally was calling from across the living room, "Come on in, you two, we are going to play a game. I know an amusing one."

She explained as we joined the others. "One person goes out of the room and the rest choose someone we all know and then the person comes back and asks questions. For instance, if it were a flower what kind of flower would it be? Or a book, or an automobile, or anything."

"You mean," said Charlie, "suppose we take Stephen—he would be a Rolls Royce?"

"Yes, and if he was a book a telephone book! And—"

"I don't think much of that game," observed Stephen, bored.

"Come along, let's try it. Who will go out?"

"Let Katharine go, she will be good at asking questions," I suggested.

After Katharine had left the room we consulted as to whom we would choose. I waited while they made suggestions, then I said, "Let's take Katharine herself?" I tried to forget the inner compulsion behind my words. It was agreed.

Walter went out to call her back and she came and sat on a big chair near the piano. We gathered about her, forming a circle. Her first glance as she entered the room was at Stephen—that fleeting, worried glance which I had intercepted between them before.

He too was watching her. She made a magnificent figure, clad in crimson velvet pajamas, the not too strong light of the camp living room obliterated everything but her best points. But I felt worse than better, as we all sat there awaiting her first question.

"Start at the right," ordered Sally, "and ask us each in turn. You ought to guess it if we are good with our answers, after you have been around the circle once."

I was absorbed in catching any reactions Katharine's guests might be receiving from her. Vally was eyeing her with appreciation. Walter's languorous gaze appraised her favorably, and questioningly. Mrs. Bacon was the only other who appeared to be noticing her, Stephen having directed his attention to Sally. She was staring, making mental notes on her pajamas with the idea of copying them, I fancied.

"Now then," Katharine remarked turning to Mr. Bacon who was next to her, "you are the first."

"Don't start with me, I won't be any good." He looked embarrassed.

"Yes, you will. If it were fishing tackle what would it be?"

Mr. Bacon, looking palpably relieved, after a moment answered, "A strong, well-balanced rod for catching big fish—say tarpon—no, maybe not quite as big as that: for catching barracuda and amberjack. A very fine rod, absolutely first class."

Ronald was next in turn. He sat on the floor smoking, a tense figure in spite of his repose.

"Suppose it were an animal, what would it be?"

I wondered if the same beast would jump into his head as had instantaneously leapt into mine.

"A puma in a cage."

"In a cage!" Katharine said. "That should be a pretty good clue, let me see. Now it is your turn, Miss Lawrence. I am hoping for something very illuminating from you. If it were a painter?"

"Gauguin."

"That makes me think of something modern and strong," I said in a rather strained voice.

"Strange and exotic," Vally murmured to me.

Katharine smiled at him. "An opera?"

After a few minutes' thought he gave her "'The Walkure' or 'Salome,' or something by Debussy."

"That's good," said Sally.

Charlie said he was out beyond his depth. Katharine looked puzzled and her hands were clasped together.

"This is not so easy," she said.

I was sitting by Vally so my turn came next. "Suppose it were a country?"

This seemed to find the inside of my head empty. Katharine a country? Certainly not America. France? Too subtle. Italy? Too romantic. Spain? Too primitive. What other countries were there? Germany, too practical, Russia too Red. Ah! England! England of course.

"England," I said.

Katharine sat very still, her arms on the arms of the chair. "Oh," she said and turned to Charlie. "Suppose it were food?"

He looked up in his droll way, "I don't like your implication!"

Our eyes all turned on him. He rose to the occasion. "A glace surprise gone wrong, cold souffle on the outside and hot ice cream on the inside."

The question asked of Mrs. Bacon was "A means of locomotion?"

Her suggestion of an airplane was repudiated by a chorus and Walter's offer of "A Roman chariot" was considered better.

It was now Stephen's turn and I was watching him with interest hidden under my eyelashes—and anxiety, too. He was not looking at his wife, his eyes were roving from one to the other of his guests as if to gauge their thoughts. When Katharine spoke, I thought her voice conciliatory though her look was icy.

"Stephen," she said, "I don't know what to ask you—well—suppose it were a business?"

"That's awfully hard," said Charlie.

Stephen looked at the floor as if searching there for some inspiration. At last he said, "I have it. It wouldn't be a business, it would be a profession." He hesitated. "I don't know—a specialist of some kind."

No one said anything. To me the silence was uncomfortable.

"Now there is only Walter left. I have an idea about who it might be, but you must give me a good answer. If it were a material?"

Walter said, "A material? That opens a vista! I think it would be a rug, one of those rugs that you hang on the wall. It would have an intricate pattern and be of rare texture. It would—"

"Go on," urged Katharine.

"It would suggest the East without being Eastern."

"I have a vague idea," Katharine looked around at us as though on the defensive, "let me ask one more question and every one of you answer it."

Sally cried, "Good! That improves the game."

"Now give me a minute to think of a leading question."

We all started talking together about some of the answers. Charlie moved over to me and said that being like a Roman chariot meant nothing to him. He thought an airplane was a good answer. "It goes up in the air and travels fast—and," he whispered, "is liable to crash at any minute."

"All right," said Katharine, "this is the best I can do. Suppose it were a house?"

Mr. Bacon said, "It would be big and built of stone."

Ronald said, "It would be French Renaissance, latter period. It would be in the country, but not in the least a country house."

Sally said, "Outside there would be terraces and gardens and statues of nymphs and gods."

Vally said, "If you went into the cellars you'd find unexpected . . . things," he finished lamely.

I said there would be a maze and a deep pool.

Charlie added, "The pool might not have any bottom—or it might be shallow and only appear deep."

Mrs. Bacon said, "There would always be hot-house flowers around the house."

Stephen said, "The house would be added onto, built at different times, you know, and it would have stables and a tennis court and a subterranean passage—"

Katharine stopped him with a gesture. "It is me."

In the ensuing confusion, while she upbraided some and thanked others, I was conscious only of the fact that she was making an effort at perfect control.

"It is flattering to be considered so interesting," she remarked in her evenly modulated key.

I was inarticulate.

It was Charlie who said, "What a beastly game! Di suggested our taking you."

Everyone except Katharine knew this, but when Charlie made it concrete it hit Ronald. A dense frown descended on his face and there was derision in his inflection as he turned to me, "Still analyzing!"

It had now become a personal matter. Katharine did not look at me as Vally passed his arm through mine and led me to the piazza. He did not speak at first, then with his writer's intuition, he said, "There is something electric in the air tonight. What is it?"

I felt I had betrayed my thoughts. "You have to be dramatic, it is your business," I said casually, sitting in the hammock.

"You feel it too." He ignored my remark.

"I think we are going to have a thunderstorm."

"So do I, but it won't be in the heavens. I love these old-fashioned hammocks—so intimate!" He sat down, necessarily forced near me.

"Katharine looked awfully handsome sitting in that big chair," I said.

"Mrs. Osmund is an absorbing kind of woman," he agreed. "Not one to treat lightly, I imagine. I should like to put her in a play."

"You probably will, then. I know you are no respecter of persons. What sort of role would you give her?"

"She would be the tragedy of the play. I don't know how, exactly."

"Do you mean the unhappy person, or the deep character or just have everything against her?"

"The things she touched would turn to sawdust in her hands. Sort of evil eye."

"Funny, I wonder why she strikes you that way? I am always surprised at the effect she produces on other people."

"She is certainly a person you can't help noticing."

"I suppose so—both you and Walter are distinctly impressed by her and you are both sophisticated."

"What did Walter say about her?"

"Of course it had to do with sex. Something about her being intriguing but not the kind of person he could ever fall in love with."

Sally, never long at ease without Valentine, came out on the piazza followed by Charlie.

"What are you two talking about?" she asked.

"The woman just can't let me alone," said Vally.

He jumped out of the hammock, threw an arm around her and rushed with her down the steps. The sound of their voices was heard as they walked along the path to the boat house.

Charlie appeared next to me in Vally's place and I lay back and closed my eyes. A breeze had found its way in from the lake. It blew away the cobwebs from my mind. Katharine's attitude, her equilibrium, her splendid appearance during the evening stood out as milestones of perfection. But the night bred another thought and it found form in the words, "Why such control? To conceal not only the energy of an inner life, but to hide the ordinary reactions toward common events?"

"I think—I think the bird is on the wing," I said out loud to myself.

Naturally my companion had no idea of what I was talking, nor could I tell him. Something so insistent that it could not be quieted was absorbing me. Bred of the night and its desire, it was tender and terrible, and terror came of it. I slipped away in the direction of my tent. I saw nothing as I stumbled into my cot, only knew that I was alone.

Coming of Rage

Natalie

ALICE DUNBAR-NELSON

NATALIE SWUNG HERSELF down from the breakwater to the white sands below, and walked along on the edge of the sea, her feet leaving prints that filled with water, and were quickly effaced. She swung her brown arms in the fading sunset light, and sniffed the whiffs of salt air with keenly appreciative nostril, swinging as she trotted along with long, clean limbed step. Natalie was happy in her little sunset world down here by the water's edge.

Suddenly she paused and her big black eyes widened angrily. Someone had invaded her territory and was coming towards her.

Down here on the sands at this edge of the beach was Natalie's own kingdom, and woe unto the trespasser who dared within its boundaries. At Mandeville, you know, there are places where the fickle Lake Ponchartrain encroaches too frequently and too violently upon the homes of men, therefore, it has to be kept back by stoutly built breakwaters, as its no less turbulent cousin, the Mississippi river is kept from swamping New Orleans across the way by levees. Then, too, there are spots here and there where the lake kisses the shores in regulation beach-like manner, or mingles with swamp and bayou over morass and tangled moss thicket. When the tide was low, one might walk on the sands below until the beachy places were found. Down here at the West End of the town, the natives called Natalie's kingdom because of the absolute sway she exercised over those sands and marshes and little beauty spots of scenery and waves.

Walking towards her now on the sunset lighted sands, evidently taking great delight in wetting her delicate slippers, came a fair-haired, rose-tinted creature, in an ethereal film of fluffy lawn and flower-covered hat. Natalie surveyed her curiously. She knew the type well; the delicate summer boarder who came to idle time away, was afraid of everything under the sun, and generally treated Natalie either with supercilious indifference or with contemptuous patronage. She knew them and hated them accordingly. But this one must be of a different kind, else how did she get down that perilous climb, and why was she unaccompanied by maid or mother? The newcomer was also surveying Natalie with admiration plainly depicted in her eyes.

Contrary to her usual custom, the queen approached the trespasser and said, "Who are you and what are you doing here?" She spoke in French, and the blonde shook her head and said sadly,

"You'll have to speak English."

Natalie's self-importance rose in a corresponding degree as the girl's eyes surveyed her healthful frame with wonderment, and she repeated the question in a mixture of bad English and gestures.

Olivia replied that her family had moved into the house at the corner for the summer. The big house hidden in red roses and magnolia trees.

"The Torrés house?" asked Natalie.

Olivia nodded her head wisely, and discussing the beauties of the place, they walked along the sunset sands. They had just reached the stage when confidences were in progress, when a sharp voice above their heads caused them to look up. They were passing beneath the fishing wharf of the house, and a fretful looking, over-dressed lady with a white lace parasol was leaning over the railing.

"Olivia!" she screamed sharply, "What are you doing down there? Come up here this minute."

Olivia started nervously; it was evident that she was afraid of her mother.

"How can I get up?" she inquired.

"You'll have to climb, yes," said Natalie, "cause the nearest slope is a leetle more than a half mile down."

So boosted up by Natalie's strong, bared arms, and clinging to the scrubby bushes that grew through the cracks of the breakwater, Olivia gained the beach smiling, flushed, triumphant, only to be met with a scowl on the face of the overdressed lady.

"What do you mean," she said sharply, "by acting like a regular tomboy, and running about with such a person already?"

Olivia hung her head, but said nothing, only walked into the house, and sat on her father's knee.

"Papa," she spoke slowly, and with tears in her eyes, "I climbed down the breakwater just now, and met such a nice girl on the sands. She's what they call a 'Cajan' here; awfully pretty, and nice, and so smart, papa! She speaks such good French, I didn't dare answer her in anything but English. Her name is Natalie Leblanc, and she lives down where the bayou meets the lake. She told me that she never liked summer boarders because they were always so stuck-up, but she liked me, because I seemed to have some sense. And she's so healthy, papa, and strong, why she almost lifted me over the breakwater. And, papa, please sir, mayn't I go with her? She says she'll show me all the beauty places, and teach me how to swim and row and fish and all that."

"Whew?" replied Mr. Spiers, "you two must have flown into each other's arms to have learned all that."

"She's a nice girl, papa, fourteen years, only you'd never think so. She's so much taller and stouter than I am."

At the supper table that night, Mr. Spiers said to his wife, "Carrie, I want you to let Olivia take off those fancy clothes and get some blood in her face; she looks like a wax doll. Let her run and jump and climb and get sunburned. It'll do her good."

"Gracious me, John," exclaimed Mrs. Spiers, "you'll have the child a regular hoyden; when will she learn dignity?"

"Six years from now is time enough. I hate these little old women that are coming up now. Let her go with the natives, they'll teach her more healthy topics of conversation than that fashionable city set."

Olivia said nothing, but her pale little face lighted with pleasure, and she flashed a grateful look at her father across the table. Next morning, Mr. Spiers went back to the city, and the family settled in their beautiful, rose-embowered, rambling old home for the summer.

NATALIE WAS SWINGING dreamily on her front gallery in a hammock made of barrel staves and sacking. A peaceful noonday silence hung over all save for the persistent trilling of a mockingbird in the moss-laden old oak tree, and an occasional hoarse grunt from an alligator in the black waters of the bayou. The persimmon tree shook a shower of snowy fragrant blossoms at its foot, as the breezes that came from Nott's Point swept its branches. It was a quaint little, one sided house, shingle-roofed, and moss-covered, its gray sides guiltless of paint. But the wide gallery that went all around the house was scrubbed white, and sprinkled after the good old fashion, with white sand, while the walk that led from the battered gate was sanded carefully, swept clean, and bordered with precise rows of poppies and larkspurs. Natalie's eyes closed as she dreamily answered the mockingbird's trills with snatches of a Creole melody. A timid knock roused her to a standing position, and there half opening the gate, stood Olivia.

"*Entrez, entrez!*" cried Natalie impulsively, "*Oh, mais, ma foi*, you look nice, you seem sensible now," with an approving glance at Olivia's gingham dress, white sunbonnet and sand shoes. "Stay with me all the day, yes, and we shall have such fun, such a nice time, yes, we will."

So Olivia stayed, and was introduced to the grandmother Mme. Leblanc, very old and dignified and gentle. She was escorted proudly around the big yard with its duck pond and plum orchard; initiated into the mysteries of the artesian well. In Mandeville, you know, slow little town as it is, everyone uses the artesian well in preference to anything else, so that every one has most clear, cold, and sparkling water at all times. This one of Natalie's fell into a big stone basin, overgrown with scarlet creepers, and water lillies on the clear pool. Upon the stone beneath the trickling stream there was a glass, and Natalie explained how glasses could be colored by simply letting them stay under the action of the water for a day, then the sulphur and iron would turn the white into a clear amber with iridescent lights throughout. Within the old-fashioned kitchen there were many glasses which Natalie had colored, and nothing more daintily clear could be imagined.

This was only the beginning of a close intimacy between the girls. There were long rambles down the bayou shores into the piney woods of the old oak, that stood sentinel-like over the water's edge, intimacies with the quaint Indians in the St. Tammany settlement; rowings around the lake's edges and up the bayou in a dory, singing French songs that Natalie could make sound so prettily; swims in the brown lake water; a healthy brownness in Olivia's face, and a pleased sparkle about Natalie in the newfound affection that was so strange to her.

But she could not be induced to visit Olivia's home at the Torrés place. "Madame, your maman, cares not for me," she would say in response to Olivia's entreaties to come to the house, "and I think it better to stay away. You come to me, we will be happy, yes."

When Mr. Spiers came over on the steamer Saturday evening to stay until Monday morning, nothing pleased him better than to see his "little country girl" so healthy, though the stylish mother grieved to see the unfashionable tan on the girl's cheeks.

One day, however, Natalie wanted Olivia for a piney woods ramble to gather pine cones which would be made into picture frames. So with bonnet and basket, she swallowed her pride, and trudged up the beach to the Torrés place. Mrs. Spiers leaned over the picket fence with a bored expression and a frown. It was dull in this unfashionable town with nothing of interest save the daily watch for the arrival of the New Camelia, which came puffing across the lake's bosom every evening, the engine's arms working up and down with monotonous precision. One regatta of very miniature proportions, with a very tame hop at Colomés' hotel, a daily drive to the post office, with an occasional visitor constituted the round of pleasures for the season. Mrs. Spiers wanted to go home, but Olivia wanted to stay, and Olivia generally had her way with her father. Natalie's voice aroused Mrs. Spiers from an unpleasant reverie.

"Is Oleevia at home?" She looked up crossly.

"Olivia?" she said.

"Yes, madame," and Natalie gave her one of her most polite French bows, while Mrs. Spiers drew herself up haughtily.

"I think you are making a mistake," she said icily, "you probably mean *Miss* Olivia."

"Yes, madame, I mean Ma'amselle Oleevia Spiers."

At this moment, the subject of discussion tripped down the flower-lined walk of the old-fashioned garden.

"Oh, Natalie," she cried joyously, and would have kissed her friend, but the mother held her back.

"Do you mean to tell me, Olivia, that this—this—person calls you by your first name as if she were your equal? Do you permit that?"

Both girls' faces crimsoned; the one with a fair flush of mortification, the other with a darker tint of injured pride and anger.

"Mama—" began Olivia pleadingly, but Mrs. Spiers was thoroughly angry now.

"In the future, girl," she continued addressing Natalie, "I want you to call my daughter Miss Olivia. I require that of all inferiors."

Natalie's dark-tressed head rose proudly, "I am not an inferior, madame," she replied, "in age and in education, I am Oleevia's equal, yes, and in birth, and breeding, I am superior to madame herself," and walked away proudly, swinging her gay-colored

Indian basket with erect head, while Olivia burst into shamed tears, and was promptly hustled inside.

Natalie did not go to the woods to get the pine cones, but walked swiftly home and threw herself moodily into the home-made hammock.

"They are all alike," she mused, "these city people with their airs, and I was foolish to try and be friendly. Serves me right, yes. Mais, much as I like," clenching her fists, "I'd pop before I'd call her mademoiselle, ah, non, non!"

Thus ended the pleasant intimacy between the girls, and Natalie went on in her old way, rowing her dory into the bayou, and fishing for the beautiful trout in its black waters; queening it over the children in the village, and dreaming the hot hours of the day away in the hammock or under the big oak. On Sundays, she would meet Olivia at the quaint little old church on the back road, and smile pleasantly as she knelt to tell her beads, or bowed at the tinkling of the hoarse, little host-bell.

The summer passed away, and merged into the autumn months; the poppies blazed red in the gardens, and the golden-rod gleamed in the woods and hedges. From all sides sounded the crack of the hunter's rifle, and the crackling of dropping nuts on the brown leaves in the crisp, clear air. It was pecan threshing time, and all the small town was busy in the work of threshing the pecan trees and packing the long brown nuts into barrels for shipping. Natalie's time was so taken with helping to thresh trees, gathering in the autumn tinted persimmons and paddling in the swampy lagoons to shoot the small birds that flocked on the water's edge that Olivia was almost forgotten.

It was on a Sunday evening that a strong southeast wind came with a rush and roar over the angry waters of the lake from Nott's Point, and sent the heavy swell booming high against the breakwater. Natalie's little kingdom down on the sands was completely submerged in about eight feet of water, and the angry waves tossed up onto the shore, dashing clouds of spray into the very houses.

ALL THE POPULATION of Mandeville was out on the beach, they dared not go on any pier, for every one of them, even to the steamer landing seemed in imminent danger of being swept away at any moment. Everyone was watching the brave little New Camelia as she battled against the wind and waves coming from Covington and the Tchefuncta river past Mandeville on the way to New Orleans. Again and again, shrilly tooting her displeasure did she skim around the landing, endeavoring to find a stopping place, but in vain, and after a final shrill squeal, she started towards New Orleans, now bounding high on the crest of a wave, now delving deep into a trough, the engine arms frantically waving up and down. Natalie, with heavy black hair, wind-blown and tangled stood in the midst of a crowd of her friends talking loudly with the rest so as to be heard above the wind and water, and at the same time furtively watching the evident distress of Mrs. Spiers and Olivia, who stood apart and wrung their hands with fright.

Everyone remembers until yet, that awful Sunday night. How in the pitchy darkness the fearful southeast wind blowing in the waters from the Gulf of Mexico through the Rigolets, upturned immense centurion oaks, and crushed solid old houses as though they were so many eggshells; how the cattle bellowed as they were swept away into the writhing, tossing waters, and how on the Monday, when the slow daylight dawned over the frightened, praying town, it revealed a complete submergment of four feet, with natives perched in every possible place, and the angry lake still tossing its heavy swells over the crushed breakwater, and dashing logs, and wood, remnants of piers and bathhouses into one's very bedroom.

Natalie's house had escaped, and the water yet lacked three inches of being in the rooms; so cheerfully making the nervous grandmother comfortable, she took her dory from its place on the back gallery, and paddled out into the desolate, frightened Louisiana Venice to give her helping smile to the distressed natives, with offers of her home to those whom falling trees or wild waves had made homeless. Picking up struggling chickens from stray bushes, where bedraggled and wild-eyed they had sought refuge, and a mewing, clawing kitten, and piling them all in the stern, too frightened to fight with each other, she rowed up the canal that had once been the main street until she came to Olivia's house. A sudden impulse caused her to ship her oars, and look up into the windows where she saw Olivia's white, frightened face.

"Natalie," called the girl, and ran out on the gallery, while the dory paddled into the ruined yard, "Oh Natalie, mama is so frightened! She is wild to go home on the Camelia, see, it is coming over now, and Mr. Colomés and Mr. Mathias have all been here, telling her she can't possibly get to the boat, and she's having hysterics, and oh, Natalie, I'm so frightened!" and she clung to the dory wildly.

At that moment, Mrs. Spiers came out on the gallery followed by M'sieu Colomés, the hotel man, who with shrugs and gesticulations was saying,

"Madame, is ver' unwise, ver' unwise; mais, non, madame will surely drown if she attempts to catch the bateau."

But madame was determined, so with a final shrug at the perversity of "dose American," M'sieu Colomés jumped into his pirogue and paddled away in disgust, determining to wash his hands of the whole affair. Madame turned to Natalie with a despairing gesture.

"You can row, Natalie," she pleaded, "take us to the landing." "Ah," thought Natalie, "I am not 'that person' now." But she said nothing, only turned and looked out upon the waste of waters. As far as the eye could reach the lake rolled in long, heavy, groundswells that sobbed in sullen anger under a gray sky at the mischief they had done. About a hundred feet from the gallery stood a row of slender storm-swept saplings outlining the edge of the former breakwater. Just at this line, the swells broke sharply throwing lines of foam into the inundated streets. The brave little Camelia was puffing and working in another attempt to reach the landing, but this time from New Orleans. The landing a half mile away showed out into the angry waters a broken pile of lumber, the pier reaching to the shore had been reduced to stumps. Natalie shaded her eyes, and took in the details of the scene at a single glance.

"Eet might be posseeble," she said musingly, "to row down the strit, yes, to the landing pier, then try the waves, but it would be dangerous, yes. Madame, the danger is over, stay in Mandeville until the water goes down."

But Madame was hysterically angry at the idea. Her husband was uneasy, she knew, and there was no possible way of letting him know that she and Olivia were safe. Then just look at those waves, and that was enough! Who knew but in the night they might rise and sweep the entire town away. Even now, the house rocked on its foundations. The servants who had gone out the night before, had not been able to return and the two were alone.

Natalie looked at her earnestly as she talked. Madame had tried all that money and persuasion could do, no one dared brave those waves to meet the boat. Moreover, all the skiffs in

Mandeville, save five, had gone to pieces in the storm. Olivia was crying silently, dreading the angry waters.

"For Oleevia, I'll take you," said Natalie at length, "For your 'Mees Oleevia,'" she couldn't help growing sarcastic under the circumstances. The few people who gazed out of windows and from galleries of the houses remaining on the beach marvelled to see Natalie's brown arms pulling the now heavily laden dory up the street. Mrs. Spiers and the valise were stored in the boat among the wet chickens and the trembling kitten, while Olivia steered. It was easy enough rowing up the street in the comparatively calm water, but the superhuman effort came when it was time to get into the lake towards the boat which had now reached the landing, puffing and blowing, and tugging at the cable which bound her to the broken anchor-post. It was only a hundred yards out, but it needed a man's herculean strength to pull against the fearful force of the heavy, incoming waves. A foot would be gained, only to be lost and beaten back for three feet or more. Mrs. Spiers, too frightened to speak, looked desperately about her, while Olivia prayed silently as she steered. From the deck of the steamer, the Captain and crew watched the dory with a field glass. "If only we could help her!" they cried, but every boat had been swept from the steamer in that awful twenty mile battle from New Orleans.

Pull, strain, tug every nerve did Natalie, and a little headway was made. Now her strength seemed gone, and it looked as if she must succumb and let the boat drift and be dashed into pieces on the shore. But onward she forged, her strong back bending as she plunged the boat through a stubborn swell.

"Oh, Marie, mere de Dieu," prayed Natalie, "dans cette heure de travail, pitie-moi; donnez-moi ton secours." For a weary hour she fought with blistered hands and failing heart against the surging swells and driving wind until near the sides of the steamer, when a lasso-like rope came whizzing to the dory. Mrs. Spiers, white and trembling made it fast to the seats, and in another instant, they were all on deck, surrounded by the wondering crew, safe, but exhausted, and sobbing, every one of them.

"And after mama being so mean to her too," cried Olivia in the first flush of excitement. Mrs. Spiers and Olivia went to New Orleans, while the captain sent one of his strongest men to row Natalie home. That night, the Torrés house crumbled to the ground, its old foundation undermined by the water.

But was Natalie ever forgotten? Go to Mandeville to-day and you'll find her there yet, though this happened eight years ago. But see the comforts around Mme. Leblanc—the books and music and pleasant little luxuries. And when Natalie goes to New Orleans for the Carnival week, Mr. Spiers introduces her to everyone as the "plucky little girl who rowed my wife and daughter out of a death-trap, by Jove!"

Girl in the Slayer Jacket

ASTRID ANNE ROSE

ALICE SAYS TO ME, "You know you can handle any kind of pain if you just breathe through it." She traces the dunes of my palm with baby-pink nails filed into teardrop points.

"Okay . . . and? Everybody breathes."

She giggles. Her bedsprings creak.

"Think about it. What do they say when you're in labor?"

"I can't remember."

Alice shoves me. "Fuck off. Think. This thing grows inside you, feeds off you for nine months, and when you're finally lying there, squeezing it out, all they can say is breathe."

She grabs the bong off the tan carpet littered with dog hair and bobby pins and old press-ons. Rips it. Blows a thin thread of smoke into the air.

Her sweatpants are black, with something printed down one leg in white.

"Where the fuck did you get those?" I ask, pointing.

"Online? Dumbass?" She coughs.

"Lemme see."

She stretches her legs out.

"Weekend . . . uhhh . . ."

She rolls her eyes.

"Weekend Nachos?" I start giggling. "What the fuck?"

"Laugh it up, fag. Sorry it's not one of your stupid Joy Division shirts."

"Nachos Division," I say, still laughing.

Alice laughs despite herself.

"You're so fucking dumb." She passes me the bong. "Anyway, listen. Listen. I was in the auditorium today. With Will."

Oh God. Will. He dresses like he literally just heard of the Sex Pistols. And he blows guys in the gym showers. Which is cool with me, whatever, just . . . the showers?

"We went up behind the top row. No one was there. You know how he seems like such a badass and stuff, right?"

"Totally."

"I told him he could put it in my ass. It took him forever to get hard enough, he busted after like three seconds, and then, guess what? He cried."

"Shut the fuck up!!"

"Bitch, he was sobbing!"

"What a pussy . . . You know he's in love with you."

"Literally. He'll do anything I say. It's kind of amazing."

"So you're gonna tell everybody, right?"

"No. Not until he pisses me off."

Alice gives me a quick, wolfish smile.

"Anyway. It hurt. But I just lay there on my stomach and felt my lungs expand. Each time I breathed in, they filled up and lifted me off the floor a little. Then I exhaled and sank back down. Pretty soon that's all I could feel. All there was, in the whole world. In and out."

In and out. I do my best not to giggle, but I can't help it. Alice groans, grabs her pillow in both hands, and starts walloping me. I fall on my side, laughing. She gives me one more thwap, tosses the pillow aside, and climbs on top of me, pinning my arms. I squirm, but she's sitting right on my hips, her weight on my belly button. I wiggle in vain.

She sits there until we both calm down. I can feel the warmth between her spread legs as she bobs on the waves of my breathing.

"See?" she says. She puts one hand on my stomach. "In and out."

She leans down. Her lips brush mine. I kiss her back. I kiss her harder. My back arches; my thighs clench. All of me rises to meet her and I know how desperate I look, bent with full-body hunger.

She pulls away. Hops off me, off the bed.

"You better go. I gotta study."

It stings, the hot and cold thing. But a no is a no. I grab my stuff and walk home; if I cut through the park it's barely a mile of overgrown grass and sagging willows. My dad doesn't blink when I come in. He's watching basketball. I hear Mom chopping something in the kitchen, *clack-clack-clack* on the cutting board. She calls my name, but I go right upstairs, lock myself in my room, and curl up under the blankets. I think of Alice: "I gotta study." Fuck off. We're in the same grade but she's a year older. Her family's rich. Her parents leave her alone. She wears her hair in a Chelsea cut to piss them off. She probably holds hands with me in front of them just to piss them off. They don't give a shit. She's an inch shorter than me, the last time we checked. I wish she'd just be honest with me. I wish she'd stop kissing me if she doesn't mean it.

I'M TWENTY MINUTES late to school. The homeroom teacher, Mrs. Tanner, doesn't say anything, but I can tell she wants to. The guidance counselor told all my teachers I have a "difficult home life," so they have to cut me slack. Even the ones who hate me.

I sit in the back corner, next to Alice, and pull my jacket tight around myself.

"What'd I miss?" I ask.

"Oh, lots. The most important thing we'll ever learn in school, I think she said?"

"How was studying?"

Alice purses her lips, playing dumb.

"Last night?" I prod. "I left 'cause you said you needed to study."

"Okay, freak. I read? For class?"

"What book?"

"Ladies?" Mrs. Tanner's voice cuts in. She glares at us. Well, at me. Alice's parents are on the school board; she's invisible.

I give Tanner a wounded smile and sink into my chair.

"Stalker," Alice says under her breath.

We head to English together. My jacket dangles off my shoulders, around my elbows. Alice's skirt flaps around her ankles, and her top is as tattered as the limits of the dress code will allow. A rainbow banner sags above the auditorium doors: Don't hide your Pride! I stop at my locker for some Tylenol. A phalanx of football players almost knocks me over. I flip them off. "Dyke," they shout, as a unit.

In English we talk about *Of Mice and Men*. For the third straight week. The teacher, Mrs. Bushey, is a pair of black glasses inside a giant nest of frizzy hair. Alice looks like she's

falling asleep until Bushey calls on her and she chirps something about itinerant workers and property ownership. I smile.
Straight from SparkNotes.

After school, I skip CCD and find Alice smoking in the parking lot, reclined on the hood of a red car. Someone else's jean
jacket is draped over her clothes.

The car looks old. Vintage.

"Hey, bitch," Alice says.

"Nice ride."

She snorts. "Fucking antique," she says, and slaps one hand
on the hood.

"Hey! Watch the fuckin' paint!"

Right on cue, Will pokes his head around the trunk.

"Oh. Hey, Liz," he says. A Cure shirt clings to his skinny chest.
Poser. I give a halfhearted wave and picture him crying after five
seconds of anal sex. He disappears again.

"If he's such a dickhead, why the fuck are you hanging out
with him?" I ask.

Alice fixes me with a stare that says "Really?"

"C'mon," I say. "I'll drive."

She shrugs off the jacket. On the back is a huge patch: some
metal band. I can never read those stupid logos. The hand-
stitching is sloppy. She drops it on the hood and hops to the
ground.

"We're out!"

Will watches Alice go like a puppy with separation anxiety. I
wink at him.

ALICE PUTS HER bare feet up on the dashboard. It's my dad's
car; he notices every little scuff. I've told her not to, but it was
enough of a battle to get her to take her boots off.

I drive us away from school, past the strip mall with two nail
salons, a bar, and a Winn-Dixie. There's a Publix down the other
way, an ice-cream stand out on an access road by the river, the
graveyard . . . Never a dull moment.

"So. Where to?" I ask.

"Dunno. You're driving, babe," she says.

"You wanted me to drive."

"'Cause I don't like driving. Duh."

"Pub sub? Starbucks?"

"Just drive, oh my God. I want an Arizona."

She turns up the music, some kind of migraine metal bullshit. There's no way she actually likes this stuff. "Whatever," I say, but she doesn't hear me. I stop at a gas station, grab a can of sweet tea and a root beer. I get back in the car and Alice starts monologuing about how she hasn't eaten for eighteen hours. I'm biting bits of dry skin away from around my nails, wondering why I put up with this, when Alice smiles at me.

Right.

I turn down the radio.

"Why didn't you get Will to take you out in his whip?"

"Bitch, I've tried. He barely drives it. He flexes it at school and drives home. That's it."

"It's his baby."

She scoffs.

"You'll never be number one . . ."

"Kill yourself. Turn my shit back up."

Under extreme musical assault, I take us to the usual spot. The rust-eaten sign out front says Lawson's Meatpacking Plant; kids call it the Meat Hole.

I turn the car off and take a deep breath. Silence. Alice gets out and stretches. Her bare legs are long and toned under a sheer black skirt. They're glowing. I stare. She looks at me looking at her. Wind picks up. Pollen and dust.

"C'mon," she says. Her bleached hair is white in the sunlight, already fading into the ink-dark cavern of the slaughterhouse.

I follow.

I USE A LOT of words, in private, to describe how Alice makes me feel. It's more than love. Rarer. Devotion. Worship. Like in catechism class, the teacher droning on about all those holy women in pain. I read and reread Saint Teresa of Avila saying, "The pain was so great, that it made me moan; and yet so surpassing was the sweetness of this excessive pain, that I could not wish to be rid of it."

I can't talk like this with Alice. She'd call me a dipshit, tell me to shut up. And when Alice tells me to do something, I do it. When Alice tells me to do something, I feel whole; every other second I'm awake, I'm shapeless, hollow, like a glove waiting to be given shape by the hand that uses me.

Does she see me? Does she see me burn?

"YOU KNOW WHO I hate?"

"Um. Everybody?"

"Not you, babe." She smiles and takes a pull off the joint. It smolders between her fingers. "Jenny."

"Jenny . . . ?"

"Ellis."

"Oh." Oh. "Will's ex."

She narrows her eyes at me. Like I don't understand anything at all.

"No," she says. "I mean, yeah. They dated."

"What did she do?"

"She's a cunt," Alice says, passing me the joint. I cash it and flick the roach into the darkness. Light drips from cracks in the roof, swells through gaps in the brick walls.

"You mean she's competition?"

"Oh, Lizzie," Alice says. Leans forward. Grazes my thigh with those teardrop nails. "You really think I have competition?"

Her face softens; maybe she's reacting to my expression, maybe a genuine moment of sweetness. My heart goes molten in turn. I can't hide from her. She knows, she has to know, what she could do to me. If she'd only ask.

We sit, limbs entwined, on a catwalk within the rusted guts of the slaughterhouse, among pitted metal piping corroded into ochre spiderwebs, concentric death mazes overgrown with rough weeds and spindly, sickly tree sprouts. I once read that abattoirs were redesigned by some lady to take advantage of the instincts of the animals, to prey on how cattle and sheep move in circles in the wild. Hemmed into those long snaking pathways, all they can see is the animal directly in front of them and feel the animal directly behind them. The idea is that they feel safe, free of stress, all the way up until the final stretch, where a chute funnels the cow forward and a bar spreads her legs while a rack presses down on her back, and all she can do is trundle forward, lumbering straight into the barrel of the bolt that punches into her skull—and maybe this is the instant at which the cow notices something is wrong, something has gone awry, the same exact instant in which she is dazed, which makes it all humane, yes, this is the humane part. A conveyor hoists her up and away, all fifteen hundred pounds of her dangling by the ankle, to have her throat cut and her body split apart like timber.

We lean into each other, our foreheads touching, and I close my eyes and fill myself with this moment: the motes of dust drifting in sunbeams, the corrugated catwalk tattooing our palms and thighs, and the stale catacomb air, all of it filling my lungs before it's gone, because I can't take the ghost-tingle of her nails on me for another second. I cup her face in my hand, my heart pounding like a battering ram, her cheek soft as snow, her breath coming fast.

I kiss her. Her lips part. Her tongue meets mine. She tastes like cigarettes and sugar.

Then she pulls away. Without a word she gets to her feet and guides me through the heart of the slaughterhouse, her hand squeezing mine, until we're outside, in the meadow, where she pushes me to the ground, pins me, tugs at the waistband of my pants. I help her; she pulls them off and moves downward. Then my panties are gone and she's face-first in my pussy.

I lost my virginity to a guy, two years ago. I remember lying there and wondering when the good part was gonna happen. The part that would make me like sex and want to shape my life around getting it, having it, obsessing over it.

It didn't. Not then, not since. Not really. And now, with Alice slurping at my cunt, all I feel is . . . nothing. Maybe nothing will ever be as good as I imagine it'll be.

She does make me cum, eventually, in the meadow outside the slaughterhouse. Then she sidles up to me, fully clothed, and rests her head on my chest. Catwalk rust powders my hands. Our breaths fall into time. I always like this part more. The smell of my own pussy clings to the air. The sun will set soon; its light cuts across the treetops and into the tall grass that glows with the fever of dusk. Alice's hand snakes around my neck.

She whispers in my ear: "Will you do something for me?"

IT'S PAST MIDNIGHT. Sequin moonlight shimmers on the wet lawn. We approach from the back, from the woods. The trees seem to part to let us through. There's one light on in the house on the top floor, a golden square between dark eaves. The streetlight flickers at random. The house disappears in between these moments, the sudden declension from bright to dark swallowing it whole. Mrs. Kendrick would tell me "declension" is the wrong word, not what I meant. How would she know what I meant? An empty vodka bottle full of gasoline sloshes in one hand and in the other a bunch of matchbooks presses into my palm. Alice clutches a ball of rags and old clothes to her chest. We scurry across the lawn like rats.

After a second of indecision, Alice stuffs her pile between a big white tank and the house's pale siding. I look at her. She jabs her finger. I hand her the vodka bottle. She soaks the rags. I try to light a match but I'm shaking. She takes the matchbook, lights one, and puts my hand on hers.

We drop it together.

The rags catch, curl, and shrivel—for a moment it seems they're gonna burn out and for a moment I think we might just laugh it off and walk away. But then a little clump of flame builds in the space between the tank and the house and then before I can blink the entire back of the house is alight.

I look at Alice. Her orange face, orange eyes entranced. The heat is insane. My eyes go dry instantly. It's so loud. I back away and stumble and assplant in the damp grass.

More lights go on in the house. Fuck. I wanted to think no one was home. Alice grabs my arm and pulls me to my feet. She keeps holding my hand as we stand there. She leans into me, vibrates with excitement.

The flames wrap around the house, blocking the front door, the side door. The exits. They have to be inside because the windows in the kitchen are full of red smoke. Someone is screaming. Alice tightens her grip on me.

A figure appears in one of the second-story windows. A silhouette in the smoke, palms slamming against the window. I see them retch and falter and disappear.

Then the window shatters; a chair flies out into the yard. Smoke heaves from inside; raw-throated shrieking pours out. The figure reappears, holding something small, both of them wreathed in fire. They fling it from their arms. It yips in the air and hits the ground and does not move. Hair sizzles.

The person bends over the windowsill, folds almost, and then goes still. They disappear inside the flames. They're probably dead. I stood here and watched them die. I've never seen anyone die before, not since I was thirteen and watching videos of Eastern European kids bludgeoning cats, suicides bursting on pavement, car crash victims twisted into wet gristle. But none of that was real.

"Is that her?" Alice asks.

I don't know.

I hear sirens. There are neighbors out front, shouting; people being brought out of the house. It's a real scene. It's fucking horrible. The noise is deafening. I sink into the grass. Alice sits beside me. She puts her head on my shoulder.

I pitch forward and vomit. It's like an arm down my throat, tugging me inside-out. Everything leaves me. I put my hands over my ears and scream, and I can't even hear myself. Alice's hand circles on my back. I think she's saying something, but I can't hear her either. The sirens wail and screech. I look at her. Sweat plasters her bangs to her forehead. She's flushed. Her lips are moving. She pushes my hair away from my face. She wipes the puke from my mouth. She's telling me something— to breathe, that it's going to be all right. That she loves me.

New York City, 1967

SARAH SCHULMAN

URBAN CHILDREN ROAM, and that is their privilege. It's a city of pigeons, laundry, and freedom where even the youngest are free. They take subways alone from the age of eight with cardboard passes issued by the Board of Ed. This is the guaranteed free ride, and they all take it for granted. By the time the girl was twelve, she had been everywhere on a whim. World's Fair Park in Flushing, okay, that's typical, but also Van Cortlandt to ride the ponies. She'd been to the wild boardwalk by the taming sea and run into the Atlantic Ocean in her underpants. She'd gone to the Elgin movie theater to see *Gone With the Wind* and smelled the grass the other kids were smoking. It wouldn't be fair to say that she was always solo, occasionally a lonely sidekick—a strange, interesting kid who no one else cared about—and the two of them would discuss and look.

This current pal was Gary. Fat boys made the best friends, because they were desperate and had become learned in the cruel ways of the popular others. In fact, Anita and Gary met crying over not being invited to the important kids' party. The pain was a lens of recognition, and the honesty became a vow.

"I promise to help you," Anita swore. "I promise to help you."

And then, as friends must do, they talked through all the reasons, the missteps, the better ways to live, and discovered together a desire to reconcile with those meanies. Extend a hand, and work together.

"Have our own party?" Anita proposed. "Then once we invite them, they will invite us back."

IT WAS A grand scheme. The two friends spent an afternoon writing on napkins, and creating little drawings of flowers, daisies. They put these handmade invitations into the lockers of their classmates and started making plans.

111

You are Invited to a Party
Tuesday, After School: 3:30 at Gary's House
Refreshments Will Be Served

On the appointed day, the two went off to Gary's place down the block and walked up the three flights to his apartment. The father, a tall, fierce red-bearded man, was a painter, and had set up the entry room as his studio. It was awkward for the rest of the family, but that was the home to two large, essential windows. Opening the front door meant stepping onto newspapers and facing the father-giant perched long upon an impossibly high stool with a rickety wooden easel before him, looking way down below in annoyance. Next was a kitchen where a long-haired, sad woman in a peasant dress made some kind of food when she wasn't dreaming of another world, sitting quietly ready to burst. Behind that, the parents' mattress lay on the floor surrounded by some items that were unrecognizable to Anita, like little drums, notebooks, books of poetry, ashtrays, peculiar toylike grown-up possessions, and sketches taped to the walls. Behind that was Gary's room. Impeccably clean. He kept his own towels and washed them with his own clothes at the laundromat, because he knew how he wanted them to be. The only uncluttered moment in his life.

Gary went into the bottom drawer of his bureau and took out his greatest possession, a Monopoly set his grandmother had sent him for Christmas. It was sparkling clean. Some nights he woke up and dusted off the cards, staring at *Boardwalk* and *Park Place*. Dreaming of *Get Out of Jail Free*.

"How many do you think will come?"

"Well," — Anita was the mastermind here, so she had to produce answers — "we invited Jeff, Nina, Scottie R., Scottie S., Robin, Tiana, Julia, Steve, Pablo. With us that makes eleven."

They looked around the tiny, dark room. Four people could fit in there if nobody moved.

"We will be four," Anita decided. She started counting out the money for four players, in neat stacks of green twenties and pink fives.

Then Gary opened the bag of groceries they had snuck in past his parents. A loaf of Wonder Bread. His parents forbade this, and Anita's parents ate rye bread. But they'd both decided, by carefully observing lunches, that the popular kids ate Wonder Bread, and that's what they needed to serve. He took out a package of napkins and a pound of bologna from Teddy the butcher on University Place. Anita had gone to him since she was born and he always gave kids a free piece of bologna. It was sweet and comforting, the way it came off the slicer and melted in her mouth. The bologna was her recommendation, and she thought it a good choice. Then Gary produced a jar of mayonnaise. This was another mystery food to Anita. She grew up with mustard, and there seemed to be two separate kinds of people: the mayonaissers and the mustardites. Gary cracked open the jar, took out a clean knife he had prepared, and started spreading it on the Wonder Bread, adding three slices of bologna. These sandwiches would be the treats for the Monopoly players. They would shake the dice with one hand, and take a bite from the other while gleefully rolling on the floor chattering about houses and hotels.

Anita watched him quietly, and then the two friends prepared to wait. After a while they stopped talking about what was going to happen at the party and started discussing Gary's fish. He had a new minnow. Then he discussed cleaning, while Anita looked out the window. Then she sat silently, and the two filled the space only with waiting. They were both readers, so, mercifully, somehow by agreement, they both pulled out the cellophane-covered library editions each one always carried. Crinkling was the sound books made. Gary read *Harriet the Spy*, and Anita was on her second tour of *The Member of the Wedding*. Gary rolled onto his back, worn striped shirt riding short above his belly. Anita leaned on her elbows and swallowed the pages. Both of the protagonists of these novels were boyish girls, with great minds and a deep, sorrowful loneliness. And soon Gary and Anita were discussing that fact, and imagining the adventure of belonging. Gary picked up his sandwich.

"No one is coming," he said. Then he began to eat.

Anita looked into the air. *Would it always be like this? How do you get other people to care?*

Gary turned on the radio.

Yummy, yummy, yummy I've got love in my tummy / And I feel like I'm loving you.

That, said the disc jockey, *was the new hit single from the Ohio Express, "Yummy, Yummy, Yummy."*

"Can I have your sandwich?"

"Okay." She didn't want to have anything to do with it.

"What's Ohio?" Gary said.

"It's a state."

And in today's news, writer Carson McCullers, author of The Member of the Wedding, *was admitted to New York Hospital after having suffered another stroke.*

"What's a stroke?" Gary asked.

"It's like a heart attack."

Anita had a reassuring quality to her assumption of authority. It didn't really matter if she knew exactly what a *stroke* was. What mattered was that she knew it could be lethal or worse, produce what was called in whispers a *vegetable*, and in that way it resembled heart attacks, cancer, and being hit by a car. Or jumping off of buildings, like her cousin had done just a few months before.

Lying together on the floor, each holding their books about wayward girls, the knowledge that no one cared about them enough to come to a party was redundant. Like bringing wet to the river.

"Now we know."

"Know what?" Gary's teeth sunk into the pasty bread.

"That no one is ever going to invite us to any parties."

Gary looked stunned. Failure had not been a consideration.

"No," he cried. "How do we make it different?" He wept. His sadness was an open gulf of pain. All his life he would cry cumulatively. But this was ahead of him. And he would die of AIDS.

THE BURDEN WAS Anita's. She had to solve the problem for them both. The problem of being unloved and unwanted. It surged through her, this responsibility. Her teeth slapped like they did when the IRT lurched and she clutched the leather straps on the subway car, colliding with a kindly crumpeted nun, whose hair was hidden from view.

"Where is New York Hospital?" Gary asked.

"Uptown."

His mother appeared at this point. "What are you eating?"

"Bologna sandwiches."

"Garryyyy," she whined, like he had soiled himself and was just too old for that. She looked sad too and then seized their contraband. Gary both protested and cried, while Anita was hushed by the larger dilemma: the mystery of sadness itself. Neither of the children attempted to explain the scenario, why they had gone to such lengths to create bad sandwiches, why the Monopoly money was set out in four separate piles when there were only two players. They were mum. Sharing the calamity that had befallen them that day would have been futile. The mother would not have understood. Mothers always predicted change that never came. They were talking to themselves. She would discount their claims, their recognition that of all the children in the world, they were the objects of exclusion forever. That when their classmates grew up and had weddings, neither Gary nor Anita would be invited. And when there were cocktail parties, they would still be standing outside.

Anita walked out as the early evening's gray started to descend. She didn't want to go home. There would be no one to talk to. Her father's disappointment, a wall of silence. Her exhausted mother putting bland food on the table. The yelling. Sometimes Anita wished that her father would look her in the eye and say something kind. But it never happened. When he did say friendly things, he was always looking away. Like he was scared, or shy. When he was angry, he would put his face close to hers, but there was still some kind of glaze. She felt like a thing. They didn't hold the same interests, that was clear. Daddy liked being at his job, and people there thought he was very important. He hated being home because it just was not that same way. Home was supposed to be better than work, but in her father's case it was not. And he hated that. It was wrong, and the culprit was clearly herself.

She started walking uptown instead, as she had done many times before. Crossing streets was a New York pastime, and walking blocks in the gray, when the sky met the concrete, was a way of life. She crossed Fourteenth Street where the bag ladies sold salted pretzels from a basket, and went through the no-man's-land of discount shops and empty office buildings. *When you walk, you are alone.* She knew that couples would *go for a walk* as a kind of date. But then they would end up at the bar of the Cattleman restaurant to have the free fried chicken, and she was too young to go to a bar. When Anita thought of her future, she thought of driving a red sports car, a convertible. Of wearing a bikini and playing volleyball on the beach. She thought of having a boyfriend who was bland and blond and looked like no one she had ever actually seen in real life.

It had been an hour now. Everyone was walking in the gray. It was the normal way to live. You go to work and then you walk. That's what life is like. Sometimes, people stopped at coffee shops and ate the bowl full of free pickles placed on each table.

Then they'd have a rice pudding and coffee or hot chocolate. That was regular life.

She stopped at a phone booth and dropped her dime. Canal 8-0151.

"Grandma?"

"What's the matter?"

"Nothing. I am going to be late."

"What are you doing?"

"My school is at the museum."

"Very nice."

SHE WALKED INTO the lobby of the hospital. It was gray and somewhat dank. Worried faces on overdressed bodies paraded the hallways. The wooden walls had photographs of men shaking hands.

"Carson McCullers, please."

The nurse was young. She seemed to be from another place, like the middle of America, where skin was naturally rubbed pink and girls put blue on their eyes.

"How do you spell that?"

"M-c-c-u-l-l-e-r-s." It was an unusual name, not like Luigi or John.

"Are you a family member?"

Anita nodded.

"6K."

Stepping out onto the sixth floor, Anita passed the rooms, almost all with doors slightly ajar. One was packed with a raucous family. Three generations. They had brought their own food and were telling jokes and laughing. Another held an Orthodox Jew with a long, yellowed beard. He was lost. Whoever was in the bed didn't have much to say. His hands were opened in prayer.

"What do you want from me?"

The next room had a young white man. He sat in his gown in his chair smoking, looking out the window. He saw Anita and looked into her eyes, just the way she wished her father would. He was the loneliest man she had ever seen. He was so lonely that he didn't even wave. He couldn't try anymore. He had to sit there and listen to the families and the lovers and the people cracking jokes trying to make someone else feel good. Then she realized that someday Anita, too, would be in a hospital. Who would be sleeping in the chair by her side? She had better learn now how to tolerate loneliness, so that later, when she needed to, she'd know how. She had to get to a place where other human beings would be unbearable. She'd be better off without them. That was the only way to go, it seemed. She'd better be prepared to lie in that bed. She'd have to learn how to dream. Or smoke.

Room 6K was painted a pale seafoam green, the color of their gym suits at school.

Anita walked in quietly, moving gently toward a lone, tiny figure, barely a bump under the sheet in the bed. Death was alive in the finished body before her, face transparent, her teeth protruding, hands clawed, her eyes glazed, staring at nothing and then adjusting as that nothing opened its heart to an unknown young girl, brown hair in a ponytail, wearing a shirt-dress, tights, and penny loafers. Carrying a book. A grim little girl, a sad girl, a smart little brown-haired Anita. A Jew. The old woman smiled, someone was there!

"Excuse me," the shy, bold child said, frightened of her own daring. "Are you Carson McCullers?"

"Yes." The voice was gravelly, hoarse, used, disappointed, broken. Anita had not planned what she was going to say.

"Mrs. McCullers, I love you."

"Thank you."

"I read *The Member of The Wedding* and it changed my life."

"I love you too," Carson said, slowly. She could not lift her head.

"Even the first line is amazing," Anita said. She lifted the book. Opened it. She knew the line by heart, but reading it gave an extra layer of feeling: *It happened that green and crazy summer when Frankie was twelve years old. This was the summer when for a long time she had not been a member.*

Carson smiled.

"You see," Anita explained, and Carson looked her right in the eye with kindness, that listening kind of understanding that the young girl craved. Carson gave her forgiveness for having barged in. She gave Anita a silent compassion and the recognition that there was something special in her that required rules to be overlooked. "It's the word *crazy* that tips it." Anita explained, comfortable. Finally, in with her own kind. "Anyone can say that it was a green summer, but to say that it was a green and *crazy* summer . . . Well, the whole world opens up and becomes filled with those dark, sad feelings of girls being alone, being too bright for their time and no one loves them."

"Thank you so much," Carson said. "I am very tired now. I want to go to sleep. Will you read to me?"

"Sure."

Anita sat down in the big chair next to the bed. It was so wide it would have held the fat man from Eleventh Street, and her feet did not touch the ground. She started reading from the end:

The world was now so far away that Frances could no longer think of it. She could not see the earth as in the old days, crackled and loose and turning a thousand miles an hour, the earth was enormous and still and flat. Between herself and all the places there was a space like an enormous canyon she could not hope to bridge or cross.

Anita understood her feelings in the process of speaking. That's what writers do, isn't it. The discovery is *in* the writing. How had *The Member of the Wedding* changed her life? It made her want to be a writer. That was it, after all, what brought Anita to this bedside. To become . . . a *writer*.

She would be a writer and sit behind a desk in a gray flannel skirt suit, cigarette burning in the glass ashtray. She would be famous and she would be loved. She would see what no one else would see, and everyone would be glad about it. They would want to know. Normal people get invited to parties, just because they are there. But Anita would have to be special. Those were the facts and she had to face them.

Cottonmouth

ELLA BOUREAU

ROSE AND LOU had been helping Uncle Jack fix up his old Chevy, when, after several hours of grease and grunting and fetching—"hand me this, hand me that"—Lou threw down her wrench in protest, announcing that it was too hot and she wanted to go exploring. A long, hot Mississippi afternoon stretched out before them, and Uncle Jack said, "You know what, it's gon' get hotter'n a whore's tit out here soon anyway, why'nt you git along with Little Lou, Rosie." Rose pulled up the waistband of her greasy jeans and wiped her palms on a corner of her oversized workshirt before pulling it over her head and wiping her face with it. Lou eyed Rose's forearms, the way the muscles roped and strained under her tanned skin as if of their own accord, each one with its own intelligence. She licked her cracked lips.

"You look thirsty, Lou," Rose grinned. "Come on, let's gon' get a cool drink of water from the pump and then I'll follow you wherever you like." Lou went after her cousin and waved bye to Uncle Jack.

They reached the pump and Rose grabbed the handle, lifting and pushing so that an icy jet of spring water shot out of the spigot. "You first," she said. As Lou leaned down, she glanced quickly up at Rose who was not six inches from her, arm pumping, T-shirt fabric straining against muscle. Lou realized with a jolt that her cousin wasn't wearing a bra; her nipples made dark Os in the white cotton, rising and falling with her breath. "Come on, cuz, I ain't gonna stand here pumpin' for you all day. Shit or get off the pot." Lou drank, and splashed a little water on her face.

"Your turn." Not letting go of the pump, Rose bent forward and put her face right up to the stream, slurping greedily. Then, without warning, she stuck her whole head in the water, right

up to the last little hairs on the back of her neck before pulling herself upright and shaking her short black hair like a dog.
Dogwater sprayed Lou. If a boy had done that, she would have
straight cussed him out, but at this moment she only became
more aware of her skin's heat against the water's coolness, and
she laughed in surprise. Rose grinned. Droplets dripped down
her neck, settling into the sweat, wet meeting wet. Lou became
suddenly anxious to get a move on, "Come on, let's go." They
set off toward the edge of the woods, the summer air filling their
mouths like honey. At first, they walked together in silence. Lou
thought only of how good it was to walk in the heat, everything
slow and exaggerated, moving to the lazy hum of the cicadas.
As they reached the mouth of the woods, the scent changed.
Dampness oozed through them, the dark power of the forest
transforming the day's clarity into sticky velvet shadow. The air
vibrated with secrets Lou could only guess at, and she suddenly
understood why Rose was always coming here.

"Didja ever see a panther in here?" she suddenly had to know.
Rose laughed and Lou reddened, feeling childish.

"Naw, there ain't no panthers here. Seen a lotta snakes
though."

"Aw, yeah? What kindsa snakes?"

"Cottonmouths mostly. You ever encountered a cottonmouth
before?"

"Naw." Lou thought of the garter snakes she used to feed
frogs to in the backyard, the way their mouths engulfed their
prey, slowly engorging until, swallow by swallow, they stretched
to take the poor things whole.

"Oh, they're nasty things. Got bodies thick as sailing rope
and teeth skinny as needles. They're brown but when they open
their mouths wide, you can see it's all white inside. That's why
they call 'em cottonmouths." Rose swatted a long-legged flying
insect out of her face and continued. "Their venom's poisonous
too. If a cottonmouth ever takes a bite outta you, best thing to
do is kill a chicken and smear its hot blood over the wound."
Lou shivered.

"Didja ever get bit by one?"

"Once. Big motherfucker snuck up on me while I was fishin'
in the creek and I stepped on it. She didn't like that one bit an'
snagged my calf. I tell you I had a job cuttin' loose from her.
My leg swole up to the size of a cantaloupe and, well, it's just a
good thing Mama keeps them chickens by the house. Even so, I

was sick for a week, with all kindsa hallucinations an' visions an' things." Lou thought of the snake, the sound of its cold scales slithering dryly through the leaves, its head rising, mouth bending open to reveal a delicately deadly white throat.

"Snakes are kinda sexy, huh?" Lou said, unthinking. Rose did a double-take. "No, really. Think about it. The way they move, all stealth, and the way their bellies curve and coil and slide. Even their poison is . . . It's excitin', knowing you gotta be careful around a wild thing like that."

"Guess that's why they say the devil is a snake." Rose threw her a sidelong glance. "You think danger's sexy, huh? What do you know? You're still a baby."

"I ain't a baby, I'm fifteen years old. There's people droppin' babies younger'n me, I'll tell you that. Sheeit."

"Don't say ain't."

Lou sucked her teeth and narrowed her eyes.

"You ain't my mama. And I ain't little anymore. I'm grown." She could feel Rose examining her. Even in the gloom, she glowed under Rose's gaze.

"I can see that," Rose said slowly. They had stopped walking and Rose placed her hand lightly on Lou's hip. Lou's insides turned to cream. She could feel even through her jeans that those hands were soft and rough at the same time. Then Rose pinched her. "Maybe I never noticed before 'cause you always wearin' them dumpy overalls."

Lou shrieked in righteous embarrassment and whacked Rose on the shoulder. "Ain't you one to talk, Rose-Anne Cartwright! Look at your stinky ol' self!" And she tugged playfully at her cousin's waistband. Suddenly Lou was on the ground, Rose on top of her, wrestling her hands behind her.

"You gon' take back what you said?"

Lou shrieked and giggled. "Never!" she choked, "You're just a stinky-ol', boy-lookin', farmhand, chicken-killer!"

"Oh, you're a nasty gal, huh? I'll teach ya. I'm just as strong as any boy you'll ever meet," said Rose as she maneuvered herself to better pin Lou to the ground. Lou stopped laughing.

"If you can do everything a boy does, does that mean you want everything a boy wants?" Lou snapped. Rose looked Lou squarely in the face. Their chests were heaving, faces slick.

"What do you mean?" Her face was inches away. Licking distance. Lou could feel her cousin's nipples on her chest, her own breasts pressed under the weight of Rose's rib cage. For the first time, she felt their roundness. The breath emanating from Rose's mouth was warm and dry. *Cottonmouth*, she thought. Every nerve in her fired its pistons as she reached up to touch the space between Rose's neck and cheek. Her cousin's pulse pounded through her like a river. She wanted to become silt. Filled with longing, her grip became more insistent. She pulled Rose's face down to meet hers. Rose's lips were as strong and hot as the rest of her. She rolled her tongue over Rose's and moaned a little. Rose tasted of sweat, elderberries, and cotton. The heat from their faces made their sweat meld and trickle. They kissed and kissed. Then Rose pulled away.

"We shouldn't be doing this."

"I know," said Lou, before pulling her down to kiss her once again. Rose came back up.

"But you're my cousin, my blood. It ain't right."

"I know. It's wrong. It's a sin—a *terrible* sin."

Lou relished bringing God into it. Their red-faced pastor and all his congregants appeared in her peripheral vision, watching stiffly from wooden benches. She pulled Rose to her again.

"Mm, but you're too young for this! We'll get ourselves in a whole heap a trouble." The congregants fanned themselves in shock and disapproval.

"Mmm, trouble."

"I'm serious Lou." Lou opened her eyes.

"Who's gonna tell? Ain't nobody's business but ours." The congregation disappeared. It was dark, and quiet.

"Is this your first time doin' this?"

"Kissing? Naw. But that's all I've done."

"Shit." Rose hung her head.

"What's wrong?"

"Well, I don't just wanna kiss you." A smile crept over Lou's face.

"What do you wanna do to me, Rose?" Rose hung her head.

"I can't tell you. You're still Little Lou to me, no matter how grown up you are."

"Then don't call me Little Lou. Call me Snake Girl, call me Devil, call me anything."

Rose smiled and said in a low voice, "Okay. Okay, Wild Thing, I want to show you how you make me feel. Can I do that?"

"Yes, Rose, I trust you."

"Good, I trust you too."

She took Lou's hand and slid it into her jeans, underneath

her briefs. The slickness there made Lou's hand slip almost all the way inside her cousin, without even meaning to. Lou shuddered with shock at the feel of her cousin's insides: hot velvet walls clenching her slick fingers. Rose moaned and gripped Lou's shoulders.

"Do you feel that?"

"Oh God, Rose. Yes, I feel it." The quiver and pulse of Rose's insides was a speech. A peach that let slip more than 10,000 words of desire. Rose's grip slackened as she hung her head and groaned. Lou loved the way it felt to pull her fingers out slow, trailing every little bump and ridge, before sinking back in. Rose inhaled sharply, her hips pushing her in deeper. Lou was a fast learner and realized that she could direct Rose's hips at her every whim. But her hand was mashed between pussy and jean, restricting her movements. "Take your pants off, Rose, I can't tell what the hell I'm doing with them on." The two of them struggled the pants off and Rose sought out Lou's hand, lifting it up to take a look. Then Lou got an evil idea.

"Taste it."

"Huh?"

"Put my fingers in your mouth, Rose, and see what you taste like." Slowly, Rose licked the sticky length of her fingers, and then put her mouth over them, sucking them dry, her head moving up and down. Lou closed her eyes. She had never known that fingers could feel this way, like extensions of her clit.

"Keep suckin' like that."

Rose's head bobbed vigorously. With her other hand, Lou searched out Rose's clit and teased it, before sliding her hand back into her cunt. The vibration of Rose's moans on her fingers only made Lou bolder and she moved the hand that was inside her cousin faster back and forth in a beckoning motion. Rose lost concentration as Lou fucked her, and the fingers she'd been sucking on slipped out of her mouth as she panted and planted her open palms on the ground. Lou held onto Rose's slender hips and guided their rocking motion so that she could get as deep into her as possible. She brought her hips up to meet Rose's and her hand became an extension of her crotch: a girldick. Rose ground her hips into Lou and soon the front of Lou's jeans were soaked with Rose.

Rose was in another universe, lost in the motion of her hips and the pressure of Lou's fingers tugging and rubbing on her. Her moans became softer, more pleading, and suddenly Lou needed to have her in her mouth. Not breaking her hand's stride, she shimmied downward and guided Rose's hips up to her face. The earth's damp was seeping through her clothing, easing its way into the fabric of her shirt like slithering, icy fingers. She shuddered. Then she pulled her tongue slowly along the length of Rose's pussy lips. Rose groaned and threw her head back. Lou smiled and pushed the soft skin aside with her tongue before gliding deeper to the inner folds. She pictured what this must look like, this pink on pink—spit on spit—before sucking up the cream that had begun to ooze thickly into her mouth. The taste was indescribable. Mouth full, she slurped and sucked, still fucking Rose with her hand— now soaked to the wrist. Lou began to moan and the tremors of her own voice in Rose's cunt seemed to send Rose over the edge, her thighs began to shake and her breathing became ragged. Lou kept steady, refusing to break focus, the little jewel of her lover's orgasm only moments away. Finally Rose dug her hands into Lou's hair and let out a long shuddering sigh, her voice breaking, body hiccupping. Lou could feel Rose flex from the inside, each spasm a smaller ebb of the last. Then Rose pulled Lou's hand out gingerly and sank down beside her, red with satisfaction.

They looked at each other and smiled, embarrassed. Lou covered her face with her aching, wet hand, a pool of guilt welling in her stomach. Rose pulled Lou's hand away, a rakish grin lighting up her face, eyes twinkling. All at once, Lou's gut seized.

"Well. I guess that's what they mean by kissin' cousins, then, huh?" Rose offered.

The guilt dam welling up inside Lou burst open and she began to laugh infectiously. Soon they were both rolling on their backs, doubled over in hysterics as if not a funnier phrase had been uttered in the history of the whole wide world.

"K-kissing, c-c-cousins! Eeheehee!!!" It took five minutes before they regained control of themselves.

Rose, wiping tears from her eyes, said, "Hushup a second. I want to make you feel the way you made me feel, Wild Thing. Will you let me?" Desire roared in Louise's ears. *Yes. Yes. Yes.*

"Show me." Rose pulled off Louise's jeans and underwear wordlessly. Then she unbuttoned her shirt, unfastening each button carefully before pulling off the sleeves. Louise watched her fingers work, imagining them flexing inside her.

Rose's hands traced her breasts and torso. The roughness of her calluses mixed with her tender assuredness made Lou's skin jump. Rose kissed the nape of her neck, sucking on it as she slid her fingers down to Louise's upper thighs, massaging the place where thigh and pussy meet. "Mm. You are so soft. I bet your pussy's soft too." Rose gently pulled her open and traced a finger delicately along the inside of her lips. It tickled lightly. Louise squirmed.

"Stop teasing me, Rose-Anne!"

"Damn, but if you ain't an impatient little thing. All right, all right, I'll put my money where my mouth is." With that, Rose spread Lou's thighs and knelt between them. Lou could feel Rose's breath on her snatch. She bit her index finger in anticipation. The first slide of Rose's tongue went from stem to stern and a wave of lust snaked from her ass to the tip of her head. Lou moaned and let her knees fall wide open to Rose like petals to the sun. Rose began tonguing her as if she were a child lapping up an ice cream cone. She was hungry for it, Lou could tell. She felt Rose's tongue searching out the center of her, trying to worm it out of her, willing to pay anything to get it. Lou bit her fingers hard, then began to suck on them, groaning, pressing her hips into Rose's face, Rose greedily slurping up anything that came at her. Lou cupped and massaged her breasts, finding reassurance in their weight. Wet leaves, Spanish moss, and dirt were stuck to her ass and thighs. She didn't care. Her eyes rolled to the back of her head and she shut them. She was falling, falling into forest time, falling into silence, into the heavy hush of her deepest self. A wave of coolness spread across her belly, purposeful and heavy, unlike anything she had ever felt before. Louise felt ancient, weighted, wise.

"Lou."

The coolness slid and rolled, coiling itself on her pelvis.

"Louise." Rose's voice was tense, measured and low, as if she were in the presence of a rabid dog.

"Don't move."

Lou opened her eyes to look at Rose, and instead was met by two oval eyes the color of gunmetal, peering out at her from a mean-looking triangular head. A cottonmouth had somehow slid its way onto her lower belly and was now sitting coiled, head raised, its gaze fixed intently on her; at once curious to see what her next move would be and daring her to make one.

"Don't get excited. Stay real calm. Long as her mouth stays shut, we'll know she don't feel threatened none, and we'll be all right." Blind shock was quickly giving way to terror as the snake studied her, and Louise tried to concentrate on her breathing. She kept it shallow, so as not to disturb the snake's body.

"Hey there, little cottonmouth," she said in the calmest, lowest voice she could muster "How'd you get up there?" The snake didn't move.

"Rosie," she said, not daring to break its gaze, "I'm scared."

"I know. Maybe . . . maybe try talking to it with your eyes." Louise tried to soften her gaze, feel warmly toward it, but all she felt was cold, cold, *cold*.

Slowly, the snake unwound itself. Its dry scales tickled Louise's skin and she shuddered. It was muscling up closer to her. It slid itself between her breasts and stopped again, a tumescent S held rigid in the cleft of her sternum, ready to strike. Its eyes were unblinking, both catlike and reptilian. Its forked tongue hissed. Smelling her smell. Could it smell her fear?

Satisfied, the cottonmouth turned and headed back down to her thigh, leaving a smooth trail in the film of her sweat. Unable to look any longer, Lou dropped her head back. Soon the narrowest part of the snake had passed from her thigh to the ground and she felt only the slick where it had been. An odor rose, sickly sweet like something rotting, a melon maybe, some meaty kind of fruit.

"What's it doing, Rosie?" Silence. "Rose?"

"I . . . I don't believe it. It's marked you. You smell that musk? I think . . . I don't know," Lou pulled herself onto her elbows to get a better look. The odor was strong, but not unpleasant. The cottonmouth approached her cunt, its tongue fanning, and lifted itself up haltingly, flicking her outer lips. Lou felt like fainting.

"Oh my god. Oh my god, I'm gonna lose it."

"Stay calm. You're all right. It's curious about you." The cottonmouth's vibrating tongue was still at her opening. Then, in one incredible moment, it pushed its way inside her. Lou inhaled sharply, then held her breath. Louise felt full, the scales undulating her inside flesh, a long earthy muscle twisting. "Rose."

"Does it hurt?" Rose stroked Lou's arm.

"No, it don't hurt really."

"What does it feel like?"

"It's cold. I can't describe it. Come lie next to me." Rose spread her clothes out next to Lou and stared at her, bewildered. The snake's head was deep in her. The power of its body was incredible. Lou felt its every twitch and she gasped at each movement it made.

"Should I try and kill it?"

"No." Lou was suddenly defensive. She was still afraid, but she began to yield to the fear, to whatever the snake wanted to give her. She felt for Rose's hand and closed her eyes again. The cottonmouth wriggled and the friction of its scales made her hips rock gently to meet its motion. It was as if the snake was pressing all the evil of the world into her. That creeping oozing gunk, the festering lies, the putrefaction of desire gone bad. She trembled, full up with it. Every hissing thought she'd ever had, in the girl's bathroom, in her bed, into the ear of the girl one desk away, was pulled out through the acrid smell of the snake's musk. It was flailing now, the smooth scales tugging her insides, its marbled head exploring the arc of her, nesting here and bending there.

"Rose," she said. "Lick me. Put me in your mouth."

Lou did not have to explain. Rose knew. She bent over the writhing snake tail and held her tongue out to taste it, then trailed its tip with easy assurance. The snake twitched in response and Lou felt a deep moan escape her. Rose picked up the tip of Lou's scaled cock and licked it, rolling its length in her hands. Then she slid it into her mouth and sucked, her eyes fixed on Lou.

Lou's vision began to blur. The darkness penetrating her was all-consuming. The snake was part of her and Rose, tugging on it, sucking it gently, was setting her—*them*—on fire. But soon that white hot feeling gave way to the tremendous cold spreading through her. She shivered, her hips bucked. The pulse of the evil thing inside her was cooling her down, turning the molten juices inside her to tar. She felt the tar escaping with agonizing languor, its stickiness twisting down her thighs in opaque rivulets. She continued the descent inward. The snake pushed further into her darkness, seeking each secret place and licking it out—every hissing thought, every petty selfishness—until every one of her desires, great and small, was unfurled and exposed to both her and the snake simultaneously.

It was then that Louise realized the darkness she was feeling was color. It was rising up as a solid wave from her cunt, from her heart, from the marrow of her spine, and all at once revealed itself in a sparking electric current. The color blue. A blue that distinguishes itself from black only in shimmering side-vision, and then disintegrates. Blue-black. Blue-black. The cunt. Blue-black. Blue-black. The chest. Volupt, volupt. The heart.

Blue sneaks into me the way you sneak into me.

When Lou regained a sense of the outside world she realized she had been speaking to Rose, but what she'd said, Louise Cartwright had no idea. The snake lay between her legs, lifeless. It had given itself to her.

Rose and Louise stared at each other, fearful that if they broke contact, they would realize they had cracked open some fundamental law of nature. They could not move. Their minds swallowed up by the impenetrable forest, all they could do was lie there, stunned and motionless. It was as if there was no difference between their limbs and the kudzu vines on the ground. Their hair was tangled Spanish moss, their expressions twisted as tree knots, the pounding of their hearts ominous and foreign-sounding as rough scales sliding through brush.

Best You Never Had

Chanson du Konallis

EMILY JONES (Lorraine Hansberry)

SHE WAS EXQUISITE.

The gown was a plain white sheath. The body beneath, one long shimmering river of movement; restrained and delicate. The arms reached up, in the mood of the song, and pulled the emotion of the taut melody to her fingertips. The voice, in Gallic tremulo, gave out at once passion and indifference. Monmartre haunted the room.

Mon coeur a de la peine
C'est qu'il pense a Paris
Au vieus Paris sur Seine.

Konnie watched the singer and listened to the words. She translated effortlessly in her mind: "When my heart is in pain— Paris . . ." Paris indeed. Men had made Paris a woman in the mind. Indeed. She fingered her drink, the narrow frosted glass with a puff of fizz crowning it and the cherry floating atop. The cherry looked like her nails; red and gleaming even in the dark room. "It's because of Paris, Old Paris on the Seine." Paris the woman. She lifted her glass and drank the coldness of the cock-tail. Paul was all but gone. The thing he had for these synthetic chanteuses. It was all he ever needed; one night like this in an intimate club with some American girl up there singing in one of those cultivated French singing voices and accents. Then, he was set for months. They moved him. She did not look at him. She knew how he looked. His eyes rather full of life at the moment, his lips moist and full of pleasure. His hand, finely manicured and beautiful, lying perhaps on the white cloth of the table, toying no doubt with a mixing stick. When they got home, he would speak French to her until he went to sleep . . .

M'a donne les plus grandes joies
Et vers lui je reveins sans cesse
C'es l'ami que l'on n'oublie pas . . .

Konnie looked up to the singer again. She *was* a marvelous looking creature at that. Paul had talked for weeks about
their coming to see *this* one. Konnie studied her. Yes—this one
was exceptional. The voice—the voice really knew what it was
doing. The rises and thrusts were honest and well placed and
the tongue seemed to love the French. That was good. French
had come early in her life and she always hated that strained
thing that Americans could do to it; only the English were worse.
But this girl—she took another drink and let the words turn into
English in her head again: "Has given me the deepest joys . . .
I always come back to her . . . She is the friend one can never
forget."

"*Bon!*" she found herself saying almost aloud to the girl singing from the middle of the night club floor, "*Bon!*" Her eyes fixed
themselves on the singer's face. It was all planes. Marvelous
planes. The cheek bones high; the full lips sensuous beyond
description; and the eyes like dark slanted slashes across the
face . . . The eyes! Konnie shifted in her seat and looked quickly
to the table. What a strange moment. It had happened before in
life. On the street; parties; in classes in school years back; the
thing of being surrounded by many people and suddenly finding another girl's or woman's eyes, commanding one, holding
one's own. It was extraordinary. Pleasant, she thought. No, not
pleasant. Terrifying because of the kind of pleasure it brought.
Yes—oddly enough the most supreme kind of pleasure. She
smiled to herself. It was, aside from whatever else, an amusing play on the sense of English words. *Pleasant* was wrong to
describe it, but *pleasure*, ah!

"Isn't she quite marvelous, darling?" Paul had lain his hand
on Konnie's.

"*C'est bon!*" she said and lifted her glass in a salute to him.
He laughed that special laugh of his to show that he knew
she was a little tipsy, and that he was delighted about it. He
longed, she knew, for an extension of any aspect of her rare
frivolity in their everyday life. She couldn't help him. He had
taken pains to marry Konalia Martin-Whitside of the Washington Martin-Whitsides, and what he got, he got! Reserve. Buckets
and buckets of reserve. Her family had grown reserve in Virginia
for generations and she was a true harvest. She smiled at her

imagery. Occasionally she had pangs about various unfortunate things, including her marriage, but she kept them rare. She had a simple design for life which made rarity of thought quite possible and desirable. It was, of course, that life was a rather simple but endurable bore. Moreover, she had everything splendidly under control; she was able to prohibit at will whatever unpleasant or rebellious thoughts that occurred to her. She had cultivated that as her family had cultivated reserve.

She looked again to the lovely one in the center of the floor who was singing something a little more lively. Her arms had come down from the air and were moving about in front of her in rhythm to the song. Konnie studied the brown skin for several seconds before it occurred to her that she was admiring it. Whatever must it be like to wander about looking perfectly suntouched all the time? She suddenly giggled aloud. It was so wild, the things one might think privately. She took another drink and the images tumbled down easily from the reaches of her mind that were still full of adolescent fantasy:

Egyptian queens . . . striding along mammoth corridors in the temples (or palaces of whatever the hell they usually strode along) graceful the way only queens could be (one was taught!) . . . in something white and tight and gathered at the hips with those long pleats hanging down to the golden sandal tops (or was that simply a movie version of a brown painted Vivian Leigh from a later time? Heavens!). Her mind lingered a moment with Vivian Leigh . . . Anyhow—Egyptian queens . . . very young, very supple, and very beautiful with the stiff black hair hidden under those curiously attractive head dresses as on all those vases and things . . . Cleopatra? No—not Cleopatra, she was Greek or something. This particular queen would be darker—like the Nile without moonlight; with high cheek bones and—and full, impossibly sensuous lips—like—like her!

Konnie sat up in her seat abruptly and put her glass down. That would be quite enough of that! This thing of allowing the mind to do what it would lately—well—it really was a little too much. She must go to the ladies' room and adjust her make-up and look at herself and quiet it all down if Nefertiti up there would ever finish! Ah! *Nefertiti*! That was the one . . . !

She looked at the singer again and there they were, the eyes, waiting. Something not unlike pain shot through Konalia Martin-Whitside Heplin, II and she trembled. She did not drop her eyes this time. Why should she. There was pleasure in the looking, she thought suddenly, wildly, yes, she would look right back at her! And she did. And the two very black ones in the center of the room smiled at her and talked to her, and the smoky, dark lashes opened and closed for her—and Konalia Martin-Whitside Heplin, II sat and looked back and felt insane with pleasure.

Pleasure. Why had pleasure so frightened her in the past? Why must one constantly run from it? Control it? Who were all those dead people who were deciding things from their graves? All those generations of highly respected poor old souls who had done this or that in their lives; founded this or that. What had they to do with her! Why was she so bound to them? Who made them right about everything? And why? Pleasure indeed. Had they ever had any? And if they had who were they to deny her? Or if they hadn't who were they to be *experts* in the matter? Pleasure indeed! Paris indeed! Paris. Paris the woman. Paris a woman. Paris and Lila. Lila and Paris. Lila. Lila pushing through the high grass of a French meadow; Lila with the small body and the golden hair. Lila. And she, Konalia, with her shoes and stockings off, racing about the hills, shrieking, wild things about France and summer, her hair flying—free and seventeen. Seventeen and free . . . free . . . free. Konalia the shepherdess—from Washington, D.C. And the overpowering memory that would not go away: that indestructible second; that flash of impossibility of a small and lovely blonde girl leaning, laughing, panting against her as they posed for a picture . . . her cotton dress damp and sweet against her . . .

Konalia lifted one hand suddenly as if to stop herself. How foolish! How destructive! Why ever must that silly image persist, so many years between, why ever must it persist! She was not, after all, a *goat girl*. And she was indeed Konalia Martin-Whitside Heplin, II. And that *was* rather that! The liquor started to fade with the thoughts. Moreover, upbringing had come to a pretty pass indeed when she could actually sit around like—like—well, one of those women—ogling colored girl singers! She certainly was not like that, *or* a blasted goat girl.

"Would you like to meet her, Konnie?" Paul was leaning toward her again. His eyes lit with his most boyish expectancy. "I know the manager here. He might—"

She heard her own voice and it was marvelously normal, cool, proper, the essence of disdain. "Are you quite mad, Paul?"

"Well, why not? I mean if she would join us—I think it would be fascinating."

"And I think you carry your fascination too far for taste." She turned her head from him, so that the total effect of the long, beautiful, aristocratic profile could work its magic. Remind him, drive him back to his senses.

"I—I thought you enjoyed her," Paul said, his voice near a slight whine.

"That doesn't mean, my dear husband, that I must have her to *luncheon* tomorrow."

"Who the hell said anything about luncheon?"

"Please don't swear."

"Well please don't work so hard at being a blasted snob. You don't have to, you know, it's built in."

"If you really wish to spend the evening insulting me, Paul, we might as well go home. I'm quite ready in any case."

Paul exhausted his hands in the air a little. "I don't wish to insult you and I don't wish to go home, either. I just want to have a nice evening. And if you could forget for five minutes that old David Whitside almost made it over on the Mayflower . . ."

"Really, Paul—!"

"Look, all I want is your permission to ask the manager if Miss Tige would care to join us at our table. It is so simple and it could be interesting. I can't imagine what all the fuss is for."

"I am not making a fuss."

"Then let me invite her," Paul pleaded, more boyishly than ever. "She'll probably refuse, anyhow. They say she's very difficult."

Konalia turned her eyes cooly, hardly looking out from under her lids at him. "Good heavens, I've married a celebrity collector!"

"Oh, Konnie!" Paul Heplin sat back then with disgust and defeat and looked at his wife with total unfriendliness. Then suddenly he sat up and lifted his fingers in the air for the waiter who was there like clockwork.

"Paul, whatever do you think you are going to do?"

Her husband ignored her and spoke to the waiter briefly in the ear. The man bowed and was off to the manager's office.

Paul sat back with satisfaction. "Well, we'll see what we shall see. If the name Heplin still means anything around here we shall soon meet Miss Mirine Tige personally." He giggled then, "Wherever do you suppose these girls dream up these names!"

"Well—!" Konalia said, "Well!" She rose from the table and Paul leaped to his feet, looking frightened.

"Darling—"

"I am going to the ladies' room, if you don't mind." Paul sat down and watched his wife make her way to the ladies' room and felt warmly how she really could go along with things when she wanted to.

When Konalia came back to the table, the singer was seated and Paul was holding a one-sided if animated conversation. Paul stood as his wife came up, grinning happily. "Darling—this is Miss Mirine Tige. Miss Tige, this is my wife."

"How do you do," Konalia said cooly and sat down. In the second she took to look at Mirine Tige close up she was startled to see that the mirage on the club floor was real and true. The young woman had apparently removed some of the heavier performing make-up, and Konnie could see that she was at least as young as Paul had insisted.

Paul rushed on conversationally. "Your command of French is simply marvelous. My wife and I have spent a great deal of time in Europe since we were quite young and I daresay our accents can't compare to yours, even though Konalia speaks it beautifully. Did you study it as a child, perhaps?"

Konnie watched the woman lift her eyes to Paul with cool, dry indifference. "On a sharecropper's farm in Georgia?"

Konalia would have let herself laugh ordinarily, but something in her consciously rebelled at the insolence that she felt exuded from the woman. She hardly represented the Old South or any of that, but really! There were just some things one maintained. Tradition, it was true, was almost mystical in the way it bound one. But nonetheless, it *did* bind one, thank God! Furthermore she could see that her husband was himself a little taken back by the abruptness of the reply. People rarely resisted Paul's social charms; and women almost never.

Paul tried again. "Did you like France?"

Mirine Tige looked at him again. "France is France."

Paul Heplin looked a little beaten, but not quite. "Yes—but the French have such a marvelous thing. I mean I think it is quite true about the French attitude, don't you?"

"About what?"

"Well." Paul Heplin lifted his eyebrows a little bit helplessly. "About *everything*. That's just what I mean."

"Oh."

"Perhaps you think differently. Having seen it from a different point of view. I mean as an entertainer."

Mirine Tige sighed a little. "I have been in many different countries, Mr. Heplin. France was simply another one. I found there what I found everywhere. That it was a country full of men and women. Some of whom were charming; others bores—still others beasts." She looked away.

Konalia looked at the woman. Her voice was certainly as compelling in speech as in song. Surely the most dramatic voice she had ever heard.

"Did you like France, *Madame*?" Mirine Tige switched to French unexpectedly and Konnie almost jumped realizing that the voice made up of guitar chords was coming at *her*.

"Uh—*Oui*—I find French culture extraordinary and satisfying. Yes, *I* think it is a unique country."

Mirine Tige nodded at her in the continental way of chanteuses and went on in French. "May I compliment your accent, *Madame*, full of the classroom but charming."

Konalia felt outrage flood through her as she forced herself to give the only possible polite reply. "*Merci, Mademoiselle.*"

Mirine Tige did not let go of her eyes and Konnie felt she was almost smiling behind the insolent lips. "What did *you* particularly adore about France, *Madame*?"

Paul shuffled in his seat. "Look—I think it's sort of affected to speak French at home. Like showing off or something, you know?"

Mirine Tige addressed him then in English. "Really? Why? I enjoy French because it is a beautiful language. Don't you enjoy speaking it?"

"Yes, of course, I *love* the language—" Paul began.

The singer's answer came back in French. "Then, *Monsieur* Heplin, why not speak it when you *feel* like it." She looked to Konalia. "And all else you enjoy. One might learn *that* from the French."

The conversational music ended from the piano and Mirine Tige prepared to leave them. She stood up and Paul rose politely. She offered him her hand and smiled at him. "It's been quite charming meeting you. I must get back to my work." She turned then to Konalia, "Madame."

Konalia murmured, "Yes. Very pleasant to have talked with you."

Mirine Tige did not offer Konalia Martin-Whitside Heplin, II her hand, but she stood a moment in front of her as if deciding something. Then she spoke. "I must tell you, Mrs. Heplin, that I came to your table because the manager told me, when he asked me, that you were the handsome young couple at the front center table. So I came. I came—"

Konalia felt that the woman's body swayed in front of her suddenly as when she sang; then she realized that they were merely waves of loveliness that shimmered in front of her. She longed to close her eyes.

"I came," Mirine Tige was saying, "because out there where the lights play tricks on the faces of those who watch—you seemed like someone I knew once. In Paris. It was a mistake of course. Forgive me for staring. But," and Konalia wondered if she only imagined the hissing sadness in the remark, "the lights do play such tricks. Goodnight."

Paul and Konnie watched the young woman walk away from them toward her dressing room. Then Paul collapsed in his seat in a fit of laughter. "Well! She *is* rather difficult all right—but enchanting I thought."

Konnie looked at him and did not see him. Pleasant she had said, *pleasant*. It had not been pleasant at all; if anything, in those terms, it had been downright unpleasant. But the other— it had been so full of the other—*plaisir*.

"It was awful nice of you to be so sweet about the way I went about it, darling. It was nasty of me I'm afraid." He smiled at his wife a little sheepishly, with what in fact he had always considered was the smile to shatter her defenses. "But I'm sated now. Curiosity thoroughly satisfied. No more celebrity hunting! Happy?"

Konalia looked away. *He* was sated. The diversion was over for him. Tonight he would sing a few songs from Monmartre and fall asleep, completely satisfied after liquor and entertainment. Happy. And she—she put her fingers to her brow—she must have another drink, more and more that made it easier, just one drink before they left. Then at home in bed, she—she would lie there until dawn . . . cursing Paris; and French meadows . . . and Egyptian queens . . . and all those eyes that seemed to turn up in life . . . cursing Lila for her sweetness—and cursing Mirine Tige; and the idiocy of Greek mythology and whoever it was in her miserable family who had ever named her after a goat girl.

Rebound

M. J. COREY

WHEN WE WALKED up from the Lorimer stop on the L train—my favorite of all the L stops—the first thing we saw was a twenty-four-hour natural food market glowing in the dark of the quiet, eerie, perfect Brooklyn street. The first time I went to Brooklyn I was grossed out. It didn't have Manhattan's anxiety or chaos; it was still and smug. We went into Sunac; we'd been damp in the armpits on Union Avenue so the air conditioning stung and I pointed to the Marlboro Lights at the register. I liked how clean the store was. It was the kind of grocery store I would want to shop at if I had money to burn. The shelves were organized—not a brown soy cereal box out of place. We trotted in our sandals out into the balmy, dirty air. For no real reason, Rachel was wearing a 1970s disco gold halter dress, and it flowed to her strong dancer calves.

"I don't know why I'm nervous," I panted, pounding the top of my pack against my palm, the way my smoker friends in high school had taught me. "I thought the cigarettes could help with the talking."

"We need to talk to people tonight," Rachel agreed. She tucked some of her thin hair behind an ear in her frantic mousy way. "You need to meet some lesbians."

A lot of the time Rachel moved as if in fast-forward. She brought her hand to my shoulder and the lightness of her touch made me twitch away. She tilted her head.

"How are you doing?"

I lit one cigarette and sucked. My veins swelled immediately; I could feel it. I was wearing cutoff shorts and a red backpack instead of a purse. I felt like a hiker. I'd just hacked my hair to my chin and it didn't suit my Arab nose.

"I cried for a few hours and now I'm better."

"You never cry," she said, her voice grave.

It was cute, how much Rachel always cared. We looked straight ahead, afraid of the eye contact. Rachel didn't like being touched either.

When we were eighteen and roomed together as freshmen, unfolding our accidentally matching blue bedding on the plastic college cots, she asked if it was hard to say goodbye to my parents. Trying to be cool in a gruff voice I said no, I didn't like hugs. The only picture I put up on my wall next to my bed was a black-and-white snapshot of Bob Dylan chasing a wheel in the street in New York when he was twenty. She taped up a collage of pictures of her Jewish single mother and all her hippie beaming friends who wore hemp chokers around their necks and said she had no excuse but she didn't like hugs either. The rib lines on Rachel's collarbone were exposed because the dress was cut low and there was a breeze and I was pretty sure she'd thrown up her dinner.

"Maybe you'll hook up with someone tonight," she tried.

We turned the corner and saw the black awning of the Metropolitan, where I had become one of the regulars. The 150 dollars I spent on a shitty fake that claimed I was twenty-three and from Philly was worth an empty refrigerator because I was becoming a City Lesbian, which was much better than a College Lesbian.

"Keep Jane Taphouse away from me, whatever you do."

Jane Taphouse was a thirty-five-year-old redheaded butch lesbian with a very long face who last time at the bar had bought me rum and cokes until I got drunk enough to lead her on but never let her kiss me. She had been talking to me on Facebook. Her wife had left her the month before.

"I don't want to be reminded that she's the best I can do." I knew this was harsh but it didn't even sound like my voice when I said it so I didn't feel any guilt.

"That's not true," Rachel squeaked.

"It shouldn't be so much to ask to be with someone young and cute and my own age," I said in the hard voice.

"We'll avoid Jane Taphouse." Rachel rubbed the spot in between her eyebrows. We went in and I went to the bar while Rachel went to the ATM. There weren't many people there yet. Some dykes were playing pool. The walls were red but it was too dark in the room to tell. The bartender was devastatingly hot.

She leaned on the counter and looked at me expectantly. She's tall and her bones stick out and she wears loose T-shirts with the sleeves hacked off and tight jeans slung low on her narrow hips. Tonight her hacked-up shirt was red so we sort of matched because my flannel was red too.

"PBR," I said. "Please."

She had black eyes that were not amused and dyed jet-black ratty hair and bone structure just falling short of being horsey. She cracked open a silver can and pushed it foaming toward me. Rachel and I walked to the outside patio so I could smoke some more. We stepped up on the deck and sat alone on a bench that looked out at the rest of the whole patio. It was all fenced in by a wood gate and if you looked up there were short Brooklyn houses with windows aglow overlooking the backyard. A few girls were sitting at outside tables, leaning on their elbows and drinking beers I wished Rachel and I could afford.

Rachel and I had nothing to say and then I saw one of my most major bar crushes walk in. She had shaggy brown hair and a weak chin and cloudy boyish eyes. She was wearing all black and she had good boobs. I'd danced with her once at some queer dance party. She'd stayed a song and then said, "I'll be right back," and went on to lose me on purpose. This is something I could not think about. She was smoking a cigarette. I looked away. I felt transparent, like the kind of deepwater fish that are so clear you can see their tiny special ocean organs. I turned to Rachel, looking at my fingers.

"I'm getting us water."

I ground my cigarette under the toe of my shoe and glanced at Bar Crush, ashamed of myself for daring to look. Rachel stood up uncertainly and I gave her no indication that she was supposed to follow me, which she was. I walked fast from the deck into the dark room while Rachel trailed after me and, noticing Jane Taphouse, I zoomed to the orange water jug at the end of the bar where they'd set up stacks of cups. I filled myself a cup and another for Rachel, handing it to her while she tried to shoot me a supportive smile that I only caught from the corner of my eye. The water was cold and frosted the plastic.

We stood by the jug. Rachel loved lesbians because she was practically raised by them in Portland and she partly wished she could be one after the way James had taken her virginity. Rachel was more comfortable in the bar than I was, looking around with a contented smirk on her face, and I wanted to hug her.

We stood in silence while I rearranged the way I rested my elbow on the counter to figure out what best conveyed a sense of ease. Jane Taphouse was circling the pool table and she was wearing a purple vest. Her face looked perpetually surprised. I hoped she didn't see me and Rachel whispered, "Let's go back outside. I saw that girl you like looking at you."

"Really?" I asked.

"Yeah, I think," she said. We went back out. The place had filled since we'd left and so there was nowhere to sit. Girls were everywhere, in dark tank tops that hung loose and Converse High Tops and 1950s sundresses and denim cutoffs and peeking-out boxer shorts. I was pleased to see that most of them had unlined faces.

I saw a table in the middle of it all with only one lady and two empty seats, so with hands gripping elbows, I approached. It was Alex, who Jane Taphouse had told us last time was a legendary lesbian. She had a black fauxhawk with red streaks in it and she looked Middle Eastern like me, her black eyes lined with smoky Lisa Frank purple.

"Hi, Alex?" I said in an asking voice that was as small and nervous as possible, which proved humbleness. "We met you last week."

It was big that we were talking to her. She was around thirty and had come to New York from somewhere in the northwest and made money babysitting an Upper East Side five-year-old during the day. I knew this because we'd talked—no, chatted—with her the week before. She'd had a Santa Claus laugh and a rascal's sandpaper voice and had told us that she was the self-appointed mayor of the bar.

"Hey!" she said in a bellow that was self-consciously friendly, leaning back in her chair to greet us. "Ladies! Sit!" She was pretty butch despite the eyeliner. She had boy khakis on over muscled calves and a green polo shirt and a black hoodie packed over a square torso. She ran her hand through her faux-hawk. I used to not know how to talk to butch girls, or anyone who would say "I'm gay." It used to make me tongue tied and almost paranoid. We reintroduced ourselves.

"There are some beautiful women here tonight," she said, leaning back in her chair. I needed her to like me. The lesbians who dressed like Tegan and Sara at my school could hate me but it wouldn't matter if the cool Brooklyn lesbians liked me. Alex squinted at me.

"What do you want out of tonight?"

"Uh—" I twisted my fingers around themselves and heard the

crack of knuckles. "I want to flirt, I guess." Admission of weakness could be wise. This interested me, that another person understood that Nights have Goals.

"It's important that she flirts tonight," Rachel piped in. "She's getting over someone."

"Oh," Alex said, her thick black eyebrows rising. "Who?" I felt my breaths getting panicky. She looked at me more closely. "How long were you together?"

Smoke was everywhere, looking like incense but smelling like cancer; the conversation of lesbians all around us was swarming the patio, and as if out of thin air Alex produced a new beer for me to drink. I sipped. Alex slapped the hand of a passing retro girl in a gray pencil skirt, glanced back at her ass, and she then turned to look at me again.

"We weren't together," I said very fast, feeling like a fraud. "Just some girl I was chasing all year. It looked like we were starting to kind of finally date." Alex nodded, being a good listener. She had black gloves on with the fingers cut off. I felt nervous telling her about it, which I guessed was a sign of maturity because I used to love to air out my own filthy laundry. "But someone new entered the picture and it's all off now." She nodded again, being a sympathetic listener.

"So what's your type?" she asked. That's what Jane Taphouse had asked me. I was learning that this was a question that mattered to lesbians. I considered Samantha and her hair and her magenta lips and her lemon-yellow sundresses. I considered the butterflies I usually got when I saw a pretty girl walk like a boy. I considered how cute girls are, the way their legs stick out from little skirts. I considered the girls who keep their keys on chains from the belt loops of their jeans because they're too proud for purses and how cool it sounds when they walk.

"I don't have a type," I said. I glanced at Rachel, who was sitting with her legs awkwardly crossed. She was looking at her nails, and stopped to rub her nose, irritated by all the smokers.

"What's your type?" Alex turned to her and leaned forward.

"Oh—I'm straight," Rachel giggled. She bit skin off the side of her thumb and her eyes crinkled like a baby. "I have a boyfriend."

Alex's smooth face cracked into a huge laugh. She slapped her knee. She fell back hard into her chair, laughing, stopped for a moment to look at Rachel, and then laughed more. "Oh, honey," she cackled. "You're going to have fun here." Rachel laughed with her; Rachel always laughs even if she doesn't know what's funny. Alex calmed down and fixed her eyes back onto me.

"You have a type," she assured me and before I could help it I frowned. This annoyed me. This was the same thing that made me worry standing before my mirror if I should keep my hair long just because I tended to want girls with long hair more. It made me feel sick at myself and it made me feel like gays were shallow.

"No I don't," I replied, laughing a little to soften the terseness of my answer.

"What did this girl you're getting over look like?" she asked.

I tried to hold my smile up and looked at my PBR. I looked around at the room. Alex was right. There were hot girls out tonight. A girl in a white wifebeater and a harsh face of dark features. A girl with wavy hair and sparkled eyes, tight jeans and heels. The girl I danced with once in all black who knew she was out of my league.

"She was girly and boyish at the same time," I shrugged, hanging my head. "I don't want to talk about her."

"How did she dress?" Alex asked. "How long was her hair?"

"She wore jeans. She dressed simple. She has sort of short hair." She had curves but she was slim. She preferred to have a bare face but her features were so thick and colorful she wouldn't have needed makeup anyway. I would have liked her in a dress or boy's jeans, I wouldn't have cared. Other girls I'd notice because they were in heels and I wanted to fuck the idea of that, or because they were trying to talk like James Dean. With her it was innocent.

"Well, I guess I'm not like that," Alex said with a wave of her hand. She pulled out some tobacco, grimy and leafy in a plastic bag, and started rolling a cigarette on the table with the tips of her dainty fingers.

Then an Asian girl, girly in navy satin, sat with us with her straight dude wingman. She spoke like a Valley Girl. Her straight male friend had a brunette lumberjack beard all over his face. My grandma told me never to trust a man with a beard. She said that it meant they were hiding something. They revealed that they were both straight and yesterday had tried out a sex club and he watched her go down on a girl. I felt dirty being around them. I went to get more beer. I stopped in the doorway to say hi to Gene, a tall trans guy who looked like Matt Dillon. My voice got severely sweet when I tried to make small talk and he nodded until I stopped talking so he could get out to the patio.

When I handed the bartender, who, remember, is devastating, two dollar coins, she sighed. "You've been giving these to me all night. I really can't accept them. Do you have bills?" I was ashamed and plunged my fist into my backpack to produce real bills. She smiled tightly and handed me a beer. I went to the platform ministage where the DJ, whose chubby red cheeks reminded me of my sister, was bobbing beneath feathered hair. In my Sweet Voice I asked if I could keep my backpack behind her turntables, and she nodded, bobbing still and smiling at me with a flush.

I returned to Alex's table where everyone was laughing and talking. Rachel stood up. "I have to talk to you," she said. She grabbed my arm and shuffled me away.

"Alex likes you," she muttered from closed teeth. "She just told me."

"Okay," I said, and noticed the pretty wavy-haired girl sitting on the bench. I wondered if it was worth trying. Tonight was the world telling me with a gentle shake that everyone decent was out of my league. I decided to try. I had a cigarette in my pocket.

"Go with them," I mumbled to Rachel, and veered in the other direction. Rachel, given a mission, nodded and returned to Alex.

"Do you have a light?" I asked, sitting next to the pretty girl. She smirked. She pulled out a lighter and handed it to me with a bored flick of her wrist. I held it to my mouth.

"Do you have any other cigarettes?" she asked; her voice slid out steadily. She had Disney princess eyelashes and her gray-brown waves were brightened by faint stripes of red-brown. She was sitting in a vulnerable-looking way because of the stilettos.

"Yeah, but they're in my backpack inside."

"Oh," she said, looking away.

We sat in silence while I smoked. I thought I caught Gene's eye, sitting at a table across from us with his timid girlfriend, so I waved, but he didn't see me.

"Do you—you want me to go get the cigarettes?" I asked.

"Would you?" she shot me a glittering smile. Even though she was girly she still had the lesbian jaw. It was comforting.

"Okay," I said, even though I didn't want to. She held my cigarette and I pushed through the mosh of people on the deck and went into the bar and avoided Jane Taphouse and retrieved my backpack. The DJ was by now making out with a cute girl in a granny sweater.

I returned to the bench, unzipped my backpack, and pulled out a cigarette. She smiled at it. My heart thudded a little harder. This was going somewhere.

"So where are you from?" I leveled my breaths. I was good enough to try to make grown-up bar talk. I had seen conversations like this on TV. The way the men approached Carrie Bradshaw.

"The city," she replied, taking a drag. "But I went to college in Ohio."

"Cool," I said. "I almost went to Oberlin." She nodded, grinning with closed lips, only opening them to suck on the cigarette. We sat in silence. I looked at her. I smiled at her to fill the silence. She raised her eyebrows and smiled at her stilettos, and then stood.

"I'll be right back," she said. She left. I heard her heels rap away. I sat alone. I sucked hard on my cigarette and looked at the ground. There was a lot of old ash and even more beer stains on the wood patio ground. I sighed and stood and returned to Alex and Rachel and all the people sitting around them. There was a redhead wearing lipstick that almost matched her hair who had joined. She was wearing a blue floral dress and she was Alex's friend.

"Hannah is my door bitch," Alex said. "For the party we do on Saturdays in Manhattan."

I'd heard about that party. It was infamous. Chloë Sevigny had gone to it and made jokes about the lesbians later in an interview. I'd tried to get in once and they'd turned down my fake ID and the bouncer said that a girl like me didn't belong at a party like that. I nodded and shook her hand. She had a sort of angelic face.

"One of the best nights," Alex began, holding up her hands for effect, "I'm sorry, Hannah, but I have to tell this story. One of the best nights was when Mark ran up and said, 'Alex, your door bitch is being fucked by a hot tranny in the coat room.'" Hannah rubbed over her orange eyebrows and tried to smile in a good-natured way. "So I go and look, and sure enough, you're being eaten out by the hottest tranny drag queen I'd ever seen."

We all laughed.

"I mean, he was a really hot girl," Alex said. "A hot tranny."

Then no one knew what to say and Alex announced that she wanted to dance. The bar was emptying. We went inside and started to dance. Rachel is an excellent dancer. She'd done ballet till twelve and then jazz till college. I was drunk enough to believe that I was an excellent dancer too. Hannah went to the bar and sat, crossing one leg over the other in an elegant motion that showed off her red wedges. I sloshed up to the DJ and said, "Excuse me," so they'd stop kissing.

"Can you play something that will make me want to lose control?" I said, gripping her booth and panting in her face. I leaned in to look at her laptop. She didn't seem upset that I'd interrupted them. She had *Charlie's Angels* hair—the TV show, not the movie.

"You want to lose control?" she repeated.

"Yeah," I said.

"She wants to lose control," she explained to the girl she'd been kissing, whose arms were wrapped around her.

"Is there someone here you want to show that you can lose control for?" she said in a knowing voice like a wink. The girl who was clutching her pecked her on the cheek.

"No," I said. "I just want to lose control."

"Okay," she said. She put a Yeah Yeah Yeahs song on. I'd been hoping for Usher. Rachel and I danced some more. Alex came up and said, "Come on," and with Hannah we followed her to the couches. There was a photo booth machine next to them.

"Let's take a picture," Alex said, so I followed her into the photo booth. She closed the curtain behind us. We sat on the bench together.

"How much does it cost?" I asked, bending below the seat to feel for a cash slot. "Where do we even put the money in?"

"It's not working," she said. I sat up and looked at her. She had very smooth skin. She kissed me. I kissed her back. I was glad someone wanted to kiss me. We kissed and it got more feverish. Her hand was wrapped hard around the back of my neck. She pushed me against the wall of the booth. I wanted to reach her boobs but they were hard to feel under all the layers she was wearing. I rubbed her chest down her waist to her hips and back up. She jerked her thigh in between my legs. I suspected she didn't like how dominant I was trying to be. She pushed my head over to open my neck up and kissed it into a bite. She yanked my necklace chain out of the way and I hoped she wouldn't rip it off because it was my St. Catherine medal from my confirmation. She bit me again and I hoped even more that it would leave a good mark. We kept kissing. I sat her on the bench and then sat on top of her. She rubbed my thighs.

"You're so on the rebound," she said through a heavy breath. I hated when I kissed people and they made sad remarks about me in the middle of it.

"Don't think about that," I said. She ran her hands up my sides. I thought about how I wasn't this kind of girl but I was probably becoming it. I kissed her more, holding her face. She squeezed my waist. She put her hand up my shirt. She put her other hand over my jeans between my legs. It was the first time someone put her hand there actually knowing where to put it and how to position her fingers.

"You're so young," she sighed. "You're so young and tight."

I laughed. She moved her hand and ran it down my thigh again. I wanted her to put her hand back. Her skill at how to place it fascinated me.

"Look at your body," she muttered. We kissed again. Our tongues got messy together.

"You're so young and tight." This bothered me. I wanted her to stop saying it. It made me think about how "young" is one of my favorite words.

"How old are you?" she asked.

"Twenty-one," I lied with ease.

"You're so young," she said sadly. "Let's go." She held the curtain open for me and stared at me until I realized we were done.

Then we all hugged goodbye and Rachel and I went out into the street. The street was dead and the air was warm. I felt smelly.

"I'm drunk," I said.

"I know," she said. "I'm not drunk but I'm high. Alex had weed."

"She knew what to do with her hands," I shook my head.

We knew where we wanted to go. We turned the corner and saw the twenty-four-hour natural food market. We went inside and got carts. The store was bright. The lights were fluorescent and the place was so clean, especially compared to the grime of the black bar we had just been in for hours. I put my backpack in the cart. I love grocery shopping and pushing down the aisles with a cart.

"This place is gourmet," Rachel exclaimed, pushing her cart a little ahead of me.

"I can't wait till we have jobs and can afford to buy all the gourmet food we want," I said, my face to the glass. Rachel nudged my shin with her dancer foot.

"So was it good? Do you feel good? Or is this going to be one of those things where you're depressed in the morning?"

"I think it's fine," I said. "She has a good personality. It's amazing what an experienced lesbian can do with her hands." I looked at the cereals. They were all organic and fancy in brown boxes. I wanted Raisin Bran. She was the first person I kissed since Adrienne.

"Do you like her?" she asked.

"Not like that," I said. I ran my finger over my throat, where the skin felt heavy like cow skin and damp like a river rock. "Come here. I think she gave me a hickey. How is it looking?" Rachel abandoned her cart and walked to me. I was holding a box of organic cookies. She studied my neck.

"No, nothing is there."

"Oh. Damn." I put the cookies back on the shelf. "I wanted a hickey. Adrienne's going to be at the party on Friday."

"A hickey would be perfect," Rachel agreed, walking on, pushing her cart again. "Should we get eggs? Then she would see it and be jealous."

"Yeah, eggs. I need her to be jealous. She'll know it came from girl's night." The grocery store had everything I needed. I wanted to buy it all. I put hummus in my cart. "I need some pita, too," I said. Rachel looked back at me.

"I think I might get some tortillas for wraps," she remarked.

"Rachel, give me a hickey."

We looked at each other for a minute. She blinked. I shrugged.

"Okay," she said. "But at Grand Central."

"Okay," I said. I put a bag of pita bread in my cart. "I'm not letting myself spend more than fifteen dollars."

We bought our groceries and then sat at a small stainless steel café table they had at the front of the store. We pulled out the hummus we'd bought and tore off pieces of pita and dipped and ate it.

"No one can know about this hickey you're going to give me," I said, chewing. I'd chosen a stupid garlicky flavored hummus that burned my mouth.

"No," she said, shaking her head, her eyes wide.

"This is a total secret. As far as everyone's concerned, I got this from Alex."

"Right," she said. "No one can know. This is one of those weird friend secrets. Like playing doctor when you're a kid."

"Right."

We took our grocery bags and got on the subway and went

to Grand Central, which still wasn't open yet and there was a gate penning people in the front. Drunk people were sleeping on the floor behind the gate. We decided to go outside, where it was silent like a vault but still somehow had the Manhattan buzz. We walked a few blocks to Madison because we knew there was a twenty-four-hour deli there, the only bright store at the base of a lightless skyscraper. We went inside and ordered a bagel with cheddar cheese to split. I put it in my grocery bag. Then we went outside again. The city air was humid and smelled like a dump truck.

There was a ledge on one of the buildings, in front of a makeup store next to the deli. We sat on it and leaned against the glass of the front window. Behind us was a display of lipsticks.

"You want me to give you the hickey?" she asked.

"Yeah."

"I've never actually given a hickey before." She leaned toward me and frowned. She pulled back and examined my neck.

"Remember when James gave you those huge violent hickeys?" I asked.

She leaned in and put her mouth on my neck. I felt her drool run down my skin. "You have to sort of bite and suck," I said. She bit down on me. It pinched and I worried about my glands.

"Suck," I told her. A cab sailed by. There were no cars out. It was five in the morning. She tried to suck. "Harder," I said. She started to suck and bite very hard. It hurt so much I had the impulse to jump away but then I melted into the pain. "A little more," I said, considering. I didn't know how long would produce a suitable hickey. I needed it to not fade too much by Friday. People passed. She continued sucking. Rachel is the kind of person who takes tasks like these very seriously. An old woman in a sweater with a cane passed and smiled at us warmly. The kinds of people who are out in Midtown at that hour are surreal and seem like ghosts. Rachel nipped me.

"Suck," I reminded her.

Rachel worked on my hickey some more and then we walked back to Grand Central. The sun had come up by the time we were home, which for some reason made it easier to fall asleep.

Notes in a Minor Key

SHAMIM SARIF

LET ME TELL you one of the things I love most about this job, especially when we're playing London. It's when the show's over, and I'm on my way to the hotel. Usually, it's well after midnight and I'm in the back of the car, looking out. The streets are quiet, softly lit, and those huge old buildings are watching over everything. I like to stop in at the hotel bar for a nightcap. Through the long panels of glass I can see across the dark, silent park and, here and there, lights twinkling in apartment rooms. There is no city in the world as romantic as London at one a.m., and I speak as a native New Yorker.

At least, that's how it looks on a good night. And it was a good night. Long overdue, too. Since I got back on tour, I've been feeling my age a little, and those kinds of nights are getting harder and harder to find. The nights when you go for every high note knowing you're going to hit it; the nights when you have those people in the palm of your hand, knowing they're feeling the emotion of the song so strongly they almost stop breathing.

"Buy you a drink?"

Buddy's sitting there, already nursing a beer. He's been my pianist, and maybe my therapist too, at times, for the past eighteen years. Even when I was out of commission, he hung in there and came back the moment I was ready.

"Great show, Buddy," I tell him. "You matched me note for note."

"You were on a roll tonight, Marianne. Felt good."

"I've always loved London," I say.

Buddy laughs. "I thought you hated the rain."

"When I sing like that, I love everything. Even the rain."

THE NEXT NIGHT we start at ten thirty, a little late. We never begin until dinner is over, and tonight they're serving a chocolate soufflé. So, we wait. That's what happens when you get a celebrity chef working the same room—secretly, they want to be up there on stage with you.

We're playing fine, no sparks, but good solid jazz, and anyway, sometimes it takes time to warm up. Until "Let's Fall In Love." I sing it low and easy, no tricks, and I don't expect any from the trio, either. But halfway through, the bass stumbles, making my own note sound harsh. Then Buddy improvises a chord that doesn't fit with my finish. Heat rises in my cheeks, a sheen of sweat forms on my upper lip. Great. I tease the guys a little between songs, part of the microphone patter, and the audience laughs.

But when the next song is off, too, I feel that old knot in my stomach. Is it them, or me? Nobody out in the audience shifts or whispers to each other, but I can sense a different response. They're enthusiastic, but that *thing* is missing: artistry, grace, or whatever you want to call it. There's an energy sometimes, a moment when you know the audience really feels every word and phrase. Tonight, they don't feel it.

When I take my bows at the end of the evening, I can see the stage lights glinting off pairs of glasses and a few silver heads. A lot of my audience has aged with me over the years, I guess. I bow again, and make a joke about being too old for the wolf whistles—and then I see her.

She's young—younger than my kids, even—and sitting at a front table, alone, applauding. I realize that I saw her the night before, too. I know it sounds crazy, but she seems kind and earnest, as though she's trying to reassure me that it wasn't so bad tonight. I try to get a better look, but I don't wear glasses on stage, and I can hardly stand there bowing forever. I throw the audience a final kiss, smile at the young woman, and go back to my dressing room. A bouquet of white roses is waiting for me. No message. I poke my head out and catch the stage manager walking past, shrugging on his coat, keen to lock up and get home.

"Eddie, who are these from?"

He shrugs. "A woman dropped them off. Young. I thought perhaps she was the florist."

I close the door. The flowers might be made of porcelain,

they are so perfect. I think about that young woman sitting out there two nights in a row. Couldn't be.

I STAY AT the bar a little longer than usual tonight. It's a grand room, all wood paneling and high ceilings, and the solid, unchanging feel of it reassures me somehow. The truth is, I feel anxious. Shaky.

"Buy you a drink?"

I don't even turn. "Only if I can throw it at you."

I can feel Buddy raising his eyebrows in that slow way he has. "Take it easy, Marianne. It's our first time back on the road since . . ."

I can feel him shuffle as he lets the sentence die. There's a painful silence during which he orders a drink and I stare at my glass, trying to summon enough anger to cover the misery rising in my chest.

"Anyone can have a bad patch," he says, finally.

"I don't want this bad patch to last the rest of my career, Buddy."

It's supposed to be a strong statement, a warning, but I find my eyes welling up and I have to look away. I take a gulp of my drink and study my hands. God, I need another manicure. Jen always used to tease me about that.

"You should've warned me, Mari," she'd say. "If I'd known what a fortune you were going to spend on those nails, I might not have married you."

I take another drink, because thinking about Jen only makes me feel worse.

Beside me, I can feel Buddy settling on his stool, taking a first sip of his beer.

"You know, Marianne, we're all getting on a little. Slowing down. Mellowing out."

"We weren't 'mellowed out' up there tonight, Buddy. We were terrible."

He pauses. "I'm sorry about that improv, I shouldn't have . . ."

"It was me," I say. My voice sounds abrasive, not the smooth tones of the jazz singer, but I'm fighting tears, and I can't bear to hear him apologizing when it was my problem. The truth is he can barely cover up for some of my mistakes anymore.

"You're too hard on yourself," he offers.

I turn to glance at him, which is all the invitation he needs.

"You can't hit a high one?" he says. "So what? Use a low finish. What you bring to a song now is different. Better, even. You don't need to sing them the way you did when you were twenty-five."

I slide down from my stool as elegantly as I can in a long sheath dress and rummage in my purse for my room key, just to avoid looking Buddy in the eye. "See you tomorrow," I say, and I leave.

I DREAM THE strangest dreams. They are about Jen, except that in the dreams she looks like the young woman in the audience. It's a rough awakening, in the gray morning light, to find no Jen lying next to me when I felt her there so strongly. Time heals, right? Well, it's been two long years since she died, and it still hurts every time I dare think about it. I spend the afternoon at the old bookstores on Charing Cross Road—the ones Jen loved so much—and then I get that manicure. While they file and paint, I think about what Buddy said the night before. Was he just being kind, or does he have a point? I am a different woman than I was thirty years ago. Sure, I've lost a little range, but life has taught me a lot about technique, and love, since then.

BY THE TIME we hit the stage that night, I feel happier. We work through the first set, and then Buddy and the boys pick up their solos. It's the only time the spotlight is off me. I stand at the other end of the piano, tapping time, and sneak a look at the audience. She is there again, at the same table. I can see her better now, without the light in my eyes: angular cheekbones, wavy hair, an intense gaze. A little like Jen—thirty years ago, maybe, but nonetheless. Her eyes catch my gaze. I smile briefly and then look back at Buddy. He's staring at me, nodding. I've missed my cue. For a long moment I can't even recall which song they're playing, and when I finally remember, it's too late. There's a terrible moment when I can feel the audience holding their breath, then murmuring, embarrassed for me. Buddy smartly finishes up the song as a bright piano solo, and as we leave the stage for the break, I glance over at the young woman again. She's on her feet, applauding.

I skip the interval drinks and go straight to my dressing room. The roses are there again. Long-stemmed, perfect. This time, I can't hold back the tears. I cry for a bit, pretty hard, then reapply mascara and try to gather my wits. I almost don't see the card, but something makes me turn back as I leave the dressing room. There's a tiny envelope nestled between the flowers. Quickly, I open it and read: *There are no songs except those sung with a broken heart.*

No name, no number, nothing. I read the lines over again, and on impulse, I grab the nail scissors from my vanity bag, clip off a creamy rose, and pin it to my dress.

Buddy's waiting outside my room. Because I'm late.

"You good?"

"I think so."

"Nice flower."

I nod. "Buddy? I don't think I can go out there and sing that set."

He looks alarmed. I look away.

"Marianne, it's the last night . . ."

"I know. And I can't sing those goddamn show tunes and smile and be happy. I just can't. Just—tell them I'm not well."

He thrusts his hands in his pockets and paces around. "Why don't we change the set?"

I begin to bluster about how he can't just change the show, what about the band . . . but Buddy puts a gentle hand on my arm.

"What do you want to sing, Marianne? Just tell me."

The scent of the rose rises. Delicate, but there. I think for a moment and list five of the saddest, most moving songs I know.

"You got it," Buddy says.

THERE'S A TANGIBLE buzz in the audience by the time we walk back out, ten minutes late, and they all clap and whistle. Whether the young woman is cheering with them, I can't say, because I can't bring myself to look at her. I feel that knot in my stomach as Buddy goes straight into the opening of "When Your Lover Has Gone"—an obvious choice, I'll admit. He takes the long route in, which gives me time to take some deep breaths. I try not to, but I can't help looking for the young woman. She's gone.

I glance around the room. How can she leave at this moment, as I stand here with my heart in my mouth and her rose on my dress? A vague ache begins to invade me, the same ache I felt that morning waking, once again, without Jen. It's a cold night and a big city to be alone in, and my heart feels weary, and without another thought I begin to sing, and it doesn't matter where

Buddy's gotten to in his intro because I can feel every note before he plays it. There is a moment of complete silence when I'm done, and then the room explodes. Suddenly, it doesn't matter so much that I feel so very bad, because every one of these people in the room feels it too.

WHEN I LEAVE after the set is finished, she is waiting for me at the stage door. She's muffled in a long coat and a scarf that covers her smile.

"An incredible show," she says. "Thank you."

"Where did you disappear to?" I ask her. As if I'm entitled to answers from this stranger.

"I was there. I moved behind a pillar. I thought it would help. I don't know why."

I nod. "It did help. So did the roses, and your message. More than you know. I don't know how to repay you."

She laughs. "You already did."

"How?"

"The way you sang." She touches her heart, and takes a couple of steps away, as though preparing to leave.

"Who are you?" I ask her.

"A fan, Miss Mark."

"I'm old enough to be your mother. Maybe your grandmother."

"Does that matter? I found your music a couple of years ago. It means something to me."

She turns up the collar of her coat and takes a step away, then looks back.

"I'm sorry for your loss," she says. And then she's gone, walking fast.

I open my mouth to call after her, but something stops me. If I've learned one thing on this night, it's that a moment of grace should be accepted. So, I watch silently as she disappears into the damp night, down this back street, toward the traffic and people in the distance. I hear her footsteps ringing against the road, and I just stand there in the misting rain, listening to them until the last echo fades away.

Rookie Mistake

GRACE BYRON

MARGO NEVER ASKED her if it was too much. That wasn't the game they were playing. The sex, the late-night drives, the drugs were all part of a high-stakes speedrun. With Margo, Hannah could evaporate into the blueness of night.

Before they got in the car, she made Hannah take a bump and a shot in the bathroom. Margo was proud of this, being able to provide.

Hannah stared at the back of Margo's shaved head, admiring the sheer roundness of it. She was too high. Her boyfriend was waiting at home, wondering what she was doing out so late.

The bridge was aglow in the distance. All around them the indigo night was dissolving. The lights of a thousand buildings flickered out.

"We're going too fast," Hannah said.

"No such thing," Margo said. "I think we should go faster."

"I took too much K, I'm gonna puke."

Margo rolled down the window without saying anything. An enigmatic smile crossed her face as she took out a cigarette and pushed it toward her new lover, who declined. Hannah looked over at the woman whose breasts she had so recently bitten, leaving tiny, plum-colored marks. She wondered if Margo had other lovers. She didn't ask, was afraid to learn the obvious; better to stay in the dark and only cling to her leather-clad lover during their late-night escapades.

Hannah stared out the window at the bay rushing past in muted pastels. The floor was littered with Diet Coke cans and napkins. Every girl addicted to Diet Coke was always addicted to more than just Diet Coke.

"You'll get better at it." Margo put her hand on Hannah's shaky palm. "Just stop thinking about whatever you're thinking about."

"No."

"Are you worried we're gonna fuck again?"

Hannah didn't say anything. She just looked at Margo's smirk. "Fuck you."

"Oh, so you can cuss."

They'd started hooking up a week after they met. Margo was chronically single, always fucking the newest trans girl to join the party circuit, inducting them into the trans-girl-for-trans-girl circle. "Like *The L Word*," Hannah had said to the woman next to her. "Not like *The L Word*," the other woman had said. Hannah hadn't expected to be cornered in the bathroom. Then she realized she'd wanted it anyway. Maybe she was becoming the Jenny of a friend group she knew nothing about.

"You're worried about whatever his name is?"

"Not at all," Hannah said, pursing her lips as Margo pushed a finger into her mouth.

"Good."

The truth was complicated. She and Cole weren't necessarily monogamous, but they didn't talk about it either. They lived together, so he probably expected that if she fucked someone else, she would tell him. Cole was nice. He just didn't get it. Or maybe he did but didn't want to know. Hannah had never told him she slept with women. To be fair, Margo was the first woman she slept with—something she hadn't told Margo, either.

Margo's hands were on her tits again.

"That's not fair."

"I don't play fair. And you're the one who wore that crop top without a bra."

The ocean was coming into view. It wasn't fair at all. Margo was wearing only a sports bra and joggers under her leather jacket. Her septum piercing annoyed Hannah but in a way that made everything a little more fun. Hannah thought back to when Margo spat in her mouth a few nights ago. It was reckless—they'd been parked outside her apartment. Cole could've seen them.

She knew Margo raced cars. She knew every time she got into the car with her she was entering into a deal with an unknown cost. The drugs were enough to keep her coming back, but the sex was more than enough to keep her trapped. Two traps intertwined moving too fast.

"Besides," Margo said, breaking her reverie, "you like when I'm mean to you."

HANNAH SAT ON the sand, examining her pale arms under the fluorescent lights. The beach looked like a void at night, something she hadn't been prepared for. Margo was trailing slowly behind, clearly on a little too much. Everything tasted green. The palm trees around them looked ghoulish, the fronds like feathery, fanged tendrils blowing in the wind.

It was lonely watching herself from the outside; Margo didn't seem like someone who ever depersonalized. Still, when they had sex, it was rough—like outlines groping desperately. At sixteen, she had been assaulted; the grimy look of satisfaction on the guy's face and the smell of metal in the back of his Toyota still haunted her. Afterward, Hannah had vowed never to cry during sex.

So she didn't. The sex with Margo wasn't like that anyway. Sex with her made the sex with Cole better, too.

A seagull landed close to Hannah as she spread her hands across the sand, which was littered with cigarette butts. Margo was finally getting closer. The seagull poked around at a plastic bottle searching for some treasure.

"You okay?"

"Of course," Hannah said too quickly.

"Stand up."

She obeyed.

"You have to learn to do things on your own."

"How do you know you're the one in control?"

Margo flinched for a moment, then dragged her hands across Hannah's back and reached inside her pink crop top.

"Don't get all weird on me."

NO ONE ELSE was in the dining room of Green Fuel. The cashier stole nervous glances at her, like she was simultaneously attracted and repelled. Hannah stood in her leather jacket, softly hitting the button to cascade more Diet Coke into her cup. She would never have opted for vegan fast food, but it wasn't her choice anymore. Hunger and poor time management had won again. The TV displayed a news report about an old woman who was gardening and found a rattlesnake under her yarrow. She wore an ugly pink cardigan. The flushed news reporter interrogated her about climate change.

It'd been six weeks of nonstop trysts. Margo was slowing down, even though Hannah was starting to catch feelings beyond mere heat. Rookie mistake.

Diet Coke was spilling out of the cup. She stopped pressing it and shot the cashier a look, her curls bouncing as she
turned. The cashier averted her gaze. It wasn't admiration, she
realized. It was anger. She waited for her stupid vegan burger
and fries and sat by the window staring at the seabirds outside
pecking at a capsized milkshake made from nuts. They were
amateur scavengers too.

It was only sixty-three degrees out. She wished she didn't
have to go to work. Checking her phone again, she had a few
texts from Cole. He wanted to get a dog together. A puppy pref-
erably, though she would've preferred an older dog. Or a cat.
He was sending pictures from a shelter. There was a new litter of
abandoned poodle puppies. She stared at the pixelated images
of white fluffy dogs attacking each other. It reminded her of a
snowstorm, like the kind she experienced as a kid visiting her
mother's parents in Chicago. Now that she was eternally cold,
she didn't miss the Midwest, but she used to. She dreamed
of the huge buffets stuffed full of casseroles, macaroni, and a
hundred varieties of potato.

The burger was gone, only a few crumbs left on the bright
green tray full of little cartoon monsters. The cashier was
nowhere in sight. A group of teenagers entered in a cloud of
noise, and she decided to go. She slipped the dog problem
into her pocket, imagining a blizzard of Dobermans chasing
her off a cliff.

EVERY SUNDAY SHE went to visit the elder trans woman in her
life. Lis and Hannah debated dating and ambition religiously.
The ethics of T4T, the loneliness, the grim reality of boyfriends.

Lis was sipping her coffee without any cream or sugar while
Hannah had loaded hers up with the stuff. Lis's apartment was
full of pictures from old events and colorful tchotchkes. There
was a large home computer, pothos, spider plants, bunches of
overgrown ivy, haphazardly stacked books, and old punk show
posters. She had an ashtray that she swore she'd got from Lou
Sullivan even though Hannah wasn't sure the timeline added
up. Years ago, she'd worked in the nonprofit industrial complex
teaching people how to serve trans people in their low-income
clinics. "It was bullshit," she always said. Still, it led to her ability to freelance and live without a roommate in the Bay.

Hannah always wanted Lis to give her advice, to unlock the
sadness she felt, to make her feel alive again. Most of the time
Lis just talked about Buddhism and pain and acceptance. She

was always trying to get Hannah to meditate, something they both agreed was utterly boring and utterly necessary. Cole meditated. Every morning he asked her if she wanted to join and she declined, preferring to drink too much coffee and listen to the news. Lis didn't listen to the news anymore. She watched old Katherine Hepburn movies and read Zen koans she rolled out to stump cashiers in the grocery-store checkout line.

Lis gripped her coffee intently and shifted in her seat. She was staring at the floor, lost in thought. Hannah opened her mouth to speak just as Lis finally got the words out.

"I don't know if two trans people can make it work. It's a lot of hurt to hold between two people."

"Encouraging," Hannah quipped.

"I never said I was going to be a cheerleader."

The early afternoon light slanted across the living room, creating a crisscross pattern over Lis's face. Hannah always stared at her nose. It was something Lis always complained about, but Hannah found sweet. If she focused on Lis's tits, she always felt bad. So she didn't.

Lis was carving her words carefully, thinking about how much to let on, how much of her own world to open up to the lost girl. Her own grief eclipsed so much, but she saw the jagged road ahead.

"Your last ex," Hannah started to ask before being cut off.

"Cis woman," Lis said. "We dated for a year. Never all that serious."

Unfortunately, their subject was always men and women. Women without men, women against women.

"What about two women?"

"I'm guessing there's a woman in particular."

"Margo."

"Do you love her?"

Hannah looked down at her pearly coffee, blooming with milk.

"Oh, babe."

Lis raised her hand and set it on Hannah's knee.

"Is she kind?"

"Not at all."

They both went quiet.

"Should I ask what happened to Cole?"

Nothing. Nothing had happened to Cole. That was the truth. The night before, her friend had posted "Shoutout to girls with boring boyfriends," and Hannah instantly knew it was about her.

"He's still around."

"What does he think about the whole thing?"

She looked back at her coffee and took a big sip.

"I don't want love to always be this whole tortured, shitty thing."

"You keep looking for something else, and sometimes, babe, there's not something else."

"I want more. I deserve more."

Lis took her hand back and stood up. She walked over to the coffee pot and turned it off.

"You do. You do. So do I. I just don't know if there's more. And I worry in trying to grab so much you'll let go of what you have."

"I don't have him," Hannah said ignoring the flurry of sexts from Cole she felt boiling over in her pocket. They felt different than Margo's. Still she knew she would ask Margo for time. Always more time.

Lis spun back around, smirking, gleaming in the kitchen light.

"That boy is yours, Hannah. But you don't seem to want him."

HANNAH WAS STRADDLING Margo while coming up on molly. It was the second time she'd done it. Margo had invited three other girls, who were now writhing on the floor under the green overhead light. Her whole apartment smelled like weed, frankincense, stale saltines, and the wet fugue of sex. Whenever she was getting fucked, Hannah stared at the Nick Cave poster on the wall, wondering over and over what had led to this exact moment. Nick Cave's stoic poise seemed like the punchline of a joke he'd just told.

"I can't . . ."

"What can't you do, baby?" Margo taunted as she stared into Hannah's pupils. The strap-on was draining Hannah of her ability to form full sentences. Unfortunate timing, as romantic thoughts were racing through her brain.

One of the girls on the floor started coming and announced it to the room. Margo turned to watch.

"That's my girl," Margo said. The girl in question was Liv, who was being serviced by the other two girls, whose names Hannah couldn't remember. They were getting close to knocking over a large lamp shaped like a tent. Even from across the room Hannah could see how wide Liv's eyes were. If Hannah could've chosen not to be there, she would have. But she was already in the car by the time she'd realized there were going to be others. Jealousy wasn't her best suit. She didn't have any ground to stand on anyway. The picture she'd taken of the two of them on the beach flashed in her mind: Margo standing with her hand around Hannah's neck, the dress she'd chosen for her protégé tight against her little breasts. Mommy, fuck mommy, fuck.

She felt a thwack as Margo spanked her.

"Where'd you go?"

Margo smiled. Her ruby-red lipstick was a little smudged, but her winged eyeliner remained perfectly in place. She hadn't taken off her floral bralette, and her nipples stood hard against the embroidered lilies.

When Hannah told Margo about her ex-boyfriends, the guys before Cole, she always told her they should've treated her better.

"You didn't deserve that."

But here Hannah was again, watching it happen in real time.

Liv let out a moan and started squirming against one of the other girls. Margo turned to watch, absentmindedly stroking Hannah's hair. Liv was beautiful. She passed, Hannah thought. She had started hormones way earlier than the rest of them.

Cruelty came too easily. The kind of girl she wanted to be didn't care, didn't have a furious mean streak. But she was watching herself become disposable in front of someone she loved. That fell out of her mouth. Like a waterfall she couldn't stop, a dam she couldn't repair. All the water metaphors, she realized, were due to the fact she was tearing up.

"I need a second," Hannah said, getting off an astonished Margo and heading to the bathroom. Liv watched her leave the room with wide, sad eyes, like she was witnessing a great personal failure.

THE NEXT MORNING she left Margo's bed for her own. She knew it was over. Margo hadn't flipped her on her stomach to go another round, but to check her phone and light a spliff. A new girl had appeared.

The worst part, Hannah thought, sliding under the covers and into Cole's sturdy arms, was that now she would be only a little trinket in Margo's mind. Would it have hurt more if she meant more to Margo? Less?

Cole kissed the top of her head. If he knew, he didn't care.

"Do you wanna watch something?"

"I have another idea," he said.

Boyishly at first, he kissed her neck. She let her head fall into the crook of his neck and his hands found her bra, unclasping it and dragging it off her body.

"It's so cold," she said as he lifted her shirt off.

"I can fix that."

He slid off her shorts and panties before going down her. It wasn't normally something she liked but there was something feral about him just now. She moaned as the cars outside passed in the morning light on their way to work. Her hands found the headboard just as he flipped her over and rose up to bite her shoulder. The garbage truck gargled outside. He grabbed her hair and turned her head back toward him.

"Watch me," he said.

NO ONE HAD seen her Before picture yet. Hannah had posted the picture of her fraying nails with an indecipherable glyph stolen from some meme about boy pussy she couldn't decipher. Everyone was fighting about Mitski online again.

Margo hadn't posted in a few days. That was the only person she wanted to see anyway. She knew that posting more made her look depressed, but she couldn't help it anymore. Nothing was going to make her feel better so there was no reason to hide her maladaptive coping mechanisms. Lis had been texting her back and forth—not about Margo, just about feeling sad. It was probably unfair to want Lis to be a beacon of trans hope. She just needed it so badly.

The walk to the nail salon wasn't too long, but she passed endless rundown cookie-cutter houses. One large, pink house with gray cacti in the front had a large empty pool in the back. She'd passed it before and stared, amazed they didn't have a fence. Maybe no one lived there anymore. The empty pool sliced her mind in half. Walking up to it over the fried grass, she saw a writhing mass of snakes collected near the drain. She'd heard of snakes growing more adventurous in the Bay. It seemed nearly every day there was another fantastic news story of some gruesome animal somewhere attacking an old woman just trying to get home with her groceries.

Snakes weren't one of Hannah's biggest fears. Even though she wasn't a Californian by birth, she felt like the stories of Dust Bowl survival women suited her. Kill a snake, raise something from the dead, drink a stiff drink, go to bed thinking of the end. In another life she wouldn't have done drugs. She would've been sturdy. She would have taken everything with cool indifference.

Nothing would make the morning feel still now. The image of the snakes intertwining their slick bodies through one another like SpaghettiOs was imprinted on her mind. It was almost impossible to see their black almond eyes; they were moving in a terrible, hypnotic whirlpool. She stole another glance for mysticism's sake. Maybe it would inspire her own survival origin story. There was no promise to make now though.

She tried to lock eyes with a snake. Maybe that would break her, she thought. They all ignored her though. Instead, the taste of Cole flickered on her tongue, her mouth still wet somehow.

Back on the sidewalk, she shivered. With each footstep she tried to load her personality of the day. Between Cole and Margo, she felt the whiplash of being a woman on the verge of becoming a brat. She had already stopped making the bed. One day she would have to end her trash goblin era and help Cole with the chores, but the past few weeks, that hadn't been her thing.

Hannah stared at the warped stucco houses and their wilting gardens filled in with rocks as she passed. Slowly the houses gave way to small strip malls, each more grim than the last. The nail salon Lis told her about was beneath a Pizza Hut. Lis told her she once fucked the manager.

To get to the nail salon, she had to descend a steep stairwell. Thank God for pink neon, she thought. The large nail art posters taunted her with cheer. As she entered, a bell rang, and she nearly kicked over a snoring white cat with her feet. An older Korean woman with thick blue horn-rimmed glasses greeted her. Hannah saw the woman was looking at a website about how to take care of pet snakes.

"Good morning."

"Can I get extensions?"

"Pick a color—over there by the wall."

Hannah wandered over to the wall and gripped the small wheel of a thousand colors. She knew it was foolish, but every time she got sad, she made ridiculous purchases like any other alienated customer with a vague brand identity. She was too high for this. It stung to remember texting Margo was no longer a way out. The dopamine hits would have to come from something else, she wasn't ready to sit in the moment without reaching for distraction. Not yet.

She chose indigo, sat down, and took a deep breath. In an hour she would text Cole and respond to his request to get a dog. For now she would watch her nails honed into talons.

pH

TRAE HIGGS

CAN'T WAIT TO DEVOUR U 2NITE (;

My Blackberry rested on a library table. I was studying for an aggressive calculus exam I couldn't afford to fail. I wasn't trying to spend another semester on academic probation.

I can't believe she is on me like this, I thought.

Butterflies. I couldn't think of anything to say that wasn't desperate.

What you wearin 2nite? I managed.

You'll get 2 c it b4 you take me out of it. don't worry.

I laughed aloud, forgetting I was in the library.

Nasty. I just wanted a lil preview.

I'll send u a pic when i'm out the shower then . . . a preview. (;

She'd sent me a "preview" before. I'd been studying then, too. I was prepping for an anthropology exam; she was sunbathing in her backyard. She was wearing a black thong bikini and took a snap of her stretch-mark-covered perfect ass from behind.

I looked up and two girls at the table next to me were staring at me, clearly irritated that I had interrupted their studies.

I thought about her, steaming, fresh out the shower.

I loved it. I hated it.

This was all so distracting and gay.

It was a miracle I hadn't drawn her breasts in the margins of a Scantron.

What started as a BBM from an unknown sender led to sexting.

Kyss told me alllllll about you!

Kyss did what now? My classmate and best friend was always starting something—something that I'd have to finish. *Who dis?*

Kyss cuzzo Xiomara. Everybody calls me Xio.

167

Pronounced See-O.
Hey Xio, I'm Trae. Pronounced Tray. lol.
Fancy, lol
You said Kyss told you alllllll about me.
Must've left out some deetz . . .

THE SEXTING STARTED 'cause my friend Kyss opened her big mouth at the family barbecue about her college "friend" that her cousin would love.

A few months later, after I'd threatened her, Kyss finally confessed how the conversation had gone down.

"Trae gets *allll* the pussy," she'd announced, mouth full of her grandma's peach cobbler.

I still wanted to strangle her.

THE DAY AFTER the sexts, I staked out Kyss's breakfast spot in the student union. She never broke routine unless something major like a hangover or period cramps had her suffering alone, quiet and hangry in her dorm, allowing the students at Einstein Bagels to, for just one morning, know peace.

I spotted Kyss's long box braids and flag football jersey from across the building. Kyss saw me approaching.

"Trraaaaeeee!" she fawned.

I caught myself smirking and snapped out of it. This was supposed to be a surprise confrontation.

Kyss and I played around once. We'd been freshmen, drunk and horny in a dorm after a joint Alpha Kappa Alpha and Kappa party, and started kissing, grabbing, humping. After waking up in her arms in a daze the next afternoon, we had a hangover talk. The consensus: We're just friends who want to remain . . . less horny friends. That didn't stop her from flirting with me. Or me from being gay.

"Hi, Kyss."

Before I could fully say "Hi," she grabbed my waist and pulled me in for a kiss on the cheek. It was something about university life and the friends you made in the bubble that made everything seem so heightened. Kyss greeted me like it'd been a semester since we last saw each other. In reality, we'd had breakfast Saturday morning, right before she drove to Ocala to see her family and put my life on blast.

Kyss came from a beautiful family. She was who she was—

loud, fun, openly bisexual—and they loved her for it. Her Nigerian dad and Jamaican mom let her major in something that would not lead to her becoming a doctor, lawyer, or engineer. She drove a 2005 Audi and didn't have to work but still picked up part-time hours at the off-campus bookstore.

The first time our little crew went to visit her massive home, her mother joked that Kyss waited until after her seventeenth birthday to come out so she didn't end up with a Ford Focus. I laughed along with the joke until I remembered that *I* had a Ford Focus. They came from different rivers and lakes, 'tis all. You couldn't tell me shit about my '02 Ford Focus Hatchback Coup. Got me where I needed to go. Most days.

Kyss once got really brave and decided to tell her parents that she wanted to double major in sociology and anthropology.

"I hear ology this and ology that, but what do these ologies do?" her dad spat out semisarcastically, in his blatant accent. *Ology this, ology that.* We made that our inside joke for whenever we'd lost the plot in class.

My pout finally registered.

"Oh no. What'd I do now?" Kyss caught my energy and switched to a serious tone.

"I'll get us a table." I said, knowing her Monday schedule like it was my own.

Kyss was so close to me I could smell the ORS on her scalp, and I could see the smudged lip gloss on her lower lip.

"Yeah Trunchbull, I have time to eat with you I guess!" Kyss shot back.

"Next! Next!" The cashier shouted and waved in our direction.

I went to walk away and Kyss grabbed my hand, "Your usual? Iced coffee with low fat milk? Bagel with scallion cream cheese? Not toasted?"

"Yeah, that works! Thanks." I smiled back, touched that Kyss remembered my orders the way I remembered her class schedule. I also noticed her tongue across her front teeth, a habit of hers.

Kyss slammed everything down on the table to get my attention and matched my dramatic energy. "Get to it, Trunchbull! What did I do this time?" she mocked.

"Xiomara? Sound famil—?!" I said without finishing.

"Oh, shit! I forgot to text you when I got back to campus last night. Shit, she already BBM'd you? You should be thanking me, really. I told her how perfect, sexy, smart, funny, and annoying you are in front of all my aunts. Two of which I am pretty sure are in the closet, so I talk about as many gay things as possible around them to see what they say. I—"

"Thanking you? She said you told her alllll about me. I've been too shook to respond, asking for what that meant, because knowing *you*, that could mean anything."

I can't front, I internally Black-girl-blushed at the "sexy, smart, funny" part like she was describing the similarly titled TLC album, *Crazy. Sexy. Cool.*

Kyss let out a cackle and threw her head back. "Oh, I definitely told her you get all the girls too, you have a crazy body and have certain skillsss," Kyss said, her tongue lingering out of her mouth for a moment.

I hit Kyss's shoulder and we died laughing. The fake tension I tried to build had died within two minutes. I cannot stay mad at a Gemini.

"Does she know we hooked up?"

"No, that's irrelevant. You're my homegirl and you're single, and a ho. That's that!"

"So how would you know about my certain skills?" I asked, mimicking her tongue move.

I showed Kyss our BBM conversation and she widened her eyes at Xio's commentary. After she was done reading, she gulped dramatically and yelled, "Y'all owe me big time. This chemistry is crazy already!"

Kyss got to the part where she saw we made plans to hang out in Orlando the last weekend in October, and began to bang her fist on the table. "*Ooooouuuuuuuuu*," Kyss whispered.

"I know, right! She really wants to see me as soon as soccer finals are wrapping. Something about sex throwing athletes off their game. She's so forward, in a way I'm not used to," I admitted.

"Why do you sound shocked? Scared, even?"

"I don't know! I have been having so many thoughts about her, some sexual, some sensual . . . but mostly sexual. I just hope the vibe is there in two weeks' time, you know? Like what if UCF doesn't win the finals or whatever and her mood is pissy? I don't know."

"Wow! I've never known you to be a nervous ho. Just a regular ho!"

We died laughing again. Kyss realized she had ten minutes to get to her next class and shot up. "All this Xio shit got me running late. I'll hit you later, baby! Movie at my place tonight?" She packed up her stuff.

"I'll bring the Amsterdam!" I confirmed.

FLASH FORWARD TO my angst about finally meeting Xio tonight. I pulled out my phone to message her. *Congrats on the big win, sexy! C u 2nite.*

She responded before I could put my phone back down to take my nap: *Thank U. Can't wait to taste my prize later. What time am I seein u?*

10-ish . . . unless I decide 2 make u wait

I doubt you'll do that. C u then.

"This bitch is so cocky!" I said out loud to myself. Cocky and correct.

It was Kyss's idea to go to Parliament House, which we called P House or pH, in Orlando. My phone vibrated: *Stoppin 4 Jay n pullin up in 5. Bring yo ass!* It was 7:58 p.m. Kyss was on time for once! I knew her pulling up in five still meant ten minutes, so I brushed my teeth and reapplied my lip gloss and patted my pits dry for the fifth time.

Being out and gay in Florida certainly wasn't incredible, but I was lucky to have my crew for sure. Kyss was openly bi and told me so as soon we'd matched on the Class of 2014 USF Incoming Freshman message board. Our other close friend Jay taught us all what being pansexual was. I had truly never heard that label before meeting Jay.

"I fall in love with humans, not genitals," she said calmly one evening during a tense game of Uno.

Kyss jokingly spouted back, "I fall in love with genitals for sure!" and slammed down a Draw 4! We all laughed, knowing what Jay meant but also reveling in Kyss's nasty-ass confession.

I was the lesbian of the crew and had been out since I was fourteen. I remember telling myself that I'd go to college without telling many people, but once I got to USF and found my people, I never really thought about that again.

We made it to pH in what felt like record time. On a Saturday night, most people living on the west coast of Florida are traveling on the I-4 E for one reason or another, so you can usually bet on traffic. We made it through Lady Gaga's *The Fame Monster* and halfway through Janet Jackson's *All For You*, and before I knew it, we were pulling into the club/motel parking lot at 9:45.

I pulled down the visor to use the mirror and refresh my lip gloss. Quiet-ass Jay yelled from the back, "The lip gloss finna be off soon anyways," and hit the back of my seat.

I shot her my best bitchy eyes and snapped back, "I know lip gloss isn't your thing, but you *sure* could use some." I puckered up in her direction, and she leaned up and slightly grazed my lips with her lips and rubbed the lip gloss on. We all erupted in laughter as Jay let it settle on her lips and said, "Mmm, peach?"

Jay was my most intimate friend. People always speculated there was something between us because we did shit like kissing lip gloss off each other, holding hands, sitting in each other's laps, hugging, and had a secret way of communicating. People would say, "Y'all just need to go ahead and date!" but we just knew it wasn't that and treasured our friendship.

The line was pretty deep to get into pH. As we were about to join, two very tall, statuesque Black bombshells cut in front of us. The taller one politely said, "Y'all don't mind, do ya?" as she smacked her gum—half question, half statement.

I smiled. Jay shrugged. Kyss ushered them forward with her hands.

Kyss leaned into my ear and whispered, "The dark-skinned one can have her way with me right *nowwww*." I pretended to elbow her in the stomach and laughed. Something about Kyss's overt affliction for dark-skinned women and men was so validating. The first time we went to the beach together, she told me that my skin absorbed the sun like we were besties. Seeing how quickly I tanned into a darker hue mesmerized her.

Once we were inside, we ran to the crowded semicircle bar. We hadn't been in a while, but one of our favorite bartenders remembered us and waved us over.

"Three vodka shots?!" she yelled over the bass.

"Only two and a cranberry and ginger ale!" I countered.

Jay was always our designated driver.

"Mmm, Grey Goose sure does taste better than the shit we be drinking," she said, smelling the shot glass.

"Yeah, Amsterdam is like flavored lighter fluid, I think!" I agreed. I shifted around and started scanning for Xio, hoping Kyss wouldn't notice.

"She'll be here in ten, loser!" Kyss said, not looking up from her phone. "Well, that was eight minutes ago, so she'll be here any minute now."

In the short time Xio and I had talked, we had exchanged so many stories about our lives. I told her how my parents had taken my brother and me to Hawaii months before they told us they were separating; I loved the photos from the trip, I said, but I was bothered that my parents had made sure we had a fun vacation, even if it meant they were miserable. Xio told me she thought her dad had cheated on her mom a handful of times, but she'd never been able to prove it. I told her how I was double-jointed in both of my thumbs. She told me about her sexual rendezvous with a girl on her soccer team that was super short-lived because her teammate's mom went through their texts and scolded her after a game. "No daughter of mine is going to be a faggot," the girl's mom yelled in the car pickup area, in front of everyone. She even threw her phone at her daughter.

The second time we were about to fall asleep on the phone together, she said, "Trae! This may seem a bit forward, but I just got a STD check and I am all clear. Just wanted to let you know."

"That's great to hear! Why are you sharing this with me? You're not assuming . . ."

"Oh my gosh, shut up, Trae!"

We laughed.

"No, seriously, thanks for telling me. I actually had trich last month, which I thought was a yeast infection or chlamydia, but thankfully it was neither. And I haven't been with anyone else since."

"Okay, good! Wow. This is so hot!"

"What is?"

"Bringing up, you know, sexual health? I'm in a women's rights and autonomy class which is all about trying to make these topics less taboo. I even carry my tampons out the back pocket of my jeans now because who the fuck cares! You know?"

"Bad ass, babe! Yeah, why do we be hiding the shit like nobody has ever seen tampons?"

We both laughed.

Kyss reached out to embrace someone. I realized it was Xio.

"Congrats, cuzzzooo!" Kyss yelled over the music as she squeezed her.

As Xio hugged Kyss back for what felt like forever, my heart began to race. Xio's gaze met mine and she looked me up and down, like she could take me right there on the bar. Xio's eyes lingered on mine for a minute, and I could feel the tension between my legs start to build.

She walked over to me slowly, never losing my gaze. She mouthed *"Damn,"* looked me up and down again, and leaned into my ear before hugging me.

"I just want to take you in for a moment," she breathed into my ear.

All I could smell was the vanilla-incense-weed combo that radiated off her hair, which was slicked into a bun. She finally hugged me and let her hands linger at the small of my back.

When we broke away from each other, Jay and Kyss were nowhere in sight. I pulled my phone out my bag and had two BBMs:

Kyss: *figg'd y'all would want your alone time. don't do anything I wouldn't do hottie. Oh and my aunt and uncle (her parents) are out of town! Tee hee hee.*

Jay: *did anyone else hear Maxxxxxxxwell start to play when y'all hugged? st3333amy=D*

I smiled at their messages. "The girls are upstairs," I said to Xio, yelling over the music.

"You're beautiful." Xio said softly, and it made me want to melt.

"Thank you. You're so beautiful. Like . . . it's like I haven't seen your pics before. Oh, and congrats again on the big win! UCF isn't celebrating anywhere tonight?" I asked.

"I am celebrating," Xio said, and leaned in to kiss me.

I felt off balance for a minute, then kissed her back, gently. When we pulled apart, she looked so happy.

Xio was maybe five-seven; I was five-six and had to slightly tilt my head to look up at her, both of us in sneakers. She had on a crop-top tank, a dark denim skirt, and fresh Air Force 1s. So simple, so sexy. Her full brows, perfect dark skin, and legs were the main attractions. I studied her lips and the mole just below her left eye, which she'd said her mom and her sister also shared. She had a small, flat scar on the right side of her chin, below her bottom lip. She'd told me the story of how a soccer ball flew at her face during practice, full force, and busted the skin right open.

"Let's dance!" Xio yelled and whisked me to the dance floor.

She was such a great dancer. Watching her body was truly a delight that I was honored to witness. Tampa DJs loved to talk over the music, but in Orlando they let the songs ride out and focused on the crowd's energy. Xio turned her ass to me when *Apple bottom jeans, boots with the furrrr* began to play. I slapped her ass a few times, and she turned toward me, put one of her legs up on my waist, and rolled backward. An onlooker grabbed her arm as if to help her get sturdy on me. The whole exchange was hilarious, and that was the thing about these Black and Brown queer nightclubs: Everybody was trying to live their best lives. There was always so much love and comradery among strangers.

We were infatuated with each other. We worked up a crazy sweat within an hour. Monica and Usher's "Slow Jam" began to play, signaling that it was the slow-down power-hour between just before midnight and one a.m. Clubs in Orlando closed at two, so it was what many considered the cooldown or hookup period of the night. Xio went from free-spirit playgirl to a sensual goddess mouthing the words to me from Usher's opening verse. When the chorus began, she grabbed my head and the small of my back, grinding my hips side to side to match hers.

When Monica's verse came on, I started mouthing it back at her. We danced nose to nose for a moment, and I went in for a soft kiss. Her upper lip tasted like sweat, and I let my lips linger just a bit longer to take in the taste.

She tilted her head slightly to deepen the kiss and asked permission with her tongue to explore my mouth. I said yes without words. Her right hand traveled up to my neck, and I felt the tension that was rising on my clit go upward into my navel. I wanted her, now. Her mouth tasted like spearmint and a cigarillo she used to roll a blunt coming into the club. I got lost in her mouth. We suddenly became each other's floss, Chapstick, and source of hydration.

Xio pulled away and led me off the dance floor onto a barstool against the wall. She motioned for me to sit down and parted my legs to stand in between them, then kissed me again. I couldn't help but fantasize Xio taking me right there with a strap-on.

She motioned her pelvis toward mine when our kisses deepened and became faster. She moved her mouth down to my neck. I let my right hand rest on her right thigh and my left hand on the back pocket of her denim skirt. This was the first time I think I had looked around in forever. "I Wanna Know" by Joe was playing now, and not a soul was looking in our direction. I saw two gay guys grinding on each other. Two friends or lovers slow dancing. Two Latin girls were pelvis to pelvis while Joe serenaded all of us into our individual little wormholes.

Heaven.

Her hands made their way hesitantly up and down my thighs. I had on a bodycon dress, and I think she was being respectful, but I didn't want to be respected. When her hands were half-way up my thigh, I wanted her to keep going so that she could feel what I wanted to give her so badly. I scratched at her thighs from underneath her skirt and she stopped kissing me.

"You ready to go?" Xio said, panting.

"Yes!" I could barely breathe.

I pulled out my phone, and it was 12:38 a.m. *Were we making out for almost an hour?*

Jay: *Don't hurt nobodyyyyyy (:*

Kyss: *We're going to City Walk boo. Love you and be safe!*

I BBM'd Jay and Kyss on the short walk to the car. I wondered if they had seen us and knew to leave us alone. I would've been pissed if they had interrupted our "Love in This Club" moment.

Xio fumbled with her keys, and it was the first time I could tell she was nervous. I grabbed her hand and the lights flashed to a black Tahoe. I expected her to be driving something cute and sporty, and this certainly was neither.

Xio licked her perfect lips, like she wanted to say something. "Would you be offended if . . . I tasted you in the back seat. I just need to." Her voice was hesitant. Her eyes softened to more of a beg.

She backed me into the rear passenger-side door; her breath was so intoxicating. Our lips were like half an inch apart, but we weren't kissing.

"I want you to!" I said, grazing my lips against hers. I pushed her off me so I could open the door and scooted back onto the leather seats. I thought to myself, *Great, much easier to clean if we make a mess in here.*

Xio climbed in after me. She moved up the passenger seat so that it was basically hitting the glove compartment, then crouched between my legs. She straddled my lap and kissed me, then explored my chest and stomach with her free hand.

I was self-conscious of how I might taste. *Fresh out of a*

nightclub . . . Florida heat . . . Thick thighs rubbing together all night . . . Did I wear a breathable thong? . . . Did I wear a cute thong?!

She looked up at me and said, "You're so damn beautiful," as she pulled down my thong. My ass got stuck to the leather seats, and I laughed at the sound it made when I thrusted my pelvis upward so she could slide them off.

Okay, I thought. *I can't smell anything from that gesture. I think I'm good.*

Xio reached back toward the ignition and started the car so she could turn the AC on low, then reached over to lock the door and cut off the headlights. She looked back at my pussy like she was starving.

When she wasn't looking, I touched my labia to see what she was giving. *Hmm, okay, we straight!*

She moved my dress up again and looked directly in my eyes as her tongue dove in between my lips. I instinctively pulled back, and her hands locked onto my thighs, signaling for me to not go anywhere.

Shit. Her tongue felt incredible; she was moving her head ever so slightly, but her tongue was doing all the work. She stimulated my labia, and then all the attention was on my clit. I was in disbelief. *Had we fucked before, and I didn't remember? How could this be possible?*

It had always been hard for me to cum from head only, but Xio had me on edge after two or three minutes. I let out a soft whimper and then a moan. I grabbed onto the arm thingy parents grab when they're teaching you how to drive and being dramatic. I opened my eyes again, and her eyes hadn't left my body. She said, "Hmm?" circling my clit, and the sound vibrated off my clit with enough force to make me shudder. I moaned again.

"Shit . . . Xio . . . I . . ." I managed to get out between labored breaths.

"Hmmm?" She hummed longer on my clit, making me want to explode all over her face.

"Shit! Uh . . . I . . . Okay," I whined, surrendering.

I couldn't believe Xio was about to make me cum in the motel parking lot of pH. Yes, pH was attached to a motel.

I asked for her to put a finger inside me. She shook her head and said, "Mmm mmm," her lips vibrating on my clit again. She raised her head and said, "My hands are dirty, baby," and went right back to sucking my clit.

. I was losing fast. Melting into her spell. I was on the edge and she knew it. My swollen clit was being cradled by her tongue when I realized I was cumming. I was hers.

I collapsed in her back seat.

"Yum," she said with a smile. She got out the back seat and into the driver's seat. "My parents are out of town, are we okay to go there? Kyss already told me you have to work at three tomorrow, so I'll drive you back in the morning if that's cool."

"Umm yeah," I said, still out of breath and slightly shaking. "That's fine, I just need a second to . . ."

"Stay back there, baby, my house is only twenty minutes away. I . . ."

Xio's voice faded away.

I woke up slowly to the sound of the garage opening and jumped upright. Xio didn't make me have just any orgasm— she triggered one of my narcoleptic nuts that I usually only get from vaginal orgasms. What the fuck!

Xio laughed and yelled, "Dammmnnn, I got you like that!"

"Shut up, I had a . . . long day," I said, looking down and realizing my dress was still up and my panties were on the center console.

When we walked inside, a huge rottweiler barked from inside an enormous cage.

"Momma's sweet baby," Xio cooed. The dog was twice her size.

"I know people always say this, but Romeo really is friendly, and I have to let him out since my parents left early this morning and he's been cooped up," Xio pleaded.

"I trust you! Plus, it looks like y'all could cover incidentals." I scanned the massive living room. I could barely hear Xio from across it.

Xio chuckled and let him out of the cage. Romeo didn't pay me any mind and ran straight to the glass doors, the outdoor pool reflecting in the glass.

"My room's upstairs, first room on your left. You can use my bathroom to freshen up," Xio shouted.

"I tasted okay, right?" I asked uneasily.

"No, actually," Xio said, her voice serious. She walked toward me. "You tasted exquisite. Delightful. Like pussy marinated just for me. A little sweaty and very sweet." She paused just before reaching my lips.

"If you wanted a taste all you had to do was ask. I'm not stingy," she teased as I reached up to kiss her and she jolted her head back playfully.

I pushed her chest back and she kissed me quickly.

"Romeo has a thing for digging holes. My dad will kill me if I'm not out there with him," she said, sprinting toward the door. Outside, she yelled, "Romeooooo," as if she had caught him mid-dig.

Upstairs, I marveled at Xio's Eve posters, her jewelry boxes, and the ocean wallpaper that gave her room a vacation bungalow vibe. She had about ten plants in her room, and I was impressed until I realized she was a full-time student who played soccer and her mom was probably caring for these beauties. I found the bathroom and immediately dived into a cold shower.

Florida fall was just like summer. It was October and it was still ninety-two degrees. The ice-cold water felt so good on my body. I lost myself for a moment thinking I had spent too long in the shower, but Xio didn't appear to be in the room or waiting for me, so I took my time.

I called out for Xio to bring me a towel and when I didn't hear anything, I just used hers. I dried off, used some of her Clearasil moisturizer, and sat on her bed airing out. I closed my eyes for a second and heard Xio coming up the stairs.

I flipped over to my side so I could look somewhat ready for her. *Play it cool, Trae!* I lay back just as she entered the room.

"Why are you sitting in the dark?" she asked.

"I didn't think we needed any lights," I said smoothly.

"Fair enough! I'm going to take a quick shower and join you." Everything she said sounded so sultry.

Ten minutes or so later, I was awoken by Xio straddling me, saying, "You even sleep cute. I hope you're not too tired for another round."

This was my first time seeing her fully naked. I wanted to suck on her collarbones. Her breasts were succulent, confident, full C's, and her torso went on for forever.

Before I could answer her fingers were parting my lips.

I let out a soft moan.

"I guess not," she snickered, feeling how wet I was.

She pushed my legs farther apart. I pulled her onto me, forcing her to revive me with her tongue the way she had at pH.

She played with my clit and ran her middle finger up and down my labia until I shuddered.

"I want to feel you around my fingers," she whispered. "Can I . . ."

"Yes," I begged. Probably in a not-so-sexy way.

The next thing I knew her middle and ring fingers were teasing my opening. She deepened her kiss and pushed her fingers inside of me at the same time.

I tensed up for a second and felt her fingers curve to fit my body.

Xio looked at me like she wanted to say something. I couldn't say anything; my pussy tightened and relaxed around her motions. I threw my head back and stared at the Xiomara airbrush sign she had over her closet.

Xio's pace increased and so did my moans.

"Shit . . . I . . . Xio . . . I . . . Baby . . . damn," was all I could get out.

She pulled her fingers out and my stomach collapsed.

"Shit!" I moaned begging for her to return. "Please . . ."

"Shhh . . . Get on your knees and turn around," she demanded, without taking her eyes off me.

She grabbed my neck and kissed it softly. *This bitch is out of her mind.*

Xio stood up and pulled out two toys, still in their boxes. "Which one, baby?" she whispered.

I pointed at the flesh-toned silicone dick with a very realistic vein pulsing through it. She went into the bathroom and told me not to move while she cleaned our new friend.

Is it crazy to want head again? There's no way she can make me cum like that twice.

Xio returned to the bed, holding the dildo in one hand and lube in the other. She kissed my ass and asked me to spread my legs a bit more. I obliged.

Xio sat behind me, parted my lips with her left hand and held the toy with her right hand, and asked me if I was ready. I moaned, "Yes, baby. I want you to fuck me."

She was inside of me, and the girth of the toy was perfect. I felt my body forming to the shape of it as she went smoothly in and out of my pussy. I looked back at her and she was lost.

Staring at my pussy, her mouth was slightly parted and then she met my eyes again.

"Xio, damn . . . I . . . Yes . . . Oh my god, yes."

I can't fucking believe she has me face down, ass up, like the Ludacris song!

"Please . . . Right there, Xio . . . Yes . . . There . . . there, uh, stay there," I moaned as I met her rhythm, swaying my hips back toward her.

I was a squirter. I found out in the eleventh grade and since then I had been terrified of how to let my partners know, so usually I didn't. It was messy and over-fixated-on in porn. If I wasn't fully comfortable with the person, I wouldn't squirt anyway, so there was no point in bringing it up. Especially because sometimes sex got too focused on *trying* to make me squirt versus seeing if I'm enjoying shit.

Yet here was Xio, her face inches from my pussy, and I could feel the build-up. Actually, at one point I could hear it and I tried hard to hold back. I arched my back a bit more so the toy could touch my pelvic floor. I wasn't going to be able to hold it for much longer. *This bitch knows what she's doing!*

"Xio . . . I . . ." I screamed as I reached back to pull the toy out of me. My juices poured out of me and I collapsed. "Damn, baby," Xio said, sounding excited.

I lay face down, trying to catch my breath. "Fuck . . ."

"Uh, wow!" Xio said while caressing and kissing my ass, my lower back, and then my shoulder blades. "You know, I feel like you want some more, and I'm ready when you are." She grinned. "I'm thirsty."

I thought she meant she was going to go get water or something from downstairs. Instead, she tapped my ass and told me to raise myself up. *Oh no the fuck she's not.*

I lifted my pelvis and she slid her head in the space between the bed and my pussy. Might I add, she was fully in the wet spot I'd left, and seemed to give zero fucks about it.

"Lemme drink you," she requested.

I repositioned myself so I could ride her properly. "Atta girl," she said as I lowered myself onto her face.

Instantly her tongue found its way to my sweet spot. We were back in the car. I was losing myself to her again.

"Damn . . . Xio . . . Okay . . . shit, uh . . ." I moaned. I grabbed her head in frustration because there was no way my body was letting her take me like this. Her arms stretched upward to my breasts and back down to my thighs.

"Uhh, baby . . . I'm about to!" I yelped.

Xio slid a finger in. I looked down at her. My request from the car, being met. I loved knowing that my person could feel me cumming. I moaned and almost collapsed. Xio held my thighs down so I could cum into her mouth. *This sick bitch.*

She kept her tongue steady on my clit as I came. I was sweaty, shaking, and really wanted Xio to know this was all her doing. When my body settled, she released my thighs and I leaned over, unstraddled her face, and fell out on the other side of the bed.

"Fuck," I sighed.

"What?" Xio asked.

"Nothing, I just . . . You know you're still in my wet spot, right?" I asked.

"And that's where I'm going to stay," she said, reaching out her hand toward mine.

Some Like It Fraught

Diana Thornton

EVE ADAMS (Eva Kotchever)

BEAUTIFUL, POPULAR DIANA. Penetrating, charming—wicked blue eyes. The perfect woman vampire of women.

Discards her ex-lovers with a grin and movement of her beautiful hands, brushes the unpleasant memories aside with ease and grace: "Can't be annoyed with notes sent by those I once loved they come too often, and in bunches," she says.

"I never read them. My maid reads them first, and if she finds something worthwhile, I let her read a passage or two for me."

Each new love is Diana's first love. Each new love she meets with childish enthusiasm, powerful passion, and forgetfulness. She honey-moons in fashionable hotels of old New York. If it happens to be a hard winter, it is Miami, a capricious spring, it's Bermuda, and sometimes, Paris.

Her honey-moons last for days, sometimes weeks, all uninterrupted. "What I want, I take," she says, and she possesses the power and charm of doing so. "Ice water, more cracked ice," is her popular demand of the bellboy, who stands wistfully in the doorway sometimes to peek at her new lover, for she is well known, it's not her first stop there, but the boy courteously obeys, courteously takes the order, for he knows there is a generous tip coming.

Diana never failed yet to win the affection of the one she wanted. They all yield to her, and they all leave heart-broken, when she commands them to go.

Her present love is perhaps just as beautiful as Diana herself. Gracia is her name, and the name well-suits her.

Gracia has been just as fickle as Diana, and there are many with broken hearts that she has left, and left them with an easy conscience.

But the two seem to belong to each other; the honey-moon is lasting quite an unusual while. Is Diana losing her power to lure? Or is this present flame stronger than all the others and therefore powerfully lasting!!!

So girls, your chance is gone!! Look elsewhere for your happiness!!

Pale Horse

AUGUST CLARKE

THE PALLBEARERS WEAR miniskirts; it's what Anaïs would've wanted. They brace her body in a box across their bare shoulders, mink lashes downcast, a vaudeville parody of Catholic grief that produces in the vicar a look of brash, delirious misery. He trails behind the casket girls, muttering to himself. He is the only man in attendance. Anaïs has a living father, but not even her favorites know his name.

Moira keeps her distance. She lounges against an obelisk, flicks the end of her spliff. Her lipstick rings the paper. The pigment matches her nails. The obelisk is a fleshy pink granite, feels cold and slick against her spine: downside of a backless dress.

She watches the procession, eyes half lidded. So many columnar thighs! Anaïs's own walking mausoleum, composed of and attended by a phalanx of weepy-eyed femmes. She would've lapped this up. *She was too material for Heaven*, Moira thinks, and it is a comfort to imagine her wakeful and watching from inside of her box. She thinks about her body moving. Not rigor mortis, something smoother. She imagines her toying with her Y-incision's corset lacing in the hot pink coffin darkness. Anaïs gloating, Anaïs writhing, foaming with formaldehyde and making Bambi eyes at God.

The procession stops at its designated hole. Moira watches the girls slowly lower her box into the ground. Suddenly, it's a funeral for real. There are lilies everywhere. Heavy petals curl out of the mist and heave perfume.

Moira peels herself off the obelisk and makes her way to the edge of the flock. Dewy grass licks her ankles. It's poor stiletto terrain. She arranges herself between a redhead in furs and a girl dressed in jet-black spandex, and it's then that she feels her absence.

187

The vicar mouths something about suffering; Moira doesn't hear it. She's been so good at not looking, at keeping her eyes to herself, at feigning the absence of her name in her mind such that a cool indifference might be maintained, but it cannot be maintained, her will is gone. A desperation shaped like hunger usurps it. Her skull buzzes. She scans the crowd, hunts through the mourners for a golden wisp of boyishness. A sport coat among the bodices. Ronnie has to be here. What kind of widow would skip?

A woman shoulders the vicar out of the way. *Chelsea so-and-so*, Moira thinks. Drinks brandy and works at a bank. She's brawny and vital, a strong contralto with a mole penciled under her left eye. "We come together to remember our fallen comrade. Anaïs was the worst of us, and I adored her for it. Adored her completely! Any sane woman would. She demanded luxury from bleakness and shared it wantonly with anybody who breathed her air. Only woman I've ever known who could make the ICU feel like a VIP lounge. She loved pleasure and indulgence and pain, despite pain. I'm glad the pain is over. I have a hunch she still lives. She's in our hearts and livers and vocal tics. We'll carry her inside us until the sun consumes the earth."

Moira rubs the gooseflesh down her arms. The eulogy feels sentimental and shouldn't ruffle her, but the truth gnaws. Bits of Anaïs did snap off inside every woman she entertained. Phantom fingers still worm around Moira's own belly. Otherwise, she might not have come.

She shakes herself. She takes a drag. She puffs smoke and thinks, *Where is Ronnie?*

A second woman replaces Chelsea. Some scrawny librarian type. She tearfully provides anecdotes about Anaïs's dread magnanimity and the times they cammed together. Work is how many of the women present met. How Moira met most of them, anyway. Chat sites in common, double bookings, the odd drink after shoots. Ms. Librarian flips up her knee-length tartan skirt, reveals a scorpion tattoo that spans her hip, matching the one on Annie's breastbone.

Annie! Anaïs would've strangled her for that.

Ash tumbles from Moira's spliff. It dots the redhead's furs. Moira takes her last hit and drops it, grinds the paper to oblivion beneath her red bottoms. She leans her cheek against Black Spandex's shoulder. She hisses—fuck a whisper—"Have you seen Ronette around?"

"Oh, she's slumped over there by the priest." She punctuates with snaps of her bubble gum. Bright, fast, clipped, coastal. She doesn't look at Moira but points across the gravesite.

Moira jerks her head up.

She locks eyes on her sweet shape.

Ronette Silverson. Ronnie herself. Her beauty is hard and innocent, hypnotic in its earnestness. Joan of Arc among the courtiers. She's got that obstinate glow. She stands (hardly slumped!) in the vicar's shadow, collar mussed, sleeves rucked, one fist lost in her short-cropped ringlets. Gives the look of her holding her own head upright. There are no tears on her face. Her brows steeple, and her cheeks and the whites of her eyes burn pink, but her look is not quite one of misery. There's something else. She makes no sound. A third woman steps up to memorialize Anaïs, and Ronnie does not look at her. She stares dead-eyed into the hole where Anaïs is waiting. It's a marvel the dirt doesn't blister.

Moira stretches. She reaches down, puts her wrist at Ronnie's eye level, waggles her fingertips. She hooks them and splays them, casts odd shadows on the grass. She makes a scene, but makes it small—a private, overlookable tease.

Ronnie's attention flickers. It lifts out of the Styx and fixes on Moira's knuckles.

Moira curls her hand, nails to heel, and jerks her thumb in the parking lot's direction.

"Anaïs was the best friend I ever had," says some stranger. "I wish I was more like her. She was so lovely. Nobody has ever been lovely like that."

Ronnie's face falls, sharpens. She turns up her collar to the wind and murmurs something in the vicar's ear, then steps backward, turns her face away. She strides off from the funeral party. Moira watches her make for her car.

Far off, the car door opens. Ronnie folds herself behind the wheel, slams the door, and waits. The sun is behind her, silhouettes her, obscures the particularities of her expression.

"It's like Anaïs always said," another stranger offers.

A moment passes. Ronnie doesn't drive away.

Moira smooths her hair, rolls her shoulders, and takes off with a casual strut. Bouncy, easy with her own sick gravity. Her heels don't touch the ground. The inside of her head is on fire.

Across the graveyard, between dirty ribbons and strewn silk flowers, Moira approaches Ronette Silverson's convertible. The engine purrs. Ronnie lolls her head back, flicks her pink eyes up at Moira. Whatever vile cosmic trick grants people ridiculously long eyelashes has made an Adonis of Ronnie. She has lashes like a calf. They brush her eyebrows when she looks up like this. Infuriating in a rival.

Ronnie's windows are down. Moira reaches to touch Ronnie's shoulder. Ronnie's breathing hard. Her pulse flutters against Moira's fingertips, even with the fabric between them.

"Moira," says Ronnie, in place of hello.

"Hello, baby." Moira smiles with teeth. Some lick of smoke must've gotten lost inside her, snakes out between her teeth now, colors her tone. "You looked like you could use a change of scenery."

Ronnie scrubs a hand over her jaw. She doesn't speak, takes a moment to search Moira's face for something. Bad intentions, probably. Moira smiles wider. She imagines that she can see the Ronnie-on-Ronnie wrestling match inside her, see the grand Shakespearean violence playing out between her head and heart. Swords banging in her throat. Or is the front in her belly? Ronnie closes her eyes. She sucks in, sinks against her leather seat. She rests her free palm on the gearshift. She says, "Get in or don't."

Moira tightens her grip and Ronnie shudders.

She lets go and circles the hood, climbs inside.

Ronnie pulls out of the lot. The cemetery recedes, and the towering pines flanking the road blur to nothing. Ronnie drives too fast, and Moira lets it happen. Neither of them fumbles for the radio.

Turning a corner, Ronnie says, "I thought you hated me."

"I've never hated you."

"Resented me, then. She left you for me, didn't she?"

Moira examines her bangs in the rearview mirror. "Sins of the father."

Ronnie curls her lip. "I didn't know she was seeing you when it started. I wouldn't have fooled around with her if I had known."

That's interesting. She had no problem staying after she learned. Funny world! "This isn't about Anaïs. This is about you. I worry about you."

The car goes a little faster. "Can you keep a secret?"

No. "Of course."

"I was going to leave her." Ronnie blinks. "She forgot my birthday, did you know that? She never told me when she'd be home late; she'd sometimes vanish for days and reappear and act like nothing happened. She'd get horribly jealous if I so much as mentioned another woman, but she's got this rotation of fifty thousand girls on call for whenever I wasn't enough. I know she wasn't well. I know, I know, she drank too much. I know there were signs, and that I must have missed them, or overlooked them, dismissed them as theater to get a rise out of me. I loved her so desperately, and she didn't let me help her, and I despise her for it." She cracks a smile. She shakes her head. "Do you think I'm awful now?"

Moira reaches for her lighter. She flicks it, lets it cough, then stows it away. Ronnie had been the special one. She had been Anaïs's favorite. She alone could tame her into monogamy, or at least extended coupled commitment. There was talk they'd get married! A real wedding, virgin white dresses and champagne, legislation, the works. Moira looks at her, at this splotchy tomboy cherub bastard, and hunger gnaws again. "Don't you worry your sweet head." She puts her hand on Ronnie's thigh. "Try as you might, you'll never be even half as rotten as me."

Ronnie makes a strangled sound. Sweat pearls on her brow. Her knees drift apart, and she turns into her driveway, Anaïs's driveway, and stops the car. She's panting. The engine carries on inside her chest. Her brows knot up. She stares straight ahead and drops her grip on the wheel, guides Moira's hand up just a little higher.

They get out of the car. Through doors and doors, then up the stairs, Moira's body thrums like a plucked harp string. Her pulse is percussive. Details flow over her, become kaleidoscopic and indistinct. Bottle-green wallpaper, meaty houseplants, crown molding over a mahogany banister. It's a spiral of wilderness, it's Eden in ruins. Time accordions and Moira swallows once, then stands somehow in Anaïs's home. Her vampire's lair. Down the hall, around the corner, in Anaïs's bedroom, with the same creamy sheets she'd had back then. Bed unmade. A Wegener hung on the wall beside a spill of frilly curtains. Her heels on a rack over Ronnie's oxblood brogues. A mirror strapped to the ceiling.

Moira is high. Her high feels like melting.

She turns on Anaïs's lover and takes her jaw in both her hands.

Ronnie's mouth pops open. The pinkness is overwhelming. Her cheekbones burning, her eyes, her lips, the flash of nervous tongue between her teeth. Moira runs her thumb along Ronnie's bottom lip. She rolls it down, exposes the neat, mean line of her teeth. Softness is an intoxicant. How malleable she is, how bendable! How she tinges the air with her body's own radiant pink! The submission feels wrathful, negatively charged. Ronnie's eyes flash, and she opens wider, sucks Moira's thumb into her mouth. She skims her teeth against her knuckle.

In heels, Moira has six inches over her. She kisses the top of her head. She slips out her thumb, fits her palm over Ronnie's nose and mouth, and presses. Ronnie's body jolts. She holds her there, a quick, gentle smothering, then eases back and lets Ronnie gasp, lets her sigh, sink into herself. Still in reach, Ronnie leans forward. She licks the head and heart lines on her hand. She moves her wrist, then the pads of her fingers against Ronnie's lips, and Ronnie devours them, takes a third when offered, making a low, brittle sound.

"Such a good girl," Moira says. She wishes it was a lie. When Ronnie slips her hands along either side of Moira's spine, she sways into the touch, hums into Ronnie's hairline. Ronnie rings her ribs, slips under the dress to touch her belly. Moira pulls her hand from Ronnie's mouth. She watches it sparkle. Ronnie kisses down her neck, brushes fabric sideways, put her teeth in Moira's neck and collar and exposed breasts.

Moira slides her hand under the waistband of Ronnie's trousers. She drags her nails through her curls. Ronnie jumps and bites down harder. Moira says, "More?"

She bucks against Moira's touch. "Or I'll die."

Moira smiles crookedly. She glides her fingertips in lazy circles, alive and untethered in soft and slick and pink and pink, lets Ronnie undress around her work. The touch is never broken. By the time Ronnie stands naked, Moira has struck some chord, and Ronnie seizes her by the back of her neck and screams into her breastbone. Her body shudders, the bones rattle inside her. Her thighs, her shoulders tremble. Moira thinks she's crying. Moira takes her time easing up.

How lovely Ronnie is in shambles. She thinks of lilies nodding. She pushes her backward onto Anaïs's bed; she drags her own dress over her shoulders and casts it aside; she looks down on Ronette Silverson and thinks she understands. She understands why her darling would leave her for her. Anaïs was sick and Moira made her worse. Moira presses bruises. She does not make; she does not mend. Shivering Ronnie, bright and clear, is sweeter and better than Moira. For Anaïs, she was better. Anaïs was just like her. There was no good way that this could end.

She saunters toward the bed, heels clacking, liquid and sure. She pulls her ankles to the edge. She crawls over Ronnie's body. Her tennis-toned calves, her slippery thighs, her belly and flat chest and long ropes of arms, she drinks in the sight of her, conceives of gazing as a kind of conquest. She pinches her pinker. She gloats at the noises she makes. She had been so jealous of sweet, earnest Ronnie! She'd despised her, mulled over her constantly with a stolen, briny love. The hilarious, seething injustice that Anaïs had to die before she could kiss her, that this mangled sweetness was all they had. The cruelty that Anaïs couldn't be made to watch. That Anaïs could still be cruel.

Moira arranges herself on Ronnie's jaw. She rakes her nails down her skull, curls her lip, grinds down on her. Ronnie's crying properly. She throws her arms around Moira's hips, keeps her close, moves her mouth. Her eyes droop half shut. Those long lashes glitter.

Moira feels good. Nothing feels so good! She lolls back her head, lolls back and then farther back, gazes up at the mirror above her bed. She admires the way her hair spills off her shoulders. She bites her blue lips, bats her lashes. The stitching between her breasts pulls taut, and she toys with her fretting, runs a nail down the puckers of ruined waxy skin. She has never been so open, so empty and pickled and good. There is so much room inside of her. Her body can hold so much love. Ronnie grazes her clit with her teeth and Moira reels with how she adores her, knows that she could adore only her, her alone. Ronnie, Ronnie, sweet, awful baby Ronnie. Moira's so close! She'll need a ride back to the memorial service. Her head foams, she can't breathe, her heart stammers. A fantasy, dripping: Ronnie's gonna drive too fast. Moira rolls her hips. Death is near. Death loves edging. She gasps a laugh. She thinks of her velvet-lined box, about warm triggers and Ronette Silverson. It hurts, and she hurts, and the mirror should crack with the sounds she makes. She imagines this as Ronnie's eulogy. She imagines Anaïs smoking underground.

Catacomb Voice

OCTAVIA C. SAENZ

I LOOK UP from the directions on my phone to find myself facing a cloud belt of concrete shapes, like an enormous death mask placed between brownstones, and I'm shocked Roy would host her orgy in such a garish place. Last event this group organized—they call themselves Catholic Guilt—was in a warehouse, and though they dressed it up nicely I really didn't get the impression they had a budget for a place like this. I bet the presence of all these dykes and trannies and old queens is lowering the median property value on this block.

At the door, a dandy with a jawline like a cliff asks me for proof of a negative test. I jokingly flash the picture of my STD battery results to get a flirtatious smile from them, and then show the actual COVID negative test from an hour ago.

"You're cool to go in," says the dandy. "Enjoy!"

Past the curtain of tinsel and red streamers, I find a foyer full of bitches in leather gear holding onto their drinks, catching up on gossip while swaying to some hard beat. Past them is a staircase, and past that a bougie kitchen—Edison bulbs hung low over the granite-top counter, ugh, you know, like, the whole deal—where two butches in white button-up shirts serve drinks and balloons full of laughing gas. On the couch next to me, a pair of bootblack dykes make out next to everyone's discarded Docs. One of them wears an LCD collar that scrolls the word GIRL interminably.

I go up the stairs. These places always have, like, rooftop gardens or whatever the fuck. The next floor seems to be occupied entirely by the line for the bathroom (women, amirite?) and I get stuck behind a duo of blonds in bunny costumes talking to a clocky dark academia bottom in front of them.

"So you know the host?" asks the shorter bunny, whose face is covered in piercings. She's white, and maybe cis—but I've learned at these events that my trans radar is not as good as I think it is.

"Yeah, we used to be in the same support group." The dark academia girl is really tall, and I can see stubble on her jaw, and she's gorgeous. I've danced up on her at a few parties; we're cordial.

"And they live here?" the other bunny asks, looking between the two other girls like she's tryna catch up. Her face has that pillowy look girls get from lots of filler. It suits her.

"Yeah, she lives—well, she was living here with like eight other people until recently," says the dark academia girl, running a hand through her brown hair. "They're getting kicked out, hence the orgy."

"Fuck yeah, fuck landlords!" the short bunny cheers, raising her bottle in the air, even though I bet there's more than one landlord in her immediate family.

"Fuck landlords." The other bunny nods, sips from her drink and swallows, looking away.

They part just enough that I can get through and continue upstairs, past another floor of women milling around—there's a coat check in one room and what looks like a sex swing and a metal table in the other room. The opening notes of several different songs stutter through from that room, like someone is skipping through a playlist.

I push through and go up one last set of stairs into a little sitting room that opens out to the rooftop. No garden, just treated concrete and lights pointing down from the railings. A pair of Asian women in leather catsuits set up a suspension rig at one end of the space. At the other end, a trio of Catholic schoolgirls stand bent over against the rails, asses exposed to a woman in a leather miniskirt and blazer holding a bouquet of flowers. The schoolgirls count up to ten while their domme whips the bouquet against their thighs.

Beyond them, past the constraints of the rooftop, and past the roofs of the neighboring buildings, the Hudson glimmers under the downtown spires, and the sky billows over us in tones of dirty gray.

I find a patio couch with enough room for me, and I sit down to smoke joint number one of the night. At the other end, two masked Black girls open a pack of cigarettes. The Bushwick sky fills with smoke from our combined exhalations.

A few puffs in, the one farthest from me asks me what's in it.

"Just sativa, Egyptian blue lotus, skullcap, and then, like, the typical herbs: mullein, damiana," I say, taking too large a hit and coughing, like an asshole. "Oh, and holy basil."

"She's smoking that witchy mix," says the one next to me, giggling and leaning back against her friend.

I offer them the joint. They look at each other, giggle, and refuse. Some joke between them I'm not privy to. But they clearly feel guilty about laughing at me, so they excuse themselves to smoke on the corner opposite from the suspension couple.

"Don't take it personal," says a voice behind me, making me jump. A woman stands there, entirely naked, nipples crinkled in the chill, her long silver hair contrasting against her clay-brown skin. "Those two once had a bad trip from one of my own herbal mixes."

I don't know what to say, so I nod and take another too-large hit, holding it in so as not to cough when I offer her the joint. She takes it and rounds the patio couch to squat next to me.

"What's your name?" she asks, passing back the joint.

"Josefina, but you can call me Jo," I say. That's flirting, right? I've never tried to flirt with a nude stranger. "How do you know them?"

"Oh, I know everyone," she says, taking the joint again and giving it another puff. "I'm with the group, I'm one of the hosts. Shanon and Ziomara have been coming to these parties for like two years now."

"Oh, so have I," I say, doing a French inhale in the hopes it'll impress her. "I'm friends with Roy—well, we used to date. Or hook up. It was unclear."

The woman laughs, then shakes her head. "That Roy, what a lady-killer. Have you seen her tonight? I wanna say hi."

I look around, trying to remember if I even know what she's wearing tonight. "I think I heard her on the floor below, with the sex swing?"

When I look back around to give her the joint again, though, there's no one there. Only a trailing wisp of smoke that could have been a strand of her hair. Maybe I put too much skullcap in this mix. Puff.

It's a pity, bitch was hot. I thought I could cruise her. But then, I only just got here. I guess sometimes I wanna get my first hookup of the night out of the way quickly so I can feel sexy and cool and desirable. Puff. Wouldn't that be a disservice to whoever that first hookup ends up being? And that silver-haired girl, she would've deserved my best. If she was real, which she might not have been. Puff.

I think tonight I just want to bask in this until whoever comes along sweeps me off my feet. Winter was long, and I haven't been around this many louche dykes in months. Puff. So I'll enjoy myself, drink in the sights and sounds and—you can't judge me—smells, and hey, even if I don't hook up with anyone, I will have charged up on enough slutty lesbian energy to last me 'til the next party.

I smoke until my head is swimming. I watch the suspension couple pinch and twist at each other until the sub is red and trembling, and the headmistress beat her schoolgirls until there's not a single petal left on her bouquet. Then, with a nod at Shanon and Ziomara, I leave the rooftop.

I don't see the naked woman in the sex-swing room, but its inhabitants have finally picked a song and are lazily making out to it. Roy fiddles with the bolts on the contraption; her long black hair draping over her face prevents her from seeing me.

"Roy," I say.

She looks up, her big green eyes meeting mine, and for a second I think she might be as nonchalant as me, but then her face erupts into a smile. Her voice, like a musical saw, whines out of her throat: "Jo, my baby! I'm so happy you're here!"

We hug, and then hold each other at arm's length for the customary barrage of compliments. Roy compliments my smoky eye makeup; I compliment her outfit made entirely of elastic straps and plastic crosses. She tells me I look cunty in my black minidress; I tell her she looks like evil Leeloo Dallas, and so on.

"So, are you having fun yet?" Roy asks, hands on her enviably protruding hips. She wiggles her eyebrows at me.

"I'm still just exploring," I say, making suggestive eyes at her. About what, I don't know. I want to ask about that silver-haired woman. Instead I say, "It's a gorgeous house! Sad to hear y'all're moving out."

I expect Roy to groan dramatically, maybe flip her hair or something. But she looks nauseous for a second—or, wait, is that sadness? Her body slumps in place, and she looks away from me. When she speaks, it's the lowest I've ever heard her voice go. "Yeah, it's really sad. After my post-op overdose we were able to keep the lease going, and I thought everything would be fine. None of us knew Ximona would do what she did."

I step in close to her, putting a hand on her shoulder. It's weird, I didn't even know Roy was capable of feelings like this. But then, maybe she's just always been guarded. "Do you want to talk about it?"

Roy shakes her head, then finally meets my eyes again. For a second, I can see the stillness in her, the worry. And then it's gone. A smile creeps back onto her thin lips and she shakes her head again. "Girl, we are here to party. Dead roommates or not!"

I laugh at that, not because it's funny but because I'm nervous about what I just saw. You see it a lot in this crowd, the Bushwick club kids and crust punks. They're like Peter Pan forgetting his friends as soon as the pirates get them. You'd think death is contagious, the way they run from it. But she's right: We are here to party.

"Has anyone else come in to say hi?" I ask, realizing how weird I must sound.

She shakes her head, her smile as solid as the swing she leans on.

"No? Completely naked, with silver hair?"

At that, Roy smirks like I'm pulling a prank on her. "Sounds like my ex-roommate. No, I haven't seen anyone like that tonight. Hey, come back in like ten minutes, I'm almost done setting up. Everyone's gonna run a train on me on this swing!"

Roy has a way of ending conversations without really telling you to fuck off that used to make it hard to pin her down and talk about what we were doing. Tonight, though, I'm grateful for the out. I leave, bypassing the bathroom line, though not without noting that the bunny girls and dark academia bottom are still there.

Downstairs, I dance to a remix of Britney Spears's "Hold It Against Me" that's cut up to make it sound like Britney is singing, "If we could escape the body somehow, would you?" The music is dreamy and sparkling, like Britney herself has dissolved all around me, the DJ, and the lone twink giving it his all in a silk robe and a leather cap. He and I float around each other, knees bending in time to the beat, both of us working up a sweat. The thing about dancing at a sex party is no one is watching you unless they want to fuck you, so you can kind of just let go and twirl, hop, undulate, and forget you ever belonged to anything but the song that's playing.

I spin, and on my third turn I see the silver hair and eyes caked in mascara. When I stop, though, I find no one familiar in the crowd. Only a strange absence, an empty space between people, or a silence in their conversations.

The song ends abruptly, and the DJ, who's been talking to one of the butch bartenders, scrambles over to her table to play the next thing. By then, I'm already headed back upstairs. Whether it's been ten minutes or not, I feel ready to watch Roy— my ex-situationship, a role no one has rules for and which has yet to be codified by Yeti-bottle lesbians—get fucked by countless strangers.

Once more, I'm stuck in the tangle of the bathroom line. The bunny girls are nowhere to be seen, and neither is the dark academia bottom. Shanon and Ziomara stand a few spots ahead of me, both of them on their phones. When I call out to them they look up, and the crowd parts to let me through, but only as far as they are. Ah well. I can mingle for a second.

"Witchy girl," says one of them. I'm assuming Shanon.

"Call me Jo," I say, doing a peace sign, which they mimic with wide smiles. They introduce themselves, too. Shanon has pink box braids, and Ziomara's wearing a one-piece made of scraps of fabric held together with jump rings.

"I'm friends with Roy," I say, even though they hadn't asked. But mentioning the hosts is always a good way to start a conversation.

"Friends, or like . . ." Ziomara trails off, then rolls her eyes, eliciting laughs from me and Shanon.

"We used to know Ximona," says Shanon. "But I guess now we'd say it's Roy, too."

"God, no," Ziomara shakes her head. "Promise me we'll make friends with some of the other hosts. No offense, Jo."

"None taken," I say. "What's the deal with Ximona? Was she, like, kicked out of the group?"

Shanon and Ziomara look at each other, and my stomach drops. I've said something stupid, haven't I? While the two of them struggle to figure out what to say, I rummage through my memories of the night for what it might be I got wrong.

"Listen," says Shanon, laying her hand on my arm. "Whole group is messy, right? Roy's in and out of rehab, that girl Alina has had, like, what, two psychotic breaks?"

"Just the one," says Ziomara. "That second time was a revenge sectioning."

I shake my head. If anyone could get this group's oral histories, it could win a Pulitzer.

"Ximona, though, she was supposed to be the normal one," says Shanon, lowering her voice. "I mean, witchy, like you. But she wasn't as messy as everyone else who lived here."

"Which is why I don't buy that she—" Ziomara starts, but she's shushed by Shanon. The two glare at each other for a second, and then Ziomara continues, her voice barely above a whisper, "They all say she killed herself, and I don't buy it."

The uneasy feeling in my stomach travels up my spine. While I try to regain my ability to talk, the two start arguing with each other, lowering their voices as the other women in the bathroom line pay closer attention. I can only get bits and pieces, something about a botched gender reassignment surgery—or, no, a botched recovery from GRS, and the cis women in the group not really understanding, or else being transphobic about the whole situation. And a death, in this very house, although they don't agree on the circumstances. Rumors are a slippery thing: They take the shape of their speakers' own assumptions. It's no wonder the entire group's being kicked out of the building, with two institutionalizations, an overdose, and a suicide. But I don't say any of that out loud. Shanon and Ziomara seem to have forgotten I'm here, and I don't fully blame them.

The line moves and I make my way through.

One more flight of stairs, and I pass the room with the coat check, then saunter into the sex-swing room. Instead of Roy, though, I find my attention consumed by a pair of hyper-femmes in medical-play gear on the metal table across from the sex swing.

On the table lies a lithe femme sub in supermodel proportions, her powerful shoulders tucked in under her leather ties, hands praying over beautiful bolt-ons with a spattering of freckles. Her face is covered in bandages; between the gauze shows only her big brown eyes, puffy lips, and the bottom of her septum. Her lashes flutter long and black.

The femme's domme stands behind her, quickly but calmly braiding up her hair, a white whip dangling from one hand. When she's done braiding her hair, weaving a red lace ribbon through it, she adjusts her robin's-egg-blue corset minidress and thigh-high, white leather boots, pulls on a nurse's cap, and pops on a pair of red-rimmed glasses. She hides the whip behind a clip-board and walks around the table, stopping once to throw a knowing glance at me.

The femme's bandages come off. Her nurse dominatrix is pinching the soft skin of her cheek, pulling at it—inches and inches of putty-soft skin—telling her how botched she looks after her filler dissolve. She squirms out orgasm after orgasm, her boots trembling at the end of the table.

When I look over my shoulder at the sex swing, I see the dark academia girl pumping away at Roy and revise my nickname for her to Vers. The line behind her isn't as long as I had pictured—or, indeed, as long as maybe Roy herself had pictured—but there's still a twinge of something in my chest at the sight of it. It can't be jealousy or envy, since I know I could hop in and do her like the old days, and I'm not as much of a bottom as Roy—no desire for surgery to make me like the other girls. If I'm envious of anything, it's the way this bitch can get more than one dyke to stand in line just like the dykes downstairs, everyone ready to pour themselves out when it's their turn on the hole.

Maybe it's time for another joint.

I descend the stairs to go back outside, where the stragglers are. I'm just better at one-on-one situations when I'm cruis-ing—or maybe feeling alone in a crowd makes me feel insecure. But either way, I'll have better luck somewhere sparse, where the music is barely audible and the air smells of cigarettes and trash.

I pull out my second joint of the night, looking up at the sky again as I hold it between my lips. It's where all the smoke in the world goes, after leaving our lungs. There is a way things disappear and leave an essence where they were, that only smoke knows.

Lighting the joint, I look back at the building I just left. On a balcony, looking out at the sky, stands the silver-haired woman, her dark skin reflecting the streetlights. I wait for her to look my way, and then I wave. She waves back, and beckons with a jerk of her head. When I exhale, the smoke obscures her and, of course, when it clears she's gone. I remember what Roy said, that it sounded like I was describing her ex-roommate. Did she mean Ximona?

"Can I have a cigarette?" a deep-voiced butch asks as she comes down the stoop. She's tall and beautiful, with close-cropped blond hair and a strong chin.

I rummage in my weed case for the cheeky ciggies I keep in there for when I'm in the mood. The woman nods her thanks, her hand brushing up against mine when she takes it. Unlike most of the bitches I've talked to tonight, she's dressed somewhat modestly in a black tank top and mesh shorts over a black thong.

We smoke in silence next to each other. I guess both of us resent the idea of having to open due to our tenuous connections to masculinity. But maybe she doesn't even realize I'm trans, and just thinks I'm another shy femme waiting for the butch to talk.

"I'm Jo, by the way," I say, exhaling smoke in her direction.

"Alina," she says, winking. "You having fun?"

I chuckle. "Yeah, in a sense. I missed having a buffet of dyke gossip to consume."

"Nothing about me, I'm sure," she says, and I shrug as cute as I can.

"How about you?" I ask.

"Well, I'm tryna avoid the gossip, that's for sure," she says, looking down and smiling at her shoes (Vans, of course) before meeting my eyes again, her gaze smoldering on her pretty face.

I sigh and slump back onto the railing as if to say, "How does one even do that?"

We smoke in silence for another minute.

"What're you looking for?" Alina asks.

I take a deep, deep drag, so deep I'm surprised I don't immediately go into a coughing fit. When I exhale, I wrap the both of us in a cloud of smoke, me and her floating in a cloud of the inside of my lungs.

"Well, it's Sunday, so tomorrow I have to catch up on weekend emails and keep up through four scheduled hours of Zoom meetings, but probably more than that actually, and then I have to clean the . . ." I start in on everything from my half-abandoned apartment building and my battle with the housing administration, and that the online pharmacy that delivered my hormones went bankrupt so I have to reteach some drugstore start-up the difference between a Luer-Lok and a slip-tip syringe, and how tired I am of Tinder and Grindr, etc. Just an unceasing avalanche of grievances. I let an unhinged edge creep into my voice because that's how I feel, and then I breathe and control myself and say, "It's like . . . I'm just looking for a way to make this night worth it."

"What kind of way?" She looks at me like she could either run or jump on me, which is more or less the effect I intended.

"Maybe your kind of way." I'm closer now, close enough to smell past the tobacco to her sweat and the faintest trace of Old Spice.

"I'm a bad way," she says, but she comes closer, too.

"But I want you—" I say, and she almost shuts me up by grabbing me by the hip. But this is a play party, and we're grown-up kinky dykes, so I'll say the whole thing: "I want you to choke me until you love me."

"That's right," she says, touching her nose to mine, the words forming against my lips. "Do you wanna take this inside?"

I nod, and she kisses me like it's a greeting, like we haven't seen each other in weeks, and she just needs me to know how much she missed me. When she walks me back through the house, explaining the scene she has in mind, I'm giddy and approve of everything she says. Something about a sacrilege kink in which she practices neo-Spiritist witchcraft on me, and I play like I'm an innocent Christian who doesn't know what anything is—which, to be fair, I don't. She lists impact play (yes, please), restraints (yes, please), possible psychoactives (don't mind if I do), and "a very small amount of sharps play, I swear, there's just this piercing toy I haven't had the chance to use yet."

She's taking me upstairs, my hand held in hers. I feel helpless in all the best ways. "Yeah, just don't cut my face and we're good."

"Why? Are you a model?" she asks, looking at me with glittering eyes. "I won't cut your face, I promise."

I let her take me down a hall. We go past the bathroom line—where bitches part for Alina in a way they simply did not for me—and through a door. It's a bedroom, tastefully decorated with posters of physics diagrams and a tapestry of a naked witch holding a skull between her legs. Bookcases overflow with texts on pagan rites, French mysticism, string theory, Hegelian philosophy, and crystals, light bulbs, and machined instruments I can't identify. Beside the bed are two wooden boxes, tall and polished.

"Was this . . . ?" I let the question hang, but when Alina doesn't pick it up, I bob my shoulders. "Ximona's room?"

Alina sucks her lips in.

"You're not seriously trying to hook up with me in a dead girl's room, are you?"

"What, too goth for you?"

That shuts me up.

We're on each other in seconds, our lips meeting in the silence, hands grabbing waists, fingers tugging at elastic, hair getting in our faces. When my eyes close for moments like this, I feel like I've evaporated into hot breaths, like the only parts of me that are real are my throbbing veins and fingertips. Right now only Alina's body exists, and even then only in the give of her flank, the hot part of her pressed into my thigh, the moisture on her tongue. There are bones, and tight bundles of muscle at the base of her spine, and there is the cold of the tip of her nose bumping into mine, and the softness of our tits pressed together.

Our eyes open as we catch our breath. Alina looks at me through her eyebrows, mouth open, collarbone heaving in the light from the window. Then, with a hand I can't see, she swings the door closed, and the only light is the glow-in-the-dark paint flecked on the walls and ceiling. She pushes me against the wall and kisses me again, then bites my neck. When I next open my eyes, the room light is on, which explains the click I felt at my back a second ago.

"So you think she'd be okay with this?" I ask. It's not like I've met Ximona, not really, but you try making out in the room of the dead girl you keep having visions of and not feel guilty.

"No lie, I think this is exactly what she wanted," says Alina, kissing me softly on my lips.

She instructs me to strip and get on the bed, and I obey. She explains that she and Ximona shared an interest in transgressing spiritual borders. What most would call heresy was, for Alina and Ximona, a form of liberation. And maybe titillation. I remember a time when I was still figuring my shit out, and I dressed as the Virgin Mary, only to reach under my cloak and dress to touch myself because my dick became rock hard at seeing myself looking so pure. So I get it.

Alina produces a black silk rope and ties my hands together, then ties both of my ankles to the legs of the bedframe. I'm shivering, but not because I'm cold; the same thing happened when I pulled the hood of that baby-blue cloak over my head. Some people describe colored auras when they're about to get a migraine, and I get those too, only the pain never comes. Just a feeling of my body functioning at a different wavelength, like I might grow a new limb or secrete a new substance.

Alina checks on the ties, asking me if they're blocking my blood flow, kissing the spots where the rope digs into my skin, running her lips up my back to make me squirm. My vision turns pink and yellow, and I'm pliable now, as pliable as that supermodel on the metal table after her bandages came off. Alina could pour me into cupcake molds and bake me if she wanted to.

"Okay, so—just tell me if any of this is freaky or triggering, okay?" she says, scrolling to a document on her phone.

"I mean, we're past freaky," I say, because what else is there to say about being tied up in a dead girl's bedroom? "But, like, good freaky. I'm so relaxed."

Alina clears her throat and begins reading from the screen on her phone.

"I name the alchemist St. Germain, who taught us death is merely time, and all time is the march toward death," Alina says, flicking the switches on the wooden boxes by Ximona's bed, making bulbs atop them light up a piercing, fluorescent violet. A laser projector inside the box flickers on, casting glowing edges onto every surface. "And in his name, I set the room ablaze in violet flame, a light wavelength of love and transmutation. May it light our journey beyond the veil between life and death and bless our march away from it."

She slinks past the door to another polished wood box with brass knobs and glass bulbs sticking out the top. From a compartment at the bottom she pulls out a brass bowl, a velvet wand rolling inside it. She rubs the wand to the sides of the bowl, holding it by the bottom and twisting both wrists to roll the two instruments together, producing a ringing lament that washes over me, through me.

Alina sets the bowl on top of the box, sitting inside the circle of bulbs coming through the top. The whole machine starts buzzing, the tone from the bowl amplified by the box, and Alina turns the knobs, adjusting the buzzing until the dual tones meet in what she calls a "reciprocal sine wave." She tells me Ximona picked it up from a set of conference notes exchanged between "Uncle Oppenheimer and Daddy Bohm," which she adapted into a workable quantum field stabilizer.

"Whatever the fuck any of that means," I say, squirming on the bed.

She runs a hand through my hair, her hand landing on my jaw, cradling my cheek. Her other hand traces down my neck, past my collarbone to squeeze my tits, one after the other. "I'm inoculating the electrons in your body against decoherence."

I worry into her caress, pressing my cheek into her palm and arching my back. "Whatever that means, too."

She pulls a tin out of her pocket and picks out a neon green capsule which she delivers, held in her lips, onto my tongue. It's slippery and citrusy, and easy to swallow down. I gulp and ask, "Weed gummy?"

"Psilocybin, actually. Low dose."

"Oh. Thank you," I say, wondering how much they cost. "Are those for reversing the neutron flow?"

"No, it's an interference adaptogen," she says, as if that explains anything.

"C'mon, slap a little more sci-fi in there. Call it a Weizman flux adaptogen or something. No name drops, nothing?"

"As if any of those academic fucks would even think to *try* operating quantum observer-interference traps while tripping on shrooms," Alina laughs. "No, the only kind of people freaky enough to experiment like that are witches like Ximona."

At that, the heat in my body dissipates. Just a little. I stop squirming and I look at Alina, searching her face for the question I want to ask. She looks down at me, and where I expect to find the smugness of what she just said, I find a fragile hope.

"What am I doing here, Alina?"

The question hangs between us, and in the gap my suspicion turns brittle, turns inward. Am I just clueless? I was here, I was in it, and maybe I'm ruining it now. Alina sighs, sitting on the bed next to me. She runs her fingers through my hair and kisses my forehead. We're strangers, still, but the kiss sparkles on my skin. "You're my sacrifice, Jo. I'm completing a ritual bridging the living world and the dead, and you're the raw material."

And it's ridiculous, but I believe her. Or I believe that she believes what she's saying, that she's saying it as plainly as she can in the hopes I'll laugh it off—because we're at a kinky play party, and there are people doing all sorts of crazy scenes above and below us, pretending they're punishing each other, or praying for a salvation that'll come in the form of a vibrator held between their legs. But this isn't that. This is personal, and real. This is me, falling through the wall we all put in front of us when we gossiped about the overdoses and the bad trips, falling into a story I didn't mean to play any part in.

"Can you please untie me?" I ask. "I just realized I don't know you."

"Please," Alina says, and the vulnerable whine in her voice scares me more than if she'd tried to be tough. "Please stay. I need you here."

"Alina."

"Jo?"

"Untie me, now," I try to be firm, but it bounces off her and I see a sort of steely anticipation coalesce in her eyes.

"I didn't want it to be like this," she says, standing up. She walks to a cabinet and opens a drawer. "I wanted you to have fun."

"I'm not having fun," I say, making my voice darker and louder. I pull at the silk rope, trying to get my hands through the loop. Instead, I end up tightening the knots. A pulsing ache blooms at the base of my skull, a cold tingling that spreads through my body.

"You'll have a choice," she says, turning from the cabinet. In her hands, she's holding a glass instrument with a large flask on one side that blooms into twisting pipes and terminates, on the other side, in a sharp, needle-like appendage. The tingling in my body sharpens, and I struggle harder against the ropes: They tighten even more, but I can't help it. I need to get out of here. Alina speaks again, her voice tight, her eyes hard. "You can take this willingly, or I can do it by force. We're going to cross the barrier between life and death, where Ximona waits for me. She's here, actually—she's been here all night, her quantum signature impregnated into the walls, ready to be born again into your body."

I scream, helplessly, until my throat stings. Alina just looks annoyed. She waits until I have to catch my breath to speak again.

"It's no coincidence you came to me," she says, coming closer. "Ximona must have guided you here, helped you find me. You've been seeing her, haven't you?"

"SOMEBODY, PLEASE! HELP ME!" My throat feels like it might bleed, and I cough, trying to fill my lungs with air.

"No one's coming. They can't hear you," Alina says. "I told you, you have a choice. You can give your body willingly, give your life for Ximona's, or I can take it by force. It'll be easier for the both of us if you consent. This equipment is sensitive, and I don't want to have to try more than once."

My breaths start coming in sharp, fast, ragged, and I can't get loose, I can't scream anymore, so there's only escape in my mind, there has to be a way I can get out of this because I sure as hell am not going to die in Bushwick on a Sunday night when nothing else has gotten me so I have to think of something I have to convince this fucking bitch to let me go to give up this insane idea that she can resurrect her dead girlfriend with sound waves and magic words! I'm not dying here! I can't! I have a launch presentation in two days!

"Breathe," Alina says, "it's coming."

I breathe. I breathe until I can think in complete sentences again. This is insane. Teeth chattering, I say, "This is insane."

"I know, I know it sounds like madness," Alina says. "But it's real. It's a miracle, and you're going to be a part of it."

"Your girlfriend killed herself and she's going to stay dead, you crazy bitch!"

"No," Alina shakes her head, determined.

"People die, and it's awful—it's not something that ever leaves you," I plead, tears streaming down my face, and I hope there's enough sympathy in my voice to cover up how fucking pissed I am. "But we move on. We keep—we keep living with their death, every day . . . every day."

She stares at me, and the stony, hard-edged anticipation melts from her face. Her cheeks fall slack, and her eyes soften, and relief floods over me. When she speaks, though, it's in a limp whisper: "If I knew how not to do this, I wouldn't go through with it. If I knew any way to live that wasn't this, I would."

"This isn't real!" I yell at her. "You're insane!"

Alina sits beside me, and for a second I try to calculate a way to hurt her, to knock over her crazy flask thing, but it's futile. I've been struggling so much the ropes have no slack left. She speaks in a low voice, almost private, almost a whisper, "But I saw your face when I said you've seen her. This is what scares you, Jo. You're terrified that I'm right."

I have nothing to say to that. I did see her, on the roof, and on the dance floor, and on that balcony.

Alina straddles me, raising the glass instrument—the flask—over her head, then bringing it down with all her weight. She screams as she does it, her thighs clenching on my sides. The violet light from the projector slides over every curve of the flask as it speeds toward my chest, its needle tip aimed squarely for my heart.

The tip breaks. And then everything does.

My brain floods with serotonin—my teeth ache and I know the psilocybin is hitting. Arching my back, I feel my consciousness atomize into a million billion particles, and I understand, as I have understood before, that every cell in my body gets a say in who I am. Each sparkling nerve of me is as much me as the nub of neurons that fires when I think, therefore am.

When I climb back to consciousness, I find myself in a dark room. The projector is on power-saving mode, displaying a trailing red logo bouncing from edge to edge.

Alina is still on top of me, writhing, but there's no one else with us. I can't even hear music coming from downstairs. The only light in the room is the faint red glow from the projector and a harsh slice of silver screen white from the streetlight coming through the sliding glass door, which cuts the room in half, catching only Alina's shoulder and the tangle of bedsheets. Something smells sweetly acidic, like rotting fruit.

Then, a sound like I'm going deep underground, my ears squelching from the air pressure change—behind me but all around me, forming words in a language I've never heard, yet my body understands. Alina can hear it, too, and I feel her shaking on top of me, sobbing or laughing wetly, and softer with every breath. The catacomb voice unmakes me, unmakes Alina, dissolves us into a we, turns us inside out until darkness becomes light.

The Perfect Pair

Excerpt from *Her Lover*

DORA ROSETTI (Nelli Kaloglopoulou-Bogiatzoglou)

IN THE NAME of this unstable and unnatural precarious love that I wanted to last a lifetime, I have decided to break all my family ties. It was time that I had my revolution. I am ready to put up a fight.

I pace back and forth between the four walls of my room in the hope that Lisa comes to comfort me. But she does not show up. I push myself to study. Examinations are imminent. If I want to pass them, I have to get out of my head, at least for a while. Even if I need her. I think about the future. And the consequences of my decision to move away from my family for her. I am afraid of my father, even though he is elderly and I doubt he will resort to violence. More than anything else he will react to my decision feigning indifference. I remember the words he said to me when I moved to Athens to study:

"From now on I am entrusting you to the care of your aunt. I know that you are a girl with a good head on her shoulders, but you are dead wrong if you think I will work myself to the bone for you if you neglect your studies and treat this time as a frivolous joy ride. I will disown you as my daughter. And don't think you will be able to sway me because you are a girl. I have raised you as I would have raised a son and I hope that you will use what I have taught you to create for yourself a serious and honest future."

He repeated the same things later in a series of letters he sent me afterward. At first I treated these letters as threats but later I considered them as just advice.

But back to Lisa, the only person I really take to heart. I am still waiting for her. I am afraid she is fed up with me. Damn! I am not going to give up on the struggle, especially now that we are on the verge of an important turning point since I have decided to change my life. I have to make her mine forever! I cannot allow this love, that cost me so much psychological suffering and the end of which threatens to throw me into an even worse hell than what I am going through now, to end.

Something strange happened at my room. My old girl-friend Popi, whom I've known since we were little girls and who is also engaged, paid me a surprise visit. She said she wanted to talk to me because she had a bad feeling about me.

She dreamed that I had been running for a long time and that at the end of my run I was teetering on the edge of a cliff and was about to fall. Popi came to my rescue after long hours of anguish. She woke up from the nightmare in a sweat and decided she had to come and warn me. She also has given me some advice. She has come to know that I spend time with disreputable people and that I do not exactly live a virtuous life. She blames Lisa. I felt compelled to defend her and within a few minutes we began to argue.

"You are dead wrong about my friend. She is only an expansive, exuberant girl, that's all, while the others are too placid. Maybe her behavior is a bit unsophisticated and candid, or perhaps she is too modern but not depraved. On the contrary. I know what I am talking about. I have no idea about what kind of life she led before we met, but now I am her only friend. And what's more, I do not give a damn about what people say."

"What would you do if, in the name of our long friendship, I asked you not to see her again?"

"No, Popi, don't ask me such a thing. I love her. She is my best friend . . . the only one I have. You are my friend but you're going to marry. Soon, I will lose you like I lost all the others. The fate of women is to forget their girl friends because of the men they marry."

Popi looked away. Her eyes filled with tears. I know that she truly loves me and that her interest is sincere but I have no intention of sacrificing my happiness for her.

"If you came here to save me, know that it is too late," I say softly.

"I know that between you and her is an unspeakable bond but I was too ashamed to talk to you about it. And then there was the fact that I thought highly of you . . . that I respected you. But these photographs! And the sofa and walls full of her name! I detest her. Actually, I hate her. Yes, and you can tell her so when you see her. She is not good for you. Leave to her despicable loves, to the vulgar men that she loves to spend time with, to her parlor flops. You are one of us. You belong to us. What about feminism and the struggle of women to improve their intellectual level? How low have they made you sink? It is time to abandon the road of error and to follow once again the laws of nature."

"Popi, the laws of nature are a sham, a silly hoax. Even death is a law of nature but that does not mean we have to die before our time. It will be death itself that comes to take us. Perhaps one day I too will be able to love a smart, handsome and rich man such as yours. But now I live and I cannot deprive myself of life."

"If only she understood you, if she at least loved you . . . But instead you have fallen into the clutches of someone who is toying with you."

"I do not know. As it is, two women understand each other better than a man and a woman. And it is exactly thanks to this mistaken love, as you say, that I have been able to appreciate other women, to understand them and to love them. It is not easy for a woman to be fond of another woman . . . let alone love her.

"A woman has a sensitive and delicate soul, and only another woman is able to ennoble it. The male yoke, however, has the unique capacity to mortify, to crush women, and to suppress their inner richness. It sometimes reemerges, transfigures, reappearing in the male offspring she gives birth to later. For women this all boils down to a holocaust, the total suppression of their selves.

Well, my dear, I am not at all disposed to suppress who and what I am . . . to sacrifice myself. I care about what little love I have won thanks to my maturity. And, moreover, this love that we are talking about here, and a woman who loves is free to love as she wishes. There are women who, blinded by jealousy, come to kill their husbands—one of the good results of your legitimate love. Others kill themselves."

Then I added, laughing, "But I am one of those women ready to die for another woman . . . my one and only."

"I am so very sorry for you," said Popi, as she rushed out crying.

MY FRIEND'S ANGUISH pained me a lot. Even though I felt grateful for her affection and her advice, I never would have considered getting engaged as she had done, to extinguish the fire of youth and the love that burned inside me.

Astarte, my sweet goddess! Come, I'll await you! I long for your ethereal figure to come into my room exuding exotic perfumes.

WE HEARD THAT Dinos, disappointed by his Lela, had also given himself over to homosexual love. I often read the poetry of Constantine Cavafy. He writes about love between men in ancient Greece and talks about Sappho and other lesbian poets which I literally devour. Dinos listens to me, sometimes carefully and sometimes ruefully. He always says that I am a lucky person because I have love while all he feels inside is a great emptiness.

One day, he told me, "Dora, you were right. Only women are capable of loving and being loved. That's why the perfect pair is formed by two women. A man and a woman are an incomplete couple and two men in a couple is idiocy."

I looked at him in amazement. It seemed to be a contradiction. Then I tried to justify it.

INSIDE I FEEL a great strength. I am studying hard for the exams. I want to get the highest scores possible. Obviously the exams don't give me happiness, but getting good marks would give me some momentary satisfaction. Generally things are going well in all fields, except with my family.

These days Lisa looks unusually unkempt. Seeing her so surprises me and makes me sad. But ultimately I do not care because I am madly in love with my Carmen, my Astarte, my Aphrodite . . . I will feel that way about her no matter what she wears.

In Asbestos

ROSE JEANOU

AUNT FLAVIE, who isn't really anyone's aunt, has too many rooms for one. Enough rooms to house a pseudo-family of farmstays. Enough rooms, even, for her pseudo-daughters to hide, to slip away from the kitchen—even though they're far too old not to help clean—and gossip in some back corner. Just like her real daughters did when they were Misty and Amanda's age. And just like that, after washing what she feels is her share of dishes, Misty slips out of the kitchen to find Amanda, who never stays to help at all.

Misty passes through the farmhouse's three living rooms, which correspond to three different times of day. On the right is a sun-spotted breakfast nook with tall windows and a long oak table, and down the hall, a reading lounge filled with books Misty can't understand, spilling from the shelves onto tables and floors. Misty thinks Amanda may have gone to the back of the house, to the evening room. This one is darker than the others, windowless, decked out like an altar. On the walls hang bad paintings of black cows, with overlarge eyes and human smiles, alongside generic landscape prints, the kind you might find in the thrift store, meant to be slid out of their frames and replaced with something more personal. Some photos show a younger version of Aunt Flavie mummified in pashminas, aprons, and bandanas. She's mean-mugging, wrapping both arms around a gaunt man Misty assumes is her husband Guillaume. This couple somehow birthed two shiny blond twins, pretty teenagers who smile out from the walls with big square teeth.

In the evening room, Misty finds Amanda sitting on the floor in Lotus position at the coffee table with a deck of tarot cards. Tea candles on the table in front of her light only Amanda's hands, while the long tapers on the bookshelf behind her glow with a warmth she wears as a halo. Amanda twitches her nose at Misty when she walks in and says, "Look what I found."

"You gonna give me a reading?"

Amanda must know Misty is joking, because Misty would know already if Amanda knew how to do something like read tarot. She says, "I'll just make something up based on the pictures."

Misty sits at the coffee table opposite Amanda. She watches as Amanda shuffles the tarot cards down into a bridge and flutters them back up. Misty can never get that move right, but Amanda's good with her hands. Misty moves her foot to touch the side of Amanda's. Amanda makes a squeak in the back of her throat and meets Misty's eyes. She looks back down but keeps her foot on Misty's, like she doesn't even notice.

After a while, Aunt Flavie floats in through the door and hovers behind the couch.

"My daughters," she says, "were just exactly like you two, but exactly. You are the picture of my daughters."

Misty fixes her eyes on Amanda, who tucks her bottom lip under the top. Aunt Flavie continues, "I miss them. Every single day. I'm not too ashamed to say this. This is what happens when you grow old. You raise children for years and years and years and years, and this is how they show you gratitude. They leave! Leave! Never call! *Mais*, I know you girls wouldn't do that. You're not princesses. You know the value of blisters on the hands. My girls are in Toronto, paying for hundred-dollar haircuts, married to Big-Deal men, staying at home with fake little dogs. Now for me, I wasn't raised on this farm. I didn't have the chance to connect with the Earth."

"Well, we're outdoor types," Misty says, removing her foot from Amanda's and shifting it back under her own thigh.

"But still! Do you see me? Where am I? I stay here!"

Amanda hides her laugh inside her smile. Aunt Flavie looks down, her face lighting up. "Ah, Amanda, you can read tarot? Oh, this is so wonderful! I never thought—"

"No," Amanda says, "I just found the deck on the table. I never learned." Misty can always read Amanda's face. *How can I put this on her?*

"Then I will read for you?"

"Oh—no, not me. Misty wants a reading. She was just telling me before you came in."

Beaming, Aunt Flavie maneuvers herself onto the couch. Misty doesn't deserve this at all. Woo is Amanda's realm, not hers.

Aunt Flavie's saggy, understuffed body lichenizes until she and the couch are all one floral mass. She's somehow changed into her nightgown already, her red hair hanging free and frizzy around her shoulders. The same candlelight which had made Amanda's face glow seeps into the folds and shadows of Aunt Flavie's, giving her the look of some long-preserved oracle, a shrunken head on a bundle of straw. She takes the deck from Amanda and shuffles. Then, fanning the cards out for Misty, she says, "Concentrate in your mind on a question."

Misty's mind always goes to Amanda. Can Amanda tell she's sending me signals? Is she aware that Peter is a pathetic, boring dickhead? Does she want to get back with me, or does she just crave attention? Maybe—when will Amanda decide to leave Asbestos?

"Keep concentrating and take three cards when you feel a *résonance*," Aunt Flavie says. Misty isn't sure what she's meant to feel, but she takes three cards from the middle of the deck and places them on the table. Aunt Flavie inhales a bit when she sees the three cards laid out in front of her and bugs out her eyes. She frowns and stays quiet for a few moments. *You're trying to die, aren't you.* An aura hovers behind the nape of Misty's neck.

"Okay, my love. I—ah, I am out of practice. Now, you don't have to tell me your question, but what was your idea? Family, health, love, money?"

"Love," Misty says, instead of lying.

"Ah! I'm so, so happy to hear this. Here I am, thinking you will never talk with me about boys! Ah, but he is a very lucky man, no?"

At the mention of Misty with a man, Amanda sucks air through her teeth.

"Ah, never mind. You don't need to tell me. I am too much like an aunt to you, no? You feel this way? This is uncomfortable to share. I will just perform your reading, then."

Aunt Flavie spins the first card around to face Misty. On the card, two figures trudge through the snow. One, crippled, limps on crutches, wincing on his bad foot. The other presses on, stoic and straight-backed, ignoring his friend's pain. Behind them, a glowing stained-glass window beckons them inside, but they trudge onward. Tiny white flecks around the two figures must represent snow still falling, but Misty's mind goes to white dust floating through the single ray of sunlight in an attic chamber, the one she used to hide out in as a kid while Mom raged. *Ungrateful*. Asbestos. *Wrong again*. Asbestos, as in Asbestos, Quebec.

"Five of the pentacles reversed. You will face a conflict in your relationship. I can see that you despair. You lack. I see some-one—how can I say?—habituated to pain. So used to suffering you see no way out. Perhaps you lack money, resources."

This all checks out to Misty, who is nearly twenty-three, with no degree, and whose only money, from tree-planting season, sits in a checking account she spends the rest of the year drain-ing. *Used to suffering*.

Aunt Flavie hands her the next card. "And dear, the Queen of Pentacles, she is your obstacle. Ah, she is one of my favorite cards. The mother, the *true* domestic. The Empress. But, I'm sorry, my dear, she is reversed. She is, perhaps, self-absorbed. Lazy, or focused on the wrong things. That is interesting. I am not really sure her meaning, dear, for relationships. It has been a long time since I read! Are you dealing with a jealous man, my love?"

Misty shakes her head. The Queen of Pentacles sits solemn on her throne, offering Misty a star cupped in her hands. She looks not at all like Misty's real mother, but more like Aunt Flavie, matriarch of Asbestos, head of the kind of house Misty hoped she'd live in as a child. A house like the one Amanda grew up in, with no one screaming. No one pulling out chunks of their hair. Warm light, home-cooked meals, books, photo albums, cards after dinner.

The final card shows a woman blindfolded and bound, stranded in the middle of nowhere, eight swords stuck in the ground behind her. Aunt Flavie becomes incensed. "You see no way out! Oppressed, restricted, driven to the edge. Madness. Paranoia. You expect rescue, but it will not come. My advice, and I am sorry, my dear, but this is what the cards are saying, I am truly sorry, my advice is—move on. Leave. Do not despair, men are not worth so very much." Aunt Flavie clasps Misty's hands and stares at Misty with her bulging tiger's eyes. "If you do the right thing, there will be a reward for you at the end of this," she says. "Your reward will not be the same as others', and yet, it will come."

Misty pulls her hands away, looks at Amanda. "Woah. Your turn?"

Amanda laughs. Her laugh, little halting grunts, lifts the dread from Misty's chest. "Okay, after that, no thanks. Hey, Flavie, why don't you braid me? Can you do Dutch style? Two braids?"

Nothing distracts Aunt Flavie like the chance to braid. She sucks Amanda into her flowery embrace, holding her between her legs. She removes Amanda's bandana, strokes out her long hair with her fingers, and arranges it in two neat parts.

"You let me touch you," Aunt Flavie notes. "Not like your sister."

"Misty's not my sister."

"Ah? Yes. I know. Figure of speaking. Friends. Well, please tell your friend that is not a very attractive haircut for a young woman. This is why it does not work with her boyfriend, hey?"

Amanda laughs sympathetically along with Aunt Flavie, then looks back at Misty to say, *I don't mean it, I'm just being polite, and I know hearing her say that must be so hard for you, what with your mom. What with how you can't deal with everything. What with you being butch.* Amanda's face says *butch* like it's a slur. Amanda thinks she knows everything about her.

"I'm sorry," Aunt Flavie responds to Misty's silence. "I don't always have the most, uh, tact. I'll tell you what my daughters said when they left me. This thing that's stuck with me all these years. They said, *Maman*, you're a crazy old bat!"

"That's not nice," Misty says.

"Well, they didn't put it like that. Not quite. They said, 'This is the end of many cycles of suffering.' Ah, you have such beautiful hair. So thick. My daughters had soft and thick hair like Amanda's. They got this from Guillaume, mind you. Mine is so frizzy—but red. Well, not so much these days, but you see, no? You know, red hair was coveted, in my day. I used to be slender. And everyone said my hair looked like fire. Except Grandmère, who said it was a sign of the devil."

"Fuck—sorry. Flavie, please—you're hurting me."

"Aunt Flavie, dear. My apologies. Imagine. My red hair. And my beautiful twins—the devil. You see, they didn't talk until they were three. And even then, hardly ever. But when they began to, they were quite eloquent."

"That's nice."

"Ah, and Misty, love? Can I ask of you a little favor? The fire?"

She's right. Misty stands to leave.

"Thank you, dear."

Amanda, stuck on the floor with Aunt Flavie stroking her hair, rolls her eyes up and sticks her tongue out to the side. Misty flashes her a sneaky peace sign.

November in Asbestos is already gray and freezing. Named for the mines that choked generations of men with cancer dust, Asbestos houses the worst plot of land the girls have stayed in on their five years of homoerotic friendship. The soil is dry, the farm sparse, its yard littered with broken appliances and scraggly rococo furniture rotted by many seasons. The past five summers have been the best of Misty's life, summers of farmstays and planting and tribbing Amanda. And respite from Mom, and everything else shitty about Forest, Ontario.

The house is heated by a black iron woodstove with no catalytic converter, old as hell. This stove tethers Aunt Flavie to the house year-round. She often tells Misty that when Guillaume isn't there, she can't travel, can't even leave for a day, because she has to be there to fill the stove and keep the fire burning through the late fall and winter. She's told Misty that her husband is married to that wood heater, having been raised with one. Aunt Flavie struggles to lift wood because of her back, and Guillaume is always disappearing, and this, she claims, is why she hosts farmstays.

Misty walks out through the back door and around the side of the house to a back room attached to the barn outside. She walks out there to fill that stove three times a day—at the crack of dawn, post-lunch, and night. She loves filling the fire. It's been nearly two years since anyone has taken care of Misty. The fire is how she keeps this alive.

Misty opens the stove door and throws the logs into her warm stomach. She's always the one to fill the stove—to do all the chores, really. Amanda likes to be taken care of, likes to play wife. Maybe she's the selfish mother. And anyway, Misty likes heaving the logs, especially when the flames lap right up against the edge and she can feel the heat almost catch her sleeve. Besides, what would happen if no one was there to fill the stove in the dead of winter, and Aunt Flavie threw her back out trying to lift a log and froze to death, there on the ground? Could she be the limping man, and Misty the one helping her through the snow? *Your reward will not be the same as others', and yet, it will come.* No, Misty can't imagine leaving yet. The thought makes her too sad.

"I CALLED IT. We're replacements."

"It was obvious," Misty says, "but you can have it anyway."

After Aunt Flavie retires at night, Amanda and Misty whisper for hours in their bedroom—the twins' old room. The twins are still everywhere in this room. Two shallow closets, Romeo-and-Juliet sinks in the bathroom, two pairs of riding boots in the corner, two sets of gardening gloves on the dresser, two large, empty suitcases gathering dust.

"God. She creeps me the fuck out," Amanda says.

"I know."

Amanda lies down on Misty's bed and pulls her pillow to her chest. She kicks her feet up into happy baby and rocks back and forth on her back, letting her long hair splay out around her. Amanda has strong, tanned legs. She's always been the object of desire between them.

"I'm thinking of leaving soon," Amanda says, dropping her legs. Her eyes fix on the ceiling.

Misty says nothing. Amanda has a chance. She's so far above this house, it repulses her. She won't sit on the molting furniture, leaves the dusty blinds down all the time so she won't have to touch them. Lives out of her suitcase because of the black smut and red hairs collecting in the corners of the drawers. Never helps with the dishes, says the crust is decades thick.

"Y'know, I do try to avoid talking about this with you—I do—but Peter does miss me. I keep dodging his calls. I feel super weird when we call—it feels like she's listening from the next room."

"She probably is." Misty picks skin off the side of her thumb. *No way out.*

"I guess I miss him a lot, too. I'm supposed to go to Grande Prairie and meet his parents next month anyways. Did I say? I'm supposed to buy a ticket."

"Oh." Someday Amanda and Peter will live in a sanitary McMansion in the Prairies with flabby office-job bodies and a couple of kids who resent them.

"Would you come back with me? You can, you know."

"I don't know." Misty's already picked the top layer of skin off her thumb. There's a satisfying skin tag forming.

"I mean, maybe it would be weird to come out to GP. But you can come back home with us for a bit first," Amanda says, sitting up and looking right past Misty's shoulder. "The 'rents love you, you know. Dad says so. His exact words were, 'It's so rare to find a friend like that.' Isn't that super sweet?"

"I was planning to stay a bit longer," Misty says. Amanda thinks Misty is obsessed with her. Amanda thinks Misty needs her. Maybe Misty's the cripple, trudging through the snow to some cold grave, and Amanda's the one who drifts safely to the warmth of the church.

Misty's thumb begins to bleed. She sits down on Amanda's bed across from her and pulls a tissue from the box on the side table to soak up the blood. Amanda and Misty sleep in two twin beds, side by side, made neatly with Quaker patchwork quilts. At the beginning of the summer, before the fight, the beds had been shoved together into a queen.

Amanda moves beds to sit down next to Misty. Maybe she notices that Misty is skin-picking again. She nuzzles her head against Misty's shoulder and says into her arm, "God. I just hate her."

Misty's heart bursts open and melts. "I know. But we've had worse hosts."

"I hate how she makes us call her Aunt. It's fucking bizarre."

"I know."

"What, you don't agree? What's up with you?"

"No, it's just that—it's not—I just feel for her. She just wants her daughters to visit more. Plus this house is big, her husband's a deadbeat. She's just lonely."

"I mean," Amanda says, placing her open palm on Misty's head and rubbing the spikes pushing up from the scalp. "I guess."

"Feels nice."

"Feels nice for me, too. Soft."

Misty loves her record player, even though it's one of the dinky fake-retro ones that makes all the music sound tinny. Off the record player, she spins themed mood vinyls from the discount section with names like Acid Jams #7 or Sapphantasmorgia. These records have combinations of music no one's ever listened to in that order before. They sound to Misty like rediscovered mixtapes from the honeymoon phase of a long-separated couple, dream pop, like stumbling around a house party lovesick and half out of your mind and hearing something beautiful playing from the other room. Amanda is always fine with Misty's music, happy with anything. She's just that kind of girl, the kind who loves dancing to anything play-ing, and Misty is the kind of girl who loves to watch. She puts one on now, a song that begins this way—

> It's the corridor of dreams that gave me everything I've
> owned,
> And I've traveled 'round the world and I never really had
> a home

Amanda stands up to dance. She raises her arms over her head and spins, her wrists loose. She's growing out her armpit hair, Misty notices. She's wearing Misty's clothes, too, a gray Gildan wifebeater and men's jeans that hang wrong on her big hips. No bra.

> And the one thing I learned was I never want to be alone,
> I was ooooooooh . . . looking

They merged during their first real, glorious spell together last summer, Amanda's brief foray into bisexuality. Now, even after having left Misty for Peter, Amanda reminds her of her other exes. Amanda had enjoyed Misty's love and from it extracted her lesbian image, as a pith from a husk.

Misty can't understand why Peter wants to be with a broad who is so obviously lesbian. All their mutual friends joke behind his back. Everyone knows Amanda wants girls, that she wants Misty, in particular, but just won't let herself. Just see how she looks at Misty now while they dance, swaying and running her fingers through her hair because she knows Misty's watching, tilting her head down and looking up with her dark, big eyes, then reach-ing up to stroke Misty's bare shoulders. Holding Misty close to her, lacing their fingers together and spinning her around as if Misty is the beautiful one between them.

What if Peter could see how Misty curves around Amanda's soft body from behind, smells her peppermint shampoo? What if he could see how Amanda turns to face Misty, pulls her in? Would he agree that this is something real? What would he think if he could see Amanda run her hand along the side of Misty's cheek, align her lips along the contours of Misty's?

"Don't," Misty says, "we shouldn't do this." And then Amanda recoils and crawls back into her own bed, where she falls asleep with her back to Misty, face to the wall. Long after Amanda's breathing becomes steady and slow, Misty stays awake, just looking.

SOME NIGHTS LATER, Misty and Amanda stay up late after Flavie has long gone into Ambien slumber. It's Misty who suggests climbing that staircase that leads to nowhere.

"Let's go ghost hunting," she says.

"God, I dunno. It's gnarly up there."

"You left all our wine up there. Remember?"

The girls find the staircase by leaving the house out the front and walking back in through a door in the mudroom along the kitchen hallway. The odd fixture is a result of the house having been initially built as something called a Boston triple-decker. Aunt Flavie explained that in the old days, Guillaume's grandmother and grandfather had lived there, along with his nuclear family and his great-aunt and uncle. When he reconverted the house for a single couple, the process had left a few odd doors and dead-end hallways and, most strangely, that staircase, with its odd, suspended landing below the attic and a view of the skeleton of the side of the house beneath.

Last week, Aunt Flavie raided their rooms and sobbed on Misty's bed for two hours about the dangers of alcoholism. After that, Amanda went up to the attic to hide their wine. Now Amanda shows Misty how to access the attic by climbing that unfinished back staircase, then ascending a ladder precariously balanced on the side of the landing, then pushing a trapdoor on the ceiling up, hard. The trapdoor opens onto the floor of the attic and is attached to the ceiling of the attic by a rope weighted down with a barbell plate. The barbell hangs in the air when the door is down. The door-and-rope system seems structurally unsound. When Amanda and Misty climb through the door, a big space opens on the floor where the trapdoor had been, which leads to a steep drop down through the frame to the stripped hardwoods below.

The attic is piled high at all corners with very old things. Two antique wooden rocking horses, bulk supplies of tampons and pads, a spare door, unopened mail, and mouse droppings. Most notable to Misty are stacks of early twentieth-century hardcovers coated in dust. Aunt Flavie will never notice if she takes one. She flips through one thin, fraying book—*La Chatte* by Colette—and tries to make out the French. From what she can tell, the book is about a man who loves his cat more than he loves his wife, unfortunately told from the wife's perspective instead of the cat's.

"Misty," Amanda's voice pitches upward from the far corner of the attic. "Come look at this."

Amanda is rifling through a box in the corner of the room. Misty peers over Amanda's shoulder. Inside the box are documents, magazines, stacks of promotional materials, and a box set for a TV show called *Le Nid*. Some old Quebecois family sitcom, starring a pair of twins, two blond girls. In many of the photos, the twins pose with a pitchfork in front of a barn that kind of looks like Aunt Flavie's, on a farm that resembles Aunt Flavie's, but almost definitely isn't.

"These are Flavie's daughters," Amanda says. "But they . . ."

"They aren't."

Amanda pulls out torn magazine covers with the actor girls on them, faces circled. Headshots of these smiling identical twins with eyes blacked out in Sharpie. Letters to the girls scrawled in Aunt Flavie's loopy illegible French, on which are stamped: RENVOI A L'EXPEDITEUR.

Misty hears herself say, "Let me see," and, "I don't understand."

"Misty," Amanda whispers like she's about to cry. *Madness*.

Misty moves Amanda out of the way. Amanda stands aside and lets her. There's some junk in the box, large manila envelopes. Misty finds herself ripping them open, looking for more—what? In one envelope she finds a stapled package of official-looking documents, but they're all in French.

"Stop, wait." Amanda pulls the top page out and reads it, raising her eyebrows to her temple.

BUREAU D'ENREGISTREMENT DES ACTIONS EN DIVORCE (PQ)
DATE: Le 15 mai 1986.
SORT DE L'ACTION: Divorce accordé. Non contesté.
DEMANDEUR 1: Guillaume Pierre Thibault
DEMANDEUR 2: Flavie Claude Lafleur-Thibault

Amanda points to a section at the bottom of the page: RESPONSABILITÉ DES DÉCISIONS POUR CHAQUE ENFANT VISÉ PAR L'ORDONNANCE. She's shaking now, almost ripping the paper. Misty grabs the paper from her hands. She reads those words, sees boxes to check off for each child under the couple's care, all unticked.

"Do you know what that means?"

Misty can't speak. She does, she thinks. *Paranoia. Leave.*

"Where's Guillaume? He's not on a trip. So. Pas de mari. Divor-cée," Amanda draws out the words, "et pas d'enfants."

"No. She has twins."

"I need to call Peter," Amanda says. "As soon as possible. Right now."

"Now? But—you'll wake her up." Of course Amanda goes right there. She can't wait to get away from Misty, crazy fucking Misty. There are so many other things Amanda could do right now besides call Peter. Amanda knows everything about her. But now, when it would actually matter, she can't bring herself to think of Misty, to imagine where Misty could go after this.

"God, I can't spend another second in this fucking place. How are you not reacting to this? Goddamn it, Misty, please! She lied to us. She's crazy. She's been lying this whole time. Why does she even have these magazines? Don't you think this is crazy?"

"No, honestly. I think you're being over the top. I'm sure she has kids," Misty says, because she has to be sure of one thing. "Maybe it's not those girls. But all over the house, there are signs of twins."

"Then why would she be cutting pictures of fake daughters out of magazines? Why pretend she's married if her husband's gone? Why have farmstays?"

"I don't . . . Maybe her family cut her off because she's eccentric."

"Eccentric? Eccentric, really? You're eccentric. She's evil."

"No one is evil," Misty says. "She's sick."

"This is so fucked up, how you're pretending you don't see this."

"What are you even trying to convince me of? You think Aunt Flavie made some setup to make us think she had twins that had lived here for years? Our room, Amanda? That room has obvi-ously been lived in by the twins. Why else would you set it up like that? And besides, to what end? I mean, if she was going to kidnap us, wouldn't she have done it already? She barely even knows where—"

"I don't even—I won't do this with you again. I'm leaving."

"To go be with Peter? You're gonna go live in Alberta with Peter in his parents' garage?"

"God. That's—that's—you know what? Okay. You know what, you're obviously holding onto a lot of baggage, and *I feel super uncomfortable—*"

Misty walks past Amanda and down the stairs. She floats through the narrow hallways, swims through the rooms filling slowly with black bile, collapses onto her bed where she lies facing the wall until she hears Amanda slip in about twenty minutes later. She's back from calling Peter, telling him about her insane obsessive dyke friend. Misty doesn't exchange a word with Amanda as she begins to pack. She's packing heavily, throwing her camping bag onto the bed and shoving everything inside. Everything from their past five months together. She's banging all around the room like Misty's mom used to do when she was threatening to leave. Like Misty's dad used to do before he did leave. Like Misty's mom used to do when Misty would stay out late with a new friend—*lying whore*—or when she'd come home with hickies, really from a girl—*I know you!*—or, when she was even younger, with her forearms sliced up.

"Are you sure you don't want to come with me?" Amanda asks from where she's perched on the ceiling. "I have the car."

The ceiling spins to the ground and now Misty is the one straddling the rafters while Amanda sits on her bed, zipping her camping pack, a noise Misty can't even hear. "No, I'll just take the bus."

"I just—I want to make sure . . ."

Amanda isn't even there. Her voice is so soft, so far away. "I'll be fine."

"Well, I'm heading out now."

"Let me walk you down."

Somehow Misty ends up downstairs in the reading lounge by the back door, holding Amanda by the hands. Blood is smeared along the side of her hand, the wound on the side of her thumb reopened. She hopes she won't get any blood on Amanda, who still isn't meeting her eyes but gazes somewhere over her shoulder. Misty doesn't look straight at Amanda either.

"Call me if you need anything," Amanda says. Then she slips out the door, which Misty considers putting a fist through, or perhaps barring from the outside so she can't get out if she changes her mind.

Back upstairs, Misty cries in her bed until she chokes. She crams her body between the window and the window ledge, where she watches Amanda drive away. She sits there in the window for hours until she wakes in Amanda's bed, where she can still smell Amanda's shampoo on the pillow. She sleeps badly, startles often. When she becomes conscious, she feels happy for just a moment. Then she opens her eyes and the memory sets in. In the bruise-throb of early morning, a black spider the size of a cat scuttles over the wall and onto Misty's chest, his spindly legs pinning her body at the sides.

WHEN MISTY COMES downstairs the next morning, Aunt Flavie says, "Well, looks like somebody's had a lie-in."

When Misty tells her Amanda's left, Aunt Flavie darts out her tongue and moistens her puffy lips. "Ah Amanda, *quelle garce*. So loud. Well, you were always the nice one. Always reading. Writing in your little journal, tucked away. Just like my Stéphane. Amanda, she was always the Noémie between you. Ah, my Noémie, I had to keep her on a leash! I mean, a real leash!"

Misty's eyes prick with tears.

"Ah, darling. Come lay your head in my lap," Aunt Flavie says. The two retire to the sun-nook, where Misty puts her head in Aunt Flavie's lap, begs for death, closes her eyes, and tries not to inhale. Aunt Flavie taps her long nails on Misty's head.

"You really should grow your hair out, darling. You have such a special face. Such potential beneath all that mess, I hope you'll excuse my saying. You'll find a good man, no doubt in my mind. A beautiful future I see for you."

On the breakfast table, the tarot deck eyes Misty in condemnation. The cards are scattered carelessly on the table. Just one faces up. The Tower. Lightning strikes the tip of the castle, igniting a small spark in the highest floor. The spinning room. On the loom, a thread ignites, alighting a roll of cotton fiber. The fire erupts, engulfs the floor. Two nuns, who had been spinning and chatting, now scream, choke, heave up blood. They collapse to their knees and crawl toward the door—in vain. A burning pillar falls from the ceiling, sets the door ablaze. Blocks their exit. Now the only way out is the window. As their lungs fill with black smoke, one nun begins to tell the other she loves her. The other, considering death by shattered bones preferable to immolation, leaps out the window. The first nun follows. She falls to her death stone-faced, her body limp with acceptance, twisting in the wind. The second falls with her face contorted, flailing headfirst toward her death, stretching out her arms to brace herself. Her wrists will snap when she hits the ground, then her arms, then her neck, and in that last living moment she'll wish she had chosen instead the warm lick of flames. The last thing she'll ever feel is regret.

"I have to fill the fire," Misty says.

She finds herself walking fast. Heading outside. Past the empty barn, the weed piles, the broken ATVs, the rotting ornate furniture. She's heading to the woodstove.

Why is the fire burning high, as if it had been lit just a few hours ago? She can't remember filling the stove. Aunt Flavie never fills the stove. Amanda is gone. Yet the fire burns so high, higher than usual, with the screams of three damned souls, lungs bursting open in welcome. Misty sees figures in the fire. Two twin girls jumping from the attic, falling, burning and screaming from the tower, their mother watching in horror. No — they're the nuns from the tower and the crone. Maybe they're all three lesbians. Maybe one will live to see everything through. *Beloved, I'd torch the sky for you.*

Amanda, after all, is gone. From the woodpile, Misty searches for the lightest log. November has been cold and barren, and the ground is bone-dry, packed dirt scabbed over with ice. The firewood, once soaked through with snow, has dehydrated. She finds the perfect log, hollow and ultraflammable, like the empty secret side of Aunt Flavie's house. She tips one end into the fire. She can't tell who has hurt her the most in this life. Misty foists the log up to the sky, carries her torch over to the skeleton-frame which will soon be nothing but white dust drifting down, glittering through the smog and landing, finally, on Misty's cheeks like snow.

Honestly

SARAH FONSECA

WHILE SCRIPTING THE finer points of Turner's Rebellion on the smartboard, Tamsen notices the child aiming the projectile. It is a benign weapon, a popularized, populist artifact from her own youth. The student, a girl named Cori with vitiligo like masterfully wrought conté, should know better than to test a public school teacher's hard-won rearview mirrors. Yet Tamsen, now facing the class, says nothing. They are so close to the end of the unit, the end of the school day, the end of remedial summer school. But there is something novel, Tamsen realizes, heart accelerating, in her uncharacteristic decision to be a pushover for an eleven-year-old who's wearing a replica Marilyn Manson tour hoodie. Exciting even, being on the receiving end of such an aim. Like a virtual reality immersion into Columbine, Sandy Hook, or Stoneman Douglas. She'll have to tell Emmanuelle. She'd assumed that, having lived forty-three years, the kinks in her tail had long been cataloged, explored, with findings documented. But this one, this one is new. A sign of the times.

The spit-mottled orb resembles a bleached model globe in miniature. It strikes Tamsen's cheek·and ricochets to the floor. She doesn't flinch, instead brushing off the transgression and blushing a bit. Some students carouse; others scowl and suck their teeth at Cori, who looks *so* pleased, as though her bull's-eye warranted a Girl Scout merit badge, a pat on the head.

And they say kids today are always on their phones, she thinks.

Take it you've heard about the shooting at a campaign rally in PA?

I have.

Tamsen is texting one number and receiving responses from another. This is not unusual. Emmanuelle returned from a war correspondence in the West Bank some years earlier "a bit tinny," as she put it, with a tender veiling of metal pins in her spine and a deep distrust of digital communications. Tamsen figures Emmanuelle also changes phones and numbers so much because she really likes talking smack, like every other femme with a preference for Android devices. One morning earlier in the summer, she found Emmanuelle in her study, contacts out and glasses missing in action, blind and cursing up a storm. *I can never tell these fucking things apart,* she murmured to herself while squinting at three separate Faraday bags, the kind that obliterate a smartphone signal. *One of these days, I'm going to end up calling my dealer to confirm a mammogram.*

Assassin missed. Tragic.

Reckon you're covering it tonight?

Yes. Tune in at seven to watch me shed crocodile tears, thoughts, prayers
xx

No. XXXO

Tamsen is relieved when she admits to Emmanuelle that she cannot bring herself to watch her anchor live television, and Emmanuelle does not mind. There is something immoral about looking at Emmanuelle doing the evening news: the invitation to look at someone she rather enjoys looking at through someone else's cameras. The silk pussybow blouses, the disappeared crow's feet, the midwestern blowout, a whorish red lip that would be devastatingly appealing on Emmanuelle in any other context. Little artificialities by committee that, in sum, invite the masses to look at Emmanuelle as though she is, in fact, nothing. Tamsen also does not want to learn the minute, pained signs of Emmanuelle subduing her displeasure for the headlines she is reciting and for the things her coanchor is saying. What Emmanuelle is not saying. Things like, "I'm going to end up calling my dealer to confirm a mammogram." Things like, "We interrupt this broadcast to inform you that, hello, the nation is on fire and has been for longer than you've cared to realize."

"HOW ARE YOU feeling?" Tamsen asks on election night.

"I feel nothing," Emmanuelle chimes. Returning home from the studio, she invites Tamsen over and continues to work, noting which states turn blue and which turn red on her laptop. Tamsen looks from her book to the television. The novel is dumb and so is the coverage. She finds herself looking at Emmanuelle's mouth, her focused expression. Her smile has always seemed like a frown to Tamsen. There is something barbed wire about it, like her lips are about to rip into something.

Emmanuelle catches her staring.

"Care to share with the class, Tamsen?" she asks, looking back to her work.

"If you were to kill him," she begins. "How would you do it?"

Tamsen thinks she sees Emmanuelle's shoulders tense beneath the wool of her Eileen Fisher cardigan, but she can't be sure.

"Is this your way of saying you need to blow off some steam? Playing pretend?"

"Yes."

"I . . . hmm." Emmanuelle thinks, chuckles under her breath, and thinks some more.

"I'd shoot him myself and bring you the corpse as an offering," she decides. "No pagan stuff. More like an alley cat mewling at your doorstep with a dead pigeon."

Tamsen is blushing when coverage breaks for a commercial. The first advertisement is for off-road vehicles. Emmanuelle rises, tall and unwieldy. She opens one of the living room windows, nestles her bottom into the fifth-story sill, and relights the joint she's been nurturing that week. Outside, someone plays a trumpet, simpering and morose and increasingly up-tempo, as though the performer aims to ward off a spirit.

"Been pumped so full of other people's thoughts, I've not had a moment to remember my own. It's been a very, very long couple of years," Emmanuelle says, folding her chest across her thighs while holding the joint outside. She's going to get chatty soon, Tamsen knows. And despite the time, Tamsen won't want her to stop. This is the real evening news.

Emmanuelle lifts her head and leans a little perilously through the window to have another drag. "You know what grinds my gears about this?" she continues. "This little feudal quadrennial game? The inverse-eugenics of it . . . engineered so anyone desiring human connection has to play a game defined by low turnouts at peaceful protests and platitudes short enough to be printed on crewnecks. Most Americans these days are freaks by virtue of precedent. My vices notwithstanding, my own blood would not pass muster as first class in five separate eras of United States history. *Five* . . . It is what it is. Yet the admission into the people's party requires leaving all of that at the door. Admission demands a goddamned lobotomy." She nods toward the television. "It's the blue on that map. And it's losing because, maybe, it needs to be retired. Shit's going to get worse before it gets better, you know. Going forward. Not just tonight. I feel painfully aware of how talk like this can get you killed because talk like this is the very thing that saves lives."

Emmanuelle adjusts her glasses and looks Tamsen squarely in the eyes, not wholly offsetting the sheepishness in her own expression.

"And because that feels so dangerous, I don't want to see other people. At least for right now. I like this, Tamsen. Would that work for you?"

Tamsen's heart explodes. She sees stars. She says nothing.

A breeze coils through the window. Emmanuelle, shuddering, wraps her sleeves around herself.

"Still feeling nothing?" Tamsen asks.

SHE IS ON her knees between Emmanuelle's after one too many shared ribs on the lost merits of grabbing, and being grabbed by, the pussy. Pussy grabbing, Emmanuel brooded while typing, had been defamed by this whole partisan farce; pussy grabbing, when both parties are on the same page, is in fact *exquisite*. Tamsen nudges Emmanuelle's computer from her lap onto the cushions and actualizes the theory, roughing her up with her hands and mouth.

"Oh, would you look at that," Emmanuelle observes, panting, legs hurting. She glances from the muted television to the head of hair balled in her lazy fist. "She—she—she just lost Georgia."

"WHAT DO YOU NEED?"

Emmanuelle is still heaving as she slinks back into her panties and folds her feet beneath herself on the couch. She strokes Tamsen's inner thigh and looks at flights. The results are all but in. She books one for the inauguration, another to a victor's rally. She will have to begin her clearance process soon.

"You'd look so hot with a gun," Tamsen finally floats, savoring the words as she says them.

"Is that what you want?"

"Well, we'd need a gun first. Could be a prop."

"Okay to keep talking about it? Not against it. Just need to wrap my mind around some things first."

"I want to be shot by you," Tamsen coos, mustering her best Marilyn.

"No you don't." Emmanuelle laughs, cupping Tamsen's jaw. "How's tying you up sound for now? Oh, look. Pennsylvania just went red."

Becoming aware of the hour, Tamsen nods in acquiescence. She takes off her top and waits for Emmanuelle; Emmanuelle, who is galloping into the bedroom on unsteady legs to glide open a closet drawer in pursuit of ethically sourced cotton rope, yards of which she will throw over her arm like an Annie Oakley for the modern broad; Emmanuelle, who glances up to the heirloom Louis V luggage set her mother had given her for work trips and then closes the closet door behind her; Emmanuelle, who is behaving as though there is another woman, when all there is is a gun.

Plus a silencer.

Emmanuelle, who slides down the train case to look, to touch what's inside. Emmanuelle, who glances at herself in a mirror, the Lebedev connecting with her palms like heavy Velcro. Emmanuelle, who glowers into the looking glass, says, "Take off your panties, baby," and promptly cringes. Emmanuelle, unable to bring herself to fuck with a real gun around her girlfriend—though the president-elect remains another story.

About the Contributors

Eve Adams (1891–1943), who published under the pen name Evelyn Addams, was a Greenwich Village tea room proprietress and realist author of the 1920s book *Lesbian Love*. A Polish Jewish immigrant, Adams was born Chawa Złoczower in Mława; she also went by the names Eva Kotchever and Eve Zlotchever. After relocation, she traveled the United States in support of Emma Goldman's political activism. In 1927, Adams was deported from the US after entrapment in a sting in which an undercover policewoman alleged the writer made sexual advances toward her. In her final years, Adams worked as a censored literature vendor in Paris, enjoying clients including Henry Miller. Though she tragically perished in Auschwitz, Adams's lost writings were rediscovered and republished by the queer historian Jonathan Ned Katz in 2021.

Trish Bendix is a GLAAD-nominated writer and regular contributor to the New York Times. Her book *Sappho Was a Pop Star* is forthcoming from St. Martin's Press in 2027.

Ella Boureau is a playwright living between NYC and Paris. She writes about sex, mediterranean myths, and female dirtbaggery. She is interested in rage and grief: when they are funny, when they are scary, when they are heartbreaking, and when they just get so twisted up that they break into something else entirely. She has an MFA from Hunter College, and her most recent play is *Quand Tu Sors du Feu*. Find her at www.ellaboureau.com.

Grace Byron is a writer from the Midwest based in Queens. Her writing has appeared in The Cut, *Vogue*, Bookforum, and other outlets. Her debut novel, *Herculine*, is forthcoming from Saga Press. Find her @emotrophywife.

M. J. Corey is a psychodynamic psychotherapist and author of *DeKonstructing the Kardashians*. Her work has been seen in *The Brooklyn Rail, The New Yorker*, and *Vogue*. She lives in Brooklyn with her cat, Baby Blue.

August Clarke is here and queer, etc. He was a 2019 Lambda Literary Fellow in Young Adult Fiction and an Amdre Norton Nebula Award, Locus Award, Dragon Award, and Pushcart nominee. They are the author of the novel *Metal from Heaven*, as well as the indie bestselling series *The Scapegracers*, which they write as H. A. Clarke.

Anna Dorn is the author of four books: *Perfume & Pain, Exalted, Bad Lawyer*, and *Vagablonde*. Her next book, *American Spirits,* is forthcoming from Simon & Schuster. She lives in Los Angeles.

Alice Dunbar-Nelson (1875–1935) was born into a multiracial middle-class family in New Orleans, coming of age in the wake of the American Civil War. A prescient thinker on racial and sexual relationships, Dunbar-Nelson published her first book—a combined volume of short stories and poetry, *Violets and Other Stories*—at age twenty-five. The educator and writer was married several times and indulged in secret relations with Fay M. Jackson, the first Black correspondent for the Associated Negro Press to dispatch from Hollywood. Gloria T. Hull first drew focus to Alice's work in her multivolume undertaking for the Schomburg Library of Nineteenth-Century Black Women Writers, *The Works of Alice Dunbar-Nelson*, in 1988. "Natalie" was subsequently elevated through Devon W. Carbado, Dwight A. McBride, and Donald Weise's 2002 anthology, *Black Like Us: A Century of Lesbian, Gay, and Bisexual African American Fiction*.

Sarah Fonseca is a writer, editor, and film programmer based in New York City who has dispatched from Cannes, New York Film Festival, and Sundance. With one eye on queer cinema history and the other on its future potential, Sarah has contributed a volume of interviews, reviews, and critical essays to LGBT and mainstream film publications including Condé Nast's *them, The Advocate, Film Comment,* and Museum of the Moving Image's *Reverse Shot.* She has also published short fiction with *Evergreen Review, Bosie Magazine,* Cleis Press, and *Math Magazine.* Currently, Sarah is pursuing graduate studies in history at the City College of New York and printed matter studies at UCLA's California Rare Book School. Find her at @sontagians and sarahfonseca.com.

Trae Higgs is a loud girl, queer writer, legal professional, event producer, and community organizer. Originally from South Florida, she has written pieces on Black womanhood, politics, queerness, and personal life experiences. Trae started her nonprofit organization Blk Book Swap in 2020. She's currently the events and programming manager at a dyke bar and has lived in Brooklyn, NY, for over a decade.

After years of complaining about the sanitization of queer women in fiction, author **Lillian James** decided to become the change she wanted to see in the world. Ranging from the sweet and sexy to the lovingly murderous, her work can also be found in 2022's *Cunning Linguists.*

Rose Jeanou (a.k.a. Roge Jean) is a lesbian writer, poet, and educator living in New England. He cohosts the *Christ's Side Wound* podcast. Contact rosejeanou@gmail.com for inquiries or follow @rosejeanou on Instagram for updates.

Emily Jones is the pseudonym of playwright and activist Lorraine Hansberry (1930–1965). Alongside her stirring contributions to American theater (*A Raisin in the Sun, The Sign in Sidney Brustein's Window*), Jones periodically published short works, including correspondence and fiction, in the first nationally distributed lesbian publication, *The Ladder.* In 1999, journalist Elise Harris interviewed one of Jones's former girlfriends, Renee Kaplan, for *Out* magazine.

Astrid Anne Rose is a Chicago writer working somewhere within the Gothic, transgressive, and erotic horror spaces. Her work can be found online on Gumroad. She cohosts the podcast *Live at the Death Factory* and edited the Swampland Press collections *The Blonde Hound & Other Strange Occurrences* and *Always Night: Tales of the Strange and Supernatural*.

Dora Rosetti (1908–1989) is the pen name of Nelli Kaloglopoulou-Bogiatzoglou, an Alexandrian writer who moved to Athens in the 1920s to study medicine. During this period, she published her first and only novel, *Her Lover*. Though destroyed and thought lost, several copies of Rosetti's epistolary work were discovered by Greek scholar Christina Dounia, one of which was inscribed to her friend, the poet Constantine P. Cavafy. Rosetti went on to practice gynecology. This is the first publication of Rosetti's work in the United States, as translated by James Johnstone for ETPbooks.

Octavia C. Saenz (she/they) is an editor and cartoonist based in El Paso, TX. She creates speculative fiction and visual narratives about queer life and temporality. Octavia grew up in Puerto Rico and has a BFA in creative writing and illustration from Ringling College, as well as a Lambda Fellowship. Find her on Twitter and Instagram @shrimpwonder.

Nadine Santoro is an artist, writer, and facilitator. She is the host of Patchwork Literary Salon, a monthly reading series, and cohost of the podcast *Thinking Straight*, a lesbian anthropological dig into the world of heterosexual romance novels. She lives in Brooklyn with her fiancée and their two senior dogs, Knives and Young Neil.

Sarah Schulman is a novelist, playwright, screenwriter, nonfiction writer, and AIDS historian. Her twenty-first book, *The Fantasy and Necessity of Solidarity*, is forthcoming from Thesis Books, a new imprint of Penguin Random House.

Shamim Sarif is a multi-award-winning novelist, screenwriter, and director for features and series. Her debut novel, *The World Unseen*, won a Betty Trask award. Her most recent novel series, *The Athena Protocol*, is published by HarperCollins US. Her new movie, *Polarized*, releases worldwide in early 2025.

L. J. Webb is the pseudonym of sculptor, diarist, arts patron, and railroad heiress Gertrude Vanderbilt Whitney (1875–1942), under which she published one homoerotic murder mystery novel, *Walking the Dusk*, in 1934. During her sixty-seven years, Webb stewarded emerging arts movements, opening the Whitney Museum of American Art in 1930. Forty years after Webb's passing, a surviving relative authorized E. P. Dutton to publish one of the manuscripts she left behind under Whitney's legal name. The novel, *A Love Affair*, is set in Paris and concerns a dressmaker's cloak-and-dagger relations with an older married barrister—and the special lady friend who commits murder so the star-crossed lovers can be together. Access to copies of *Walking the Dusk* remains limited to two research libraries.

Acknowledgments

Labor. If we knew how much would be required of us and our communities when we embarked on this book, we may have tucked our tails and ran. We only knew that our predecessors had done it, and that it was incumbent upon us to do the same, with greater skill and care than the pulp medium has previously necessitated. Our forebears' own histories suggest they didn't know what they were getting themselves into, either. Lesbian arts and letters are a unique hall of mirrors, showing one the light when the dark is on the cusp of becoming unbearable.

To that end, we extend deep gratitude to Feminist Press's Jeanne Thornton for giving this project a spine; Lucia Brown, Rachel Gilman, and Tyler Kristin Hubbert for giving her a mouth; and Alicia Lim for helping us bring order to the admittedly mega-lomaniacal project of both reviving and rescuing the lesbian pulp tradition. Likewise, we remain grateful to Leslie Hung and Drew Stevens for taking on the hefty responsibility of designing *The New Lesbian Pulp*'s cover. Prolific bowing is due to lesbian emissary Trish Bendix for her enthusiasm for the project, and for volunteering to write the book's foreword.

Thanks go to author and activist Sarah Schulman for being an unrelenting champion of Ella Boureau's "Cottonmouth" and for assistance in locating a long-lost report on lesbian writers, to the Astraea Lesbian Foundation team—including Joy Chia, Kristin Gardner, and Robin Wilby—for unearthing said report, and to Courtney Gillette for using it to sound the alarm regarding institutional funding for lesbian writers in her book reviews for the Lambda Literary Foundation. Historian Marcia Gallo has heroically ensured that issues of *The Ladder* remain accessible online. Outsized gratitude must also be levied at historian Jonathan Ned Katz for elevating one featured author beyond the realm of queer urban legend in his 2021 book *The Daring Life and Dangerous Times of Eve Adams*—and to Nina Alvarez for chancing upon Adams's *Lesbian Love* in her apartment building in Albany, New York.

Many scholars and researchers' efforts informed this book's contents, including Gloria T. Hull, who should be lauded for her painstaking editing of three volumes of Alice Dunbar-Nelson's writings for the Schomburg Library of Nineteenth-Century Black Women Writers imprint in the 1980s; editors Devon W. Carbado, Dwight A. McBride, and Donald Weise subsequently elevated Dunbar-Nelson's profile in *Black Like Us: A Century of Lesbian, Gay and Bisexual African American Fiction* in the 2000s; and we would be remiss if we did not note that we had the pleasure of first encountering the late abolitionist author in a Buzzfeed article penned by RedBone Press's Lisa C. Moore in the 2010s. We are indebted to Enzo Terzi at ETPbooks in Athens, Greece, for the publisher's translation and willingness to have Dora Rosetti finally published stateside. The late art critic B. H. Friedman began the delicate, divisive act of probing Gertrude Vanderbilt's private life and writings in 1978, enabling Barbara Goldsmith to name the artist-heiress's queer affinities in *The Wall Street Journal* in the early 1980s.

In addition to the institutions named above, we are thankful to the Smithsonian Institution of American Art, the Library of Congress, the Jerome Foundation, and the University of North Carolina–Asheville's Queer Studies Conference for affording us access and providing material support for *The New Lesbian Pulp*. Finally, we are grateful to those, names unknown, who have leveraged to keep elements of queer history accessible to all through queer community gossip (that time-honored medium) and newer open-source initiatives like Internet Archive.

Permissions Acknowledgments

"Revenge of the Roadkill Bodysnatchers" by Rose Jeanou
Song lyrics from "Born in XIAX," copyright © 1982 by Nina Hagen, are reprinted by permission of Nina Hagen.

"A Parlor Game" by L. J. Webb
(Gertrude Vanderbilt Whitney)
"A Parlor Game" was previously published in *Walking the Dusk* by L. J. Webb (Coward-McCann, 1932), copyright © 1932 by L. J. Webb. Reprinted from The Gertrude Vanderbilt Whitney Papers, series 7, Smithsonian Archives of American Art, Washington, DC. The Gertrude Vanderbilt Whitney papers were donated in 1981 and 1991 by Whitney's granddaughter, Flora Miller Irving. Funding for the processing and digitization of this collection was provided by the Terra Foundation for American Art.

"Natalie" by Alice Dunbar-Nelson
"Natalie" was written in typescript by Dunbar-Nelson before 1896 and was previously published in the Schomburg Library of Nineteenth-Century Black Women Writers' *The Works of Alice Dunbar-Nelson (Volume Three)*, edited by Gloria T. Hull, copyright © 1988 by Oxford University Press. "Natalie" was subsequently anthologized in *Black Like Us: A Century of Lesbian, Gay and Bisexual African American Fiction* (Cleis Press, 2002), edited by Devon W. Carbado, Dwight A. McBride, and Donald Weise, copyright © 2002, 2011 by Devon W. Carbado, Dwight A. McBride, and Donald Weise.

"Chanson du Konallis" by Emily Jones
(Lorraine Hansberry)
"Chanson du Konallis" was previously published in *The Ladder*, volume 2, issue 12, in September 1958.

"Rebound" by M. J. Corey
"Rebound" was previously published in the *Brooklyn Rail* in December 2010. Reprinted by permission of the author.

"Diana Thornton" by Eve Adams (Eva Kotchever)
"Diana Thornton" was first published in *Lesbian Love* (1925), a self-published book by Kotchever that was limited to around 150 copies. *Lesbian Love* was republished in Jonathan Ned Katz's *The Daring Life and Dangerous Times of Eve Adams* (Chicago Review Press, 2021). Reprinted by permission of Jonathan Ned Katz.

"The Perfect Pair" by Dora Rosetti
(Nelli Kaloglopoulou-Bogiatzoglou)
"The Perfect Pair" was previously published in *The Two Lovers* by Dora Rosetti, translated by James Johnstone, copyright © 2017 by ETPbooks. Reprinted by permission of ETP Books.

"In Asbestos" by Rose Jeanou
Song lyrics from "Corridor of Dreams," copyright © 2012 by The Cleaners from Venus, are reprinted by permission of Martin Newell.

The Feminist Press publishes books that ignite movements and social transformation. Celebrating our legacy, we lift up insurgent and marginalized voices from around the world to build a more just future.

See our complete list of books at
feministpress.org

THE FEMINIST PRESS
AT THE CITY UNIVERSITY OF NEW YORK
FEMINISTPRESS.ORG